PRAISE FOR

A BREATH OF SCANDAL

The characters, the setting, and the relationships that bind them all together create a world of staggering beauty, filled with heartache, hope, and love. People are flawed, but Essex has created a world that highlights why romance is important and why people all over the world want happily ever after. —*Fresh Fiction*

ALMOST A SCANDAL

Almost a Scandal is a bold and brazen fast paced romance with a daring heroine and smoldering hot hero! With an explosive danger and red-hot romance this book is most definitely a book to treasure! —*Publisher's Weekly*

Almost a Scandal eschews the balls, gowns, and clever conversation that characterize most Regency romances. But the love affair between Sally Kent, midshipman, and David Colyear, lieutenant, is utterly engrossing and (once Sally and David are sent on a mission to engage the French navy) thrilling as well. —*Eloisa James*, New York Times Bestselling Author

A SCANDAL TO REMEMBER

Set sail with Essex as she cleverly pits a bluestocking against a stiff-upper-lipped British naval officer and lets the sparks fly. Essex spices her fast-paced tale with fascinating details of ships and sailing and adds plenty of sexual tension, high-seas adventures, danger and desire. Readers will be on the edges of their seats reading this latest Reckless Brides tale. —*Romantic Times*, 4 ½ stars and TOP PICK!

Mad
About The
Marquess

HIGHLAND BRIDES, BOOK 1

ELIZABETH
ESSEX

This is a work of fiction. All of the characters, organizations, and events portrayed in this novel are either products of the author's imagination or used fictitiously.

For information, address Elizabeth Essex at elizabethessex.com

DEDICATION

To Lori Freeland, writer, critiquer, advice-giver par excellence, and friend, who wanted to call this book "The Earl and His Girl," and in so doing, helped me find the characters.

The race is to the strong, not just the quick, my friend.

Chapter 1

Edinburgh, Scotland
June 1792

LADY QUINCE WINTHROP had always known she was the unfortunate sort of lass who could resist everything but temptation. And the man across the ballroom was temptation in a red velvet coat. There was something about him—some aura of English arrogance, some presumption of privilege—that tempted her beyond reason, beyond caution, and beyond sense. Something that tempted her to steal from him. Right there in the Countess of Inverness's ballroom. In the middle of the ball.

Which was entirely out of character. Not the stealing— she stole as naturally as she breathed. But because the other thing that Lady Quince Winthrop had always known, was that the most important thing about stealing was not *where* one relieved a person of his valuable chattels. Nor *when*. Nor *how*. Nor even *what* particular wee trinket one slipped into one's hidden pockets. Nay.

The tricky bit was always *from whom* one stole.

When one robbed from the rich, one had to be careful.

Pick the wrong man, or woman for that matter—too canny, too important, too powerful—and even the perfect plan could collapse as completely as a plum custard in a cupboard. Which made it all the more curious when she ignored her own advice, and picked the wrong man anyway. Whoever he was, he stood with his back to her, his white-powdered hair in perfect contrast to that red velvet coat so vivid and plush and enticing that Quince was drawn to it like a Spanish bull to a bright swirling cape. Unlike the gaudily embroidered suits worn by the other men, the crimson coat was entirely unadorned but for two gleaming silver buttons that winked at her in the candlelight, practically begging her to nip one of the expensive little embellishments right off his back.

A button like that could feed a family of six for a fortnight.

And while her itchy-fingered tendency toward theft was perhaps not the most sterling of characteristics in an otherwise well brought up young Scotswoman, no one was perfect. And it was so very hard to be *good* all the time.

She had much rather be bad, and be *right*.

So Quince took advantage of the terrific crush in Lady Inverness's ballroom, slipped her finger into the tiny ring knife she kept secreted in the muslin folds of her bodice for just such an occasion, and sidled up behind Crimson Velvet.

She did not pause, nor give herself a moment to think on what she was about to do. She ignored the chitter of warning racing across her skin, and set straight to it, diverting his attention by brushing her bodice quite purposefully against his back, while she nipped the button off as easily as if it were a snap pea in a garden.

The elation was like a rush of blood to the head—intoxicating and addictive.

And because that was what she did—regularly stole fine things from finer people in the finest of ballrooms—she wasn't satisfied with only the one button. Nay. Another six mouths could be fed, and Quince could live all week on the illicit thrill of having taken the second button as well, and gotten away clean.

Except that she didn't get away clean.

She didn't get away at all.

A very large hand clamped onto Quince's wrist like a shackle. A red velvet-clad hand.

Alarm jumped onto her chest like a sharp-clawed cat, but Quince kept her head, automatically tucking the buttons and knife down the front of her bodice, and winding her now-empty free hand around that crimson velvet waist. She pressed herself to his backside more firmly, and familiarly, and said the first unexpected thing that came to her mind. "Darling!"

Crimson Velvet went as stiff as a bottle of Scotch whisky. "Good Lord. What's this?"

Alarm faded as recognition, and something that really oughtn't be delight curled into her veins. She knew that deceptively easy tone. Strathcairn. Earl thereof.

Oh, holy clotted cream.

The Laughing Highlander, she had once called him. But the Highlander was not laughing now. He was looking down at her with a sort of astonished wonder. "Wee Quince Winthrop, is that you? Good Lord." He stepped away—though he did not let go of her wrist—to case her as thoroughly as she ought to have done him. "I would not have recognized you."

She had clearly not recognized him. But the man gripping her wrist was neither the powdered dandy she had imagined from across the ballroom, nor the amusing, carefree Earl of Strathcairn she remembered. This man was different, and as dazzling in his own way as the shining silver buttons she had secreted down her soft-pleated bodice.

Firstly, he was as irresistibly attractive as that red velvet suit—all precise, well-cut shoulders, and long lean torso that seemed a far cry from the rangy, not-yet-fully-formed man in his youth. But secondly—and more importantly—he was much more controlled, more...curated, as if he had carefully chosen this particularly splendid view of himself to show the world. As if he not only wanted, but demanded to be *seen*.

Quite the opposite of Quince, who minded her appearance only to make sure she blended into the crowd—if her sister told her this season everyone was wearing white chemise dresses, then a white chemise dress she wore, disappearing into a sea of similarly dressed swans.

By contrast, Strathcairn looked every bit an individual, and quite, quite splendid. His waistcoat was of the same saturated color as his coat, and his snow-bright linen with only the barest hint of lace was the perfect foil for his immaculately powdered hair.

On any other man such a look might have appeared plain and underdone, but on Strathcairn the blaze of unadorned velvet served to highlight the force of his personality.

And there was nothing she liked as much as personality, unless it was a challenge.

The earl appeared to be both.

"Why, Strathcairn." She made her voice everything breezy and cordial. As if her heart were not beating in her ears, and dangerous delight were not dancing down her veins. "It's been an age."

"Too long, from the looks of it." He stepped close—too close, not that she particularly minded—and looked down at her in a perilously attentive way, like a great, green-eyed tomcat eyeing up a wee mouse. The effect was most unsettling. It put her right off her stride. "Do you often embrace men you haven't seen in years?"

It had been exactly five years. He had briefly been one of her eldest sister Linnea's suitors then—newly elected a Member of Parliament, and headed to London, brilliant and ambitious. Quince remembered thinking the lanky Highlander was too tall, too clever, too canny, and far too insightful for tiny, fluttery Linnea, who adored nothing more than to be made a pet of.

Strathcairn hadn't seemed the type to keep pets.

Quince had been little more than a fourteen-year-old lass, but she had quite liked the young man's intelligence, nearly as much as his vibrant charm. Though what she liked best of all was his lovely, buttery smile that had made her feel like she was melting in the sun.

Strathcairn was certainly not pouring the butter boat over her now—his eyes might have been smiling, but from this angle, his chiseled jaw seemed to have been carved out of Grampian granite.

No matter. Quince was not Linnea—she was no one's pet. "I thought you were someone else," she lied without effort or qualm. "You've changed."

"So, my indiscreet young friend, have you." The barest hint of amusement in his glorious baritone was all that was necessary to bring back all the delicious torment of her youthful infatuation. "What in heaven's name did you think you were doing, calling me 'darling'?"

"Thought you were my Davie." Quince made up a convenient beau on the spot. "I must find where the darling lad's got to."

Strathcairn let out a low, disbelieving bark of laughter, but didn't let go of her wrist. "You can't be old enough to be making assignations with men, wee Quince."

He trespassed easily on the old acquaintance by calling her by her Christian name—if Papa's botanically inspired names for his daughters could even be called Christian. Strathcairn also crossed the lines of familiar behavior by turning her toward the door, and somehow settling her against his side in such a subtle, but insistent, way, that not a person in the place would have suspected she was being all but frog-marched from the ballroom.

Even though she was grown up now, and towered over tiny Linnea, Quince still had to leg it to keep up with Strathcairn's long strides, all the while craning her neck to get a proper close look at him.

He looked so different, with his hair powdered white, and this controlled look upon his face, as if his smile had been put away in a cupboard, like a cravat that no longer fit. This new Strathcairn was far more imposing, and much, much more intimidating looming beside her like one of the great statues at Holyrood Palace than he had ever seemed all those years ago when she had keeked out at him from behind the drawing room curtains.

But she was not four and ten now. Quince let him tow her only as far as a conveniently empty alcove at the end of the entrance hall, before she rounded her elbow out of his grip, and served him a sharp, instructive jab in the ribs— anger brought out the Scots in her. "I'd be much obliged if you'd take your great paws off of me, Strathcairn. You're creasing my gown."

He subdued his grunt of discomfort, but put a hand absently to his side. "My *paws*"—he gave the word a wry intonation—"are not great in the least. They're rather average. For a Scot." At last he let the gorgeously rough Scots burr rumble beneath the town polish of his Member-of-Parliament accent. "Your gown is barely creased, and not by me, but by that interminable crush. Or more likely by this Davie fellow. And who the devil is he?" Strathcairn's green gaze poured over her like chilly water. "He can't possibly be a worthy mon if he lets a lass like you caress him in public. You're too young for suitors."

By jimble, but he had grown into an even more attractive man himself over the years, despite this polished, urbane facade. Or perhaps because of it—his worldliness gave him an attractive look of experienced wisdom. Quite irresistible.

"I'm not young anymore, either. I'm nineteen."

This he acknowledged with a wry sideways slant of his head, as if she were so out of kilter that the acute angle somehow made it easier to see her. "A very bad age to be an accomplished liar. And flirt." Strathcairn finally released her arm.

Much to her chagrin—which was all the emotion she would allow to account for the strange warmth suffusing her face—she found she missed the contact. How disconcerting.

So she changed the subject. Without flirting. "What are you doing in Edinburgh?"

"I've come north to see to Castle Cairn now that my

grandfather's passed on."

Something that must have been sincerity stabbed her hard in the chest. "I am sorry, Strathcairn. He was a grand auld gent."

It was the right thing to say—Strathcairn's whole demeanor softened enough to show her more of the young man she had admired beneath his curated veneer. Even those glittering eyes went soft at the edges. "Thank you. He was, wasn't he?"

"Aye." The Marquess of Cairn had been a cavalier of the old school, gentlemanly, generous and bold. He had raised Strathcairn when his son, Strathcairn's father and the prior earl, had passed away suddenly during Straithcairn's youth. "He'll be missed. Oh—that means you're Cairn now."

Strathcairn—for she could think of him no other way even if he were now Marquess of Cairn—lowered that chiseled chin, and nodded in rueful agreement. "Aye. And he's left large boots to fill. So I'm seeing to Cairn." He took a deep breath as if he were collecting himself before he raised his head, and added, "But before I head north to home, I've also been asked to see to a rather persistent problem plaguing Edinburgh."

A softer sense of alarm—or perhaps it was guilt— padded across her shoulders like a stealthy barn cat. She made light of it, as she always did. "The persistent plague of too many ladies and not enough gentlemen? I do hope you've come prepared to dance."

The first hint of a smile began at the far corner of his lips, as if he were not yet ready to commit to the strenuous exercise of a full-out grin. "No. I rarely dance." He shook his head in rueful apology. "No, the problem I speak of is a rash of thefts from some of the better households in the district. I've been asked to restore some sense of law and order within Edinburgh's society."

"On guard" was too simple and sensible a phrase to describe her reaction—Quince's skin went a little cold, and that sharp-clawed sense of alarm scratched its way down her spine. But she rose to the occasion—she knew better than most how to put up her weapons. To win any sort of fight, one had to attack, not just defend. And satire was the sharpest sword of them all.

"*Restore* law and order?" She made herself suitably wide-eyed and breathless. "I hadn't realized we were lacking it. Ought we to be on watch for gangs of housebreakers?"

"No, no. Nothing like that." He looked sage and worldly with all his unruffled calm, but she could see a tinge of riddy heat creeping over his collar. "Though it's too early to tell. But certainly too early for worry. Pray don't be alarmed, lass."

Quince's skin went all over prickly—nothing put her back up like being condescended to.

She sharpened up her sarcasm so he would not be able to so easily evade her point. "Holy sticky toffee pudding, Strathcairn"—she decided if he could trespass upon her Christian name, then she would trespass upon his old title—"imagine that. A gang of cutthroat housebreakers carting off priceless *Louis Quatorze* commodes to furnish their tatty tenement houses. How have the newspapers and broadsheets not been full of that?"

His smile confined itself to the outer corners of those intelligent green eyes. "No priceless commodes have been carted off."

"Auld occasional tables, then? Scaffy, mismatched chairs?"

"You needn't mock, lass. It's not ladylike." He put a hand up to rub the back of his neck, as if she really were succeeding in making him uncomfortable. Marvelous. And he had to subdue his growing smile—it started to hitch up one side of his mouth, as if he wanted to be amused, but was sure he oughtn't be. "If you must know, it's been very small items—smelling salt bottles, buttons, and the like."

And her with his two buttons down her bodice. She could feel them press into her skin as if they were biting her. Unsurprising since they were *his*.

Quince was too larky a lass to let a bit of her discomfort show. "Really? You've never abandoned Westminster, and come all the way north from London for some missing smelling salts?"

He had the good nature to look chagrined—that wary smile turned down sheepishly at the corners. "Not exactly. It's more complicated than that."

In fact, it was a great deal simpler than that. And she could not resist telling him so. "Well, it's a very good thing you told *me*." She lowered her voice in mock confidence. "Because I'm sure I know exactly what's happened to them."

He did not lean down to share her confidences. If anything, he became more upright, and even tilted away from her, as if he thought he could see her better from a distance. "You, lass?"

"Aye." She seized him by the upper arms, and manhandled him around—and by jimble if he hadn't the brawest, most firmly shaped musculature hidden under that soft, plush velvet—so he could follow the direction of her gaze. "There. Mr. Fergus McElmore has misplaced his snuffbox there, right under that vase of heather and broom. See? And there"—she pushed him in the other direction— "the Dowager Countess of Chester has abandoned her silver vinaigrette bottle in the cushion of her seat. Q.E.D. as you parliamentary types say." She made a dramatic flourish as if she were a theatrical barrister in court. "There is the *modus operandi* of your thefts, Strathcairn—silly stupidity at worst, simple thoughtlessness at best. Though in Fergus' case particularly, I think the thoughtlessness has come from an excess of Lady Inverness's fine Scotch whisky befuddling his poor wee numptie brain."

A fine coloring heat crept up Strathcairn's neck to his jawline. It lessened that impression of Grampian granite nicely.

He shook his head, but smiled nonetheless. "You think me foolish."

"I think whoever complained of their missing baubles is foolish, when they are likely only victims of their own excess—how *can* they be expected to keep track of so many possessions?"

He looked at her then—really looked, as if he finally saw more of her than the ghost of her pigtailed past. "You've a remarkably jaundiced view of society for a lass your age."

She was more than jaundiced. She was nearly lock-jawed with disdain. "I have a realistic understanding of human nature, Strathcairn. I think people are forgetful, and don't want to appear foolish, so they bluster and blame others for their own mistakes. And it is easy enough to blame the powerless"—she nodded toward the servants, who were most often the first to be accused when anything went amiss—"from the safe position of privilege."

"I take your meaning, lass." He acknowledged the right of her argument with a nod. "Nevertheless, it is my duty to look into the matter, to determine if it is indeed only a case—or cases—of forgetfulness."

"Then I should advise you to start with our hostess, and ask her what she does with all the flotsam and jetsam her guests leave behind after her balls." Because not even Quince, terrible magpie that she was, could take everything that was available—her bodice could only hold so much. "Perhaps she has the footmen cart it all up, and take it to the poor box at Canongate Kirk where they'll get better use of it."

The moment the words were out of her mouth she wished them back. She'd let her tongue run away from her mind, and run far too close to the truth for comfort.

And her suggestion brought Strathcairn's perilously attentive green gaze back to her. "What an agile mind you have, Lady Quince." And then for no reason she could fathom, he smiled at her—that gorgeous, gleaming grin she remembered of old. That mischievous, sideways curve of lip that made her feel as if she were being blessedly bludgeoned over the head with a five-penny slab of butter.

Quince nearly had to pinch herself to call her wits back under starter's orders. "Oh, pish tosh. Practical is what my mind is."

His smile settled back down to the corner of those sharp

eyes. "Perhaps, but you've given me an idea—perhaps what I'm looking for is not a hardened criminal, but someone with the dowagers's vice."

Nay, nay, nay.

Clever, too clear-eyed man.

She had to divert him with something equally clever. "Carrying a vinaigrette is a vice? What do you imagine the ladies keep in there? Undiluted opium?"

Strathcairn shook his head, but he was amused enough to still smile. "The dowager's vice is the irresistible tendency toward theft. That is, the compulsive stealing of objects which are not rightfully theirs. It is commonly practiced by maiden aunties and elderly companions. And dowagers, of course. Hence the name."

Oh, by jimble. That sounded far too apt.

And the skeptical Scot in him had taken over—he was frowning at the row of seats at the far side of the ballroom where the older ladies, including some rather impecunious relations and companions, sat with their heads together in a comfortable coze. "They look perfectly harmless, but one never knows what might be hidden in their reticules, or tucked into their bodices."

Heat blossomed in that very place where Strathcairn's purloined buttons dug into her skin. Oh, he was clever.

But so was she. "Down their bodices?" She quite purposefully, and quite inexpertly, straightened her trim bodice, drawing his attention out the side of his eye to her small, but nevertheless eminently serviceable breasts. Mama always said a man couldn't think and look at breasts, no matter their size. No fool, Mama. And the clever padding Mama had insisted her maid sew into her stays made up for any natural deficit. "How do they find any room? Must be dreadful uncomfortable."

His brow rose as slowly as a guillotine over that acute eye. But his self-control was not equal to the task at hand, and his gaze strayed exactly where she had meant it to.

"Lady Quince." Strathcairn's lowered voice was absolutely irresistible when he forgot himself enough to let the Scots burr rumble. "Let me make right sure I understand you—are you *flirting* with me?"

"Am I?" Quince ignored the blaze of heat his voice and gaze kindled under her skin, and gave him her bright, knowing smile—all pleased lips and mischievous eyes. "What I am doing is trying to make you remember your duty, and accede to my wish to dance with me."

He regarded her with those too canny, too bright green eyes for another long moment before he answered. "Perhaps I will." He reached for her hand, and held her at arm's length for a lengthy perusal, as if he had not yet decided to grant her wish. "Yes, I definitely will. But before I do so, perhaps I ought to warn you, wee Quince, to be good. And be very, very careful what you wish for."

The heat that had blossomed under her bodice spread like wildflowers across her skin along the whole length of his gaze. And she liked it.

She raised her chin and gave him her slyest smile yet. "Oh, I am always careful, Strathcairn. But I had much rather be bad, and be *right*."

Chapter 2

THE WEE SLIP of a lass was astonishing. Young Lady Quince Winthrop was just as willowy and witty and amusing as Alasdair had always hoped she would grow up to be. And grown up she had. In the five years that had passed since he had seen her last, she had become a damnably attractive young woman.

Alasdair Colquhoun, formerly fifth Earl Strathcairn and now fourth Marquess of Cairn, had not foreseen that—her being so attractive. Dangerously, distractingly attractive.

Which was strange. Because she wasn't a raging beauty— no one in London would have called wee Quince Winthrop a diamond of the first water. She was pretty without being beautiful, ordinary without being plain.

But what she was, was animated. And intelligent. And *interesting*.

Even with that appalling name.

Quince. It was bad enough as a boy's name, but it was nothing short of ridiculous for a girl. But Lord Winthrop was Edinburgh's Gardener Royal, a botanist who had long ago been bitten by a particularly virulent horticultural bug, given to erecting glasshouses and planting pinetums and arboretums, and giving his daughters ridiculous botanical names like Linnea, Willow, and Plum. And wee Quince.

Alasdair had always thought of her as *wee* Quince. She had been the baby sister in the Winthrop household—the naughty one wearing long chestnut braids, the one as spare and silent and sly as a she-fox. But she had also been entirely sympathetic, always laughing at his jokes. He could still see wee Quince in his mind's eye, peeping out at him with those bright golden-brown eyes as big as saucers, smiling with mischief from behind whatever chair or curtain she had hidden herself when she was supposed to be practicing the pianoforte.

She was still clearly naughty. Delightfully, unapologetically so.

Most young ladies of his acquaintance were the opposite—they pretended not to be naughty or vain or cynical, or interested in putting their arms around their beaux, and would never call the damned fellows darling. But Lady Quince Winthrop seemed impish and open, uncensored by society's opinions.

How damnably, dangerously refreshing.

She was tall for a lass, though she barely came up to his chin, even when she tilted that formidable nose in the air. But there was something about her—a largeness of presence that did not have to do with size. And although Lady Quince was dressed like almost all the other young ladies present, in the same sort of soft white dress the Duchess of Devonshire had recently made the height of fashion, wee Quince stood out like a bright-furred fox—all sleek, un-powdered chestnut hair, and neat, elfin features in a heart-shaped face.

But wee foxes could bite.

They could be provoking. And enchanting.

So enchanting he did not object to her next proposal. "You really must dance with me" —she began to tow him toward the ballroom—"if for no other reason than the pleasure it will afford me when you make the figures of the *ceilidh* dance badly."

She breezed onto the dance floor to take her place in the set without waiting for his agreement or say so. He had half a mind to abandon her there in the middle of the floor.

But it was as if wee Quince could read his thoughts. "Come, come, my Lord Cairn." She raised her voice loud enough for everyone in all of Edinburgh New Town to hear, and ladled on a broth of Scots brogue. "Don't be shy and stand-offish. I'm sure ye'll dance well enough, though ye've been in London so long with your parliamentary set, ye can't be expected to remember all the complicated *ceilidh* steps."

Guests turned their heads, just as she had wanted. There was nothing for it but to bow, and accede to her wishes as gracefully as possible. "You are a brat."

Her vixenish smile was all in the corner of her eyes. "A *clever* brat." She spun herself into a gracefully melting curtsey as the first fiddler scraped up his bow. "You do ken how to dance a proper Scottish *ceilidh* like Strip the Willow, do you not?"

He offered her a deep, if somewhat ironic, courtly bow. "Though I was educated in France, my lady, as all good Scots gentlemen are, I have not forgotten my country dancing."

"Were you really educated in France?" She narrowed her eyes, and then looked at him all askance. "And still they let you into the English government, with all the revolutionary uproar going on in France nowadays? How shocking."

He would love nothing more than to shock the tight, uplifting stays right off her trim little—

Devil take him. Best not to think of trim waists and uplifting bodices, or he wouldn't be able to call himself a gentleman. And he had worked long and hard—too long and too hard—to make himself into a proper British gentleman, to abandon that title five minutes after reacquainting himself with this provoking young lass.

A provoking young lass who was not yet done twitting him. "Mayhap we will be so fortunate as to have a small collision that will knock your wig askance, and amuse the onlookers, who stare to see you dance so." She pressed an unhelpful hand to her luscious little bosom, and let out a sigh of anticipatory pleasure. "I live in hope."

He was beginning to live in something else entirely.

But it would not do to say so. "And I live to serve, brat. Though I assure you I wear my own hair powdered, and not a wig."

"Do you? A pity." She let out a dramatic little sigh. "But perhaps we still might amuse, for we do look ridiculous together—me so small, and you so tall."

Alasdair was about to protest that however wee she was, she wasn't in the least bit small. But it would never do to tell a young lady—even a witty, amusing lass like Lady Quince Winthrop—that her strange impression of largeness was a product of her over-sized character. The damn lass should have been a field marshal, the way she had maneuvered him.

Once the music began, he found his feet easily enough, following the lilting lift of the fiddles as they skipped along. And Lady Quince was both uplifting and diverting in her own way—she executed the little jumps and turns with such gracefully careless enthusiasm that Alasdair's gaze became increasingly fixed on the top line of her bodice, from whence her lily white bosom threatened to spill over the top of all that sublime, silky lace.

When had she grown such superb breasts?

Oh, devil take him for a damned fool. Thank God he was dancing, or he'd have no way of explaining the astonishing heat sweeping across his face. Alasdair could only pray people would think his color was due to the exertion of the dance, and not to his musings on Lady Quince's remarkable little breasts.

To combat that heat, Alasdair lowered his gaze to the floor, which he hoped would be a rather more prosaic view, but the skipping steps of the dance conspired to give him more than one glimpse of the brat's trim, stockinged ankles. Enough of a glimpse to make him think of the calves above those well-turned ankles, and of the knees above the calves, and of the garters above the knees, crossing her milky thighs—

Alasdair pinched his eyes closed, and forced himself to take a deep, calming breath. Why he thought said thighs might be milky was pure hallucination on his part. Clearly the young lady's thighs were likely to be as tricky and dangerous as the rest of her—even her smile was devious, as if she were daring him to like her.

If ever there was a lass in need of a husband, it was daring, darling Lady Quince. She needed a man who could keep all that mischievous potential in check, and keep her too busy to flirt and cause ballroom havoc. "Why are you not married?"

Bloody hell. He had asked the bloody question out loud—loud enough for the couple next in the set to hear him, and give him a horrified, cautionary look.

Any other lass would have instantly rebuked him, or burst into tears, or perhaps even slapped him at so forward and intrusive a question. But because wee Quince Winthrop was not like any other lass, she laughed. "Why on earth would I want to be married? Give up my freedom for wedlock at my age? What an appalling, auld-fashioned notion."

For some reason he could not fathom, Alasdair felt compelled to defend the institution. "Sometimes the old-fashioned ideas are best."

Her scornful look told him she did not agree. "When did you become such a sorry auld grumphus?"

When he had realized being ambitious meant choosing sides. But, "grumphus?" He could feel his face split into another ill-considered smile. "Lady Quince, you're havering—there is no such word as 'grumphus.'"

"There is now—I just made it up. And you are most assuredly a very sorry auld grumphus thinking that way. Though you do dance tolerably well."

Even her rebukes had an air of sweet mischievousness. Which was growing decidedly hard to resist. So he stopped resisting, and let his smile stretch out and make itself comfortable in a grin. "Only with you, my lady lass. Only for you."

She accepted his fealty as her due, with a roaring laugh that threatened the integrity of her bodice. "You're getting there. Another five minutes and we'll have you laughing full out, like a proper Scot. Admit it—dancing, and laughing, is good for you. You should do it more often."

"Perhaps," he conceded as they took hands to go down the dance. "Perhaps I will."

But when they got to the bottom of the line, the fiddlers drew their bows to end the dance, and Alasdair was forced to relinquish her hand. "Thank you, my lady. You were quite correct. It has been a distinct pleasure."

"You are quite welcome." She curtseyed very becomingly, and then led the way off the floor. "But as lovely as it has been to renew our acquaintance, and dance, and match wits with you, Strathcairn, I'm afraid you'll now have to go."

Go? Alasdair was not about to be so easily dismissed. Not when he was having fun matching wits with her. "I think not."

"Strathcairn." She frowned mightily, and made a more obvious shooing motion with her agile, animated fingers. "Go away. You musn't talk to me anymore. Someone will notice."

"I thought that was what you wanted when you cozened me into dancing with you."

She smiled, but blithely ignored his logic. "Nay. I won't allow you to be such a danger to yourself. And don't pretend you don't understand. If a mon like you, a *marquess*, for pity's sake, who ought by all rights to be married off by now—what *have* you been doing with your time?—is seen talking to *me*, who's nobody, it can only be for devious or nefarious purposes."

Her logic was categorically flawed. But vastly amusing. "What I have done with my time is work for the Prime Minister's government. And thus no one who knows me will think that I am being either devious or nefarious. And you're not nobody."

"Don't be absurd." The lady made a decidedly un-ladylike, disparaging sound. "Then it will be worse, Strathcairn—they'll think you're being *serious*."

He decided he liked the irreverent way she called him by his old name Strathcairn, man to man, as it were. "That is a chance I am willing to take, lass. Perhaps I *am* being serious. Perhaps, because I am *old-fashioned*, I shall appoint myself to watch over you, and keep you from slipping out into the night to embrace ill-mannered, callow young cads named Davie. You must understand how dangerous that is?"

"To be seen talking to you for over a half-hour now? Oh, aye, undoubtedly. My friends will think I have lost my good sense, as well as the better part of my good humor, if they see me talking to a politician, even a 'New Tory'— which is a ridiculous thing for your set to call yourselves, because you're all as stodgy as any old Tory, if you ask me, which you do not. But what my friends will think when they see us together talking after dancing in so slim a period as a half an hour, is that you *like* me. Or worse, that I like *you*." She shuddered with mock horror, as if such a thing were akin to contracting the influenza.

"You used to like me." Five years ago, she had been the invisible audience at the passion play of his wooing Lady Linnea. It had been a game, guessing which chair or curtain she would be hidden behind, stifling her giggles.

Funny how it had seemed just yesterday.

Lady Quince was not a party to his reminisces—she was all of the here and now. "Aye, I suppose I did like you once." She heaved another theatrical sigh at him. "But I can see you've grown scruples to spare now that you're Cairn. How tedious."

"Have I?" He frowned, even as he felt himself smile. "I'd like to think I had my scruples all along. Maybe you just couldn't recognize them yourself—as you seem not to have many a'tall."

It was very nearly an insult, though he didn't really mean it as such—he meant to be teasing.

But she was herself, and though her smile momentarily slid off to one corner of her mouth as if considering its options, she didn't take offense. She laughed. "Quite right. I sold every last one of my scruples for a lively profit some years ago, since I wasn't using them." But then she poked him hard in the chest. "You used to be fun."

"Ah, well." What could he say? Time marched on. "That was a long time ago, lass, when I was younger, and untested in the ways of the world. And when I became a man, I put away childish things—"

"Oh, for pity's sake, don't quote the Bible at *me*. That's *my* gambit," she muttered. "Talk about fallow fields."

"Aye." He could feel his face stretch into a grin. "I can see you're unrepentant. But I do thank you for that assessment of my former character." He leaned back against the wall, and crossed his arms over his chest. "You saw and heard an awful lot from behind those chairs of yours."

"I saw enough." She peeked up at him from the corner of her eyes. "I saw Linnea throw you over."

Alasdair felt his jaw go tight. It was galling to find that anyone had witnessed even a part of his come down—it was not a moment he liked to remember. But it was also a moment that he could not allow himself to forget—that moment, and the nascent scandal that had given rise to Linnea's rejection, had shaped the man he was today.

"Poor staid Strathcairn." Lady Quince repeated her opinion of the man he was today rather emphatically. "Perhaps Linnea sensed that you were destined to become a grumbly auld grumphus."

Did wee Quince not remember the reason behind her sister's terse dismissal? Perhaps she had been too young to understand the fullness of the brewing scandal. But she was not so young now. "You are too old to be trying to provoke me in this childish manner." So was he, but he could not seem to stop himself from crossing verbal swords with her.

"Never," she contradicted. "And I am only trying to provoke you into having some *fun*. Larkiness is good for the soul, and you, Strathcairn, could use a great whopping dose of larkiness."

"I should think you've enough for all of us."

"I have. And I take it as my solemn duty to spread all available larkiness around."

"Rather like manure on a garden?"

She roared laughing again. "Quite right, Strathcairn. Rather exactly like manure. Manure for the soul!"

"Quince, my dear?" Lady Winthrop stood no more than three feet away—close enough to have heard their conversation.

But how much? He had been too absorbed with his wee nemesis to notice.

"My Lord Cairn." Her ladyship dropped a graceful, if economical, curtsey to him, before her eyes shifted toward her youngest daughter. "What can the two of you have been having such a heated *tête à tête* about?"

"Parliament, Mama." Wee Quince surprised him with the speed and ease of her lie. "Strathcairn reveals himself to be a strict, dedicated politician."

He had quite purposefully made his career the entirety of his existence. So why did wee Quince Winthrop's opinion of him sting so much, like a tiny, but biting nettle, working its way under his skin?

"How interesting, my lord." Lady Winthrop's voice held the quiet yet commanding tone of a lady who knows very well when people are saying one thing, and meaning another. "I did not know you had been introduced to my youngest daughter."

That daughter again answered before he could speak. "His lordship trespassed upon the old acquaintance." Her mischievous little smile dared him to contradict her. "Though I almost did not recognize him, it has been so many long years since he courted Linnea. And she such an old married matron, now."

"Quince." With a single word and a singular look, Lady Winthrop stopped her daughter from saying anything more provoking. "I daresay his lordship has grown tired of your taunting style of conversation. And your Aunt Celeste bids you attend to her."

To his surprise, the lass did not argue, or protest, or offer her mother the slightest cheek. She did as she was bid, but not before she shot him a warning look—all leveled brow and direct stare—that told him he was not to reveal the true nature of their conversation—all that *flirtation*—and silently excused herself.

He watched her go with a strange and entirely unexpected pang of relief and loss, as if he had forgotten to breathe, and was just now catching his breath.

"Well, my Lord Cairn." Lady Winthrop's pleasant social smile did not falter in the least, but her gaze was as direct and forthright as her daughter's. "Might I inquire as to what sort of *manure* you've been spreading around?"

Oh ruddy, bloody hell. Clearly, Lady Winthrop remembered the old scandal full well.

Alasdair had to call upon all his politician's tact. "Just a metaphor for my rather execrable attempt at matching young Lady Quince's wit."

Lady Winthrop's look—all high brows and inquiring eyes—showed her astonishment. "You were attempting to match wits with Quince? And how, pray tell, did you get on? Though you don't look like you're bleeding about the face and ears like the rest of them. Dare I hope you held your own?"

Alasdair was so astonished, he gave her the truth. "I haven't the faintest idea."

"Yes, her style of conversation, to use a polite phrase, is rather a bit too...acrobatic. But you don't look the worse for wear." Lady Winthrop gave him a consoling pat on the shoulder. "Well done, you."

"I don't know how well done it was, but I can tell you that lass of yours is wasted in Edinburgh. She'd take Parliament by storm if she unleashed that acrobatic, agile mind of hers in serious debate."

"Would she?" Her ladyship's brows rose, though her gracious smile never faltered. "Pray don't tell her that, or you'll have a petition for ladies' suffrage on your hands. But what an *interesting* assessment of my daughter's character, my lord."

Oh, devil take him. Now she thought he was, as Quince had said, *serious*.

"I'm sure she's a lovely enough lass." Alasdair was anxious to change the topic, and save himself from any further scrutiny. "And how is Lady Linnea these days, ma'am?"

"Ah." Lady Winthrop was kind enough to turn the conversation his way. "Well, I thank you. She is Lady Powersby, now, and the mother of two rambunctious children. Their Aunt Quince is therefore a favorite of theirs."

Of course she was. Like attracted like.

Alasdair forbade himself from smiling. "Lady Powersby is to be congratulated."

The lady's mother nodded in acknowledgment. "I will give her your greeting, my lord."

"Thank you, Lady Winthrop. Please do."

The lady again nodded cordially, but there was still something of her youngest daughter's straightforwardness to her gaze. "Your attentions to my youngest daughter have been noted, my lord. I do not say so entirely to censure—as I have heard nothing but good of you these past years—but to warn. Quince likes to…" She searched again for an appropriate word for her blithe youngest daughter. "…stir the pot. And I should think you would prefer not to have your particular pot stirred."

"Indeed, ma'am." He had been duly warned off—for his own good, as well as her daughter's. "Just as you say, my lady."

"Thank you, my lord." She inclined her head cordially. "I bid you good evening."

"Good evening, ma'am." Alasdair bowed deeply, and as soon as Lady Winthrop had disappeared into the crush, he made for the card room where he knew a good drink—meaning a decent, large glass of brandy—could be had.

But there in the doorway to the card room,

absentmindedly patting down his coat pockets, was the Honorable Fergus McElmore.

"What ho, Fergus my lad," Alasdair greeted his acquaintance. "Misplaced something, have you?"

"Hello, auld mon." Fergus McElmore returned the greeting. "I say, Alasdair, have ye seen my auld snuffbox? That one of my father's? Damned if I *haven't* misplaced it somewhere again."

Perhaps wee Quince Winthrop had the right of it. Perhaps the thefts he had pledged himself to end were nothing but the product of whisky and forgetfulness. "Do that often, do you, Fergus?"

Fergus reddened enough for his cheeks to match his nose. "More than I ought."

"Well, lad, you're in luck this evening, because as a matter of rare fact, I have seen your snuffbox. Right this way." Alasdair led Fergus toward the spot where he had begun his wordplay with the intriguing and infuriating Lady Quince Winthrop. "Saw it just here," he indicated the small table with the vase of heather spilling over the edge.

"Here?" Fergus peered around the base of the vase. "Don't see it."

"Nay. Just at the side there. I'm sure of it." Alasdair picked up the vase, so there would be no mistake, no missing the wee silver box.

But there was no mistaking that the table was now empty. The snuffbox was gone.

It *had* been right here—he had seen it himself. It had to still be right there. Unless... "Did you pick it up from here, and then misplace it perhaps somewhere else?"

"I don't think so," Fergus answered Alasdair's first question. "But I say, auld mon, ye seem to have lost something as well. The buttons on the back of your coat. They're gone."

"The hell you say." Alasdair whirled around, grabbing up his coattails to have a look. And there, where only an hour ago the shining silver buttons had winked at him in the mirror, there was only plain, unadorned, blood red velvet.

Well, damn him for a fool.

Chapter 3

THE HONORABLE FERGUS McElmore's snuffbox was all but burning a hole in her pocket, but it was really her conscience that was on fire.

She ought not have taken it. She really, really ought not. But the box had just been sitting there. Calling out to her. Reminding her that one tiny silver and enamel box could feed many, many little mouths.

But the very bad fact of the matter was that she could resist neither the temptation, nor the slippery jangle of anticipatory excitement that had set her pulse to beating from the moment she'd decided she would take the glittering little prize. Nor the illicit thrill buzzing through her veins now that she had the tiny container safely stowed away. The thrill that was as addictive as any opiate. And addicted she was—she would always be tempted.

Yet, even such clear-sighted self-awareness did little to curb her magpie habit.

Quince escaped the ballroom by slipping into the withdrawing room, where she might splash some cool water on her cheeks, and calm her hectic pulse. As nervy as she felt, it would quite likely show. Someone—meaning her nearly omniscient mama—would think she *had* been doing more than sparring with Strathcairn if she looked all flushed and giddy.

No fool Mama.

And then there was Strathcairn, no longer earl thereof but marquess, who might put one and two together, and come up with a sovereign—which was about as much money as she would get from melting down the silver from the buttons and snuffbox.

Speaking of which—the ruddy buttons were still digging into her skin. She tried to shift the press of her stays, but nothing worked. "Jeannie?"

"Mileddy?" The withdrawing room attendant, a local dressmaker who had once been Quince's personal maid, came to her feet. "May I help ye?"

There were other young ladies taking advantage of the withdrawing room as well, so Quince would have to be discreet. She gave Jeannie a subtle nod before she adjusted her bodice in a way that made the two buttons fall silently to the floor at her feet, and raised her voice. "Yes, please. I'm afraid I've torn the lace on my bodice. If you'd be so kind?"

"Certainly, mileddy." Jeannie picked up her basket full of sewing notions and spools of threads in every color, and set it on the floor before she got to work, while Quince smiled over her shoulder and murmured greetings as other young ladies and matrons came and went.

"There ye are, mileddy." Jeannie bit off the thread, and scooped the buttons into her basket amongst all the other notions. "And let me get ye a cool cloth. Ye've gone a bit pink in the cheeks."

"Thank you, Jeannie." She pressed the linen to her face, and adjusted her clothing "That's better."

She had been smart to come, and take a moment to calm down and collect herself. There was a time to rise to a challenge, and a time to hide away, and save temptation, like dessert, for later.

Quince smoothed down her skirts in preparation for

disappearing back into the crowd in the ballroom, where she would do well to find an unobtrusive spot to keep a wary eye on Strathcairn. "Thank you, Jeannie, Once more into the breach, dear friend."

Only to find the breach of the doorway filled with Strathcairn.

"Taking snuff, are we now, Lady Quince?" he growled as he clamped his hand around her elbow, and hauled her down the corridor with a great deal less subtlety, and far less good humor, than he had displayed in whisking her from the ballroom earlier.

Oh, nay, there was nothing gentle or humorous about the way he reeled her into an empty, unlit room—there was anger and the potential for violence in his grip. She would have to tread a very fine line indeed.

Because her own unruly anger was rising to the occasion.

Quince rounded her elbow out of his possession. "Strathcairn." She polished her voice down to a hard shine. "I wish I could say this wasn't a terrible surprise. What on earth do you think you're doing?"

"I might ask the exact same question of you, Lady Quince." His voice had lost every last ounce of its pleasing, teasing intonation—the refined Scot's burr was now as thorny as a thistle. "What have you done with them?"

"With whom?" She narrowed her own gaze down to a matching frown—she had the measure of him now, and would give as good as she got.

"I am speaking," he bit out, "of the buttons from my coat and Fergus McElmore's snuffbox."

Oh, holy iced macaroons. It was he who had the measure of her, and was weighing her up as accurately an undertaker.

Thank goodness the only light came from the moon filtering through the windows, washing her in silver, or he might have seen her face pale. As it was, she had everything to do to control her breathing, and act affronted and confused, and not give into the impulse to chafe her arms to warm the skin that had suddenly gone cold and clammy. "My dress does not have any buttons. And I don't take snuff. The occasional nip of whisky, aye. But not snuff." She did not have to fake the shudder that worked its way up her spine. "Disgusting habit."

The darkness of the room made Strathcairn look even more grim and unforgiving as he advanced upon her. "I should advise ye, brat, to stop attempting to bamboozle me. Just give me the damn buttons."

Bamboozle. In any other instance she would have delighted in his pronunciation of the word—no man should be able to make the words themselves jump up and dance to his tune. Especially when he was angry. And he was very angry. Inconveniently so.

Because she had some serious bamboozling to do.

She began with misdirection. "Strathcairn, clearly you have misunderstood something." She put up her empty palms to keep him from advancing any farther. "What buttons?"

"The buttons from my damn coat." He pulled up the tail of his coat to show her the bare swath of crimson velvet.

"Your coat doesn't have buttons." Misdirection worked best with the obvious. "So there is certainly no call for you to shout at me so."

"I am not shouting." He crossed his arms over his chest as if it were the only way he could keep himself from throttling her. "I am everything calm and reasonable considering the circumstances. And so I will warn you not to lie to me, wee Quince Winthrop, though you do it alarmingly well, and without a shred of remorse. You're altogether too convincing, and too larcenous, for a lass your age."

Not convincing or larcenous enough, apparently.

"Now," he instructed succinctly. "Give them to me."

She had much rather put the buttons up his gorgeously fine, straight Scots nose, but alas, such a feat would undoubtedly be unwise. Not to mention terribly messy. And utterly impossible.

One must pick one's battles, Mama always said, and fight only upon firm ground.

Quince put up her chin. "You are grievously mistaken, if you think I have them. There were no buttons upon the coat when we met. I have nothing of yours, Strathcairn. Nothing."

He uncrossed his arms, and stalked closer, as if he were trying to read her face in the frosting of moonlight. "Have you always lied so well, lass? Or have I just forgotten?"

It was the hint of actual admiration in his tone—at least it sounded to her a *little* like admiration—accompanying the affront that almost made her answer truthfully. Almost.

But she did not. Because she was not suicidal. And because lying *was* a skill she had cultivated as carefully as an exotic seedling in one of her father's meticulously tended glass houses. A skill she had mastered out of necessity. A skill as necessary to survival within society as breathing. Or finding the right dressmaker.

The trick lay in adding just enough of the truth. "Nay, you have not forgotten. But everyone lies, at least a little. Don't you?"

"Nay." He answered straightaway. "Deception of any kind is abhorrent to me."

Well. Quince deliberately made her tone light, as if she were too much of a flibbertigibbet to understand the gravity of the topic at hand. "Pish tosh, sir. I thought you were a politician. You'll not get far in *that* racket if you can't tell a well-told lie."

"It's not a racket." He ground the last word down as if it were grist from a Glasgow mill.

"Oh, aye." She batted his protestations away with an airy wave. "I'm sure the English Parliament is as important and necessary as all get out. But that doesn't give you the right to come back to Scotland, and just accuse people of things. Goodness, Strathcairn, did you listen to nothing I said?"

"Oh, I listened. Which is exactly why you're here." His gaze pored over her, cataloguing every blemish and defect, as if a closer look might reveal the deeper flaws of her character. "Your conversation told me you're clever and curious and observant and bored. And you had your hands on my back. I am not stupid, so don't you be, wee Quince. I am not a man to be trifled with."

That was clearly true. And she was not stupid either, so she abandoned her plan to trifle with him. "Then I will go."

He came at her with such speed she could not prepare herself for the rough grasp of his hands upon her shoulders, as if he meant to try and shake the truth out of her. "For God's sake, lass. Don't. Don't willfully misunderstand how dangerous this is."

"To be closeted up in a dark room with you while you're in the grip of some violent passion?" She tried very hard not to be intimidated by him looming above her. "I completely agree. It must end immediately. And now that you've made your point so clearly, I'll heed your advice, and go."

She tried to duck around him, but he snagged a strong arm around her waist, and pulled her back against his chest. "Not so bloody fast." He slid his big hands to either side of her waist, so that his thumbs pressed at the side of her stays with just enough pressure to make her bodice gape away from her body, while he looked over her shoulder, straight down into the shallow valley between her breasts. "If you won't show me, I'll just have to see for myself then, won't I?"

Quince immediately put up her hands over the rise of her breasts to preserve what modesty she could, but she could feel the angry heat of his body searing into her—feel the power he had over her, and feel her own fear burning its way down her throat—the sliver of space between them felt as wide as a gulf.

"Strathcairn!" Her voice was as thin and frail as a willow. "I have no idea of what—"

"You've some idea," he countered with another rough shake. "You probably had the idea to slide the damn things right down your trim wee bodice." And with that, his big, clever fingers slid straight down along the line of the busk, beneath the thin protection of her chemise, completely against her bare skin.

Oh, holy ice picks.

But instead of swearing as she might be forgiven for doing under the circumstances, she let out an undignified sound very much like the frightened squeak of a mouse. And managed no more. Her breath was trapped inside her chest—a fist of aching heat stopping up her throat. Her stupid brain was entirely incapable of thought.

She was frozen, though knew she ought to do something. Laugh. Or slap him. Hard.

But this was the new Strathcairn. He might just laugh and slap her back.

And his arm was still wrapped around her waist, girding her like a sapling he could snap in two if he but chose, while his other hand was groping under her breasts.

Heat prickled everywhere on her body. Everywhere.

How ridiculously lowering. How entirely infuriating.

No matter what she had done, she did not deserve to be groped.

"Strathcairn!" She abandoned modesty to dig her sharp fingernails into the soft skin inside his wrist, and screw his thumb out of its socket, and out of her bodice. "This is not the way a gentleman treats with a lady."

"Devil take you" He wrung his wrenched thumb out of her grip. "If I do not act the gentleman," he countered grimly, "it's because you do not act the lady. Where have you stashed them?"

She took advantage of her freedom to simply haul back and slap him hard across the face. Hard enough that her hand left a vivid print across his cold cheek. So hard, the crack of her palm against his flesh echoed against the four walls.

The force of her fear and anger left her stunned. And livid. And very nearly afraid. She was alone with a man twice her size, three times her strength, and four times her influence. She had waved her cape at the wrong bull.

Seconds of stunned silence ticked by. She stood her ground, and braced herself for the force of his reprisal. But somehow, sense prevailed.

Strathcairn was thankfully gentleman enough not to slap

her back. Or worse. Instead, he took her stinging rebuke like a man—he stepped away. "My apology, my lady."

Quince was too vexed to be properly relieved or grateful—she was still shaking with the awful admixture of guilt and fear and unholy, desperate anger. "Your apology is barely sufficient."

"I am sorry." He took another step back from her. "I thought— I was sure—" He shook his head as if he might realign his thinking. "I seem to have made an error."

Indignation spurred her on where common sense might have held her back. "You've made more than an error, Strathcairn. You've made an enemy out of a friend. I am no one's pet or plaything. No matter what you think, my body is my own, and I play by my own rules." She tried to speak with heat and force, but her voice was strained—the hot ache of tears threatened to rob her of bravado. Every bit of her, from the top of her head to the bottom of her shoes, was pinched tight with the awful tension. Her stinging right hand was fisted at her side, her fingernails digging into the flesh of her palm.

His righteous anger faded in the face of hers. "Indeed, my lady." He spread his open hands before him in apology, and shook his head in wonder. "I don't know what I was thinking. Devil take me, but I was sure—"

He had been sure because he was diabolically clever, as well as correct in his assumptions—she *had* taken his blasted buttons. And the snuffbox. Only she did not have them now. Her well-honed instinct for self-preservation had urged her to rid herself of the evidence, and pass the items off to Jeannie as soon as possible. Or, perhaps it had simply been that the buttons digging into her skin like a brand had made her too uncomfortable. Too guilty.

Which was made worse by the fact that Strathcairn seemed rather genuinely contrite. "Lady Quince, please accept my most abject apology."

"Aye. All right." She nodded herself, and took the moment to pull a lungful of air into her tight chest as they stood there restoring themselves to a pale, wary approximation of their former equanimity.

He shook his head again, as if his brain were still not clear. "I can't believe I just put my hand upon your wee bre—"

"Do not say it." She crossed her arms over said breasts. "Do not. Or I'll be tempted to skelp you again. I must not have hit you hard enough the first time."

"Oh, you did hit me hard enough." He reached up to test his jaw. "Cracking good skelpit. Knocked some sense into me, you did. And again, I apologize. I'm sorry I thought you capable of such deception."

There was nothing she could say that would not make her feel the veriest blackguard. The truth was that she had secretly practiced her pugilism, as well as her swordplay, almost as assiduously as she had her deception. They were all necessary skills to the strange, larcenous life she had made for herself.

And the sincerity in his voice placated her more than she liked. She was safer being angry with Strathcairn. Anger might keep her from playing any more stupid tricks on him.

Because he was not stupid. Far from it. He was a more than a worthy opponent. If she were not very careful indeed, he could become her nemesis, and then she would be most sorely sorry.

She had baited the bull more than enough for one evening.

Quince made her tone more purposefully light and mocking. "If this is what comes of having an excess of scruples, then I am glad to say I haven't any. At least *I've* never assaulted anyone." She was far more backhanded than that.

Strathcairn continued to weather her scorn like a gentleman—that is to say, with sincere remorse. "I'm heartily ashamed of myself. And which is worse, I know my suspicions are like to cost me your friendship."

It wasn't the suspicions, but his way of handling them. "Aye," she agreed. "Which is really too bad. For I did like you, Strathcairn, in spite of your wretched scruples. But now—" There was really nothing else she could say. Quince took a deep breath to push the nervy tension out of her lungs. It really was tiresome business, this anger. "I liked it so much better when we were sparring along so amicably. It was *fun*." She had felt alive and happy and thrilled in a way that she only ever felt when she was stealing something, and getting away with it.

But that was the crux of it all—their evening and her conflicted feeling toward him—she *had* stolen from him. Strathcairn's reasons for suspecting her were sound—she would do well to be warier of his cleverness in the future—even if his actions were not. "But even if it was fun, and I did like you, that was not an invitation to put your hand down my bodice."

He chafed that same hand across his face and into his hair, disrupting the sleek white queue. "Nay. You may be assured that I shan't do so again." He took another step backward to emphasize his intentions to keep well away from her.

"I should hope not. Or next time I might not be content to only skelp ye."

"Nay." The faintest trace of a smile cobwebbed up the corners of his eyes. "Next time I expect you'll try to put a bullet in me."

"I expect I'll do more than try if you ever try to get handsy with me again."

"*Handsy*," he instructed, not unkindly, "is not even a proper word."

"It is a properly useful, made-up word. Which is why I made it up."

A quiet huff of laughter escaped him. "You really are the most extraordinary lass, Quince Winthrop."

She would not give in to the pleasure of his admiration. She would not. "Oh, don't you dare pour the butter boat over me now, you dreadful man. I am still properly cross with you."

But it was a lovely feeling—warm and slippery. And dangerous.

Quince had to remind herself she could never be wholly candid, wholly herself, with him. Because she lied and stole just as well, and just as easily, as she danced. And deception of any kind was abhorrent to him.

"More than cross," she added for emphasis. More to convince herself than him.

He continued to be everything contrite. "As well you should be. You've every right." He heaved a sigh out of his chest. "But no more cross than I am with myself. And I am no closer to finding out who has been stealing people's valuables." He looked up at the coffered ceiling for a moment, as if seeking divine guidance. "Do you really think it could be one of the dowagers or maiden aunties?"

"Oh, no. Don't think just because your suspicions are no longer pointed at me, that I'll fall in to help you. I am no gossip." Of her many faults, rumormongering was not one—which was rather unfortunate, since an affinity for gossip was the one fault society favored.

"Nay. I don't suppose you are. You're too straightforward." His smile warmed his eyes to a lovely shade of green that made her think rather absurdly of arbors and quiet, peaceful gardens. "But this kind of opportunistic theft is called the dowager's vice for a reason. The old ladies, especially those in some financial distress or hardship, are the logical place to look."

Nay, nay, nay. She spoke before she could think to her own advantage. "I don't think it would be any of the maiden aunties, honestly."

Oh, holy iced lemonade. Why could she not just shut her mouth and let him chase his tail about the chaperones and companions? Why could she not just let angry tomcats howl? Because.

Because it would not have been fair to those poor old ladies. Life was hard enough for them without letting Strathcairn prowl his intimidating way around the poor old tabbies. It would be truly upsetting to ladies like querulous old Miss MacDonald, who worried enough about where her next shillings were coming from without Strathcairn looking over her shoulder counting up her coins.

Nay. Quince needed a plausible alternative—a better form of misdirection. "Why is it called the Dowager's Vice? Why not the Bachelor's Vice? Or the Dandy's Vice? Why must such thefts be motivated by feminine poverty instead of something far more compellingly masculine, like jealousy or greed—which is what leads to most of that feminine poverty in the first place, if you ask me, which you don't. Why is it less plausible that someone coveted Mr. McElmore's snuffbox for their own collection? Or was so jealous they wanted to mar the perfection of your absolutely stunning velvet suit?"

"Stunning, is it?"

"Oh, don't come coy with *me*, Strathcairn. I shan't give you a polite lie. You've both a mirror and valet—you ken you look very well indeed, you great vain popinjay."

"I think I preferred it when you were politely lying."

"I don't lie when the plain truth will do." Truth was fine, only if it was accompanied by misdirection. "Though I am not so averse to the necessity of lying as you seem to be, poor sad politician that you must be."

He made a warm sound of amusement, a lovely low rumble from deep in his chest. Which would have been wonderfully gratifying had she not remembered that his amusement was just as perilous, if not more so, than his anger.

"As much as I have enjoyed *some* moments of becoming reacquainted with you, Strathcairn, I do not want to be found locked up in a room with you."

Which was almost a lie. In any other circumstance, he was just the sort of man—the *only* sort of man—she would consider being locked up with. A smart, amusing, attractive, experienced man.

Who spoke before she could go. "I should like to make it up to you—my terrible lapse in judgment."

Oh, here was the real danger—the rush of pleasure that flowed through her like a floodwater, sweeping all other concerns aside. Especially the concern that she *was*, in fact, a thief. She *had* stolen from him.

"Best not, Strathcairn." She firmed her voice. "Best to go our own separate ways."

"Which may prove difficult. Edinburgh is not like London—its society is not so large that we'll be able to avoid each other entirely."

She would find a way. "Nay. But—"

"It were better if we were allies instead of enemies. And I could very much use a friend." He took the time to warm the butter boat of his smile for her. "In fact, I could use your help."

"Help?" This temptation was the most dangerous of all. "I couldn't possibly help you."

"Certainly you could. You're clever, and quick, and you see things others don't—like Fergus McElmore's snuffbox hidden on a side table. And you know Edinburgh society in a way that I don't, having been in London these past five years. You could help me."

Oh, holy blasted gunpowder. She had never been so torn, so pulled in two entirely different directions. If only he had come home three years ago, before all this—all the stealing and lying and *bamboozling*—had started. If only *she* wasn't the one he was searching for. If only it wasn't utterly and hopelessly impossible.

Too impossible for her to resist.

Because she was who she was. And he was here, now, and *interested*. And he was a man, the likes of which she was not like to meet again.

This was the time to take the chance fate had been kind enough to give her.

"All right, Strathcairn. I'll make you a deal."

Chapter 4

ALASDAIR WAS INTRIGUED and tempted, if only for the naughty note of mischief that had crept back into the lass's voice. But his hard-won habit of prudence warned him to be wary of any proposals, especially when the mercurial Lady Quince was involved.

After all, she had just slapped him—skept him damned hard.

Not that he hadn't deserved it. "What sort of deal do you have in mind?"

"Not a deal, per se," she amended, "but more of a...proposition."

"Oh, aye?" The fine hair on the back of his nape prickled in awareness. Every instinct he possessed told him the lass might *not* have taken his buttons, but she knew *something*—everything about the lass shouted *knowledge*.

"As you've noted, I am clever, and bored. And very, very curious."

That prickling awareness changed, and spread under his skin like warm honey. "What in particular are you curious about, wee Quince?"

"About…things." She tipped her head to one side, as if she were just thinking out loud, deciding as she went along. "Life. Courtship. Gentlemen. The reason your face went an alarming shade of red after you put your hand down my bodice."

Hell. She could not have surprised him any more if she had skelpt him again.

Alasdair gave his cravat a tug to loosen it, and hoped his face wasn't turning the same alarming shade of red now—steam was all but seeping out from under his collar. But with the mischievous wee Lady Quince, there was no profit in being coy or disingenuous. "Well, as you seem to want to be candid, I'll tell you the reason my face went such a telling shade of red was that your breasts were magnificent."

Wee Quince Winthrop's mouth dropped open in a silent "o" of astonishment. Or pleasure. He could not quite tell.

"Magnificent?" She treated the word with skepticism, as she looked down at the breasts in question. "No one else thinks so."

Alasdair passed a hand over his eyes, as if the thought pained him. Which it did. "Pray do not tell me their names, or I will be obliged to kill them on the spot. And that would surely ruin my coat."

She pleated her lips together to subdue her smile. "I know I oughtn't say so, but it would be lovely if you would kill them, Strathcairn. Run them straight through. I doubt the blood would even show with *that* coat."

"What a remarkably bloodthirsty lass you are." He pretended to be aghast. "You oughtn't know about such things as sword fights and blood stains."

But the truth was that she was *exactly* the sort of lass who would know about swords and dueling and blood stains. He could see her in his mind's eye, experimenting with cutlasses and rapiers. Attired in alarmingly tight-fitting white breeches.

Alasdair gave himself another mental shake. It wouldn't do to be picturing her wee snug arse any more than it would to think of her luscious wee breasts. She was as like to run him through with a sword, as she was to put a bullet in him.

"I oughtn't know— Honestly. Men." Her smile was all wry resignation. "Clearly you're the delicate ones, if you can't imagine women knowing about blood stains."

He felt heat scorch up to his hairline. It was remarkable how quickly she managed to turn the tables upon him.

Devil take him, but she was an extraordinarily clever lass. "Quite right." He cleared his throat. Time to put this topic to bed. "Now you know why my face—and yours, I might add—went red. What else do you want to know?"

"I want to know…if my magnificent breasts make you want to kiss me?"

"Aye," he said before he could think better of the fire that lit his lungs, making it a pleasurable discomfort to breathe. "That and more. Since we're being so bloody candid."

Perhaps Quince felt the singe of the scorching heat, because she walked away from him—prowling the edge of the room like a fox perusing a hen house. "What more?"

She was insane to be so provoking. And he was insane to let her provoke him.

"Are you really even nineteen?" Devil take him, but he needed a drink to douse the heat in his gut. But alcohol would undoubtedly only fan the flames. "Has no one in your family—your mother or one of your older sisters— ever told you the facts of concupiscence, as it were?"

"Concu-what?" She gave him a strangely blank frown. "I don't think so. Or if they did, I wasn't listening."

"That I doubt," he muttered half to himself. "If they'd told you, you'd have listened. I'm sure you would." He reeled another breath deep into his lungs, and prayed for strength. "I'd think a lass like you'd be all agog to hear all the sordid secrets of marital relations."

"Oh!" Her smile lit up like a Guy Fawkes bonfire, blazing across her lips. "Marital relations? You mean the act of sex. Why then, that word, *concupiscence*, is just a fancy, ten guinea way of saying fu—"

"Don't you say it." He waved his arm at her like a

constable. "Don't you dare." Even the thought of her saying such a raw, earthy word was like throwing gunpowder on banked embers. "Remember my delicate sensibilities."

She gave him one of her slippery, mischievous smiles. "I will. Well, then I reckon I do know about *concupiscence.*" She pronounced the word with delicate relish. "My father is a botanist, after all, so I know that all plants as well as animals have sexes, and all the trees and flowers and insects out in the garden are busy day and night with the need to pollinate and copulate and reproduce."

The last—the very bleeding last—thing he needed to think about was copulation and reproduction. No matter her astonishing frankness, he had to remember wee Quince was a lady, and young, and only making an act of all this jaded worldliness to nettle him. But she had to be stopped from going on in this provoking manner. For her own good as well as his.

"Quite." He put his hands behind his back, pressing them hard into the wall with his weight, so he wouldn't touch her. Yet. "But enough of talk. We have got away from the point, which seemed to a bargain you wanted to strike."

Her eyes met his, ghost bright in the moonlight. "But that *is* the bargain I wanted to strike."

"Copulation?" He flung the strangled word out of his mouth. "Let me understand you with no mistake, Lady Quince—you want to strike a bargain to *copulate?*"

At last he managed to shock her. At least a little. "Oh, holy lemon ice, no!" A fine spot of color appeared high against her cheekbone. "No, I've no interest in ruination. But in something considerably less."

"How much less?" His tone was a bare mixture of disappointment and relief.

She looked at him from under her lashes. "Just kissing."

She might as well have said just *fucking* for all the effect it had upon him—every muscle in his body simultaneously tensed and relaxed. And tried to move toward her. "Let me make right sure I understand you—you want to bargain for kissing?"

"Aye." She frowned and nodded her head, as if she were firming her resolve. As if she had to talk herself into kissing him.

Alasdair was astonished to discover it a blow to his pride. "Why me in particular, and not say…your fellow, Davie?" Perhaps she had frightened the lad off with the prick of her sharp, acrobatic tongue.

Another wave of heat scorched his face. Thank the devil the room was so dark.

Quince was uncharacteristically circumspect—she gave nothing about her other beaux away. "You seem an experienced, thorough-going mon of the world. You've lived in London, and France, and no doubt enjoyed their reputations for pleasure."

He could feel his better judgment start to give way. "Well, damn my eyes, I have."

The damn vixen smiled back. "Good. Because if what just occurred between us has taught me anything—and it has taught me a number of useful things—it is that you're a mon of both power and restraint. You can be trusted to act like a gentleman. In short, I can trust you."

"Not with those breasts." Since they were being so bloody candid.

Delicate color flooded her cheeks, but she kept her gaze level. "Then we will leave breasts out of it, won't we, and settle for just kisses."

"Wee Quince, there is no such thing as *just* kisses."

"Certainly there is, if you concentrate, and do it properly."

Despite his better judgment, Alasdair felt the last of his resolve crumble. There was something in her—that dark fairy combination of mischievousness and glee—that made it hard to resist her wayward charm. He tried harder. But not too hard. "You're incorrigible."

She was also unrepentant. "I should hope so, my lord. Now come. You want a favor from me, so you must be prepared to offer one in return."

"And the favor you want in exchange for helping me

with my inquiries into the thefts is a nice slow bout of kissing?" He asked again, just to be absolutely clear.

"Aye. And kissing alone, thank you very much." She held up one elegantly obstructive finger. "I've no interest in the rest of it."

"A shame. You've no idea what you'll miss."

"Oh, I've an idea, Strathcairn. A very good idea. But while I've faults enough, I am not so taffy-brained as to want to add ruination to the list."

Clever lass. "At last, we agree on something." And what he had to agree was that despite the risk, or perhaps because of it, he was having *fun*. Everything about this lass was fun—a lark. A lark he could control, and keep from getting out of hand.

"So you agree to kiss me?"

He decided to prolong the negotiation, to heighten the wonderful lazy feeling of satisfaction and anticipation strolling through his chest. "To be clear—just the once?"

She gave him a smile full of shrewd consideration. "Why don't we think of it as a *trial* kiss. To see how well you do. To see if I'll be wanting another."

"Fair enough. And I'll see how *you* do, as well. To see if *I'll* be wanting another."

"Fair enough." She nodded and stuck out her right thumb. "We'll proll thumbs on our agreement."

He debated telling her his hesitation was not because he had forgotten the ancient Scots custom of touching thumbs to seal a bargain, but because he had instantly imagined grasping the hand she extended, and then pulling her to his chest and holding her there, so she would be pressed flush against him from neck to thigh, and he might feel those luscious, magnificent wee breasts hard against his chest.

And that he was still debating doing that very thing.

But he decided doing so would be too precipitous—too much, too soon. With a lass as clever and curious as wee Quince Winthrop, he needed to let her take her time, and let her take the lead.

He pushed himself off the wall, and bowed over her

wrist like a proper gentleman. So he could hold on to her. "We are agreed. Shall we commence with the trial?"

"Aye. I suppose." She retrieved her hand, and almost instantly had a qualm. "But you must stay as you were. With your arms behind you, against the wall, so I know you won't get all handsy."

In his efforts to quash his smile, he could only hope that he didn't look grim. "As my lady desires."

When he was properly installed back against the wall, she stepped closer—close enough that he could smell the subtle scent of rose and orange blossom wafting off the warmth of her skin. Alasdair drew in a deep breath, and felt his chest expand with the pleasure of anticipation. He was going to explore that delicate, delicious skin in just a few moments. He could almost taste the sass on her sweet lips.

She turned her face up to him. "You may kiss me now."

He decided that this time, he was going to be the one who did the unexpected—he didn't take the lips she so freely offered. "You're a bit fast off the mark, aren't you, lass?"

"Absolutely." She didn't so much as blush. "Do try and keep up."

"A fool's errand, that would be," he half muttered to himself before he cleared his throat. "I don't think I will kiss you."

Her arms went straight to her muslin-clad hips in indignant protest. "But you just said you would. You agreed."

Alastair felt his smile spread full across his face, as he ducked his head nearer. Near enough to whisper. "Oh, no, my devious wee lass. If I'm to keep myself from getting *handsy*, then you're the one who's going to have to kiss me."

"Oh." She took an unsure step or two back, flustered, her eyes wide with confusion and unexpected indecision.

"Do you mean to say you, Quince Winthrop, haven't kissed anyone before? You? At nineteen, I'd have thought you'd have sampled half the lads of Edinburgh."

"Don't be insulting, Strathcairn. I've been busy. With

other things."

"If you say so." He contemplated her dilemma for a moment or two. "I didn't realize it was instruction you wanted, and no just greater experience. So"—he dropped his voice to a low, encouraging murmur that brought out the brogue he had worked to eradicate from his accent— "I'll gie ye a proper lesson in kissing. I'll tell ye how to begin, and then how to get on."

"Oh, all right. I can't resist when you talk like a proper Scot." She tipped up that chin in a gesture he was coming to recognize as willful determination. "What do you suggest first?"

"I'd suggest ye fetch yourself a wee bit closer, lass, so it's not such a fair reach." If it was a proper Scot she wanted, it was a damn proper red-blooded Scot she would get. He leaned his own head down, and angled it slightly to the side for her convenience. "So ye can take your time considerin' and decidin' what part o' me you'd like to kiss first."

She drew back, so she might get a better look at his face. "Well, your mouth, shouldn't it be?" At such a slight distance, her voice had fallen to a whisper—she wasn't nearly so cool and collected as she might like him to think.

"Only if ye desire, lass. A cheek, perhaps"—he dutifully turned the cheek in question—"might be a less demandin' place to start. But what ye'll want to do, is just come in close..." He waited while she inched closer. "That's it, lass. Now just take a good long gander at me a'fore ye decide. Slowly, now. Have a good, long look. And remember, even if I can't touch, ye can."

She was an apt pupil, clever, curious, fey Quince Winthrop was. "Ooh. I see what you mean." Her breath warmed the side of his neck above his collar for fraction of a second before her finger followed, drawing a light, evocative line down the side of his neck. "Aye. I do see."

He himself could see nothing—the scent of her filled his head, all but blinding him. She smelled like a warm summer day, all blue sky and fresh breezes. He closed his eyes, and inhaled until he fancied he could smell the wild roses that grew in the hills around Cairn. "Oh, aye."

And then, there it was, the merest warming just below his cheekbone—a murmur against his skin. A hint of warmth, and then the slight press of sweet firmness, her lips touching his skin. So soft. So very surprisingly soft, when all the rest of her was a bundle of sharp, stinging nettles.

Alasdair squeezed his eyes tight so he might take it all in—his anticipation, the pleasure and newness of their wary dance toward trust, the eroticism of her surprising restraint—and turned carefully to present her with the other cheek.

Her second kiss was less tentative. More sure, more emblematic of that characteristic bold curiosity of hers. She let her lips linger against his skin, and then meander across his face, making their slow curious way toward his mouth.

"Aye, lass." It was everything he could do to stand and wait and hope her lips would soon find his. To pray that she would like her first taste of him enough to take a second, and a third kiss. And want to delve deeper.

Her hesitation—the delicate approach that seemed so out of tune with her brash character—nearly did him in. It made him want to take her in his arms and hold her and draw her close and tell her all the words he should not say. Encourage her to do her worst, because he was more than prepared to do his best.

But he was suddenly unsure if his best would be good enough. If his experience would prove equal to her native wit and natural curiosity.

It would be a monstrous thing to disappoint wee Quince Winthrop.

And with that realization, Alasdair could no longer fathom what he thought he was doing alone in a dark room, kissing wee Quince Winthrop. All he knew was that if he didn't taste her lips with his, he would go mad.

"That's fine, lass, fine," he murmured encouragement, and held himself scrupulously still as her lips skated along the line of his jaw to his ear, and back. "Take yer time. No need tae rush—"

"Strathcairn," she breathed into his ear. "Do shut up."

And then she was there—her lips sliding along his, pressing against his with the beginnings of desire, learning the texture and taste of him. And he was falling and flying and yearning, already dying for her. Already addicted to the astonishing sweetness of her lips on his.

His arms ached to hold her. To cup her moonbeam face, and stroke the line of that stubborn chin. To run his fingers into the artfully tousled disarray of her bright chestnut hair. To explore all the secret places that would set her passions alight, and leave her too flushed with pleasure to lead him a merry dance.

But he had to go slow, and let her set the pace. No matter her veneer of brashness, every fiber of his being told Alasdair that wee Quince Winthrop was an innocent. Every instinct he possessed told him that she was a lass rife with secrets, and that he had to go slowly and carefully if he wanted to uncover them one by hidden one.

The temptation to surrender himself to desire was nearly too great. She smelled too delicious. She tasted too sweet. "Quince." He breathed her name like an endearment, repeated it like a prayer. "Sweet Quince."

In response, her hands slid up his coat, crushing the velvet lapels. He let her draw him in, let her pull him closer as curiosity became pleasure, and pleasure began to grow into passion. Let her decide to press herself fully against him so he could feel the hard boning of her stays through the soft layers of frilly muslin fabric.

He opened his mouth to her, and her tongue stole across his, sly and questing. She drew his lower lip between hers, and he had everything to do to mute the moan of pure, unbridled lust that tunneled out of his chest.

His back came away from the wall, and he leaned into her, hungry for the warm pliancy of her willowy frame. His hands stole up to cup her face, and angle her head just so. Just so he could kiss her more deeply, just so he could hold her steady while he kissed her deeper and deeper still.

She kissed as she was—agile and acrobatic, curious and

capricious, delightful and determined. She was light and air and sunshine in the velvet dark of the empty room. She tasted of danger, dark and bittersweet like morning chocolate, and after one kiss, already deeply addictive.

He could lose his head over this girl—he very nearly was losing his head over this girl. She was water, clean and fresh and cold at the bottom of a deep, dark well. And he wanted to drink his fill of her.

It was only when his hand crept down the long slide of her neck, and around the delicate curve of her shoulder, and across the cage of her stays toward those magnificent wee breasts, that something deep within Alasdair's brain—some cautious, wary shred of self-preservation—told him he ought to stop. Told him he must stop before a lesson in kissing became a lesson in something entirely less innocent.

"Jesus God, Quince." He let go of her before he gently took her arms, and carefully set her away.

Her eyes opened slowly. "I don't think God had anything to do with that." Her voice was full of wonder and lazy happiness. "But if he did, tell him I want more."

"Sorry, lass." He held her at arm's length, and then stepped back himself. He had to. Because warm, welcoming wild roses were wreathing his brain, and giving him permission to do stupid things. Stupid, pleasurable, necessary things.

The moonlight slanting through the window revealed a look of perturbation on Quince's face that told him she did not share his misgivings. "Why ever not?"

All the reasons he thought he had marshaled quit his brain. Why not, indeed?

He fell back upon platitudes. "Well, wee Quince, this is neither the time nor the place."

"Why not?" she repeated with more heat as her hands came to rest defiantly on her lovely lush hips. "We're alone in the privacy of the dark. No one knows we're here."

He felt his own frustration rise to keep up with hers. "Because we are alone, in the dark, and someone will soon know we are here, because someone is bound to miss you, and come looking."

She waved his concern away. "Not for me. No one ever does."

It was his turn to ask, "Why not? Does no one have a care for your well-being?"

She nearly laughed. "Why would they? I'm perfectly capable of looking out for myself."

That fact was entirely debatable. Mostly because she was alone in the dark with him. And he had already had his hand on her magnificent breasts. And because she was still in a room with him after he had had a hand on her breasts. And because he wanted his hand back around those breasts. "If that were true, you wouldn't be here, wee Quince Winthrop."

He liked calling her that—wee Quince Winthrop. There was music and magic in her name.

"I am here because you agreed to our bargain. But if you won't keep to your half, then there's no need for me to keep to mine." She took a deep, almost purifying breath. "So that's done, then."

"Not so fast, my wee lady." Alasdair reached out, and almost caught her muslin sleeve to hold her from leaving. But he remembered his pledge, and left his hand out between them in the empty air. "We're not done, Quince. We've only just begun. You can't think you've learned how to kiss properly from one wee buss."

"No, I can't. But if you aren't willing to teach me, then I'm sure I can find someone who is." She turned for the door.

He knew she was goading him. Knew if she had wanted to kiss some other man she would have bloody well done so long before now, and not waited to strike a bargain with him.

"Well. You'll not get what you're looking for with some callow youth. Nay." He shook his head, and gave her what he knew was a knowing smile. "Because they won't understand you like I do, and they couldn't possibly ken what it is you really want, wee Quince Winthrop."

Like the curious clever creature she was, she could not help being intrigued. "And you do?"

He gave her a slow nod. "Aye, lass. I do."

She did not answer, and for a moment, he wondered if he had played the wrong hand with this card player of a girl. "Come, Quince, lass." He could not keep his feelings from his voice—it mattered too damn much. "You're too young, and too pretty, and come from too nice a family to fall into such an idle, destructive vice as going into dark rooms for kisses. It might not be opium, or dallying with callow cads, but once the thrill of the mere dangerous wears off, you'll be on to more forbidden pastimes to give you the same guilty thrill. Because that's what you really want—not kisses, but a cracking good thrill."

She paled stark white in the moonlight. Finally, he had hit a nerve. "Nay. I—" she denied, but all the heat had gone from her voice.

"Oh, aye, my wee Quince Winthrop. I reckon I know a thrill seeker when I see one."

Because he, Alasdair Colquhoun, sixth Marquess Cairn, diligent, upstanding member of the Westminster government, had himself once done almost anything just for a thrill.

And damned if he didn't want to do so still.

Chapter 5

HIS WORDS MIGHT have been insulting if they hadn't been so awfully true.

Strathcairn had her dead to rights—she had become inordinately attached to the sweet, coppery tang of danger. She might tell herself she lied out of necessity, and stole to feed hungry children and families, but the naked truth of the matter was that she was in it for the risky, illicit thrill.

And she had kissed Strathcairn to try to replicate it—her lips still tingled with something too heady to be mere excitement.

But this was no time to give Strathcairn and all his inconvenient, insightful scruples the upper hand. "Perhaps," she conceded. "But the particular problem of the moment is that the poor kiss never quite reached the level of 'thrill.' Though I am given to understand that happens sometimes." She tossed up one shoulder in a resigned shrug. "Unfortunate, but there you have it."

"Nay, lass." His ire brought out the marvelously musical roughness of his brogue. "Fortunate is what you are. It takes a great deal of care to be left wanting. And you were certainly thrilled enough to be left wanting more."

Insightful, inconvenient man.

"Well, I don't care much for being left wanting. It smacks of unfulfilled bargain."

"You'd care if I left you ruined. Or perhaps not." His smile was so knowing it was nearly intimate. "If I left you ruined, you'd be bloody thrilled enough not to care."

Now *that* was insulting. And promising.

But she'd be damned if she would let the sting of the insult show. Though he was Strathcairn, she was no meek little miss to be intimidated by the fact that he seemed to have acquired a great deal of cleverness and experience along with his scruples. "I may be bereft of scruples, my lord, but I sold them for a profit I later spent on backbone. You keep to your part of the bargain—thrill without ruin— or I won't hold to mine."

Strathcairn smiled at her in that lethal, tomcat way. "Why then," he finally decided, "you're nothing but a wee, opportunistic scoundrel."

Quince raised her chin, and smiled to show him she was a species of mouse that would bite him back. "What I am, my lord, is an *ambitious* scoundrel."

"Scoundrel all the same," he insisted, but there was at least a little amusement crinkling the corners of his eyes.

And she had to admit, she was coming to rather like the idea of being a *scoundrel*. Men were scoundrels. The hint of respect that the masculine term implied went a long way to mitigating any insult.

"Just so." She gave him her best smile yet. "I told you, Strathcairn, I've long since done with being good. And the bare truth of the matter is that I had much rather be bad, and be *with you*—if you'll agree to accommodate me."

"Depends on how you'll accommodate—"

She gave him her flat terms. "We've already made the bargain—I'll only accommodate and help you if ruination is not in the cards."

"It's not." His voice told her he was both frustrated with her obstinacy and very obstinate himself. "And that's why

I'm over here, and you're all the way over there. But if we're to go on, at some future point you'll have to bow to my greater experience and superior judgment in these matters—matters related to 'thrilling.'"

Quince wasn't a lass who bowed much to anyone, and she rarely trusted anyone's judgment but her own. But Strathcairn did have a point. "I suppose I might—just this once, mind you—accede to your greater experience. For the common good."

His smile widened, gleaming in the moonlight. "Aye. The common good is a very good thing indeed."

"Then we're agreed." This time she licked her thumb before she held out her hand, as a proper Scot would when making a bargain. "You'll give me regular lessons in kissing."

"If you'll help me with these thefts."

"Agreed." Quince kept her smile to herself. Because the thefts weren't going to be a problem anymore. She could guarantee it. "There's my thumb."

Strathcairn was enough of a Scot to do the proper thing—he licked his own thumb and struck it against hers. "Aye, we've a bargain."

It wasn't very romantic as propositions went, but she was a realist, and she'd take honesty over romance any day.

THREE DAYS LATER, Quince wasn't so sure—it was harder than she had thought to stop stealing. For a number of reasons she had not anticipated.

The first was now that she was on the straight and narrow, time weighed heavily on her hands. The jangle of excitement and anticipation that had speeded her days and spiced her evenings was now replaced by an unbearable dragging tension that could not be relieved—Strathcairn had disappeared.

Three long days had gone by without her seeing or

hearing from him. And she really, really wanted to be kissed. She *needed* to be kissed.

To mitigate her itchy, idle discomfort, she took to long, athletic walks, and bruising hell-for-leather rides into the Pentland Hills surrounding Edinburgh. But nothing worked. It was annoying and nearly painful—like trying not to scratch a particularly venomous midge bite.

Oh, by jimble. Perhaps the dratted man was right. Perhaps the stealing was a compulsion she could not control. It certainly had been a thrill to take the snuffbox despite the risk, and a double thrill to know she had defied him.

But maybe, just maybe, this prickly feeling that she was coming out of her skin was because she simply wanted to see Strathcairn. Maybe his kisses *had* been so thrilling that she was indeed itching for more. But there was no way for her to test out her hypotheses.

Dratted, inconvenient, nowhere-to-be-found man.

"Who are you looking for?" Plum pulled Quince out of her contemplation of all things itchy and inconvenient as the three of them—Quince, Plum and Mama, followed by Mama's maid and a footman—walked the short distance up the narrow close from their home at the foot of Calton Hill to the Canongate, which ran like a granite spine along the cobbled ridge of the old town.

"Whom, Plum," Mama corrected. "For whom are you looking?" But Mama in her way already seemed to know the answer. "So you have renewed your acquaintance with the Marquess of Cairn, Quince. How did you find him?" Her tone was everything casual, conversational and disinterested, but Quince was not fooled.

She settled immediately upon the truth as the surest way to deflect any further interest. "I found him opinionated."

Mama laughed, just as Quince had hoped she would. "And who do you not find opinionated, my dear?"

"Everyone and anyone who has an opinion contrary to hers," Plum was quick to criticize. "How on earth did *you* meet Lord Cairn?"

By not making mad cow eyes at him. But Quince was saved from actually uttering the remark by Mama's quick censure.

"Plum." Mama kept her third daughter in check with a word and a look, much as she had with the fourth, youngest and most wayward. To whom she now looked. "After I spoke with Lord Cairn at the Inverness Ball, I thought you and he had another, very long conversation."

Oh, no fool Mama.

What could Quince say that would hold as much as possible to the truth, without giving anything else away? Lying was much like stealing—the best defense was to take offense. Or evasive action. "We spoke of politics, as I said. Or rather, he spoke of politics, while I pretended to listen."

"How interesting." Mama's tone was as spotless as her lace kerchief and cuffs. "Such a long time for you to pretend to listen. I would not think your patience was up to such a task."

Oh, by jimble. Quince was all appreciation for her mother's subtle wit—it kept her on her own toes. "I fear Strathcairn's conversation did about wear my patience out. And we did not even speak of the new government's proposed Poor Law."

"Ah. I begin to see how he might engage you in argument instead of conversation. But what, I wonder, persuaded Lord Cairn that he needed to closet you away to talk politics in the first place?"

"So she couldn't escape," was Plum's answer.

Plum might have been happy to poke fun, but Mama was not—she was too clever by half. As was Quince. "He did closet me away, didn't he? Oh, holy lemon tarts!" Quince pretended to gasp. "You don't think he has"—she paused for dramatic, and hopefully horrified effect—"any designs upon me?"

Mama raised an acute eyebrow, but did not stop walking, taking care to keep the full skirts of her *robe à la française* well above the dirty cobbles. "His lordship does not strike me as the type of man who has 'designs.' But other than that, I cannot yet tell where his interest in you lies," her mother admitted.

"No," Quince and Plum said at the same time.

"He can't be interested in her," Plum carried on before Quince spoke over her.

"You cannot think that he means to *court* me?"

"Again, I cannot tell what the marquess means to do," Mama said. "It is a strange man who makes love by talking politics. But I would caution you now to be wary of him, Quince. He has…" Mama searched for the right word. "…History. You would be wise to be leery of him."

"Mama!" Plum and Quince chorused for entirely different reasons.

But Mama had her own ideas about what Quince ought to do with Strathcairn. "The Marquess of Cairn is hugely influential. And handsome to boot. Not to mention quite attractively rich, and apparently attracted to you. As are you attracted to him, though you try to hide it—you never would have talked to him at all if you were not. But there is an old scandal still attached to his name."

"What scandal?"

Mama pursed her lips closed, and didn't answer the question. "I know you well enough to know that warning you off will only increase his attraction for you, so I will only caution—be very careful how you take anything the man has to offer."

And Mama didn't even know what the man had actually offered.

"Yes, Mama." She would be very careful how she conducted her improper acquaintance with the most proper man in all of Edinburgh.

Perhaps this little time away from thievery was going to be *fun* after all.

And speaking of fun—out of the corner of her eye, Quince spied a penny that had wedged itself between the cobbles. She quickly bent to pick it up—waste not, want not. She was such a magpie that she couldn't pass up even a single penny for the poor box.

"Good morning, Lady Winthrop."

Quince whirled upright, and there he was, as if they had conjured him up with their talk, looking as polished and urbane as a gem in a jeweler's shop. Strathcairn was again magnificently turned out in an impeccably tailored suit of the darkest forest green silk, not a hair out of place, nor so much as a fleck of powder marring his sleeve.

She felt her cheeks grow warm with embarrassment—an emotion she rarely felt—from having him catch her grubbing for pennies in the dirt. She hid her clarty, soiled fingers behind her quilted skirts. It wouldn't do to have him wondering if she were as hard up for money as an old lady's companion.

The marquess was doffing his tricorn hat to her mother before he turned the focus of that acute green gaze toward her. "Lady Plum. Wee Lady Quince."

Pleasure swirled into her veins like warm cream into her morning chocolate cup.

"Strathcairn." Quince took care to let nothing of over-friendliness or intimacy warm her voice, because not even that off-putting "wee Quince" could curtail Mama's interest, or Plum's competitive instincts.

Her sister's greeting was everything effusive that Quince's was not. "Why, good morning, my Lord *Cairn*." Plum emphasized Quince's mistake in calling him by his former title, before she swanned into a graceful curtsey, spreading her immaculate, embroidered lawn skirts like a fan. "We were just talking about you. So very nice to see you."

"Likewise, I am sure, Lady Plum." Strathcairn touched his hat, but wisely ignored Plum's invitation to appease his curiosity. Instead he addressed them all impartially. "And where are the lovely Winthrop ladies headed this morning?"

"We are shopping," Mama answered in a politely neutral tone. "Costumes for the Marchioness of Queensbury's Midsummer Masquerade Ball. Do you plan to attend the masquerade, Lord Cairn?"

"I do plan on attending, Lady Winthrop." His glance shied toward Quince—she felt his attention like a physical touch. "And you, Lady Quince? Will you also be attending the Marchioness of Queensbury's masquerade ball?"

"Perhaps." Quince tried her best to be equivocal, while she slid her eyes obediently toward Mama. At just nineteen, her attendance at something as potentially risqué as a masquerade could not be taken for granted. And Mama had just warned her away from the marquess. One must pick one's battles, Mama always said. "If my mother approves."

Mama's tone was as careful as the look she passed from Quince to Strathcairn and back. "As the ball is a private, and not a public masquerade, I have no real objection. The Marchioness of Queensbury will see that her revels don't fall into the debauchery and licentious behavior so common during the ticketed masquerades at the Theatre Royale."

Plum had not yet given up on attracting Strathcairn's attention. "Of course, *wee* Quince will only have an unimaginative costume sewn up, made from some old, pulled-apart gown—she's so thrifty she picks up pennies. The only reason she's even remotely fashionable is that I give her my cast-offs. If I didn't, I daresay she'd be an embarrassment to us all."

"Plum." Mama's tone was like water dousing the flame of Plum's malice before it could singe anyone else.

"It's quite all right, Mama," Quince put in swiftly before anyone could remark any further upon her thriftiness, nor any potential reasons for it. Let them all think she was too tight with her purse, or too disinterested in fashion to spend her allowance on new clothing. Anything to keep them all from the truth—that she dressed not to impress, but to blend into the scenery. "It's too true that Plum is all that stands between me and fashion ignominy. Without her, I wouldn't know the difference between a *polonaise* and a round gown. Alas, if I only cared a whit about it. But I don't. Wit and not wardrobe, is my motto."

Plum made a huffy sound of derision. "What you think passes for wit—"

"—is really just sarcasm. Yes, thank you, Plum." If Plum thought that calling attention to Quince's admittedly myriad faults would bring her Strathcairn's attention, good luck and Godspeed to her. "I'll leave you and Mama to the fashionable dressmaker of your choice, while I go on to the unfashionable one of mine, though you ken full well her needlework is exquisite." She gestured meaningfully to Plum's elegantly embroidered skirts. Quince might not care overmuch for fashion, but she cared about Jeannie. But she also had to be careful not to call too much attention to her friend, either.

Quince decided more discretion was the better part of valor, nodded to both Plum and Mama, and made Strathcairn the shallowest of curtseys. "My lord."

"Look at her, going on her own without so much escort as a maid. Really, Mama, it's too bad of her."

But her sister's protestations had the opposite effect of her intentions. "With your permission, Lady Winthrop," Strathcairn broke in, "I'll leave you ladies to the accompaniment of your maid and footman, and give wee Lady Quince the safety of my escort to wherever it is she is going."

Poor Plum, hoisted on the petard of her own complaint. She'd never learn.

"Thank you, my Lord Cairn," Mama answered carefully. "That will be acceptable. Although I can easily see your progress up the High Street to Menleith's Close."

"And so you have been warned," Quince said under her breath as Strathcairn touched his hat to her mother, and they turned westward up the pavement, "that we are watched."

"Not for the first time, I'll wager." He fell into step beside her, far enough apart that not even the hem of his fine coat brushed her skirts, but not so far she could not smell the subtle hint of warm vanilla and citrus spice that wafted off him like an evening breeze.

The scent slid under her skin like an opiate. It was a sort of exquisite torture to be this close to him, and not touch him. Not fist her hands in his lapel, and pull his lips to hers. Not knock his hat to the ground, and muss that perfectly powdered hair. "Nay, not for the first time. My mother has warned me away from you."

"Just as she has warned me away from you."

As there was nothing she could say to that, they walked on in silence, until they came to the narrowing of the street at Nether Bow. There, she stopped on the pavement. "I thank you for the courtesy, my lord, but I had much better go on alone. My dressmaker's shop is just down the close." She indicated the long alleyway reaching north off the High Street. "And her shop is so tiny, you'd be entirely in the way. So I'll thank you"—she gave him a perfunctory curtsey—"and bid you good day." She waved back to Mama, who gathered her full skirts in one hand, as if she were making ready to go.

Strathcairn, smart fellow that he was, understood what Quince hoped had been polite caution in her voice, and without being obvious, positioned himself around the corner, where he could not be seen. And he did not dally, but came straight to his point. "I have thought much about our last conversation, wee Quince. And the bargain we struck."

She couldn't decide if she liked or loathed his continual reference to her as "wee Quince." It made her feel small in a way that had nothing to do with age, or height. Mostly. Because he also said it so nicely that it felt almost…intimate.

"Have you? Thinking better of your half of the bargain, Strathcairn, and wanting to get out of it now that you've been warned off? That would account for the fact that you haven't been seen in days. I assumed you'd decamped to Cairn."

"I do have a profession, my lady. Unlike you, I cannot spend each and every day strolling idly to my dressmakers."

"Oh, aye. I'm sure I'm quite the stroller." She waved her annoyance away, and strove not to say something overly cutting. If she had a profession—which she did—it was far better kept a secret. Especially from him. "Just as I'm sure your business is as important as anything."

Her obvious irritation had the correct effect upon him.

"Your pardon, my lady. The fact that I have been busy with some of the more meddlesome details of my grandfather's will and estate, as well as in gleaning information regarding the rash of petty thefts—and you were quite right in deeming them petty—is what has kept me occupied, and out of your amusing and highly entertaining company for several days. But I assure you, our bargain, and fulfilling that bargain as soon as possible, has been very much on my mind. I have pleasurably passed some otherwise tedious time planning out the curriculum for your lessons in kissing."

But Quince heard nothing of kissing. That stealthy sense of alarm was back, hissing and scratching against the backs of her legs like a stray cat. Her mind was now entirely taken up with wondering what "information" he might have gleaned, as well as plotting a chess move six moves ahead, and how best and unobtrusively to ask about that information. "I suppose I'm meant to be flattered."

His wry smile alone was flattery enough for half the city. "You are. Patience, wee Quince. Rome was not built in a day. And speaking of Romans—"

"Which we were not."

"Which I was." He carried on without stopping, though he did smile. "Because I will lay a groat someone comes to this damnable masquerade as a Roman general."

"No bet. However, to be sporting, we may lay odds as to how many Roman generals and emperors there might be."

"No bet." Strathcairn shook his head even as he smiled. "But does not a masquerade—where our identity will be disguised to all but our intimates—strike you as a particularly auspicious place for us to meet, and make good on our bargain?"

Ah. Quince felt the relief fall neatly into puzzle pieces. "Oh, aye." She favored him with her brightest smile. "It does."

He nodded as if he were pleased with himself. "So you must tell me what costume you are planning to wear, so I might find you more easily."

"If you can find me easily, Strathcairn, it means other people will be able to as well." It was something she had learned in her first forays into robbing the rich—never stand out from the crowd. Even at a masquerade. "I shall endeavor to dress as alike to other costumes as possible, so I shan't be missed should I escape the ballroom to further our *bargain*."

Strathcairn smiled his approval. "Clever lass. Commendable logic. But if I cannot find you, then you shall have to find me."

"I am confident I shall know you instantly, Strathcairn. You'll be the tall, imposing fellow with the white hair."

His smile snuck up the corner of his mouth. "Perhaps I won't be."

"Tall and imposing?"

She was rewarded by an actual laugh. "Nay. That can't be helped. But now I have an idea not to wear my hair powdered white so you'll have as much trouble finding me as I shall you."

"Oh, holy confectioner's sugar, Strathcairn. What shall the other New Tories think of that? Don't tell me you shall crop off your hair, and sport an auld-fashioned wig?"

"Nay. And they shall think nothing of it, I assure you, as very few of my fellow politicians will even be at the masquerade. And to the few who do attend, I shall take care to remain anonymous."

She could not reconcile the idea of such anonymity from the man who had worn—and was currently wearing—such an austerely ostentatious suit. A suit that practically begged people to pay him heed. "And why is that?"

And there was the hint of color that loosened up that austere Grampian granite. "I think I would do well to heed your example. What you've said makes me think that it would be far better to go about unobserved—to be more anonymous. And I've another friend in London who once counseled me that one needs to set a thief to catch a thief, as it were."

All the pleasure leeched out of the day—it was as if the

sun had that moment been eclipsed behind the moon, so completely did her pleasure evaporate into the air, and leave her chilled and uncomfortable.

"Quince? Wee Quince, are you quite all right?" Strathcairn moved closer by increments, peering down at her as if he feared she might dissolve into a puddle at his feet.

"Why do you keep calling me that? I'm not wee in the least." She fought to recover her wits. "And are you are going to set yourself as the thief?"

His smile was the first answer. "Only to steal you away for a good long while."

Oh, by jimble. Her heart was going to be worn out from all this starting and stopping. It would help if she remembered to breathe.

She pasted a smile upon her face. "And just so I might fulfill my part of our bargain now that you appear ready to fulfill yours… You mentioned the petty thefts? What sort of information, if any, have you managed to glean?"

"Aye." His serious, magisterial look settled back upon his face like a mask, diminishing all his natural warmth. "No one has been fencing the goods—which is the term for dispensing with stolen property—with any of the known pawnbrokers in the city, even the shadier establishments. Which makes me think that the thief is someone who moves within society."

And just like that, the cold chill in the air seemed to burrow deeper into her bones.

Quince knew perfectly well what a bloody fence was, but she'd be a fool to admit it. And while she was obviously a fool about any number of things—including Strathcairn and his kisses—she'd be damned before she'd be a fool about stolen goods. "How can you be sure that someone as scaffy as an auld pawnbroker is telling you—an outsider to Edinburgh—the truth?"

"I have the help of others," he admitted. "Others well outside the bounds of polite society, to help me along, while you help me within society."

"Suddenly, I don't feel so special." What she felt was nearly sick to her stomach with dread, not only for herself, but for the others who helped *her*. One of whom was only steps away.

But her light rebuke had the desired effect—Strathcairn was smiling again. "Oh, you're most assuredly special, wee Quince, though it is likely to my disadvantage to tell you so."

Now she was flattered, as much by the humor in his voice, as by the fond feeling chasing the chill away from her bones.

But she batted such a dangerous distraction away. "However you say. But I must be along, Strathcairn. No matter our private arrangements, it won't do to be seen debating the terms in the public street."

He replaced his hat, and touched the brim to her. "As you wish, my lady. I am very much looking forward to our next meeting." His low tone was just encouraging enough to spark a low fire of anticipation in her blood. "I hope you'll save me a... dance?"

Oh, holy apple tarts. He was already leading her a very merry dance as it was. But there was so much promise in that lovely low rumble of a voice that she simply could not resist.

"I'll save what I may."

Chapter 6

QUINCE TURNED HER back on Strathcairn—and by jimble, she needed every ounce of self-discipline she possessed to do so, when all she wanted to do was watch his lovely long legs stride all the way up the street—and made for the safety of the close confines of Jeannie's shop.

Once through the jangling door, she waited for the familiar quiet to realign her sense of purpose, and calm the strange tension that came from Strathcairn playing his cat to her mouse.

Only Strathcairn didn't know she was his mouse. Or did he? He had already suspected her once—was he prolonging or advancing their acquaintance merely to keep his eye on her? Or was his interest in her strictly personal, and as amorous as her mother feared it might be?

She would not get an answer by asking herself. "Jeannie?" She called through the curtain separating the front of the shop from the workroom. "It's me, hen."

"Back here, mileddy," came the response.

Jeannie, whom Quince had not seen since their timely

meeting in the withdrawing room at Lady Inverness's ball, was coming to her feet next to her worktable. "I was wonderin' where ye'd gotten yerself to, my Leddy Q."

Quince greeted the talented seamstress with a kiss, more like the friend she was now than the servant she had once been. Jeannie had been Quince's maid, and while Quince was no slave to the whims of fashion, she had been quick to recognize both Jeannie's talent and her ambition—which were entirely wasted on her—and had set Jeannie up in her own dressmaking shop. It had been Quince's only non-charitable use of her ill-gotten gains.

Ill-gotten they might have been, but not ill spent. Not by a long shot.

"I've been a bit fashed about ye," Jeannie admitted. "Hadn't seen ye for days. Thought som'at a goon wrong after ye passed me them buttons at Lady Inverness's."

Even if she were no longer her personal maid, Jeannie was still Quince's confidant and confessor. "Nothing's gone wrong, exactly," Quince hedged. "More of a slight hitch in our proceedings." Jeannie was one of the only people she had entrusted with her secret, and one of two people who were trusted to turn Quince's stolen bits and bobs into ready money.

"Don't tell me." Jeannie set her hands to her hips with resignation. "Ye've a change o' heart. Tho,' I knew ye would someday."

Quince hastened to reassure her. "Not a change of heart." It was far too late for that—it had been too late from the first moment three years ago when she had pocketed a vinaigrette bottle Mrs. Neville Campbell had dropped in the stairwell of the George Street Assembly Rooms, and felt the unholy satisfaction of turning rich people's portable chattels into ready money for the poor. "Only a temporary change of plan. I had to stop the business, as it were"—she peered back through the shop's curtain to make sure they were not being inadvertently overheard—"while a certain party is in the city looking into petty thefts."

Jeannie dropped back down to her bench with a sigh. "I

thought that mon were trouble. Saints preserve us, he's the look of a knobdobber."

"He's not so hard-headed, Jeannie, really. He can be quite lovely and larky when he sets his mind to it." She couldn't seem to stop herself from defending the inconvenient—and inconveniently attractive—man. "He's just forgot where he's come from, is all. That's what comes from living too long in London, I suppose." But Strathcairn the man was not her problem—Strathcairn the ambitious politician, government minister and investigator of crime was. "And while the saints might decide to preserve you, I'm going upon the principle that they're far too busy to help an unrepentant sinner like me. So we'll have to work it out for ourselves."

Jeannie nodded her acceptance. "Then what do ye ken?"

"Best to take a wee break from the pilfering for a bit— save our breath to cool our porridge, as it were. At least until the mon in question leaves the city for his highland estate."

"Aye. That sounds a'right. I'll be fair pleased when ye see the back o' him." The dressmaker made a clucking sound. "I'd not like to cross that mon. But I will say, at least he's a fair face to goon at."

Jeannie knew her far too well.

"He does have a fair face, indeed. If you like that sort of thing."

"And ye'd be blind and daft no to like that sort o' thing." Jeannie chuckled. "And ye may be many things, my Leddy Q, but yer no daft."

She was daft enough about some things. Strathcairn-shaped things. Kissing things.

But she was not stupid. "So you can see how it is? You'll let Charlie know that things are going to be at a stop for a while?"

Charlie was Jeannie's brother, and the third spoke of their wheel. Quince deposited her stolen goods with Jeannie—for it was nothing out of the ordinary, or strange, for a young woman to regularly visit her dressmaker. Then

Jeannie could easily and unobtrusively pass the goods to Charlie, who was the reason Strathcairn wouldn't find any of Quince's stolen items cluttering up pawnshops. Charlie was a blacksmith, with a forge on the muddy south side of the city, down behind Back Wall Street, near the riding academy and livery yards, who routinely came up to Menleith's Close to check on and look after his younger sister, just as a good brother should. It was Charlie who had the wolves's share of the work, melting down the metal objects, and then bartering or selling the ingots for ready coin, which he then brought surreptitiously back to Jeannie on one of his daily visits. She passed the purse back to Quince, who then deposited the proceeds—minus a small but fair commission for Jeannie and Charlie—into the poor box at the old West Kirk of Saint Cuthbert's, on the edge of the city, near the Charity Workhouse where dispossessed crofters who had been evicted from their highland farms seemed to gather like lambs huddling together before the slaughter.

Lambs that needed to be fed, and sheltered, and shepherded into new lives. Which took a vast deal of money. Which she gave.

And so their little alms-producing operation turned efficiently, but more importantly, invisibly, both salving Quince's spotty, but strangely ardent conscience, and giving her a reason to keep stealing.

Until Strathcairn had almost caught her.

"Aye, Charlie'll ken how 'tis." Jeannie was nodding. "He's already been by to leave the wee purse frae the Tuesday." Jeannie fetched a small suede purse out of a locked drawer, and poured the coins into Quince's outstretched palm. "I don't mind tellin' ye, my Leddy Q, I'll be fair relieved to have a wee break frae it. Stretches my nerves somthin' thin, it does, having them things, and then the money, here."

"I understand, hen. Me, too." The strain was so constant Quince had mostly gotten used to it. Mostly. But she hadn't thought of the toll it might be taking upon Jeannie, or Charlie. She hadn't realized they, too, might feel the sick sense of relief that came when she passed the goods off, and then when she took the purse, and again when she deposited the coins in the poor box. "Would you rather we stopped for good?"

Maybe that would be for the best. Maybe Jeannie and Charlie wanted more than a temporary relief from the constant nagging tension—the worry each of them must feel for what might happen to them if they were caught. Jeannie and Charlie were far more vulnerable than she, who had a family of influence to speak for her. All Jeannie and Charlie had to speak for them was her, and who would believe a girl who had robbed her peers blind?

No one. Not even Strathcairn.

"Och, I don' ken 'bout that." Jeannie knitted the stiffness out of her fingers. "I've nearly enough saved ta hire on another lass tae do the seaming. And Charlie'll hae another mouth to feed soon, with his wife expectin' another bairn."

Quince nodded her understanding. "All right. Just a break, then."

"Aye, mileddy. A wee break."

That is, if Quince could actually make the break. She had never before managed to stop her pilfering. Everywhere she went, there was something—some jeweled hairpin or cravat pin, some silver comb or earbob left carelessly behind, forgotten on some table.

Everywhere she went, temptation was waiting.

But what if something—someone—else was waiting? What if she could alleviate her itchy fingers by clutching up Strathcairn's expensive lapels, and rumpling his perfectly powdered hair? What if kissing him gave her as good a thrill as it had the other night, in the close dark of Lady Inverness's bare spare room?

The thought calmed her fears, and spread a smile upon her face. "Now then, dearest Jeannie. All that remains is for you to make me a masquerade costume that will blend in with the wallpaper."

BY THE TIME the Winthrop party arrived at the reception hall of the Marquess of Queensbury's majestic mansion near Holyrood Palace, the crowd of costumed revelers awaiting admission stretched into the street, and Quince's nerves were stretched as taut as the lacing of her stays—she felt as if she could barely breathe.

Days of waiting, of not stealing, and of still not seeing Strathcairn, had worn on her. She was not a person suited to inactivity. Wit and not wardrobe was only the beginning of her ethos—action not idleness was the beating heart of her character.

And so the moment they made their way through the doors, Quince abandoned the reception line by making herself both useful and scarce, taking her mother and sister's silk evening cloaks, and depositing them with the footmen in the small chamber beneath the stairs. Which also gave her access to the servants' stair, by which she could slip away from the crowd.

She made her way by back corridors to the narrow mezzanine above the ballroom, from whence she could take stock of the gathering. Below, the whole of the ballroom had been done over in a harlequin theme, with black and white diamond patterns painted onto the floor, and pastel garlands of flowers festooned above the doorways and windows, as well as all the chandeliers, perfuming the air with the scent of carnations and lavender. The effect was bright and gay and perfect for the longest day of summer, when the golden evening sunlight stretched through the windows, and bathed the room in gilded light. The marchioness was assured success—it was utterly enchanting.

And Quince was ready to be enchanted—she was beyond ready for something, anything to happen. Unable to even stand still, she passed down the length of the railing to the darkest corner, where she might observe the scene below, while being unobserved herself. The ballroom was filling rapidly with revelers of all sizes, shapes and costumes, all so busy with their own intrigues that none of them thought to look up into the dimmer corners of the balcony above.

It was the perfect place for a tryst.

The perfect place for her to forget everything but the sure pleasure of Strathcairn's kisses. The lovely taut texture of his lips. The delicious rasp of his smooth shaven jaw against her cheek. The wonderfully generous way he had let her take her time, and explore at will, clenching his hands into white-knuckled fists against the wall to keep to her rules. Teaching her control by showing her power and restraint.

Her own fists gripped the railing in nervous, heady anticipation.

The feeling was almost as good as stealing. And nearly as dangerous.

Dangerous because there was something about him— that devilish combination of power and restraint—that called to her, and made her want to bedevil him. Something that, even as it appealed to her own mischievous nature, called for her respect.

That was a very rare thing indeed in her world, respect. There were only a handful of people she truly respected, but Strathcairn had to be counted as one of them. And so she would take care to keep him from being her enemy, and make him her friend. And maybe even, if she were very good and very careful, something more than a friend.

"The marquess is not here." Plum appeared at the top of the small stairway with a pleasantly snide simper upon her lips, and flourished her embellished shepherdess's crook with, well, a flourish. As if *she* were the one expecting someone to come upon her looking fetching in her short-skirted costume which exposed her trim ankles.

Her sister had somehow managed to follow her through the crowd. Quince would have to watch herself to make sure it didn't happen again—it certainly would not do to have Plum witness her trying to entice Strathcairn into kissing her.

And she was not about to play Plum's little game, by either asking *whom* she was talking about, or pretending she had not been looking for Strathcairn. "How inconvenient," she said, instead. "Strathcairn owes me money."

Plum's expression blanked to astonishment, immediately followed by outrage. "The Marquess of Cairn owes you money?"

"Aye." Quince let her voice slide deeper into the local dialect that always infuriated Plum, who was far more aspirational that any of the sisters, even fussy Linnea. "Lost a bet, he did."

"You know you're not supposed to bet, Quince, or play cards for money. It's not ladylike. Wait until Mama hears."

Quince was glad she had left her wee dirk at home as an aid to resisting temptation, or she might have been tempted to poke her sister in her interfering arse then and there. It wasn't a nice thought, but there you had it—she wasn't good. But she managed to resist that temptation as well.

"Then you'd better hasten off to tell her, hadn't you?" And leave Quince alone to find a new place to hide. Which should not be a problem—the Queensbury mansion was a wonderful hodgepodge of different additions tacked onto the main house through the ages, with nooks and crannies to spare, as well as a wide sweeping garden down the south side of the walled property. Perhaps tonight Strathcairn would be Scots enough to take his ease under the shelter of the blackthorn tree—*Prunus spinosa*, her father would correct her—growing in the back corner of the garden.

"Not before I've made you over." Plum immediately began to fuss and tug at Quince's gown.

"What do you think you're doing?"

"Keeping you, to use your own words, from fashion ignominy. That dress is revealing enough, but the drab color doesn't do you much justice. Here." Plum plucked two pink roses from the bodice of her own costume, and insinuated one down between Quince's breasts, and tucked the other behind her ear. "That's better. It warms your skin, and helps you look less afraid."

"I'm not afraid!"

"You ought to be." Plum looked her in the eye, as if doing so would make Quince hear her more clearly. "I've done what I can, and I'm going back to Mama now, so mind yourself. And don't be with him too long."

Before Quince could puzzle out such bizarre behavior, her sister was gone back down the stair. She followed Plum's progress across the floor to where she met their parents on the far side of the ballroom. Mama was costumed as the constant Pole Star, with a glittering diamond ornament in her hair, while Papa was more predictably dressed as the esteemed botanist Carl Linnaeus—which meant he was dressed almost exactly as himself, but with a mask.

But while Quince knew how her parents were dressed, she had taken care to cover her own costume with her evening cloak. Because the simple truth was that the costume Jeannie had devised was a great deal more revealing than what Quince was used to, or what her lady mother would allow. But the risk had been worth it. From the vantage point of the balcony, Quince could see that at least five other ladies were dressed in the same costume as she— as Diana the Huntress. Jeannie's intelligence from dressmaker gossip had been correct, and as a result, even with the addition of the roses, Quince would be just another masked girl with her hair in Grecian curls, dressed in ivory-toned muslin drapery that blended with the wallpaper.

Perfect. And perfectly anonymous among the crowd of dark dominos and be-wigged cavaliers.

And there he was—her own cavalier, moving purposefully through the throng, a vision out of another age. She would have known him anywhere—no mask could conceal the glitter of those green eyes, nor any domino shroud the delicious breadth of those strong shoulders. But most of all, not even the wide, plumed leather hat could cover the deep Scots russet of his hair.

Oh, holy apple carts. With all his staid white powder, she

had quite forgotten the blazing glory of his brilliant hair.

A memory dropped into her mind like a cameo into her pocket—a younger Strathcairn with his bright ginger head bent, earnestly trying to inveigle her older sister into a kiss. A kiss which fussy Linnea had evaded.

Quince wouldn't have.

And she certainly wouldn't tonight. Not when he looked so gloriously magnificent. So devilishly kissable, with his hat and his plume and his pair of patent flintlock pistols bristling from his belt. The Marquess of Cairn. The man *she* would soon be enticing into kisses.

But not up here on the balcony—Plum might have revealed both her hiding place and her costume to Mama by now. Quince bolted for the stair, determined not to waste another minute that could be spent more profitably with Strathcairn, learning everything there was to learn about the taste and texture of his lips. Discovering just how far the sweet joy of kissing—

"Lady Quince."

She came up short on the second to last step, to find her way blocked not by the man she sought, but by a man she hadn't thought to avoid. The man who had for three years been the beneficiary of her larcenous largesse, though they had never met—The Reverend Mr. Adam Talent, medical doctor, vicar of the West Kirk of Saint Cuthbert's, and principal administrator of the Charity Workhouse there.

Quince felt her face flush scarlet to the roots of her hair. Of all people to recognize her whilst wearing gossamer drapery in the middle of planning a tryst, she had to meet with the only clergyman in all of Edinburgh who seemed to know her by name, though she had taken pains that he should *not* know her.

Her heart plummeted to her sandals—her conscience, it seemed, had come to call.

What on earth had possessed the marchioness to invite such a Friday-faced, sober man to a revel? And what the devil could have possessed a reverend to accept? Unfortunately, Quince could think of nothing that would account for the clergyman's presence—nothing that didn't have to do directly with herself.

The Reverend Talent had planted himself across the foot of the stair like a solid oak tree—*Quercus robar,* her father would have classified him, tall and dependable. It was the gravely responsible Reverend Talent who tended, body and soul, to the crofters who seemed to be pouring out of the highlands, dispossessed of the hill farms their families had inhabited for generations by what the powers that be were calling "clearances." Wholesale evictions were what they were, made by landlords eager to "improve" their agricultural yields by turning arable land into more profitable pasturage for sheep. West Kirk workhouse was about as far as people made destitute by dispossession could get.

And it was there that Quince's ill-gotten gains were turned into very well spent assistance. She loved the deeply ironic symmetry of it all—stealing from the very people who owned the land and had dispossessed their crofters so they could make more money, and using that stolen money to finance a new start for those same crofters.

Justice was indeed blind, and daft to boot, if you asked her. Which nobody did. Nobody except, it seemed, the reverend. Who made her decidedly nervous.

"Lady Quince," Reverend Talent repeated, doffing his round-brimmed hat to hold in his large, capable hands. The reverend was attired in his one and only costume, which was what he wore every day—the black suit and white linen collar of the sober clergyman. "We have not seen you at Saint Cuthbert's for quite some time, my lady. I hope you have not been in ill health? We have been greatly missing your… prayers."

Quince suppressed her agitation, as well as her irritation. The reverend may have been young and stodgy, but he possessed the age-old ability to appear to be saying one thing while meaning entirely another. Quince did not go to West Kirk to pray. She had only ventured into Saint Cuthbert's to slip money—a vast deal of money over the past three years—into the poor box. She had never intended for anyone to know the money came from her. Although she was not particularly religious, she knew her bible well enough to adhere to the admonition to do good by stealth.

Unfortunately for her, the good reverend seemed to be annoyingly good at sussing things out—almost as good as Mama, and Strathcairn, for that matter. But she obliged the clergyman's sense of propriety by speaking in the same way—she was as fluent in double-speak as she was in outright lies. "My apologies, Reverend." She made her curtsey of respect, and tried not to let her gaze wander past his shoulders into the crowd, where her cavalier was hopefully looking for her. "You must have me confused with another."

"Ah, good. Yes." The tall young vicar twisted his hat in his hands, and lowered his voice, as if he were imparting a strict confidence. "I must admit that I came tonight in the hope of seeking you out, my lady. I cannot help but notice that your visits—for which we are, and always have been supremely grateful—have fallen off of late. I grew worried for your... health."

Her health was fine—it was her state of reawakened guilt that was not. By jimble, it had only been a few days since she had decided to cease her pilfering. But to the reverend who, in his defense, had destitute mouths to feed, she supposed it might well have been a year.

But she was not about to explain that she had traded opportunistic thievery for kisses to a vicar. "I cannot think what you mean, sir."

"Ah, I understand." He glanced around at the costumed crowd. "You wish to remain anonymous. I don't want you to think we are ungrateful," he hastened to add in an exaggerated, overly confidential whisper. "It is only that the need is so great at the moment. So many new petitioners every day. We have, it seems, gained a reputation as something of a savior for the dispossessed at Saint Cuthbert's. And while it is gratifying that our modest successes have helped so many people and families in need, our very success has outstripped our ability to help."

Though Quince had over the past three years contributed what felt like a fortune—and a very hard, dangerously earned fortune it was at that—the money she gave wasn't enough. It was never enough. And on days like today, when the reverend's pale gray eyes implored her, the small amount she stole felt like it was never *going* to be enough.

"You have been such a great supporter," he continued in his sermon-like way. "I suppose I've come to rely on you, and your generous donations. And I should hate to turn away someone in true need. And there are so many. So very many. So you see why we are especially in need of contributions?"

She did see. It was why she was able to look herself in the mirror, and sleep at night—doing good for people in desperate need. But it was really just an excuse, the do-gooding.

Talent sighed at her silence, and throttled his hat within his hands, before he launched one last appeal. "We received three new families, with at least three children each, one with four—thin, peaked looking children—just today."

It was Quince's turn to sigh. The amount she had yet to place into the poor box—the take from Strathcairn's silver buttons and Fergus McElmore's snuffbox—wasn't enough. And the plain truth of the matter was that she would never have enough if she kept on the way she was going—pocketing small items that lost half of their value the moment they were melted down for safety's sake.

But certainly she could not do more. For all her bravado and enthusiasm, she was only an opportunistic thief—an amateur. And she could not even do that effectively with Strathcairn snooping around, mucking everything up.

Which he did at that very moment, looming up behind the reverend like the ghost of sins past. Which was a feat—the looming—as she had thought the reverend so tall. But Strathcairn was taller. And far more flinty-eyed behind his black mask.

"Clever Diana." Strathcairn's voice was as cool and

polished and London-ish as it had been that first night. "Does this clergyman importune you, or are you shielded by the armor of chastity?"

Quince bit her lip to keep from making any sort of expression—only Strathcairn could manage to woo and insult all at the same time—but his tone made her put up her chin. "It is a very good thing I ken my Shakespeare, sir. And the answer is nay. The vicar was just leaving." She didn't want anyone, least of all Strathcairn, associating her with Reverend Talent. It would never do for anyone to think her religious—it would absolutely ruin her reputation as a flibbertigibbet.

She shifted her gaze back to the clergyman. "I'm sorry for your troubles, Reverend. Good evening."

Poor Reverend Talent took his cue, and with an awkward bow in her direction—oak trees didn't bend easily, did they?—he took his leave of them.

Which left her with a wildly attractive, but wary cavalier. No, not a cavalier.

Oh, holy burning bonfires.

Strathcairn was dressed as a *highwayman*, with a brace of pistols bristling from his belt.

It was as if a beacon had been lit in her brain, lighting her way, heating her blood. There it was—the brilliant idea that would solve all her problems, salve her conscience, and please the vicar to no end—the way to infinitely more money.

"Who was that mon?" Strathcairn's green eyes probed from behind his mask, making him look hard and dangerous. Just as she liked.

But she could not attend properly to his attractiveness for all the shouting in her head—a highwayman. "A vicar," she answered at last.

"A friend?"

A highwayman. A masked thief who stole outright from the rich. In the dead of the night.

"An acquaintance." She could feel her heart thumping against her throat. "Jealous?"

"Appalled." His glittering eyes softened behind that severe mask. "Flirting with a vicar."

"Aye." What was appalling was that she had never thought of it before, that she had gone on so long thinking herself competent, satisfied with the pittance from her little bits and bobs. "You're a highwayman."

"Aye." He dashed his cape off one shoulder, and set his fists onto his hips, showing off a smashing pair of flintlocks, matched and well balanced and perfectly lethal from the wicked look of them. Then he pulled them from his waist, holding the barrels up, giving her the full brazen stand-and-deliver effect.

Oh, holy highway robbery. That was the way to do it. A gun in each hand—one for the coach, and one for the driver—and the reins between her teeth.

She could picture it all in her mind's eye, from the way she would sneak her dark mare out of the stable, down to the set of pistols her father kept tucked away with his court sword in his book room, and the black leather gauntlets she would wear to protect and disguise her small hands.

"And what do you think?" Strathcairn was asking. "Not exactly a thief, but more dashing."

"Very dashing. I think it's brilliant." Her heart was beating so fast it was a wonder it didn't jump right out of her bodice, and run amok about the room. She was as excited and unnerved as she had been the first time she had realized she could take people's forgotten things and get away with it. "I think *you're* brilliant."

"You're not so bad yourself, lass. That's an awfully attractive gown you're almost wearing."

Quince barely heard his backhanded compliment. She had rather be wearing his highwayman's costume. Out on the roads. Right now. "How kind of you to notice."

"Every mon in the place has noticed your magnificent bodice." An equally magnificent frown was etching its way across his forehead beneath the hat.

The dark intensity of his tone wrenched her wayward mind back to the present. Strathcairn was *flirting* with her.

And she was going to make her hay while the sun shined, and flirt back for all she was worth. "One does one's best. But I admit I am rather taken by the sight of you thus. I might quite look forward to meeting you on some misbegotten stretch of lonely heath." Aye. She could imagine just the place—a suitably darkened patch of wood on a moonlit night. Like tonight.

Strathcairn's frown disappeared as a smile slid across his face, treating her to the full flash of that marvelously mischievous grin of old, and it was as if she had been bludgeoned by that five penny slab of butter, knocking what was left of her good sense right out of her. Making her reckless. Filling her with the jangle of excitement.

He spread his hands wide, and made her the courtliest of bows. "One does one's best."

One might do better than one's best, if one had the nerve. If one planned and was careful, one might do the impossible. The unexpected.

It was all coming crystal clear, showing her the way forward—a black domino, a wide brimmed hat, and a long, dark cavalier's wig—there were easily such things in trunks in Winthrop House's attics.

She could do it. And who would stop her? The roads of Scotland had been full of daring highwaymen half a century ago, long before she had been born. But nobody had played Captain MacHeath upon the roads of Edinburgh in years—and certainly nobody with an expensive pair of Manton patent dueling pistols fresh from London. Which were only needed for show, as there were no patrols—the garrison up at the Castle never seemed to do anything but march up and down the parade grounds.

It was indeed a brilliant idea. A terribly brilliant idea. It would be daring and totally unexpected.

Tonight she would get everything she wanted—kisses and thrills and gold.

The excitement—the sheer brazen possibility of it all—gave her that intoxicating rush of blood through her veins. She felt lit up from inside—all reckless enthusiasm.

And here was the perfect way to exercise it.

"Take me outside, Strathcairn. It's time to stand and deliver."

Chapter 7

HER WORDS WERE exactly the sort of talk Alasdair had been waiting to hear. He had spent an interminable few days forced to sit in stuffy rooms with magistrates and solicitors shuffling papers back and forth, and arranging with unwilling bureaucrats for off-duty soldiers from the Castle to assist him in his searches, when all he could think of was wee Quince Winthrop. And her acrobatic, laughing mouth.

So stand and deliver he would. At his first opportunity.

The heat of anticipation spread through his body with all the subtlety of a bonfire, goading him into action. "Wit and not wardrobe," might have been her motto, but the motto of the family Strathcairn was *Incipe*—Begin at Once.

"I've a mind," he said as he shoved his pistols back into his waist sash, and took her by the hand, "to see directly to our bargain and your education." He headed straight for the door leading out to the long, walled garden full of conveniently lengthening shadows cast by the golden twilight that made dark corners and hidden spots aplenty. He was sure he could hide them away where they wouldn't be found by inconvenient, interfering vicars or eagle-eyed mothers.

"How entirely impetuous of you, Captain Wigamore." She was nearly running to keep up, but still that clever mind of hers kept ticking on, challenging him at every turn.

Oh, she was a trial, this clever, curious, teasing lass— Captain Wigamore being the name given to a legendary highwayman of the last century, and also a very good jest at his reputation as a moderate, Whigish Tory.

"You can call me whatever you like, fair Diana"—he was as careful as she not to use her real name, which might alert bystanders to their identity—"once you give me what I came here to get."

Such frankly indelicate talk seemed to encourage her more. Instead of blushing, she laughed, and challenged him just as frankly. "And what is that, my fine captain of the road?"

"Your mouth," he growled as he swung her behind a hedge, and underneath the canopy of the trees. "On mine," he finished before backing her up against a particularly sturdy looking trunk.

He kissed her laughing lips with all the heat and force of his want, built up over days and days of waiting and wanting. Of having had only one brief sip of her that had left him hungry for more. A hunger that was always held in check by good manners and breeding and political necessity. And a damn lack of opportunity.

But he had the opportunity now, and he bloody well meant to take advantage of it.

She didn't object at all to such treatment. She smiled, and settled her back against the tree, and tipped up that stubborn chin in expectation. "No sweet words to soften me up? That's how you used to inveigle Linnea into kissing ye."

"Linnea always refused." Her sister, Linnea, had been something of a prude.

Quince gave him that mischievous, incendiary look from under her lashes. "I won't."

Devil take him, she was spark to his bonfire.

Alasdair settled into her, comfortably close. Close enough to inhale the delicious mixture of rose and orange blossom perfuming the hollow at the base of her neck. Close enough to whisper the Scots burr she liked into her ear. "Ye don't need soft words, wee Quince Winthrop. Ye need hard kissing. And I aim to give it to ye."

She tasted of rain and whisky. And hesitation, which proved as darkly provocative as any whisky and twice as potent. She went to his head in a way nothing else did. Nothing else ever had. "Had a wee dram, did ye, wee Quince?"

"Aye. For courage."

He felt his lips curve into a smile even as his mouth found the delicate lobe of her ear. "Ye don't need courage with me, lass."

"Easy for you to say. You're the one with the guns. Which are rather sticking into me." She pushed him away enough for him to miss the pliant warmth of her body. "Do you mind?"

She pulled the pistols out of his waistband without waiting for an answer, and put them God-knew-where, but he didn't care, because she was already back, looping her hands about his neck, and plastering herself against his chest, offering her sweet, kissable lips.

She felt so very good. So very alive. So very right.

"Easy for me to do," he murmured as his lips found hers in another incendiary kiss. He filled his arms and hands with her, holding her tight, tracing her lithe curves, angling her jaw so he could better take all she so generously offered. She was curiosity and confidence, all nubile warmth and comfort, despite the fact that she kissed with more enthusiasm than finesse, with her lithe torso plastered to his chest, her bare arms clasped around his neck, and her lips pressing ardently to his.

"Strathcairn," she sighed between kisses.

"Aye, lass," he encouraged. "That's the way of it." He angled his head to deepen the kiss. To teach her something more of tongue and tasting. Of patience and subtlety, and taking her time. Of drawing out the pleasure to make it last.

Oh, the things he could teach her. "So impatient."

"It's one of my better qualities." She fisted her hand in his hair, and pulled his mouth back to hers, breathless and ardent.

"Just as patience is one of mine." He covered her hand with his, entwining their fingers, and eased back from her, determined to slow things down. They didn't need to seduce each other, but there was no need for them to rush. He smiled at her, open and relaxed, full of lazy satisfaction. The way he used to look, he supposed, all those years ago, before he had gone to England and learned to be staid. "You can't just rush into the theory and system of kissing."

She matched his smile, and cozied herself flush against his chest. "A System of Kissing devised by the Marquess of Cairn? That is a book I would actually read."

"Says the lass who knows her Shakespeare. You just want people to think you're a flibbertigibbet, don't you?"

"A flibbertigibbet gets kissed more than a scholar."

"Does she?"

"Oh, aye. Because she needs to be educated in the ways of kissing."

His laughter ruffled the soft curls along her temples, and he smiled down at her, gently chafing her soft bare skin of her upper arms with his palms, warming her to his touch. "I'll give you an education, lass. But you may not go teaching it to anyone else without proper authorization."

"And would you give authorization?"

"Nay." His voice turned gruff—almost revealingly so. "For some reason I cannot currently fathom, I don't like the idea of you kissing other men, and teaching them what you've learned from me."

"To be fair, I haven't learnt much from you yet, so it's hard to reckon if I'd want to share your techniques with the wider world."

She was teasing him, he knew, but he couldn't seem to stop his arm from encircling her, and gathering her tight so the top of her stays rested against his chest. "In my opinion, the wider world is generally not worthy of such advanced techniques."

"Such a cynic," she teased.

He could not kiss the sass from her lips when all he could do was smile.

"And frankly, Strathcairn. I'd rather have your kisses than your opinion."

"Then you shall have them." His hands came up to cup her face gently between his palms. "Wee Quince Winthrop," he murmured. Such an interesting, intriguing amalgamation of contrasts, this lass. "That's the first element of the system, lass. Saying each other's name. Sweet like. Soft and easy, as if the name itself were dear." He bent his head to nuzzle against her ear, and her head fell back, her eyes closed.

"I'm only dear to you because I'm letting you kiss me."

"True," he admitted in the same teasing vein. "But I do believe you're becoming dear to me because, kissing or no kissing, I haven't had this much fun in years."

And it was true. He had denied himself for years. He had held himself back. Until he had met her, and his need for her—for fun, for a *thrill*—had built like a wave of want behind a dam. He'd never met a young woman like Quince Winthrop—a woman who challenged his wits as much as she appealed to his senses. A woman he could not—try as he might—get out of his mind.

"Careful, Strathcairn. Don't go getting *romantic* on me." There it was again, that teasing tone that equated romance with the influenza.

"Not a chance. I'm only here in the service of my fellow mon to give ye a thorough lesson in kissing. And the second lesson is go slow. Take your time. Savor the kiss. There's no need to rush." They had all night. He could kiss this lass until the cows came home, and then went back out again.

"What if I am in a rush?"

He could not tell if she were teasing. "Are you? What else could you possibly have to do that is nearly as much fun as kissing me in a dark, secluded garden during a masquerade, where no one kens who we are, and when we have all the time in the world to do what we want to do? Where else are you going to get yourself such a thrill?"

Her smile was sly and delightful and utterly incandescent. "I have several ideas, but none so easily to hand as you."

"That's it, lass." He settled a little more of his weight into her, pressing his chest against her enticingly trim bodice, easing his growing arousal. "You've so much more to learn. I'm afraid you need more instruction in the various systems and theories of kissing before you're properly thrilled."

"Less theory." Her hand curled around his nape. "More kissing."

He let his own fingers explore, sliding up into her artfully disarrayed curls. Her hair was as soft and slippery as the rest of her, sliding through his fingers. "I promise, my clever, curious Quince, that I will make the wait very much"—he skimmed the very tip of his finger along the delicate skin at the side of her temple to make her head tip obligingly to the side—"worth your while."

"Will you?" She sounded out of breath, as if she had been chasing after her usual teasing bravado, and lost it along the way.

"I will. I can." He eased closer, until his mouth was but a hairsbreadth from the sensitive shell of her ear, and whispered. "I promise."

Her eyes fluttered shut on a whisper. "I'm beginning to believe you."

He kissed her lips again, without reservation, without holding back or thinking or even breathing. He kissed her with his mouth and his tongue and his longing, setting fire to the bonfire of want burning within him.

She was so warm and alive, clinging to him with supple strength. She kissed him back with equal amounts of ardor and playfulness, laughing and smiling as if kissing him were either the greatest joke or the greatest fun ever.

They fell apart from sheer need for breath. "Please tell me it's the greatest fun."

She somehow followed his obscure reasoning. "The

greatest fun," she confirmed. "So far."

The groan that tunneled out of his chest was laced with his own laughter. Even her torture was fun. "Ah, wee Quince, don't tempt me like that. Don't tempt me to do things we'll both regret."

"I regret nothing so far. But—"

"Quince?" A low voice came from the other side of the hedge. A woman's voice.

Alasdair instinctively shielded her from view. "Who is it?"

"Shh." Quince clamped a hand across his mouth. "My sister, Plum," she whispered. "Oh, by jimble. She's such a bossy, interfering hen of a busybody." Quince let him go, and ducked deeper into the shadows of the hedge. But she was not inviting him to join her. "You'd better go." She pointed back toward the house. "Quickly. She may have my mother or father with her. Hurry."

Alasdair didn't like the thought of leaving her. But he liked the thought of coming face to face with Lord Winthrop, or God help him, Lady Winthrop, even less. It would put paid to all his best-laid plans for the future if he were discovered in the shrubbery with his hands all over wee Quince Winthrop.

If he wasn't careful— and he was always careful—well, nearly always—he could end up married to the most unsuitable lass he'd ever had the blessed good fortune to meet.

But there were worse fates.

It was as if the ground shifted beneath his feet—he felt unsteady, lightheaded. Not at the thought of marriage— which he had long contemplated with all clear-headed seriousness, drawing up a list of suitable society misses—but at the thought that there would be worse fates than being bound to wee, unsuitable, unpredictable, but ever-so interesting Quince Winthrop.

Who was staring at him the way a vixen might eye a hound—wishing him elsewhere. "Strathcairn. You have to go."

"You're always saying that to me," Alasdair grumbled.

But she had already turned away from him, was already straightening her bodice—if the gauzy drapery she was passing off as a gown even had a bodice—and adjusting her mask with a finality that said she had taken enough tuition for this evening.

"We're not done with the lesson, Quince. In fact we've barely even started."

"Aye. I am sorry. But if I'm caught with you, Mama will come after me like a— Well, like a mother. That's likely why she sent Plum. I'm sure you understand."

He did not understand.

He understood only the need to feel her lips beneath his. The need to hold her face between his hands. The need to taste the sweet tartness that was wee Quince Winthrop.

But go he did, after one last quick kiss upon her lips. "You have tree bark in your hair. Meet me later. Please."

And then he swallowed his need, and his hunger, and his pride, and left. This is what he had come to—slipping through the shrubbery like a naughty schoolboy.

All because she'd asked.

And damned if he didn't already know he would do whatever she asked, whenever she asked him again. Damned if she wasn't going to be his fate.

IT WAS FATE. Fate that had put such an outrageous idea into her head. Fate that put Strathcairn's guns in her hands. Fate that sent Plum busybodying her way into the garden to break them apart.

And Quince decided she was too smart to ignore fate.

Or too stupid.

Because it was an entirely irrational idea. A daft, dangerous idea. But an outrageous, audacious idea that set off a thrill of excitement so strong, her breath felt tight with unholy, addictive anticipation.

And she knew that once the idea had taken up lodging in her head, she would not be able to resist the temptation.

She could not resist hefting the absolutely cracking pair of matched Manton patent dueling pistols in her hands—trying them out for size. They were heavy but beautifully balanced, with long octagonal barrels set in polished and checkered walnut. The perfect weapons for holding up a coach.

But whose coach?

The name came to her in an instant—Sir Harry Digby, a man whose name and reputation were well-known to her, but whom she had never met.

Aye. She would learn from her mistakes, and take great care not to repeat them—she would choose *from whom* she stole with the utmost care.

Sir Harry and Lady Digby were an older, steady couple, not given to fits of drama. Nor were they connected to the government or judiciary in any way—all it would take was for her to rob some judge or former magistrate, and the full crushing weight of the law would come down upon her head. And around her neck.

Nay. Sir Harry and his lady wife were known for their genial temperaments, their success in prize monies won running their horses on the sands at Leith, and Lady Digby's superb collection of family pearls. But most importantly, Sir Harry was known as an inveterate, habitual gambler, who most often won—very often from her own father. According to Papa, Sir Harry liked to start early and take the first few pots, and so could be relied upon to be one of the first to leave the masquerade. He liked to head for his estate several miles out of the town as soon as he had won a hand or three, and had a purse full of coin.

A purse full enough to feed a family of five for far longer than a fortnight.

Aye. Sir Harry was perfect.

And so would she be. She would take only the purse—not the pearls, which would have to be fenced—this very night, when the moon was full, the weather was balmy, and the full heat of the idea was still burning like a beacon in her brain.

She would give herself no time to think, to turn prudent and turn back.

She, wee Quince Winthrop, Edinburgh's most thoughtless flibbertigibbet, would rob the lucky man blind.

And she needed to begin immediately. There was no time like the present—the full moon was already rising in the cloudless sky to the east of the city, providing the perfect light to be riding the roads. She needed to prepare— horse, route, costume, guns. Immediately.

First, the guns. She could not hope to conceal them on her body in her present costume, so she stashed them carefully in the hedge before she pushed her way through the shrubbery. "Plum?" Quince ran to catch up with her sister, who had already given up, and started to return up the lawn.

Her sister whirled around, shepherdess's crook and all. "Quince! I knew you were out here. What were you doing?"

The best defense was always an offense. "I might ask the same question of you."

"I came looking for you." Plum peered toward the shrubbery from whence Quince had come. "Are you alone?"

"Not anymore." Quince linked her elbow with her sister's. "I'm with you."

Plum wasn't so easily turned from her point. "What were you doing out here alone?"

"I came out to get some fresh air, but despite that, I've developed the most intolerable megrim." She stopped Plum at the edge of the torch-lit terrace. "I think I had best go home."

"Are you sure?" While not exactly convinced, Plum was at least concerned. "Do you want me to get Mama for you?"

"Nay." The last thing she wanted was for her sharp-eyed Mama to get a good look at her no-doubt flushed cheeks. Or worse, to send anyone home with her. "Just tell her I've gone home."

"What about the marquess?"

Quince tried to play her metaphorical cards close to her chest. "What about him?"

"Quince, really." Plum all but stamped her shepherdess's crook on the ground in frustration. "It's obvious you're mad about him. Just as he is for you." Plum glanced briefly around the terrace, and lowered her voice. "I saw him in the ballroom, looking for you. And I saw you come out here with him."

"So you followed." Her sister was worse than a shepherdess—she was more of a sheepdog in the manger.

"Only after you'd been out here too long. Mama had begun to look around." Her sister let out an exasperated sigh. "Honestly, Quince. Disappearing into dark gardens? I don't want to interfere, but you're out of your depth with the marquess."

Plum wasn't the only one exasperated. Quince was more than a little tired of Plum's constant jealousy. "And you wouldn't be?"

"Quince." Plum turned her name into a scold. "Don't be daft. No matter what you think, I'm not jealous. I've purposefully tried to throw you two together—maneuvering him to escort you the other day. I know you like nothing more than a challenge, but I'm beginning to fear that the Marquess of Cairn is too much of a challenge—too polished, too much of a politician. He'd make anyone, including me, but most especially *you*, a dreadful husband. And you'd make him a dreadful wife."

"I'd make anyone a dreadful wife." It was the bare truth, though it was painful to admit it, both to herself, and especially to Plum. But though Quince had often enough lied to others, she had never lied to herself. She had made herself un-marriageable with her flippant tongue, her passionate contempt, and her compulsive stealing.

It all came back to the stealing.

So why not go all the way? Why not make it entirely worthwhile? Why not dare greatly?

But Plum surprised her by not agreeing—at least not

entirely. "That's not true. Or at least only partially true, and only because you never think about what you're doing. You never have. You always rode too fast, and played too hard, and climbed too high, and you still do. You dash in headlong, never thinking about tomorrow, or what people will think."

Another bare truth. Mostly. She didn't care what people thought of her, but she did think about what she was doing. All the time. She was always planning, and thinking about tomorrow. Except at that very moment, when she was thinking, and planning, about tonight. "If Strathcairn asks after me—and I doubt he will." He was too clever for anything so obvious. "Tell him the truth—that I've gone home."

"But you can't go alone. It's not safe."

"Of course I can." Quince had never subscribed to the strictures that ladies ought never to venture out alone, and never walk anywhere they could be carried. "It's only a few furlongs."

"Quince." Her sister laid a protective hand to her arm. "It's nearly two miles."

"And most of that is straight up Canongate. But if it makes you feel any better, I'll take a chair." There were bound to be a raft of sedan chairs and their porters waiting along the street in front of the Queensbury mansion.

"It would. And get a link boy to light the way." Plum produced a few coins from her purse. "The last thing Mama needs to worry about is you being held up by footpads."

"Plum, the last thing that's going to happen tonight is me getting held up by footpads. I can guarantee it."

Chapter 8

NO ONE ACCOSTED her. No one paid her the least bit of attention. She walked home along the familiar streets with only Strathcairn's heavy patent pistols for company, slapping against her thighs from deep inside the pockets of her evening cloak. Keeping time with her footfalls. Pressing their steel-barreled urgency upon her.

Adding weight to the arguments in her head.

She could do it. If only she dared. And dared greatly.

Robbing a coach wasn't really that much different than the opportunistic pilfering of bits and bobs from a ballroom, was it? She had already made the moral compromise to take what wasn't rightfully hers—why not make it a much more profitable compromise? She had tried to do good by stealth—now was as good a time as any for a more direct approach.

But did she really dare? Robbing a coach was a hanging offense. And even though there had not been a case against a highwayman in decades, Quince doubted the law had become any more lenient. If anything, the current attitudes were becoming more draconian, not less—Strathcairn's presence in response to petty thievery was proof enough of the enduring rock-like immutability of the law.

But Strathcairn was safely masquerading the night away, and there were no troops of horse patrolling the roads. She would take great care, just as she always had, not to get caught. She would very careful, and would plan with both flexibility and precision. She would not give in to her fears, nor let them overwhelm her and make her stupid.

She could not afford to be stupid. The poor of the West Kirk Workhouse were counting upon her—people who had nothing, through no fault of their own. She would not let them down.

Quince stopped for a moment, closed her eyes, and pictured him—the scaffy lad in the street all those years ago—the raggedy child, the beggar boy who had started her off down the road of righteousness, and who had turned her itchy compulsion toward theft into a crusade.

She made herself remember his thin hands, and the over-wide look of his hopeful, ill-nourished eyes. Made herself remember what he had looked like, curled up on the cold pavement like an abandoned kitten, dead on the corner across from her father's house in the gray morning light. Dead because they, who had the power to help him, had not. Dead because she, who had tried to help him, could not.

She had not tried hard enough.

But she was not an inexperienced sixteen-year-old now—she had backbone to spare.

Once Quince made up her mind, she did not pause, nor give herself even a moment to think on the enormity of what she was about to do. She ignored the cold shiver of warning chilling her skin, and set straight to it. Up into the attic trunks to dig out one of her father's old, voluminous, black dominos, and an out-moded court suit of midnight velvet, with a matching, broad-brimmed beaver hat decorated with a wilted white plume. A dash down to the bottom of the dusty cabinet in his book room to retrieve his ceremonial court sword. And finally, a stop in her own room to don her rakish costume, and dust her face and hair ghostly white with rice powder.

The black suit and breeches made her feel strange and new and strong. Strange, because it was bizarre to see her legs walking beneath her. New, because the white mask and powdered hair pulled out in old-fashioned full curls flattened and hid her features so no one should be able to tell it was she. Strong, because with her height, and on horseback, no one should even be able to tell she wasn't a man.

But she was still herself who had never done anything so bold or daring before, and her hands shook, spilling powder across her sleeve. It was one thing to plot highway robbery in theory, and another thing entirely to actually take to the roads—to take that first step out the door and into the night.

She hesitated in front of the mirror, searching her image for flaws, raking over each part of her spur-of-the-moment plan. Knowing that once she committed herself, and stepped through the doors of her father's house, there would be no turning back.

No telling herself that it was all a lark or silly mistake.

It was not a mistake. It was the very rightest thing she could possibly do.

She looped the bright tartan sash of her father's sword belt over her head and across her chest, and pulled on the leather gauntlets. And there in the mirror was a complete and perfect highwayman. Rakish, and daring. Ready to dare greatly. Ready come what may.

If only Strathcairn could see her now—what would he think? Would he still think she was magnificent? Or would her deception be abhorrent to him?

Most likely abhorrent.

But she wasn't going to let Strathcairn's inconvenient scruples stop her, because he need never know.

With one last tug on the broad brim of her hat, Quince finished her preparations—fetching a satchel in which to hide the mask and plume and sash once she was done.

With the house quiet of both family and servants, it was easy to sneak unseen across the meticulous garden into the silent stables. It was child's play to tiptoe into the tack room to stealthily retrieve her father's saddle and bridle, and the work of a moment to slip into her mare's stall unobserved by the lone, dozing lad left to watch over the place while the coachman and grooms were still out, idling in the yard of the Queensbury mansion, waiting for Lord Winthrop and his family party.

All of her father's horses were coal-dark Thoroughbred and Warmblood crosses, matched to draw the glossy black town carriage in style. And since her mare, Piper, was meant to be a spare should one of the four carriage horses come up lame, she, too, had almost no distinguishable markings beyond a dash of white at her rear fetlocks. And that Quince was able to quickly cover with a pinch of bootblack.

And then there was nothing left for her to do but walk the mare out into the close, cinch the saddle girth tight, and mount astride.

Quince swung herself up and into the saddle, and—

Oh, holy hoof claps. It had been a long time since Quince had ridden astride, and her mare wasn't used to having a rider with legs on both sides of the saddle either—Piper jibed and shied to the left so strongly Quince feared she was going to come to muddy grief right there on the cobbled close before she ever had a chance to stand and deliver.

Quince took a firmer grasp of the rein despite her slick palms, and set the poor animal down the close at a smart trot, before their clattering antics on the cobbles could wake the stable lad. And if Piper were going to throw her off, best the mare do it now, when she wouldn't have so far to walk home.

But she didn't end up in the gutter—the two of them sorted themselves out soon enough, helped by the fact that Quince quickly adjusted the fall of the sword sheath so it didn't ride against the mare's flank. For her own part, Quince liked the feeling of surety and control of having two feet in the stirrups. Tonight of all nights, she was going to need all the extra control she could get.

The Digbys's estate, Fairleith Manor, stood in wooded seclusion some five miles north of the city proper, off the shore road along the edge of the Firth of Forth. Which meant that Quince had to chance taking the more heavily used Leith Walk to head northeast before she could reach the more countrified lanes to skirt north around the edges of the town. Her plan, should she encounter anyone along the way who might inquire after the strange manner of her dress, was to say that she had been at a masquerade in the city. To pretend, in fact, that she was Strathcairn.

Since the idea for her larcenous masquerade came from him, it was only right that he be included.

But with or without Strathcairn, her bravado could not overcome her nervy uneasiness—the only time she met with a rider coming toward her from a distance, she hid herself behind a hedgerow, quickly dismounting and concealing herself in the warm shadow of the mare's neck, until he had safely passed.

Even with such an interruption, it seemed no time at all before she reached the cool wood that hid Fairleith Manor from the coast road. The moon was still high in the night sky, warming the cool dark of the forest with a sheen of golden light. With luck, she would rob Sir Harry, have the mare back in her father's stables, and herself safely back in bed within the hour, long before the revels of the masquerade had drawn to an end.

But first, she had to be successful. And to be successful, she had to think like a highwayman.

Accordingly, she chose a secluded spot at the bottom of a rise, where the rolling wood opened up just enough to let the moonlight illuminate the road, but where that road was also so narrow it would be impossible for the coach to turn or run. And she ensured it would be impossible by rooting about in the undergrowth for a few minutes until she found a suitable limb, downed in a recent storm, and dragged it out into the middle of the road at the far edge of the pool of moonlight, where it formed a natural barricade.

Everything was set so the carriage would stop.

All Quince had to do was sit tight and wait for it to arrive.

Only she couldn't. It was impossible. She was far too nervy to sit, listening to the thumping of her heart in her ears, while her mare fell to dozing beneath her. So Quince practiced her ploy, urging her mare back and forth between the concealment of the trees and the open road three times, rehearsing the path she would take, counting the eight paces that would take her to the exact right spot at the exact right time to be seen and stop the coach.

And still the road remained empty.

Patience was a virtue she did not normally possess. She could not quiet her mind, or still her body, and her nerves communicated themselves to her mare—poor Piper shifted just as restlessly, her ears flicking backward and forward in alert annoyance.

"It will all be over soon," Quince whispered. If everything went according to plan. If Sir Harry acted according to his custom, and left the revels earlier than most. If she had the nerve.

And then it was too late for second thoughts—the first faint jangling of harness, and the rhythmic clomp of hooves could be heard closing the distance, though it was suddenly hard to hear anything over the thunderous pounding of her own heart.

Quince had to adjust her reins through hands that had suddenly gone nerveless, slick and damp within the confines of the leather gloves, so she decided to loop the belt of the reins around under her right thigh so she could keep her hands free for the guns, and her mouth free to give orders.

The jangle of the harness grew louder and louder, until a pair of white horses seemed to evolve from the shadows into the moonlight, drawing an open landau with a single ancient coachman up front, and Lord and Lady Digby nodding with sleep at the back.

The horses knew their job better than the driver, and the

whole of the equipage was rolling to a slow stop some thirty feet in front of the makeshift barricade before the old coachman seemed to realize something lay in his path.

And then he turned to find her eight paces away, just as she had rehearsed.

Without knowing exactly how she had gotten there, Quince set straight to the business, tossing back the domino's cape, drawing the first pistol staunchly from her belt, and pointing it directly at the old coachman's heart.

And nothing happened—the old man just sat there on the box, gaping at her.

As the strange moment extended itself, the weight of the gun made her arm wobble rather too much for the picture of a professional highwayman that Quince had intended to present. She had also intended to say something cool and clever, but her throat closed itself up tighter than a dowager's purse.

Faced with the continued threat of her pistol, the coachman finally broke the silence. "Ain't you supposed to say stand and deliver?"

"Don't have to, do I?" She tried to push her voice low, but her mouth was so dry, and her voice strangled the words, and instead of sounding manly, which is what she had intended, she somehow sounded rather French.

Which was a monstrously good idea. "You understand me alreadee. Your choice, *cher Monsieur*—your monee, or your life."

As the coachman probably had little money, he wisely chose his life, slowly pushing his hands into the air.

"I thank you, *Monsieur*. But you may drop the reins, first, *mon vieux*. Care-fully." It was a safe enough command—both because her schoolroom French seemed to be rising to the occasion, and because there was nowhere for the horses to bolt with the branches across the road. "Keep your hands where I can see zem, eef you please."

Sir Harry chose that moment to shake himself awake. "What goes here, Rackham? Why are we—" His voice gave out the moment he saw her.

Quince gave him what she hoped was a courteous, courtly nod of introduction. "As your good coachman Rackham tells mee, *Monsieur*, zee custom of your country is to ask you to stand and dee-liver. And so *mon vieux* milord, I ask you to do just zat. Stand down from your coach, keeping your hands all the times where I can see zem."

Sir Harry seemed at first too stupid to accommodate her request—he gaped at her. "What is the meaning of this?"

"Zee meaning is zat you shall be robbed, good sir. Out of zee coach," she repeated her command for good measure. "Eef you may be counted upon to keep your Engleesh manners, zen we will all get along swimmingly, and no one shall be hurt."

"By God. I'm not English, I'm Scots. But if you—"

She drew her second pistol with a flourish, and aimed it squarely at his greying head. "I have no quarrel wiss your God, milord. Nor wiss you, eef you will be so good as to hand over your purse."

Sir Harry clambered down from the coach with such ill grace that he woke his lady, who had the good sense, or good terror, to stay mute while her husband emptied his pockets of a few assorted coins, throwing them to the ground at the mare's feet.

She marked the fall of the coins before she slid her glance back to Sir Harry. She hoped her smile looked as riled and rude as she felt. "Milord, I pray you would not insult me wiss your leettle copper pennies. I will take zem, you may be sure, but I also detect a purse, and a rahzer fat one at zat, disturbing zee cut of your plain, ill-fitted Engleesh coat. I will take it, eef you please. Eef only to ameliorate zee offense you make to fashion."

"Damn your head."

But the purse with his evening's winnings chinked gratifyingly as he pulled it from his waistcoat pocket.

"Excellent. You may hold zat zere, for zee moment." Quince kept her eyes constantly roving between the three of them—the coachman, Sir Harry, and his lady. "And now we arrive at your most compliant and silent ladee."

"But I have no money," Lady Digby dithered. "And… And I don't think I could stand for the life of me."

Quince nodded her head regally, letting the playacting go to her head, and throwing her well-planned caution to the night wind. "You may sit and deliver, *Madame*, eef it please you, so long as you deliver to me zose most ancient and becoming pearls."

"My pearls!" The woman threw a hand across her bosom as if blocking Quince's view of them might deter their loss.

It would not.

Quince decided it was an opportune moment to cock back the hammers of her guns—the menacing metallic click serving rather effectively as her answer. Though she also prayed that at such a distance, neither Sir Harry, nor his coachman, could tell that the guns were not actually loaded.

She added a soupçon of threat to her tone. "Your pearls, *Madame*." In the past, Quince had always shied well away from taking items of jewelry. Trading in gems was too far out of her—and Jeannie and Charlie's—experience and understanding. But she was playing a different game now, and in for a penny, in for a pearl. The luminous beads would be easy enough to unstring, and sell at some later date, when the furor had died down—when Strathcairn was gone away to Cairn.

Or better yet, months from now, in the autumn when he had safely taken his inconvenient scruples back to London. Aye. And then perhaps she would send the jewels to Amsterdam. There were plenty of merchant houses in Edinburgh who traded across the North Sea, and would take any sort of small cargo without asking too many questions. Her father often traded plants, bulbs and seeds with botanists all across the globe, with no one the wiser as to what was in his packages.

Aye. And while she was convincing herself that the pearls were safe enough to take, she took another look at the diamond and pearl ear bobs swinging from the lady's thin lobes. And the emerald cravat pin adorning his lordship's lacy jabot.

"And because you have discommoded me by making me wait, I will take all of zee jewels—earbobs, brooch, and pin of zee cravat." She punctuated her words by pointing to each item in question with the barrel of her gun.

She was very nearly enjoying herself.

Which was very nearly a mistake, as her attention was almost diverted from Coachman Rackham, who had been trying to nonchalantly lower his tired old arms, and reach under his box, no doubt in search of a weapon. "Move anozer inch, *Monsieur* coachman, and I shall be obliged to blow you into several thousand terribly messy pieces." Her voice rose dangerously high, exposing her, she was sure.

But her victims thankfully heard only the angry desperation—enough to make the coachman halt, and quickly raise his hands back to the air.

It was past time for her to finish what she had come to do. "Take zee gems from your wife, milord, and put zem all in zee purse." She paused while he did so. "And zee sparkling emerald in your lace as well. Now," she commanded, "leave zee purse on zee ground at your feet for *mes confrères,* the men of *Monsieur Minuit*"—she made up some imaginary conspirators as well as a highwayman's name on the spot—"to retrieve. Ah, yes, just so." She complimented him when he complied. "I sank you for your exemplary cooperation."

She was so close. The money was so close, just lying there on the ground. Waiting. Almost hers.

"*Mes braves, je l'avais,*" she shouted toward the wood, as if her imaginary friends were watching and waiting, hoping her memory of schoolroom French had conjured up the correct conjugation.

But Lord and Lady Digby did not seem to be parsing her French grammar. Instead they obligingly glanced to the woods surrounding them, as if in expectation of a gang of cutthroats.

It gave Quince the confidence she needed to plot out the last moves of this particularly dangerous chess game. "You may remount your coach, milord. Drive on," she instructed the coachman in a voice made louder from the dangerous surge of power and relief and hope spilling into her veins. She was so close, so very nearly there. "*Allez*! Go!"

There were only about ten yards of ground between the team and the downed tree limb, but while the coachman was busy gathering his reins, and moving the equipage forward, he would be too busy to shoot her. So as soon as the landau jolted forward, Quince threw her leg over the pommel of the saddle, ready to jump down.

But she had forgotten the damn rein looped around her thigh. The leather strap twisted around her leg and held fast.

Quince plunged arse over teakettle over the mare's neck, losing her hat, and landing in a tangle on the ground. It was a long, fraught moment before she could clear her head, and catch her breath, and free her leg from the rein enough to scrabble forward on her hands and knees to snatch up the purse.

She had the suede pouch in her hand, and was pushing to her feet, swiping up her hat and reaching for the reins so she could circle around poor skittish mare and remount, when she heard Sir Harry exhort his coachman. "The gun, mon! Where's your damn gun?"

Quince didn't wait to hear anything else. Indeed, she could not hear anything else over the surge of terror pounding like an ocean in her already ringing ears.

She shoved the purse down her front, and charged straight for the wood on foot, tearing in the opposite direction from the coach, pulling the mare along, praying that it would be harder for the coachman to retrieve his blunderbuss, and turn, and take aim over Lord and Lady Digby's heads, than if she had run for the trees closest to her.

She hoped and prayed it would be harder to track her on that side—there was no time to do anything but clap her hat onto her head, haul hard on the mare, hunch herself against the shelter of the poor animal's bulk, and pelt for the trees as if hell and all its flaming minions were pouring after her.

The mare's momentum kept her going a good forty feet

into the welcoming cover of the wood. Once hidden by the dark leaves, and with no fatal gunshot chasing her, Quince vaulted into the saddle and spurred the mare into a gallop down the narrow path along the burn that tumbled and churned through the woodland, covering the sound of their headlong flight.

Quince let the canny mare run her own course, while she checked the path behind, twisting in the saddle to peer blindly into the shifting darkness of the wood. But she could see nothing, and if she couldn't see them, she reasoned, they couldn't see her.

Cold comfort, but she would take whatever comfort she could get. Her heart was still pounding away like the cannon at Edinburgh Castle on the King's birthday, she was panting like a frightened dog, and her stomach didn't feel so equitable either.

Still, she did not rein in until she had gone several miles, and reached the temporary sanctuary of a small stone bridge that forded the stream and marked the spot where the larger wood gave way to open fields outside the city. In the sheltering dark beneath the bridge, she waited, listening over the babble of the burn for any sound that might signal pursuit.

There was none.

Quince slid from the saddle, and all but collapsed into the knee-deep water, trying desperately not to spill her quivering guts into the stream. Waiting for the little firefly flickers of light to recede from the edges of her vision.

She cupped some water into her hand to drink, and willed her fractured nerves to knit themselves back together again. So much for the image of the cool, rakish highwayman. She could only be glad that Strathcairn couldn't see her now, pale and sweating and chilled.

And laden with ill-gotten gain.

Quince touched a hand to the bulge beneath her waistcoat, to prove to herself that the fat purse was real. That she had indeed done it, just as she had so audaciously planned.

Fortune favors the bold, they said. Well, damned if that wasn't true.

She had done it, hadn't she? Well, so far, anyway—she still had to get home undetected, and dispose of her loot. And the only way to accomplish it was to set straight to it, erasing all traces of the highwayman.

First, she dunked her head in the frigid waters of the burn to wash her face and scrub her hair free of the white powder. Then, she scooped up handfuls of sand to clean the bootblack from her mare's fetlocks. Next, the white plume and mask went into the jute sack she had rolled at the back of the saddle, as did the pistols, and the colorful sword belt. The rest, she hid under the dark cover of the domino, which she tied across her chest like a silk evening cape.

Now she looked like any gentleman headed to the town for a night of revelry—albeit a thin, damp, nervous young gentleman. In fact, it wasn't much of a disguise, but it would have to do. All it had to do was get her home safe, to end the night prudently, in her own narrow bed.

She set Piper to a swift canter down the lane, and with every pounding stride, every moment that passed without alarm, the nervous distractions of imminent peril wore off, and prudence seemed less and less necessary. With every hoofbeat her heart grew more and more giddy with relief, and the addictive elation of accomplishment.

And she knew that once she was home and safe, she would still be too thrilled to lay still.

She couldn't possibly sleep. Not when Strathcairn might be awake.

Chapter 9

ALASDAIR WAS PROPERLY put out. Stymied, even.

After five years of hard learning and practice in the art of never letting anything stand in his way or impede his progress, wee Quince Winthrop had managed to utterly confound him.

The lass was nowhere to be found, and it seemed nothing short of a pack of hounds was going to find the vixen now that she had gone to ground—he searched the garden without finding a trace of her. Or of his pistols, which he had last seen somewhere under the hawthorn tree.

Or at least he thought he had seen them—he hadn't exactly been paying attention. He had had other, more nubile, kissable things on his mind.

How did she manage to put him so off-balance?

Alasdair damned his weakness for his Diana with a pair of flintlocks, and went to check in with the men he had assigned to act as footmen, watching for thefts. "MacGilvray."

The man snapped to attention as if he were holding a long gun, and not a pitcher of ratafia. "Milord."

"Anything?"

"No' a thing, sar. Though it may be just as ye sayed 'bout folks just leavin' things—some auld hen come up to me, and hands me her fan she does, and off she goes. Still got it, if she do return." The stout man gestured to the silver tray upon which sat a pitcher of punch, two silver punch glasses, and an ivory handled fan. "Jes' hopin' I don't get no punch on it, sar."

"Just so, MacGilvray." Damned if it wasn't just as wee Quince Winthrop had said—people simply didn't bother to keep track of things that were easy enough to replace with another trip to the drapers or haberdashers.

Alasdair stepped around a toga-clad Roman emperor—and there were six of them to report to Quince when he did see her again—only to come smack up against Lady Plum Winthrop brandishing a shepherdess's crook.

"Come, my lord," she ordered presumptively. "We can't have you standing around in this stupid manner, spending all night looking for her, asking footmen about her. People will think you're *serious*." She passed her crook into the hands of one of his nonplussed footmen, and began towing Alasdair toward the dance floor, in much the same presumptive manner as he had earlier towed her younger sister away from that same floor.

They certainly weren't shy, these Winthrop ladies.

"It won't do, you know, for the whole of the world to know you've developed a *tendre* for my sister. It will make her insufferably smug, for one thing, and we can't have that."

"We can't?" There were many things he might have called wee Quince Winthrop—flirtatious, infuriating, unapologetic—but smug was not one of them. "Have I?"

Lady Plum Winthrop gave him as withering an eye as ever her sister might have. "Have you not?"

Damn, but these Winthrop women certainly had a way of plain speaking.

He supposed, when faced with such a bald fact, that he *had* formed something of a *tendre* for wee Quince Winthrop.

Which thankfully wasn't quite the same thing as an attachment. Nor an understanding. A *tendre* he could manage. Perhaps.

With luck. And patience. And a great deal of brandy. And a great deal more kissing.

"And exactly what, Lady Plum, would you advise me to do?"

"Well, for one thing, stop wearing your interest, like your heart, upon your sleeve. And for God's sake do not take my younger sister out into the garden at a ball to have your experienced, London rake's way with her."

Damn his eyes. That was plain enough. Alasdair felt heat singe his collar. "Your pardon, my lady. I did not think my affections were publicly known. I had not thought us observed."

"You are at a masquerade, my lord—everything is observed. And you have a reputation. Not everyone is blind to a mask, my lord. And is it affection, really?"

The heat scorched across his cheeks, but he was honest enough to give her the truth. "It is," he finally said. Though it felt strange to admit such a truth out loud. "And I am not a rake."

Lady Plum remained entirely unconvinced. "You certainly seem one, with your *rendezvous* in the shrubbery, and your stylish London ways. My sister is young and inexperienced, and out of her depth with you, my lord, and I beg you not be so ungentlemanly as to take advantage of her for it."

Ungentlemanly.

Lady Plum's accusation slapped him as hard as her sister's palm ever had. Harder. The word was a dagger to his pride. To his very sense of self.

Everything he had done over the past five years, every alliance he had forged, every word he had spoken, had been to prove one thing above all—that he was a gentleman worthy of the marquessate of Cairn.

That wee Quince Winthrop has hardly out of her depth with *anyone*, let alone him, was a minor quibble in comparison to the charge that he, Alasdair Colquhoun, might not have acted like a gentleman. He could practically hear his grandfather roaring and rolling in his grave.

And Lady Plum was not yet done rebuffing him. "I've heard the old rumors, even if she hasn't, and I shan't let you amuse yourself with her as some sort of a diversion while you rusticate north of the Borders, my lord. My sister is not a plaything."

Only when she herself wanted to be. But he took Lady Plum's meaning. "I understand, Lady Plum. Your sister told me much the same thing herself."

"Did she? Good for her." But she looked at him with narrowed eyes, as if she were still not prepared to trust him.

Him, the most trustworthy, loyal, honest man in all of London. Everyone said so. He had built his entire reputation there, both in the government and in society, upon the bedrock of upstanding, gentlemanly behavior. He was a Strathcairn. He could do no less.

"Please forgive me if I gave any impression that I have anything less than the utmost respect and admiration for your sister, Lady Plum. But I shall take your advice, and take care with how I am seen with her."

"Good," she repeated with more surety. "Because if you don't act the gentleman, I will make sure that everyone in Edinburgh knows how you have treated her. I shan't let her be cowed into silence. So you'll have to be a gentleman one way or another."

It was as uncomfortable a thing as it had ever been, to be threatened with blackmail. But he took her point. "I understand you, Lady Plum."

They seemed to have arrived at the end of their discussion. But still they stood on the edge of the dance floor. "Do you still care to dance, Lady Plum?"

"It is unnecessary now," she admitted. "But I suppose it will do my reputation no great harm to be seen dancing with a marquess. And it seems only fair that we Winthrop sisters get some *public* use out of you, my Lord Cairn. So yes, you may have this dance with me."

"I am honored." He led her into place in the set. "And pray tell me, Lady Plum," he asked as they joined hands for the lead around. "Do you Winthrop sisters spend all your time trading quips and sharpening your wits in order to skewer the unsuspecting?"

"Indeed we do, my lord. Not *all* our time, but enough, I should think."

"Indeed, my lady. More than enough."

"Thank you. But you, my lord, are hardly unsuspecting. Or undeserving."

She had him there. Lady Plum deigned to complete the rest of the set of the cotillion in blessed silence. But when the dance was done, and before he walked her back to her mother, he had one more question. "Could you tell me, Lady Plum, if I promise to be circumspect and gentlemanly, where in this cavernous place your sister might be hidden? Or am I not allowed to know?"

"You are allowed, my lord." She retrieved her crook from the waiting footman. "But she is not hidden away in this cavernous place. She has gone home."

Gone? Or sent? He didn't have the heart to ask which. This time, Alasdair knew the tight, hollow feeling of the air leaving his lungs for what it was—disappointment.

"Thank you, my lady." Alasdair decided he had been the victim of more than enough Winthrop wit and whimsy for one day. He bowed. "Your conversation has been most edifying, my lady."

"Was it?" She put her nose in the air in much the same way her sister brandished her aggressive little chin. "It was meant to be terrifying."

Oh, aye, these girls had certainly practiced sharpening their wits to well-honed blades.

He bowed more formally, as to an opponent at swords. "A hit, my lady. Acknowledged. I will count myself lucky not to have been mortally skewered, and take my leave of you."

"Good night, Lord Cairn." She swept him a very commonplace curtsey, and turned away, as if dismissing him completely from her thoughts.

Would that he had the ability to do the same. But he did not. Her words—along with those of her mother, Lady Winthrop—stayed with him. The thought that he might not have acted in a manner fitting the house of Cairn haunted him all the long way home, across New Bridge to the New Town.

Were his intentions toward wee Quince Winthrop strictly honorable? Was it gentlemanly—was it right—for him to take advantage of her curiosity and inexperience so he could have his "London rake's way" with her?

Never mind that he wasn't a rake, and never had been. Never mind that wee Quince Winthrop had asked him for lessons in kissing. Never mind that despite her inexperience, wee Quince Winthrop was certainly no innocent.

If he answered as the gentleman his grandfather had raised him to be, the answer was a resounding nay. He had no business giving wee Quince Winthrop anything, much less lessons in kissing.

But devil take him, he had certainly enjoyed the tutelage.

It had only been six days since he had returned to Scotland, and only a few hours of those days had been spent with her. But every other intervening hour had been spent thinking, hoping, planning, and simply indulging in fantasies about her. Six days and he had formed a *tendre*.

Clearly a brandy was needed to help sort out the matter.

And mercifully, his secretary Sebastian Oistins—a young freedman originally from the West Indies island of Barbados who had, under Alasdair's patronage, become a formidable writer of essays against the slave trade—was awake, and had a keen sense of occasion. Sebastian took one look at Alasdair as he crossed the threshold of his rooms in Prince Street, and gestured to the well-stocked tray. "The decanter is full, my Lord Cairn."

"Thank you, Sebastian." Alasdair made straight for it. "And don't 'my lord' me."

"If I may inquire, my lord?" It was a game they played, this battle over titles and formalities. A battle the young abolitionist always won. "The pistols?"

"Misplaced." Alasdair was too embarrassed to admit the whole of the truth— that he had given them up for a kiss, and promptly forgotten them. Instead he poured himself a healthy splash of brandy—desperate times called for desperate measures. And he felt desperate, so he poured himself another desperate measure.

He would send a quiet inquiry round to the Marchioness of Queensbury's butler for the pistols in the morning. It would be just as wee Quince Winthrop had said. The footmen were probably even now collecting the flotsam and jetsam of the revel—finding discarded masks, forgotten shepherdess's crooks and lost pistols strewn about in dark corners around the house and grounds.

Alasdair sank into the down-filled upholstery of his favorite chair, and propped his booted feet upon a leather ottoman sofa.

"Shall I see to your boots, my lord?" Sebastian asked.

"You're my secretary, not my valet," Alasdair groused. "I'll get myself out of them, thank you." He was in a fine mood, wasn't he? Too restless, too unfulfilled, too empty to take pleasure in anything.

Which was precisely why he aimed to fill himself to the gills with brandy. So he would not spend the next two hours in the same manner that he had spent the two previous— thinking, hoping, and fantasizing about wee Quince Winthrop.

Alasdair took a too large a gulp of the heady liquor, and found himself gasping for air. Much like he had been under the blackthorn tree with Quince kissing him into oblivion. Which was precisely his trouble—she was so mischievously enthusiastic. And it had simply been too bloody long since he had allowed himself to misbehave.

Alasdair took a more measured sip, closed his eyes and let his head fall back against the cushion. He felt exhausted, as worn out as if he had spent all day convincing MP's on a vote, instead of doing nothing but getting dressed for a party and kissing a lively lass. Kissing a lass, followed by several hours of fruitless searching so he might kiss her some more.

Sebastian's voice interrupted his inner tirade. "I can't help but notice that you've been spending a great deal of time with the piquant Lady Quince Winthrop."

"Have I?" Nonchalance seemed the best defense.

"You have, my lord." Sebastian's smile was all at Alasdair's discomfort. "You have singled her out. It has been noticed. People will talk."

"People with nothing better to do."

"Quite true," Sebastian acknowledged. "Yet such people are often acute observers."

There was something in his careful tone that chafed. "Do you object to the lady?"

"It is not my place to do so, my lord. But I can't help observing that she does seem an odd choice for a man of your character."

"Staid? Without a trace of larkiness?"

"Just so, my lord. While the word I hear most commonly associated with Lady Quince is flibbertigibbet."

Alasdair could not help but smile. Even Quince had called herself that. The word was apt, conjuring up that dark fairy mischief.

Sebastian misread his smile. "Then is it serious, sir? Am I to be wishing you happy?"

"Don't be ridiculous." Alasdair would have shied his boot at his friend, except that he hadn't bothered to take his boots off. "She's an interesting enough girl, but she's…" Troublesome. Too intriguing. Too exciting. For reasons he could not quite articulate. "She's inappropriate. Now leave be, I beg you."

Sebastian's own smile was all at Alasdair's expense. "Never thought the day would come when I'd hear you beg."

"You'll be the one begging—for a position—if you don't leave off. I've had more than enough twitting for one night."

"Then may I suggest a bath, my lord? The housekeeper

has heated the water. And from the looks of you, a good soaking might do you a world of good."

"I suppose it might." Alasdair knocked back the rest of the brandy and refilled his glass before he excused himself to head upstairs to his dressing room where a bath indeed stood steaming in readiness.

He set the drink aside as he disrobed. Thus far, the brandy had only served to make him restless and exasperated with himself, and he took out his frustration in the senseless rebellion of tossing his clothing in heaps on the floor, instead of folding them neatly as was his usual habit.

He settled into the oversize copper tub, took another drink, and let the heat and alcohol wash away the lingering feeling of disappointment. He allowed himself the further rebellion and pleasure of not thinking for a minute or two. Not thinking about Quince Winthrop, or her lessons in kissing, or her lips, which he reckoned were the color of the inside of a seashell. Or a summer peach. Ripe and soft and—

The window in his dressing chamber rattled, as if a sudden rain squall had driven in across the firth. Alasdair turned his head to listen. The night had seemed clear on his walk home, but perhaps he hadn't been paying adequate attention. Perhaps his mind had been too full of lips and lusciousness.

He took another swallow of brandy, let the pungent liquor sear its way down his throat to warm his gut, and closed his eyes to lean back against the rim of the tub and—

And the rattle—this time he could distinguish it for a spray of pebbles against the glass at his back—returned. Followed by a familiar, mischievous voice.

"Strathcairn. Straaath—"

Alasdair rose, dripping wet and steaming, irate and irrationally pleased. He didn't even have to ask to know who was wandering about his back garden in the middle of the night. The elation singing in his veins was identification enough. He unlatched the window. "Damn your eyes, lass.

What in the hell do you think you're doing?"

Chapter 10

"WAKING YOU UP." Quince felt her face split into a wide, unbridled grin—he hadn't even bothered to ask who it was.

"I wasn't asleep."

"How obliging of you." She cupped her hands around her mouth to project her voice upward. "Come down."

"I'm naked. And wet."

"How *very* obliging of you." She was smiling like lunatic, rocking up and back on her toes, trying not to laugh out loud. "Come down."

"Come—" The warm light from his chamber practically flared blue at the invective he sputtered just loud enough for her to hear every off-color word.

"Though you do curse prodigiously well, Strathcairn, I shan't be put off." Not when she had come so far—both figuratively and literally—to be with him. It had been a near-run thing to make it back to the city, dump Strathcairn's pistols over to the back wall of the Queensbury estate near enough to their trysting spot to test her theory about footmen collecting all the forgotten bits and bobs. And then she'd had to sneak back into her father's stable to rub down and put up the horse, and then tiptoe into the house, up to her room, and out of the costume, and into a bath, and back into her own normal clothing with no one the wiser.

But she couldn't have come to Strathcairn smelling of horse and victory. He would sniff out her misadventure—which was how he would label her evening's activity, if he knew about it, which he wouldn't, because she would take great care to keep such a thing from him—like the great tomcat he was.

But she had to come to him. She couldn't not. She was too keyed up, too full of the thrill of success, and she wanted to turn that thrill to kissing. "You said to meet you later."

Quince's neck began to tire from all the craning upwards. Strathcairn's house in the New Town, stood at six stories tall—though what a single man in possession of both his wits and a castle in the high hinterlands to the north could need with a house six stories tall, she could not imagine. But that was the rich for you.

The window above snapped shut, and she rested her neck for the two minutes it took for Strathcairn to appear, clad in boots, breeks and shirtsleeves, at the kitchen door. "What in God's name do you think you're doing sneaking around my back garden, throwing rocks at my windows? Why could you not knock on the front door, like a civilized person?" His tone might have been grumpy, but he was very nearly smiling that slippery, begrudging, one-sided grin that made absolutely every trouble worthwhile.

"Oh, certainly, Strathcairn." She gave him her own version of a slippery smile. "Next time I'll walk right up to the front door, and ply the knocker. I'm sure that kind of straightforward behavior wouldn't be in the least bit ruinous. Nay, I'm sure your neighbors are all as discreet and silent as the grave."

He saw her point. "Come inside before one of them sees you."

"Oh, no thank you. It's much better—much safer, and far more atmospheric—if I stay out here." Though she did move under the cover of one of the ornamental flowering birch trees—*Betula utilis*—that lined the narrow walk from the house to the mews. "Much more seemly."

"Lass, I fear I need to tell you there is absolutely nothing seemly about making your way to a gentleman's residence in the middle of the night."

"No," she agreed. "But it is a grand lark."

He tried not to laugh. He really tried, poor man. He looked up at the stars and worked to keep his mouth in a straight, stern line, but she could see the telltale white glint of his teeth in the moonlight. "You're going to give me grey hairs."

She gave him her most encouraging smile. "Think of what you'll save on powder."

That coaxed more of his smile from him—one side of his mouth curved upward without his permission. But he wasn't entirely ready to be pleased with her. "I waited for you at the masquerade, but you disappeared. Your sister said you went home."

"Aye." A plausible, or at least believable, lie was best. "I am sorry. But sometimes it is best to retreat from the field of battle in order to fight another day."

He reached out absently, as if he could not help himself. As if some other power made him want to run his hand through her hastily pinned, and still very damp hair. She had come in a rush, throwing on the first pieces of clothing that had been to hand when she had jumped out of the bath—a fitted forest green jacket and a short quilted petticoat in moss that had undoubtedly seen better days, but which were dark enough to blend into the night.

"And have you come here, straight from your bath, to fight?" he asked.

"Not a'tall," she assured him. "I am all serenity."

"That would be a first." He let a long strand of her hair run through his fingers before he dropped his hand. "Wee Quince, as happy as I am to see you again, it's the middle of the bloody night—"

"Can you think of a better time?"

"Aye, I can." He was all helpful clarity. "This evening. At the masquerade. When we were safely hidden amongst half of Edinburgh."

He had a point. "This is better," she cajoled. "More private."

"You're incorrigible, wee Quince Winthrop." He shook his head, but his smile was spreading beyond his control. "What am I to do with you?"

"You're to kiss me of course, while the moonlight gilds my hair, and makes me irresistible. Which you already are— the moon has given your lovely ginger hair an almost saintly halo. Although I must admit, I rather hope you're prepared to act more like a sinner than a sain—"

He kissed her to shut her up. Clever man.

He kissed the way he did everything—with a sort of easy, effortless control. She had thought herself so firmly in charge, calling him down to her, but the moment his lips moved over hers, she forgot all her best intentions. She forgot everything except the heady pleasure of his lips on hers.

His clever, careful hands cupped her face, and slid along the edge of her jaw, urging her to tip her head ever so slightly to the side, so that she fit against him just so. So their mouths and lips could play and taste and explore. He was all around her, his arms encircling her back, holding her tight, leaning her against the side of the house, and his mouth—his glorious, educated, experienced mouth—was doing impossible things to hers. Impossible, wonderful things. Warm, wet, wonderful things.

Clever delicious man. He tasted of brandy and apples— of the sweet, intoxicating comfort of the familiar. Of reliable warm and sure solidity.

What an inane notion. But no odder than the thought that when he held her in his arms, when he cupped her face, and drew her lips to his, she felt safe.

As if she could never fall. Never fail. Never let anyone

down.

Never let *him* down.

Oh, that was surely the most dangerous thought of all. She would eventually disappoint him. It was inevitable. But just now, at this moment, she was too happy to worry about the future when the present was so, so overwhelmingly delightful.

She laced her fingers through his damp, gilded hair, tugging him closer, nearer, tighter. So close there was nothing but him—nothing but the firm press of his lips and his tongue and his scent and his weight.

Everything in the world she wanted at this moment.

Oh, aye, he was everything safe and solid and dangerous. But he was also challenge and excitement and pleasure. So, so much pleasure, coursing through her body everywhere his lips pressed, everywhere his hands touched. Heat and warmth and bliss stole under her skin, robbing her of breath. But she didn't want to breathe, she wanted more of the lovely heady bliss that made her want more than just a kiss in a garden. More than just a temporary thrill.

This time, it was she who turned, and backed him against the garden wall. This time it was she who fisted her hand through his damp hair, and pulled his mouth down to hers. This time it was she who pressed her weight against the solid warmth of him.

"Aye," he whispered into her hair.

It was all the encouragement she needed to guide his hand to her rib cage, to press the warm heat of his palm against the underside of her breast.

He stilled. "Are you— Are you not wearing stays?"

"Nay." She ducked her head down against his chest, afraid that he might see the excitement, the anticipation, and the need to be thrilled written across her face. "I am not."

"Oh, devil take me, Quince." His hand snaked around the curve of her spine, pulling her tight so he could bury his face in her hair. "Your hair is damp," he breathed into her ear, "and you smell as fresh as the dawn, all golden and dewy. All I can think of is you, in your bath, naked and warm and wet and—"

She kissed him to stop him from saying anything more incendiary. She was throwing herself at him, she knew, but when he talked like that—on the cusp of his breath, with all the words roughened up as if he'd taken them on a roll in the heather—she wanted to be naked and warm and wet and in his arms.

"Quince."

"Aye," she answered, even if he had not asked anything. Because she would do anything for him. He made her so happy, he almost made her want to be good.

Oh, holy thunder claps.

That was the most dangerous thought of them all. That was the impossible, wishing its way past the reality of the life she had chosen—she had chosen to be bad just as assuredly as she had chosen Lord and Lady Digby to rob. And wanting it to be otherwise was just wishing into the wind.

And there was so much more possibility in being bad. And in being bad with him. Why should she not have everything she could want from him while he was close and willing and backed up against a wall?

Before she could think better of the idea, she guided his hands to the contours of her breasts, and then set her own fingers to the buttons on the front fall of his breeches.

"Whoa, whoa, lass. I don't think you know—" His hand fisted into the material of her jacket, holding tight.

She ignored his halfhearted protest, and slid her hand into the placket, and found just what all the fuss was about. She wrapped her hand around the heat of him.

He sucked in a hiss of air. "Devil take me. You do ken what you're doing."

"I do," she assured him. "I've always been prodigiously curious." And never more so that at this moment. His flesh was soft and amazingly hard all at the same time. Curious indeed. "And I have been prodigiously curious about your cock."

"Jesus God, lass." His voice was all breath and dark whisper. "Where did you learn such a word?"

"I'm nineteen, Strathcairn, not some green girl. I've heard all about cocks from my sisters—the wicked married ones. It's amazing the things people will say to each other when they don't think you're listening."

"You're incorrigible. For a lass who didn't ken how to kiss a few days ago, you're going a damn fine—" A sound of inarticulate pleasure drowned out whatever else he had been going to say when she grasped him more firmly.

"Like this?" she asked.

"Aye, lass, aye." Another near-moan tunneled out of his chest. "Two hands for beginners," he advised, and then sucked in a long breath as she wrapped her second hand around the lovely length of him. "God help me, you're a quick learner. So quick, I may have to—"

"My lord?" a voice from the house broke into the privacy of the darkness.

Strathcairn froze for the merest fraction of a second, before he pulled her around behind his back, shielding her from sight—just as he had done earlier at the masquerade— while he swiftly put his buttons to rights. "Don't speak," he ordered in a harsh whisper. "Or show your face."

There was an uncomfortable clearing of throat, and then the voice tried again. "Your pardon, my lord."

"What is it?" Strathcairn finally answered.

"The Lord Provost is here, sir."

"What in hell does the magistrate want with me this time of night?"

The question was purely rhetorical, but with her head held pressed to Strathcairn's chest, the words rumbled ominously through her, chilling her to the bone.

There could only be one thing.

"He did not say, sir." The messenger paused. "Though it appears most urgent, my lord. A number of other gentlemen have come with him."

"Thank you. I'll be there presently." Strathcairn's voice was everything calm and polite, but she could feel a livid stillness come over him, a wary pent-up power, like a tomcat scenting a rat.

He took a deep breath, but didn't release her. "Something has come up." But then he placed a kiss in the sensitive hollow under her ear before he whispered, "Wait here by the bench, and I'll be back as soon as may be to escort you home."

Quince wasn't the sort of girl to wait quietly, nor was she the sort who wanted or needed an escort home—she'd just been out on the high road robbing a carriage, thank you very much. And she also could not resist the temptation to listen to every word that was said. So she found herself a shadowed spot to conceal herself near the open terrace door, and hoped the conversation would carry.

"My Lord Elder." Strathcairn's voice, crisp and polished, entirely parliamentary, without the least bit of Scot's burr. "What brings the Lord Provost to my door this time of night?"

"Something more than a missing snuffbox, I assure you."

"I am all attention, sir."

Quince scooted closer, setting her ear to the door casing.

"A highwayman, my lord. Attacked Sir Harry and Lady Digby, of Fairleith Manor, and robbed them in their carriage in the wood beyond the Coast Road."

"Bloody damn Frenchman." Sir Harry himself could be heard in Strathcairn's entryway. "*Monsieur Minuit*, he called himself. Riding a huge black horse. Took everything, cool as you please.

"Well, damn him indeed." There was a wealth of warning in the volatile mixture of anger, astonishment and—most revealing—satisfaction in Strathcairn's voice.

A warning she would do well to heed, instead of being absolutely delighted at this version of herself. Her disguise had succeeded beyond her wildest expectations.

"Why come to me?" Strathcairn's voice again, civil and cool. "Surely this is a matter for the local magistrates, and presents no great mystery. Lay the fellow a trap, and you'll be done with him."

"Aye. I daresay." There was an awkward clearing of throat from the Lord Provost who stood beyond Quince's line of sight. "There seems to be some…misapprehension regarding your…involvement."

"Then don't involve me," Strathcairn countered. "I have my hands full with enough other business before I leave for Cairn within the week, and—"

"Nay." The Lord Provost's voice gained in volume what it lost in surety. "You misunderstand me, my Lord Cairn." There was another awkward pause while the Lord Provost seemed to be swallowing his hat—his voice came out strangled and thin. "Sir Harry has attested that he recognized the fellow, the highwayman. He said he had seen the very fellow earlier in the evening. At the Marchioness of Queensbury's masquerade. And…and several of the guests attested that you, my Lord Cairn, were seen wearing the very same highwayman's costume. And that you were missing from the revels for quite some time."

Oh, nay, nay, nay.

Quince's hand rose to her mouth in something more than astonishment. More than horror. Poor, poor upstanding, honest Strathcairn, to whom deception of any kind was abhorrent.

In the deathly silence that followed, Strathcairn's voice was so powerfully quiet it was lethal. "The hell you say. I was present for the entire time of the masquerade," he asserted. "If you be so kind as to consult with the colonel of the Royal Dragoon Guards, he will tell you that I was supervising a contingent of his men at that very masquerade."

"Oh, aye. I see." The Lord Provost sounded eminently relieved at such a proof of un-involvement.

"You can account for the whole of the time?" Sir Harry again, agitated and querulous. "Rumor has it you disappeared from the ballroom."

There was an awkward silence before Strathcairn answered. "Discretion forbids me from saying—"

Another voice with a careful English accent interrupted—the servant, or secretary, who had come to fetch Strathcairn from the garden. "Does my Lord Cairn stand formally accused?"

"God, no," the Lord Provost stammered. "Nothing so foolish. I came in the hopes of preventing any such thing. I am quite sure this can all be sorted out."

"It was only a costume," Strathcairn's explanation was both exasperated and reluctant. "Worn to impress...someone who—"

"Quite. A Frenchman, you say, sir? Is there a sworn affidavit? May I see it?" The secretary was still speaking for Strathcairn. "Firstly, and most obviously, my lord is not French. And he does not ride a black horse. He rides a grey—who this moment rests in the mews, unused and clearly not ridden this night—and does not own any black horses."

"Good, good." Quince could hear the relief in the provost's voice. "Good to know. Probably just coincidence. You know how tongues can wag at a masquerade, and things can get quite confused at a revel. All those masks, don't you know."

"Indeed." Strathcairn's voice was honed down to a sharp edge. "Yet it is never comfortable to find oneself the subject of even idle gossip. I can only give you my word as a gentleman—my oath—that I had no part in this highway robbery. And I can only pledge to help you in any way that you should deem necessary."

"Thank you, my lord. I much appreciate your candor, and your offer. It has been a long time since we've had any highwayman business here in Edinburgh. I'm afraid we've grown lax and rusty."

"Anything that I might do to assist you in remedying that, you have only to ask."

"Again, I thank you." There were sounds of shuffling feet, and the creak of the front door opening on it hinge. "I will take my leave. I bid you good night."

"Good night, and thank you, my lord. Please keep me apprised."

"I will. Good night."

The door closed quietly, and Quince heard the sound of

the lock being thrown.

"Well, hell." That was the other man, the secretary, she now assumed, given his defense of Strathcairn and his obvious understanding of the law.

"Fuck all," was Strathcairn's rather more vulgar but understandably heated response.

And that was her cue. For all her daft, idiotic daring, Quince was too smart to stick around for Strathcairn to re-appear and read the truth of her guilt—and her own horrified satisfaction—written large across her face. She was under no illusion that she was a good enough card player to lie to Strathcairn effectively enough to hide *this*.

She bolted for the gate.

Chapter 11

THERE WAS NO such thing as coincidence.

The fact that someone had just bloody well robbed a coach while looking enough bloody like him to have him implicated, was no coincidence. At least not a coincidence he would believe.

Someone was deliberately making a fool of him.

And Alasdair had let himself be made a fool of by spending all his time and energy thinking about kisses and costumes and impressing wee Quince Winthrop, instead of concentrating on the business of the prime minister's government and on Cairn. He had made himself an easy target.

Again. But no more.

"First thing in the morning," he informed Sebastian, "I will interview Sir Harry Digby myself, without any interference, when he has calmed down, and ask my own damn questions. And then, I'm going to find my bloody pistols and hunt down the bast—"

"My lord?" Sebastian tilted his head toward the back of the house. "Your guest?"

Quince. In his bleeding anger and ruddy resentment, he had all but forgotten her.

"Thank you, Seb. Correction, first, I will see my *uninvited* visitor home"—it seemed important, in the face of such an accusation, that Sebastian know he had not abandoned all standards of gentlemanly behavior by inviting lasses to kiss him in the dark under the birch trees—"and then I will find out who is riding about Edinburgh making an utter bloody ass of me."

Alasdair strapped on his sword belt and threw on a coat before he stomped his way out to his back garden, which was empty—the wayward subject of his wayward thoughts was gone.

That was all he needed to make his evening complete— for wee Quince Winthrop to be waylaid by a highwayman or footpad, or worse, a drunken aristocrat.

He took the length of the garden at a run, just in time to see her disappearing through the mews gate. "Quin—" He stopped himself from making an even greater ass of himself by broadcasting her name throughout the mews. "Wait!"

Characteristically, she did not. She disappeared through the locked gate—at least it was supposed to be locked—and was making her cautious way down the darkened mews when he caught up with her. "Quince."

She practically jumped out of her skin. "Oh, Strathcairn, it's you."

Something about her tone—the strange, panicky nervousness—gave him pause. "Were you expecting someone else?"

"Yes, frankly." She gave him a nervous smile. "I thought it might be your servant come to shoo me home."

"Nay." Her explanation gave him relief—he hadn't wanted to face the ugly possibility that she was running away from him because she thought him an ungentlemanly brigand who had spent the better part of the night robbing a coach at gunpoint. "I've come myself to shoo you home, or at least to escort you there, just as I said I would." He reached to pull up the hood of her evening cloak over her head, so she might be concealed should they be seen, but she flinched away from him. "Quince? What's wrong?"

She let out a tight little breath. "I'm sorry. It's just—I ken I shouldn't have, but I was listening at the door. About the highwayman."

It was so like her—both to have listed at the door and to have admitted it—that he wasn't angry. Disappointed, perhaps. And definitely apprehensive. "You needn't fear the roads are filled with brigands, Quince. It was only one incident. But I'll escort you home, just to be safe."

"Oh, I wasn't afraid. Not of highwaymen." She shook her head a little, as if she had changed her mind. "It's just that…you're very angry."

Alasdair let out the breath he hadn't realized he was holding. "Aye." It was the bare truth. "But not at you." He made a point of taking her hand, enlacing his fingers with hers. "I'm angry at whoever is making such a comprehensive ass out of me."

And this wasn't the first time someone had set him up to take the blame for a crime he did not commit. The ramifications were enormous, as was the coincidence. But there was no such thing as coincidence.

Quince bit her lower lip. "They cannot possibly think you, of all people, are a highwayman."

"Nay." Her disbelief was more than comforting—it was a relief so profound and heartening, it shored him up for the fight he was going to have to make to save what was left of his good name. And if Quince didn't know of his past brushes with infamy, he'd rather not enlighten her. He wanted there to be at least one person in all of Edinburgh who did not automatically think ill of him. "The misapprehension is likely all due to my bloody costume."

What an ass he had been to choose it, wanting to surprise and impress her. If his grandfather had been moaning in his grave at Lady Winthrop's caution, or Lady Plum's assertion that he had acted as less than a gentleman, the old man must be positively thrashing about his coffin now, to find his grandson taken for a highwayman.

Devil take it. How could anyone who knew him think it possible?

But that was the trouble, wasn't it? No one in Edinburgh—including the Lord Provost and the rest of the Winthrop family—really knew him. They only remembered the rather feckless young man he had once been before he had gone to London, and learned to be serious and earnest and ambitious. It was as if everything that he had worked for, every sacrifice he had made for five long years, had vanished in an instant.

"It was a very good costume," Quince said sympathetically. "I can see how someone might have convinced themselves that you were the genuine article. Are you going to be in a great deal of trouble?"

The compliment salved his wounded pride a little. A very little, because he didn't deserve to have his vanity soothed. "Nay." He tried to assure her. And himself. "It is just a mistake—a case of mistaken identity—not a serious charge. Or someone at the masquerade attempting to make trouble. My petty thief, most likely, wanting revenge for me making life difficult for him. Who knows? It's too hard to prove a negative."

"*Your* petty thief? And what do you mean, prove a negative?"

"It means that it is very difficult to prove that one did *not* do something. Much easier to prove that one did. The fact of the matter is that I didn't rob anyone, but it is going to take a great deal of time and effort on my part to prove that fact." The roiling admixture of seething anger and outright shame was burning a hole in his gut—in his very person.

Quince cut straight to the heart of the matter. "Strathcairn, do you need me to lie, and say that I was with you the whole time? Because I will, if you ask me." She smiled up at him from under her brows in that openly appealing way that had already inveigled him into so much trouble. "And ask me nicely."

"I would never ask you to lie for me." For one thing, it was plain wrong. And for another, were it known that he had spent even a small amount of time alone with wee Quince Winthrop, it would only add to the scandal—to have his name linked with another innocent young woman would do far more damage than good.

"Pity." She let out one of her theatrical sighs. "Because I would, Strathcairn." She looked him in the eye. "Lie for you. Anytime. You have but to ask."

He couldn't quite tell if she were joking, or dead serious. "Thank you. But however well-intentioned, it would be wrong to let you do so." If he had learned anything in the past five years, it was that one lie never made up for another, no matter how well intentioned. "And a gentleman would never ask that of a lady."

But this time, he wasn't only going to do the gentlemanly thing and keep silent while others slandered his good name. This time, he was going to put all the lessons he had learned about justice and the law to good use. And no matter the time or effort, he wouldn't stop until he had brought to account the miscreant who was setting him up for the fall. And he knew exactly where to look for the bastard.

"We both ken I'm not much of a lady."

He didn't like to hear her talk, or even think about about herself like that. "You are lady enough for me. And to prove it, I'm going to see my lady home." Alasdair, like Falstaff, let discretion be the better part of valor, and kept his peace, simply leading her down lesser-used closes behind the Register Office toward Calton Hill.

He would have liked to pull her close, and walk with his arm around her, as several other couples—albeit working class couples—were doing. He would have liked to wrap his arm around the trim span of her un-corseted waist—and oh, God, best not to think of that—and inhale the warm scent of roses and orange blossoms from her damp hair one last time. But they were neither working class, nor a couple.

They were two very different people who were, due to no reason either of them could seem to fathom, unaccountably attracted to one another. At least he was. In her inexperience, she was probably less so.

She turned up a long empty close that ran alongside her father's property, and stopped halfway up the incline. "Well, here we are."

"Here?" To either side of the narrow cobbles were nothing but six-foot-high brick walls. "There's no gate."

"Don't need one," she assured him. "And this spot is closer to the house. Just do this"—she cupped her hands together to show him—"and give me a leg up."

He did so, mostly to show her he knew well enough how to leg someone up, but as soon as he cupped his fingers, the blighty lass promptly stepped right into the stirrup he had made of his hands. And before he could stop her, she had legged it over the top of the wall.

Which she sat astride, giving him a gratifyingly unimpeded view of her bare legs atop her mannish riding boots. And from what he could see in the silver moonlight, her thighs were every bit as milky as he had dreamed. He couldn't stop himself from reaching out to touch the soft skin above her knee.

She instantly laid her hand over his. "I don't suppose I'll see you for a good long while?"

"I don't know," he said with all honesty. It was going to take a great deal of effort on his part to clear his name—effort he meant to exert immediately. His experience in government had taught him that things almost never "blew over" unless they were given a solid push.

And then there was the inconvenient fact that his attentions to wee, mischievous, inappropriate Lady Quince Winthrop had been both noted and remarked upon. He would have to be a vast deal more circumspect. "I fear I'm going to be entirely at the Lord Provost's disposal for the next few days."

"I suppose it can't be helped." She patted his hand consolingly. "Thank you for seeing me home. Clear your name quickly, if you please, Strathcairn. I've grown rather fond of these little trysts of ours."

"Only fond?"

"Oh, aye. Very fond." She smiled at him in her strange

older-and-wiser-than-she-looked way. "But you needn't worry, Strathcairn, that I'm more. I'm no romantic."

"Of course not, wee cynical, realistic Quince Winthrop. I'm surprised you've let yourself grow so sentimental as to admit to being *fond* of a person."

"Let's just say that I've grown fond of kissing," she hedged. But she was giving him that full, mischievous smile.

"Clever lass, then." He turned his palm upward to hold her hand. "But it's no use alone, is it? To have any fun, you have to kiss another person."

Her smile turned warm and mischievous. "And they have to kiss you back."

"Oh, aye." He interlaced his fingers with hers. "Kissing back is the best fun. Especially when you're fond of each other."

"And are you grown fond of me, Strathcairn?"

"Oh, aye. You've grown on me, lass. Even if you do talk too much." He tugged on her hand, and just as he had hoped, she leaned down, bending at the waist to meet his lips with hers.

What started as a bittersweet last taste of her lips quickly became something more. Something hungry and wrenching and desperate. Something that made him cup his hand around the back of her neck, and hold her so he could give her a kiss she would not soon forget. A kiss that would tide her over until he could resume their lessons in kissing.

But the truth was that he was the one who wanted tiding over. He was trying to subsume her, as if he might take every last bit of joy, mischief and larkiness she could give, and store it up to see him through his current difficulties. "You're a terrible vixen, wee Quince Winthrop," he whispered against her skin. "But I like you all the more for it."

That was not what he had meant to say, but now that he had said it, he wasn't sorry. Because it was the truth. He did like her.

Quince's face shone like the moon in the thin silver light. "Do you really like me, Strathcairn?"

"I wouldn't be going to so much trouble to kiss you otherwise."

His other hand stole along the fine line of her jaw, his fingers fanning across her high cheekbones, and stealing into her hair. Anything to stop the aching fist of regret tightening in his chest. Anything so he might bind her to him.

Because that was what he wanted. He wanted her even when he shouldn't. He wanted her to wait for him to sort out the ugly mess he had created through carelessness and inattention. He wanted her to wait through whatever carelessness and inattention he might have to serve to her in order to do so. He wanted her to be more than fond of him. He wanted her to like him. Enough to let him come back one day to finish the lessons they had started.

And perhaps she wanted to, too, because she was fisting her hands in his hair, holding him just as close as he was holding her. Kissing him with as much hunger as he was kissing her.

It was everything he could do not to tumble her off the wall and into his arms. Everything to let her hold herself to him as long as she wanted, and not a moment longer.

Which was a moment before he was ready.

"Oh, by jimble, Strathcairn. I'm going to miss you."

"I'm already missing you." It was the most honest thing he had ever told her. And he was a scrupulously honest man.

"You poor mon." She smiled down at him. "It'll all come right, Strathcairn. See if it doesn't."

He wished he could believe her. But it wasn't that simple. "Are you counseling me to patience, wee Quince?"

She have him a strangely solemn smile. "I am. Be patient, and remember that whatever I am—and I ken I'm a vixen and not good—I'm loyal and sincere."

The relief and pleasure that swamped his chest were dangerous, not least because he could not seem to stop himself from basking—however briefly—in her admiration. "Does that mean you like me, too?"

"I don't know," she admitted. "It's not that I don't want to, but liking someone is difficult. Liking someone implies a certain sameness of spirit. Fellow-feeling, if you will. I'm not sure exactly what it is we share, but it's not quite fellow-feeling, is it?"

"Nay." Because what he felt for her was nothing like he had ever felt for any fellow. Because what he felt for her—and what he was sure now they felt for each other—was pure animal attraction. "Quince, we don't have to like each other to be attracted to each other." Although it seemed to help him enormously.

"I ken." She looked unhappy, but determined to put on an unconcerned face. "So there you have it."

But what exactly, did he have? He had a bloody great problem that he wasn't going to solve kissing wee Quince Winthrop.

And he wasn't going to kiss her anymore that night. Because she was already gone from him, over the wall, and blending into the dark, enveloping night.

Chapter 12

QUINCE WINTHROP KNEW exactly what she had to do—she had to ride out as *Monsieur Minuit*, and put paid to the accusations against Strathcairn. She would strike quickly, before their iron was hot, and Strathcairn and the Lord Provost ordered a troop of horse to patrol the roads.

It was easy enough to get out of the next evening's scheduled entertainment—all she had to do was hint that she had rather not go to that particular musical soiree, as the Marquess of Cairn might be attending, and her mother immediately left her to her own devices. That her own devices would include finding a coach to hold up, she kept entirely to herself.

Actually, she didn't even need to hold up a coach—all she had to do was be *seen* as the highwayman, while Strathcairn was being seen as himself. He was more important than any money. But if she should happen upon a likely coach while she was at it, so much the better.

This evening, she didn't rush headlong onto the roads, but took her time preparing, knowing it was more important than ever that she get it right. Once her parents were out for the evening, she poked through the dusty bottom of her father's cabinets until she found a beautiful presentation set of flintlocks to replace Strathcairn's heavy patent pistols. The elaborately engraved pistols looked so perfectly polished she doubted they had ever been out of their felt-lined case. But they would glint and shine menacingly in the moonlight, and no one would ever know they had never even been fired.

She gathered all of her accoutrements—black velvet suit, plumed hat, rapier and tartan sash, as well as an assortment of other disguising bits and bobs—away from the house and the prying eyes of sisters and servants alike. In the quiet privacy of her father's glasshouse, where the moonlight shone brightly enough, she could powder and disguise herself without the need for a light that might give her away.

The musical soiree her parents were attending was to be up in the New Town, where the elegant houses and wide, precisely laid-out squares contrasted so perfectly with the twisty, narrow closes of the Auld Town along the spine of the High Street. Quince ducked her mare into the low vale between the two halves of the city, along the seam of the old Nor Loch, which had been drained and manicured into a public garden below the cliffs of the Castle. She knew the way well from her trips out to the West Kirk of Saint Cuthbert's, and hugged the shadow of the high battlements, until she reached the fields where the town gave way to the countryside, and she could ride unobstructed to the north, skirting around the tollbar at Kirkbraehead.

Actually— Quince reined Piper into the shadows of a copse to strategize. As her purpose was only to be seen as *Monsieur Minuit*, perhaps the tollbar was exactly where she ought to go. There was always a keeper on duty that could assuredly be counted upon to report a sighting of a highwayman to the authorities. She had only to make herself memorable without actually robbing the tollgate keeper, who would most certainly be armed—which certainly made it an entirely different proposition than robbing an old coach with an elderly couple and an even more elderly driver in the woods.

But if she were fast, and if she took the toll keeper by surprise—

If she dared.

She would. She had to—Strathcairn's reputation was at stake. And even if she had no care for her own reputation, she was sincere and loyal enough to have a care with his. And she wasn't going to get any lessons in kissing until he was free of suspicion, so she would do all she could to hasten that end.

Quince made her way slowly through the field until she was at the crest of the hill, hard against the Queen's Ferry Road, and took another look, determined for once not to be hasty.

From her vantage point she could see the tollbar across the roadway two furlongs away. All was quiet—smoke wafted intermittently from the tollhouse, where the keeper sat idly with his pipe. If she went at the tollbar at a run—

Quince didn't allow herself to complete the thought, but dug her heels into Piper's flank, and set them to it before she changed her mind. She urged the mare into an easy canter, while she grasped the reins firmly in her left hand, and gripped a pistol with her right. Her pulse quickened in time with Piper's hoof beats, but her heart clutched up in her throat, and she nearly pulled up, when a hired coach— the driver being attired in the well-known livery of the local carriage jobber Thornton's—rumbled out of St. George's mews onto the roadway in front of her.

But in the space between one heartbeat and the next, Quince decided to take advantage of the fact that the coach would draw the keeper from his house—away from whatever gun he might be armed with—and gave the mare her head.

The pounding in her blood rose to a veritable tattoo of drumbeats as Piper charged ahead at a gallop, and Quince set the mare to jump the high gate.

Not that she had jumped much before, never having ridden extensively astride. But she had seen it done often enough, and it was too late to pull back—they were passing close by the coach, and the mare took a great soaring lunge into the air.

Up and over the gate, as if they were swimming through the sky—as if the night was made dark with inky molasses that stretched every moment out like sticky toffee. She could see the whites of the passengers' wide eyes as she sailed past the coach, and watch the open, astonished mouth of the toll keeper, and hear her own shout come out of her mouth as if she were at the other end of a tunnel and not four feet away from him.

"*En garde!*" her *Monsieur Minuit* cried, brandishing her pistol high above her head.

What a sight they must make in the moonlight!

And then the mare's head went down, down, down, and they were falling—tumbling through space as if the road had disappeared beneath them. They fell so far, they landed with a terrifyingly jarring jolt that made the mare stumble to her knees. Quince grabbed for Piper's mane, but with her hand full of reins, it was a near thing to keep from coming to a cropper on the dirty cobbles. But luckily, the mare regained her balance and surged on down the hill at a clatter.

The surge of elation—of pure unbridled vainglory—was more powerful than any other sense of pride or accomplishment she had ever felt before. It was a slippery rush so intoxicating, she laughed out loud, and recklessly set Piper to jump the wall into the concealing shelter of Saint Cuthbert's churchyard, and then out again into the dark expanse of the parkland.

But the last jump proved her comeuppance—Piper refused, stumbling on the uneven ground, and the two of them nearly went down in a tangle of horse and leather.

Holy thundering fools.

Quince found herself fair puckled, panting and blowing as hard as the mare. She immediately pulled up and dismounted to check Piper's legs—the mare had a bloody scrape on one knee, and needed to be taken home and tended to. She had done more than enough damage for one evening.

She walked the mare in a few slow circles, taking a moment to catch her own breath while she did so, stripping off her hat and fanning her face to let that slippery elation subside. There was a lesson here for her, about not overreaching, about being more cautious, and being satisfied with what she had managed to accomplish.

But she wasn't much for lessons or caution—never had been.

Because the night was young, and so was she, and on the other side of the stone wall, she could hear a lone coach slowing to turn down the lane cutting through the park. The carriage was so close, she could hear the passengers' conversation through the open window.

Quince peeked over the wall to see the same hired carriage from the tollhouse, carrying two cup-shot young men—all pink faces and voluble high spirits—in the well-lit interior.

Over the jangling of harness and creak of wheels, a young man spoke. "... the most bloody exciting thing! Bloody hell. Imagine, Monsieur Midnight, in the flesh. I never would have believed it if I hadn't see him with mine own eyes."

"Aye, we'll dine out on this for days—being held up by the infamous highwayman."

"Well, we weren't exactly help up by him, what? But still—"

Quince didn't wait for the fellow to finish his thought. Instead, she let the intoxicating excitement still coursing through her veins lend her strength and speed, jamming her hat low on her head, and running for the wall diagonally opposite.

She managed to vault atop the wall just as the lead carriage horse turned into the narrow confines of the lane. Her heart was pounding a terrific thunder in her ears as she drew both pistols from her belt.

"Allow me to change that circumstance for you young gentlemen. It will be so much better if you can tell your dinner companions that you were made to stand and deliver," she cried.

The driver immediately sawed on the reins. "I told 'em it was a fool's errand to come along after ye this way," he groused, while he raised his empty hands. "But, no, they were keen as flamin' mustard fer another damn look. Well, they got it now!"

"Just so." Quince addressed herself directly to the flummoxed man. "We'll keep this simple, shall we? You and I"—she belatedly remembered to inject her spurious French accent into her speech—"we are professionals, *non*? You help me weeth your young gentlemen, and you weel keep your own purse. Agreed?"

"Aye," came the ready reply.

At his businesslike agreement, Quince's pounding heartbeat evened itself out into a steady but lively throttle. Not that she wasn't still as nervy as the devil's manservant— her hands shook slightly though she gripped her guns tight. "*Bon*. Tell them to come out weeth their hands in the air."

"Aye." The driver turned and obediently spoke through the latch into the carriage. "Come oot handsome-like, gents, or 'e'll blow ye to bits, 'e will."

An exceedingly rough translation, but it would more than do, especially since the drunk galoots complied immediately, tumbling into the mud of the narrow lane in their haste to have a look at her.

They themselves had the look of newly made professional men—solicitors just come to the bar, or medical doctors just setting up practice in the fashionable stretch of George Street—with polished but slightly ill fitted clothes, and less-than-polished accents.

"Are ye really 'im?" the taller of the two galoots said in a broad northern English accent.

"*Oui*. Purses," she demanded in as disdainful a manner as possible, flicking her gun menacingly at their empty heads. The less said—and the quicker said—the better this evening, when word of *Monsieur Minuit* might already be spreading from the tollbar to the garrison at the Castle.

"'E's too short to be the Marquess of Cairn," the other numptie commented. "Tho' he do look a bit like 'im."

"*Non*. Enough talk."

"Gie 'em yer purses, ye gammy gits." The driver took his part seriously, and seconded her instruction with enough force that the young men complied immediately, tossing their purses straight to Quince, who had her hands too full of guns to catch them.

But the suede bags clinked enticingly as they landed in the soft grass on the other side of the wall, fueling another rush of satisfaction through her veins.

"Excellent." She nodded her plumed hat approvingly. "That weel be all, good sirs," she said to the drunken gits, gesturing them back into the coach. "Whip up your team, man, and be gone!"

The driver needed no further instruction, and was speeding his coach away before his unlucky passengers had even fully closed the door behind them.

Quince jumped down, and snatched up the purses in a trice, immediately stuffing them into her waistcoat, before seeking out Piper, grazing under the dark cover of the trees.

The heady thrill of victory was twice as potent now, and in order to exercise the intoxication from her veins, she led Piper across the churchyard to the door of Saint Cuthbert's, and immediately stuffed the two purses through the slit in the doors without even looking at their contents.

It was a fitting end to her night, which had started out for one purpose, but been diverted to another—that unholy throttle of satisfaction from having dared and done it, and bested someone. It was mad and dangerous and addictive, and she knew in that moment that clearing Strathcairn's good name had only been an excuse to scratch her secret itch.

It wasn't the most sterling of characteristics in a lass—or anyone for that matter—but there you had it. And it was too hard to be good even *most* of the time.

It was time to go home, and only home. Her exercise for the rest of the evening would be to keep herself from going back up to the New Town to throw pebbles at Strathcairn's windows.

She busied herself switching out her highwayman's garb for the nondescript coat and cap she had appropriated from her father's stable, and stripped the saddle from the mare, rubbing the sweat from her flanks with dry grass, before heading homeward through the dark woods at the base of the Castle cliffs.

Hide in plain sight, she had learned in her years of pilfering, and so she would tonight, pulling the stable boy's cap low over her eyes and the saddle over her shoulder. She led the mare onto the narrow twisted cobbles of the Tod's Close stretching up toward Castlehill Street, and into the wake of an ox cart trundling through the Lawn Market.

Not a soul gave a stable boy and his charge so much as a second glance—her only companion, besides the mare, was the warm satisfaction of knowing she had done right, both by Strathcairn in clearing his name, and by the vicar.

She would not push the boundaries of her luck by going up to the New Town and throwing pebbles at Strathcairn's window, no matter how badly she wanted to. She would have the patience she had counseled of him, and would wait for everything she wanted to come back to her.

HE CAME TWO nights later, just as she hoped he would. Because Mama—and Papa, too, she supposed, though Papa didn't have anything to do with the preparations that were proceeding at a fever pitch—was holding Winthrop House's annual summer ball. Just as she did every year on the first of August, when Edinburgh society swelled with English peers heading north to their otherwise vacant highland estates for the shooting. Which would mean plentiful pickings for her. If she were still stealing snuffboxes and vinaigrettes.

Which she was not.

Not with Strathcairn, still looking for his petty thief, as

well as the mysterious French highwayman. The broadsheets and newspapers had been full of the tales of the dashing foreign fellow, with each new version growing more and more fanciful and exaggerated in the re-telling. By the end of the week, the highwayman had become a giant of at least seven feet tall, riding a pitch black, flying stallion, whose hooves struck sparks out of the bare earth.

It was all so pleasingly ridiculous. Which was exceedingly gratifying, as it gave her the pleasure of doing right by Strathcairn while she was doing wrong. The only trouble was that she couldn't share her triumph with him—she couldn't share it with anybody. And by jimble, the temptation was nearly killing her.

What she needed to assuage the itchy feeling was a nice slow bout of hard kissing.

With Strathcairn. At the ball.

So in order to ensure that she would get what she wished for, Quince surrendered herself to Plum, and let her older sister save her from fashion and social ignominy. And while the white muslin chemise dress Plum chose was the current height of fashion for young ladies, and would doubtless be seen on any number of other girls, Plum knew just how to make it unique by adding a bright blazing sash of apricot silk gazar at the waist, loaning her sister delicate coral ear bobs, and pinning exquisite Euphorbia blooms fresh from Papa's glass house into Quince's elegantly curled hair. The effect was every bit as subtle and enchanting as Quince could have wished.

Tonight she would not blend in to the wallpaper.

"Why Quince, you look quite lovely." Her mother complimented her when she came downstairs. "Where is your sister?"

"Taking care of her own toilette now that she has finished mine."

"I hope you thanked her." Mama swept her along down the corridor toward the east wing of the house, where the ball was to be held in the spacious orangery "Now, the gardeners should have seen to the removal of the majority of your father's specimen trees from the orangery, but I need you to remind Railey to see that the gardens are illuminated with torches. The night promises to be mild, and while there is still a good portion of a moon, your father will want our guests to be able to stroll the gardens. So—" She looked at Quince as if her very presence had brought something to mind.

"Aye?"

Her mother gave her a level stare. "And tell Hobbs that we will need to have the extra footmen stationed throughout the garden to discourage any untoward or lengthy trysting in the dark shrubbery at the far end."

Quince felt her face go riddy with heat so quickly, it was a wonder her hair didn't catch on fire from embarrassment. But it would do no good to try to dissemble. No fool, Mama. "Yes, Mama."

"I said it before, and it bears repeating—be very careful how you trust the Marquess of Cairn, Quince."

"Don't tell me you believe all this nonsense about him being the highwayman?" Quince could barely contain her ire. "'Tis nothing but idle, vicious gossip."

"That may be. Indeed, I'm sure it is, but there are auld rumors, of an auld scandal that I should not like to repeat."

"What auld scandal?" Quince could not believe such a thing of Strathcairn, for whom deception of any kind was abhorrent.

"I said I should not like to repeat it, and I shan't. What I will say is that I forbid you to make assignations with him in the garden. Do I make myself perfectly clear?"

Quince could only hope her face was not the same bright color as her sash. "Aye, Mama."

"I will expect you to act in a manner befitting a hostess, Quince, and dance with each and every young man who seeks the honor, not just stand around looking for the Marquess of Cairn."

"You needn't worry, Mama. I can promise that there will be no assignations in the garden. And I promise that I will dance each and every dance with those who seek the honor, including the Marquess of Cairn, if he is smart enough and quick enough to seek a dance."

"Quince," Mama sighed. "I do hope you know what you are doing with that man. He's not the kind who can be led about by the nose."

Quince tried not to let embarrassment turn into resentment, and only partially succeeded. "I'm not leading anyone about by the nose."

"Good. And don't let yourself be led, either. Be careful."

Her mother was, as usual, entirely right. Quince forced herself to take a deep breath. "I won't, Mama. I do know what I'm doing with him, honestly—"

Mama cut her off. "Pray spare me the details of how you acquired any such wisdom." Her mother let out a pent-up sigh. "I am not the kind of mother who is ill-advised enough to ask for perfection from her daughters, Quince, and I have never sought to make you anything but who you are. But for God's sake, do be careful. For once in your life, don't stir the pot."

"I won't, Mama. I promise."

She would be everything poised and circumspect and correct. She would not give in to any of the temptations that came her way. She would be strong.

Chapter 13

SHE WAS STRONG until the very moment she saw Strathcairn walk through the door of the orangerie. How could she not see him, when she had been watching the door like a sentinel? It seemed all of Edinburgh had been on watch as well—every head in the room turned to look at him as he strolled into the ball as if he had not a care in the world.

He stopped just inside the doorway, and stood, letting the gawkers look their fill. Letting them whisper and wonder and judge and gossip about the marquess who was rumored to be a highwayman one day, and exonerated the next. Letting her insides go all topsy-turvy with some terribly wonderful combination of excitement and guilt— excitement that he was here, at last. And guilt, because she was the reason he was being stared at so rudely. Poor man.

Poor, clever, magnificently unapologetic man.

Strathcairn had clearly abandoned any and all attempts to blend in. He wore an austere suit of midnight blue velvet, unadorned except for the rows of shining silver buttons marching two by two down the front lapels.

Practically daring her to try to snip even one of them off.

Clever, annoying, infuriating, magnificent man.

She wouldn't even try, of course. She had learned better. She would have her thrill from him another way. Because even if her mother had warned her to be good, and not disappear into the shrubbery, there was no way she was going to resist the sheer force of Strathcairn's magnetism.

He had left off powder, and wore his blazing ginger hair in a simple queue tied with an uneven length of blue velvet ribbon that trailed off on one side, grazing his shoulder. Practically begging her to pluck it off.

Talk about baiting a bull.

Of course he didn't know she was his bull, did he? And she was going to take care to keep it that way. The only thing she was going to attempt to steal this evening was a piece of his heart.

Or perhaps a different, less tricky piece of his anatomy.

But she was getting ahead of herself. First, she had to dance with the man.

Who was making it extraordinarily difficult. Directly after his entrance, he confined his conversation almost exclusively to the gentlemen present—perhaps his brief tenure as an accused highwayman had him shoring up his personal battlements with the New Tories. But he was also engaging to speak to each of the footmen.

Which was rather odd. Because the Winthrops normally employed only two footmen, Thomas and his brother, Roderick—all of the other liveried young men standing about the doors, or circulating through the room with trays of punch and lemonade, were hired on specifically for Mama's ball.

And now that Quince was paying enough attention to have a good look at them, the hired men had none of the characteristics typical of footmen, who were chosen for their imposing, uniform height and good looks. These fellows were of varied height, and not one of them could be considered anything close to handsome. How curious.

What on earth was Strathcairn up to?

Quince skipped the next dance in order to suss it out, prowling down the side of the room, trying not to let her attention wander to the diamond earbob Lady Farquhar fiddled out of her ear. "My, lady, if you please," Quince called. "You dropped this." Or the silver card case the Honorable Mr. Edward Enwright was leaving on the side table. Or the loose button on Lord de Lacey's coat.

Tonight she was going to be good, and confine herself to the challenge of Strathcairn, and Strathcairn alone.

But it was almost as if people were trying to lose things.

Oh, by jimble. Abominably clever man. She had the measure of him now. "Setting thieves to catch your thief, are you, Strathcairn? Or just setting a trap with footmen?"

"Lady Quince." His bow was everything courteous and correct, but the smile he gave her was full of equal measures of admiration and annoyance. "How could you tell? It's meant to be a secret plan."

She did not even try to hide her pleasure in impressing him. "Well, since you asked me, which you normally don't, but you should, because I will tell you that you really oughtn't use men to play footmen who are so obviously soldiers."

"So obviously?"

"They walk like guards. All—" Quince demonstrated the rhythmic, slightly rolling, side to side gait of men who were used to marching in formation. "And look at Roderick, there." She pointed to her family's footman. "He's attentive, but he's not 'at attention' the way your men are. I should judge your footmen to be straight from the Castle's garrison of Royal Dragoons."

"Damn my inattentive eyes." He shook his head even as he smiled. "Just as I said—you see things others don't."

"Pish tosh. Don't waste your time flattering me, Strathcairn. I'm not allowed to disappear into the shrubbery with you this evening. Mama has warned me expressly."

He had the good grace to flush, and it certainly did warm that impression of Grampian granite nicely. "Are you allowed to dance with me?"

"I am, and I should like nothing better."

"I hope you'll be kind enough not to mind my missteps. I've been away from Edinburgh so long, you see, I may have forgotten how to make the proper figures in a complicated Scots *ceilidh*."

The riddy warmth that heated her face this time had nothing to do with embarrassment, and everything to do with pleasure at this charming echo of their first meeting. "Strathcairn, are you flirting with me?"

"Aye, I am. Is it working?"

Too well. But it would never do to tell him so.

Her answer was instead a low, melting curtsey. "Come along, my lord, and I'll do what I can. And if nothing else, I am sure we'll serve to amuse."

She threw herself into the enjoyment and excitement of the dance, a rollicking reel called the Dashing White Sergeant. Every time his eyes met hers was exciting. Every touch of his fingers was a thrill. Every minute that she spent in his presence was a minute that she was simply and utterly happy—she did not know when she had ever been happier.

For the first time in three years she relaxed, and stopped thinking and watching and worrying and planning, and gave in to the sweet temptation of the moment.

And the most tempting thing in that moment was that midnight blue velvet ribbon, hanging so perfectly imperfectly from his queue. Her fingers brushed against it once, then twice as the steps of the dance required her to lay her hand across his shoulder. By the third time the dance brought them together for the step, her fingers acted without asking her brain for permission, catching one end of the ribbon end between her fingers, and gently tugging the loop from the bow as they crossed back to back.

Strathcairn turned his head toward the gentle pressure, but Quince was already circling around in the opposite direction, weaving her way in and out of the other couples, winding the ribbon discreetly around her hand.

Oh, it was lovely, the secret slippery joy. It was brilliant and beautiful and as balletic as anything she had ever stolen or ever hoped to steal, this single thin piece of ribbon that had no value to anyone but her.

It would be her secret souvenir, a treasure to savor alone in the comfort and quiet of her room, a token of whatever affection they felt for each other. Like a maiden with a medieval knight's favor.

Quince laughed at such a fanciful idea. She was no innocent maiden, though Strathcairn just might make a convincing crusading knight with his pleasingly granite jaw. But he looked much better in a suit of midnight velvet than ever he would in a suit of armor—chain mail would likely be atrocious at showing off a gentleman's legs.

The musicians drew their bows in the concluding notes of the dance, and Quince surreptitiously stuffed the soft velvet ribbon deep into her lacy bodice. She knew her smile was all across her face, but she did not care. She was with the handsomest man at the ball, and he was smiling back at her, and reaching for her hand.

"Thank you for that dance, Lady Quince." As he escorted her off the floor, his hand came to rest lightly in the small of her back, just at the spot where her laces were tied.

The touch was all that was gentlemanly and correct, but she felt the contact all the way up her spine. Heat, and something that certainly wasn't fellow feeling, blossomed in her chest. "You are very welcome, my Lord Cairn." She gifted him with his correct title. "It was a pleasure."

"A pleasure which I assume we may not repeat?" His fingers played lightly against the lacing of her stays beneath the muslin fabric of her chemise dress, and pressed, just enough. Just enough for her to understand him. Just enough for her skin to warm and her breath to catch up in her chest.

She had to collect herself to speak. "At least not for a little while. I have been tasked with being agreeable to all the guests, not just the handsome ones."

"Why, my wee Lady Quince, does that mean you think I'm handsome?" His smile was not quite the full butter boat, but it would do.

"Strathcairn. I have said it before, and I will say it again. You have a mirror and a valet—"

"I don't have a valet, actually. I have a secretary of uncommon, and even exceptional abilities, but he leaves me to dress myself. So I should like to take your compliment all for myself."

"Well, then you shall have it. You ken you look very well indeed, you great vain popinjay."

He laughed out loud, just as she'd hoped he would. "My head shall swell with such praise." He paused, and tugged her hand gently, so she remained close by his side. "All teasing aside, my lady"—he did not even bother to ensure they might not be overheard—"you must know. You must know that it has been an awful few days, until the bastard showed himself. And even after— But just knowing that I would see you this evening, and that you would be yourself to me, and not be looking at me askance, as if I might have held Sir Harry Digby up in a wood." He smiled. "And you have been yourself, and been lovely. I don't know when I've ever had so much fun dancing. Even more than the last time."

Oh, she felt the veriest blackguard. Something that had to be those scruples she claimed not to have tangled up her breath. So she gave him her sunniest smile as an antedote. "So have I, Strathairn. Don't let anyone tell you you're not a marvelous dancer."

"But now I must return you to your mother, mustn't I, and show her that I have not secreted you off to the dark of the garden. And—" He stopped and frowned down at her. "What's that on your dress? There's—" He reached down as if he would flick away a piece of lint or—"Is that my ribbon?"

He put a hand up to find his neat queue had indeed come untied, and his lovely thick russet hair was spread across his shoulder. But he smiled at her, even as he frowned. "How did you—? You must give it back."

"Nay. I think not." She was not done twitting him. He

couldn't have everything his way. It would go to his head. "Be happy you still have all your buttons."

Oh, holy, holy, holy—

The moment the words were out of her mouth, she wished them back. But there was nothing she could do. Nothing she could say. Her chest and throat strangled tight from the breath she was holding. "I mean," she stammered. "I—"

"Don't." His voice was as sharp as a guillotine. "Don't say anything."

She could not have done so if she had tried. Her throat was as hot and tight as her palms, clenched into fists at her side. But she forced herself to look at him, to face what she had done.

Strathcairn's sharp gaze cut into her like a blade, carving up every one of her misdirections and evasions and lies. "It was you all along."

It was a statement of fact, not a question.

There was nothing she could say to fill the gaping, growing void between them. Nothing that could stop the unbearable agony of the moment. But she had to try.

"Don't." He stopped her before she could begin. "Please don't deny it." His voice had gone quiet, and weary. "You lie far too well, far too convincingly for a lass your age. And that would only make things worse. Much, much worse."

"Nay. I can expl—"

"Oh, I'm sure you can. I'm sure you'll have me bamboozled and besotted in under a minute. You're altogether too convincing. Ought to have trained you up for the government—the army is always looking for low, back alley spies."

The cool cruelty of his assessment hit her as hard as the slap she had once given him—the burning pain was the same.

"What am I to do with you, wee Quince Winthrop?" His voice was lethal in its softness.

"Why, you're to kiss me, of course," she said, but her voice was the merest shred.

He let out his breath. "I don't think that's possible now."

A low ache started hard in her middle.

"Or ever again." He stepped away, as if the touch of her skin against his—as if her very presence—was painful to him.

The loss was like a blow. "Strathcairn. Please. I can explain."

He set his face like flint. "You couldn't possibly."

She could no longer meet his eyes—no longer endure the raw betrayal she knew she would see reflected in those dark green depths. She closed her lids against the heat building in them, as if she could block the thought of him looking at her so. But it was impossible. He was everything she saw. Every pain she felt. Everything she regretted.

Because she knew she was abhorrent to him.

Chapter 14

"LADY QUINCE?"

Quince nearly jumped out of her skin at the intrusion. The sober voice belonged to the black suited clergyman who stood less than two feet away. "Reverend Talent."

"My lady." He had planted himself like an oak tree in the middle of the floor.

What a strange triangle they must make—the clergyman in black, the liar in palest white, and the politician with his indignation blazing red.

"Is this gentleman importuning you?" The reverend asked in an ironic reversal of their first triangular conversation at the masquerade.

"Nay. I—" She pulled a lungful of thin air into her chest. She did not know what to say to the vicar either. He was certainly the last man she thought might come to her rescue. Especially as he had not even been on her mother's guest list.

"I came in the hopes that I might speak to you, to thank you, most ardently, for your recent assistance."

"My dear sir." She had to stop the vicar from saying

anything more, especially in front of Strathcairn. "I cannot think what you mean."

The reverend was intelligent enough to look from her to Strathcairn. Who looked from the reverend back to her. Who looked back to Strathcairn.

Oh, holy rolling eyeballs. "Would you please be so kind as to give us a moment?" She had to stop the situation from going from bad to worse.

"No," Strathcairn said, all unyielding granite. "I think not."

"My lord," she began, putting up her chin, and finding something of her former bravado. "You *will* excuse me." And to prove it to them both, she took a step away from him, toward Talent. And then another. Leaving Strathcairn no option but to let her go, or make the most horrendous scene.

"I will be waiting to speak to you again, Lady Quince," Strathcairn said to her back. "We are not done here. Not by a long shot."

Nay. She didn't doubt him in the least. But she didn't stop walking.

"Your pardon, my lady," Talent was saying as he caught up with her as she headed for the doors. "I was not sure whether I ought to interrupt your conversation. But you appeared distressed."

That was putting it mildly. And if Talent could see that she and Strathcairn were at a total impasse, who else had seen? "Thank you for your timely intervention, Mr. Talent. The interruption was most welcome."

She needed the moment away from Strathcairn to think, and figure out what he was going to do next, so that she might come up with a plan. A plan that did not involve her groveling for forgiveness.

But then again, perhaps groveling was in order—she did have a lot to be forgiven for. So many, many things, and the appalled look in Strathcairn's eyes was enough to make her wish she had never stolen a single one of them. And he didn't even know she was the highwayman.

And she must keep it that way.

Which meant keeping the Reverend Mr. Talent quiet. "Reverend Talent, why don't we go outside, where we can talk more privately."

"Yes, I thank you for the invitation." He escorted her out the long glass doors that gave way to the torch-lit lawn. "I am glad then that I took advantage of your family's hospitality to take the chance to speak to you. I came so I might tell you that your great act of charity—"

"Pish and tosh, sir." Quince cut him off before he could say anything more damaging. Who knew if Strathcairn had footmen hiding in the hedges? A glance over her shoulder revealed that the marquess had not budged from the spot where she left him, and that he was still watching her. Let him watch. As long as he didn't hear. "You must have me confused with another."

The Reverend Talent did take at least some of her meaning. "My apologies, my lady. But, for the life of me, I cannot think of a reason that you might not want your beneficence known."

She could think of several reasons, all of which centered on the man staring a hole in her back. Even through the glass door, she could feel the cold heat of his anger.

"Reverend Talent," she began. "You're laboring under a misapprehension. You must stop thanking me. You must stop seeking me out, and speaking to me." She had not given him the money to receive accolades. "It won't do. Does not the Bible say one ought to do good by stealth, and not broadcast any such reports across ballrooms?"

"Yes, I suppose it does. But surely a report of your beneficence can only be to your benefit?"

"Nay." She tried to make her tone less sharp, less combative, but she had to keep the vicar quiet. She had to think of what Strathcairn was seeing, staring through the glass door. She had to think of Jeannie and Charlie, and how to keep them safe. "I care nothing for my benefit, Mr. Talent, but for the benefit of those in need. Say nothing of me, please. Nothing at all," she insisted. "Only then will I account myself satisfied."

"But I must be allowed to tell you your most recent gift of funds has allowed us to assist a number of families, and even go so far as to purchase tickets for them to emigrate to Upper Canada."

"That is very good, sir." Quince let a small measure of satisfaction ease into her lungs. But she was not done. "I congratulate you on such good work. But I assure you, I had nothing to do with it."

The vicar smiled at her, and reached for her hand, which she did not want to let him take—Strathcairn was still watching. "You are too good, my lady. And I admire you greatly for it. But I fear that our work is not yet at an end. Our need, my lady, is still so great."

The need was always so great. The need was endless. It was like a death knell only she could hear, quietly reverberating in her ears until she thought she would go mad—more, more, more.

She had nothing more left. "What did Christ say, Mr. Talent? The poor will be with us always?"

He made a sound of pleased demurral, and patted her hand. "But I don't think, my lady," he chided, "that the Lord meant for us to take that as an excuse. Not when so many have so much, and others have so very little."

He gestured to two gentlemen who had come out onto the lawn from the card room—Sir Harry Digby, and a well-dressed African man she did not recognize. A man who smiled and shook Sir Harry's hand, and tucked what looked to be a brown suede pouch full of coins into his brocaded waistcoat pocket. A man who had beaten Sir Harry Digby at cards.

And there he was. Her next victim.

Fate was all but handing him to her on a silver platter. Because she had tried to be good, and confine herself to stealing hearts and ribbons, and she had failed spectacularly.

And because if she was going to be bad, she might as well be utterly rotten.

And so she didn't even bother trying to resist the

temptation.

She abandoned the vicar. Right there on the lawn. In the middle of her mother's ball.

"Lady Quince? Where are you going?" The Reverend Talent gestured awkwardly back toward the house. "I— what should I tell...them?"

Them? "You may tell *him* that I've gone to the devil, Reverend. And that I aim on enjoying the trip."

She went away at a run, down through the maze of dark yew hedges, across the lawn to the long glass house, where she locked the door behind her, and secreted the key safely down her bodice. Strathcairn could stand all night on the edge of the dance floor, for all she cared, waiting for her to come back and atone. She wasn't atoning. And she wasn't returning. Not without a sack of gold to show for her trouble.

The soft, pungently scented air of the glasshouse slowed the hard rush of defiance, but filled her with that calm determination that had always seen her through. The determination to plot her own course, and face down whatever was going to happen now that Strathcairn knew she was his thief.

He would undoubtedly tell her parents. And the Lord Provost. And who knew whom else— in his present state of mind, he might be angry enough to tell all of Edinburgh.

Not that she cared. All of Edinburgh could go to the devil as well—she would be happy to show them the way. She would once more become *Monsieur Minuit*, her Captain Midnight. She had been successful before, and she would be sure to be successful again. And this time when she held up a coach, she'd be damned if her hands were going to shake.

This time, she was prepared. After her last foray, she had stored all the accoutrements of her highwayman's costume—black suit, mask, boots, rapier and guns—in an old trunk she had hidden under the seedling flats in the overfilled glass house. The only thing she did not have to hand was the hair powder. But no matter. The hat and mask were enough to hide her identity from this man she had never seen before, and if all went well, never would see again.

This time, when she shed the innocent white of her ball gown, and unceremoniously stuffed the wad of muslin into the trunk, she did so with defiance, and the knowledge that this was a change in character as well as in clothes. The last time she had donned her disguise, she had still felt like she had everything to lose in the attempt. But this time, she had already lost everything. This time, when she pulled on the black velvet coat and rakish breeches of the highwayman, she clothed herself in recklessness.

Reckless, because she didn't have a plan. Not that she couldn't make one up as she went—it was one of her greatest strengths, improvisation. So she took stock. She knew *what* she was stealing—the purse full of gambling winnings.

But the tricky bit was always *from whom* one stole, wasn't it? And she knew nothing about the dark-skinned gentleman, except that he had a fat purse. She did not know where he lived, or what his carriage looked like. She did not know where she might best relieve the fellow of his winnings.

She would have to watch, and think, and plan out her opportunity.

Once dressed, it was easy to slip out of the glass house, and sneak along the shadow of the hedge toward to back gate of the stable. The stable yard was so full of guests' unhitched, idling carriages and teams, it was child's play to tiptoe to the dark end of the stalls unnoticed. It was the work of only a moment to tack Piper up and lead her out into the crowded close.

Quince pulled her hat down low over her eyes, walked the mare along the shadow of the wall where the muddy edges of the pavement muffled the horse's hoof falls, and blended unobserved into the mist that rose with the moon.

It was almost too easy. But she would take whatever beneficence fate was prepared to hand her and be glad of it.

Away from the torchlight, the night felt closer than it had

in the garden. The waning moon was obscured by clouds, and the low fog rising from the ground deepened the dark, hiding her more completely as she approached the end of the close.

To the right was the front gate and drive leading to the house. Across from the gate was Calton Hill, rising in all its steep splendor to preside over all of Canongate. It was the best vantage place from which to watch for the African gentleman's departure. From there, she could sit hidden in the mist-shrouded undergrowth, and keep a close eye on all the comings, and especially the goings.

The front of the house was a hive of activity. Carriages and sedan chairs came and went as passengers arrived and departed. Light from torches danced across the stone facade, jewels sparkled, and silks glistened. Footmen hied to and fro, escorting people in and out of the house, and running messages back and forth to the mews, calling for carriages.

Quince tethered the mare to a gorse bush, and sat on a rocky basalt outcropping, letting the angry determination that had sent her storming into the glass house recede enough to let something resembling common sense take its place.

Except there was nothing common about her situation. There was nothing common about the itchy compulsion that had first set her down her present road—a dark, increasingly twisted path. And if she continued—if she did what she set out to do this night—the path would likely get darker yet.

Yet how did she stop? How could she leave the past behind? How did she disappoint the Reverend Talent? How would she ever face Strathcairn again?

But as fate would have it, she had no time to think it out, because the man with the winning purse was already coming out of Winthrop House, and already mounting his waiting carriage. There was no mistaking him for someone else. He was not the only dark-skinned man at her mother's ball— Edinburgh was an international, cosmopolitan city with traders of every nation and stripe—but he was clearly the richest, attired in exquisite, embroidered satin, and his bearing—with elegant, faultless manners—marked him as a gentleman of considerable means.

A means she meant to take.

One man's gold spent as well as another's, and the possessor of that gold had already climbed into a plain, unmarked black town coach with four horses in hand and only a young groom and an ancient-looking coachman hunched over the box, and was already off, trundling east down the road behind Canongate, picking up speed.

Quince was on her feet, already snatching up Piper's reins and running down the twisting scrubby path with the mare in tow, already chasing the retreating coach before she had come to any sort of decision. And before she could think about mounting the horse, the coach was over shoulder of the hill, passing through the Watergate, and swinging north onto the Easter Road toward Leith. And she was after it.

She threw herself up into the saddle and urged the mare down the dark hillside as quickly as possible, joining the Easter Road at the bottom of Abbey Mount. There, Quince kicked Piper into a hard canter, chasing the swinging carriage lights as the coach disappeared into the swirling dark.

There wasn't much along the narrow road between the Auld Town of Edinburgh and the walled seaport, Leith, some two miles north. If she didn't catch the coach before the road ran out, or the gentleman arrived at his address, she would be dead out of luck.

Quince put her heels to Piper's flanks and let her fly toward the wide heath of the Leith Links, where the Royal and Ancient Company of Golfers had once kept their course until the lot of them had moved north to St. Andrews.

Tonight, nothing but the north wind filled the empty grounds as she charged blindly through the dark.

Until suddenly, out of nowhere, the coach was upon

her—the jangling team loomed up out of the darkness, headed toward her at a run.

Oh, holy flintlocks. They had changed direction as well as putting out their lights, so the whole ruddy equipage was bearing down upon her where she had reined the mare to a hasty halt in the middle of the roadway. And thinking of flintlocks—she drew her guns out of her waist and pointed it at the coachman. But she really wasn't thinking, because if she were, she would have ridden straight off into the darkness at the side of the road, and stopped her headlong descent into madness. But she did not.

She did not pause. She did not quaver. She held her ground as if she were made of stone, and willed the carriage to grind to a screeching halt.

And when it did, she lowered her voice to her version of a masculine growl, and shouted, "Drop your ribbons, and put your hands high in the air where I can see them."

The coachman and groom said not a word, but immediately did as she had requested, reaching their empty hands into the air, so she was emboldened to go on. "Set the brake," she instructed. "Climb down from the box, slowly and carefully. No sudden movements. And come forward so I can see you."

And amazingly, they did so. Except that the two men started the climb down on opposite sides of the carriage.

"No," she stopped them. "You'll go together." She gestured with her barrel for the groom to follow the driver down the left side of the box. "And come out here"—she urged Piper to a better position, where she could cover both men, and gestured with the gun again—"and lie down in the center of the road."

Yes, that was a much better idea than letting the driver stay up on the box as she had auld Rackham with Sir Harry's carriage. Much less to worry about. Yes, that was perfect. She would add it to her new list of larcenous rules—remove driver from box and proximity to potential weapons.

As if there were going to be more larcenous occasions. As if she had already decided to become *Monsieur Minuit* on a permanent basis.

Except that she had forgotten to use *Monsieur Minuit*'s spurious French accent.

Oh, holy foppish Frenchmen. But because Quince lied as easily as she breathed, on her next breath she was already formulating a new plan—an exaggerated English accent. Perhaps a new accent would even add to the mystery and confusion, giving credence to the rumors that there really was a gang of highwayman of various and sundry nationalities roaming the roads. Perhaps next time she should be an American.

Another rule for her larcenous list.

Once the coachman and groom were safely on the ground, Quince kneed the mare cautiously toward the near side of the carriage, keeping the dark, empty expanse of the heath at her back, easing toward a spot where she could comfortably cover both the men prone in the road, and also the door of the coach. Which remained steadfastly closed.

"It won't do, my good fellow." She imitated that clipped, Member-of-Parliament accent that had made Strathcairn sound so English. "I know you're in there, old man. And it will be in your best interest to stand and deliver."

The response from the coach was silence.

Quince's heartbeat kicked up harder in her chest. But she ignored the warning hiss of fear scratching its way across her skin, and firmed her voice. "Open the door slowly now, keeping your hands where I can see them," she called loudly, but her voice was as strained and creaky as an old stair. "Or I shall be forced to shoot it open."

"One moment," came the response. But no movement. The door remained firmly closed.

Quince could feel her heart churning in her throat. A sheen of sweat broke out between her shoulder blades. "Come out, damn you!"

At last, the door swung slowly open. The dark man finally emerged, moving at a snail's pace, every movement of hands and feet slow and cautious and deliberate, as if he had taken her command entirely to heart, and was moving as slowly as he could.

She waited patiently until he finally stood next to the open door. And looked straight at her with his wide, solemn eyes, as if he were memorizing what he could see of her face in the night.

And then he smiled. "My Lord Cairn," he called over his shoulder into the coach. "You're going to want a look at this." He met her eye again. "You would have done better, young sir, to have loaded those pistols."

Chapter 15

"HOLY FUCKING FLINTLOCKS."

Cairn. Bloody, inconvenient, interfering—

Quince did not wait to see her Lord Ruddy Cairn emerge from the coach, nor wait to hear what his lordship might have to say on the subject of young highwaymen who didn't know how to load their bloody pistols.

Quince abandoned all thought and took immediate instinctive action, digging her heels into poor Piper's flanks, wheeling and spurring the mare into a dead gallop straight into the heart of the dark expanse of the rough heath. She leaned low over her neck, and rode as if the devil were at her heels.

Which he was. A devil with loaded guns.

Which she knew because she heard the muffled roar of a pistol discharging, and listened as it grew louder and louder, until the deafening noise caught up with her at the same moment that her right arm was suddenly flung into the air so forcefully that her own pistol flew out of her hand, arching high into the air.

The steel engraving on the pistol glinted as it spun upward in the moonlight slashing through the clouds. She lunged out to catch it, but it was impossible. The air turned thick and impenetrable, and her body grew strangely heavy, filling with pain that weighed her down even as she reached upward.

And then she was on the ground, hitting the turf hard enough to crack her teeth and knock the wind out of her. Agony ricocheted throughout her body, leaving her ears ringing and red blotches dancing before her eyes. And the pain was everywhere, everywhere, swallowing her whole.

She curled into herself to try and block it out, hold it back, and breathe, just breathe. But she had no time to breathe—she couldn't just lie there and wait for the world to right itself. Strathcairn was likely after her already, and would find her in a trice.

Quince struggled onto her knees, and dragged herself into the gorse bracken—*Ulex* damn *europaeus*—that covered the links' undulating hills. The thorny brush scratched her face, and clawed at her eyes, but she pushed on blindly, diving headlong into the demon dark.

Quince went as far as she could before her strength deserted her. She could only hope she was completely concealed by the thick bramble. She could only pray she would catch her breath enough to think, and take stock.

She was alone—the mare had kept running. Smart horse to run when someone was shooting at her.

And not just someone. Strathcairn.

Damn the mon.

He was out there. She could feel the heavy vibration of his footfalls, and hear his harsh breathing and muttered curses as he ran past her, chasing the runaway mare.

He wouldn't catch Piper. She was as wary of being caught as her owner. Warier, even.

Quince thought of trying to push deeper into the thorny bracken, but couldn't seem to summon the wherewithal to move. Her arm was strangely numb, but throbbing with a sort of livid soreness.

She could think enough to claw the bright white mask off her face and shove it deep into the peaty dirt to hide it, but couldn't think of what she should do next. She blinked the sluggish bleariness from her eyes, and shook her head to clear it. She had bashed and bruised herself up pretty badly in the fall. Her hat was gone, either tumbled from her head in the flight, or stuck on a gorse branch—hopefully far enough away that it wouldn't lead Strathcairn straight to her hiding spot in the brush.

"Fuck all!" His roared curse filled the night.

He was closer than she thought—she could hear him kick the bushes no more than ten or fifteen yards away. She crawled away from the thrashing bushes—grubbing inch by stubborn inch through the thorns, retreating as far as she could into the thicket to curl up into a tight ball and pray that he came no further. She felt strange, and disembodied, and in terrible pain all at the same time, staring upward through the brambles, waiting to see his ire-filled face loom out of the night.

"I know you're out there, damn you. I can feel it." Strathcairn was livid in his rage, but farther away.

At least he hadn't called her by name. And he didn't seem inclined to get down on all fours, and crawl the twenty-five thorny yards nearer, and drag her out.

Quince squeezed her eyes shut against the ache that crept through her bones, and closed her mind to everything but the need to breathe quietly.

Time stood still. Or perhaps she slept. Or passed out. Either way, she must have waited for a very long time, because when next she opened her eyes and listened, there was nothing but the low moan of the wind across the heath. She braced herself against the pain lodging in her middle, and slowly pushed herself upright enough to look through the bramble. Across the heath, the carriage—lanterns, equipage, team and men—was gone.

Quince didn't entirely trust her vision—she could barely see for the red spots dancing across her eyes. And she oughtn't trust her judgment while the pain was working its way up her jaw and around the back of her skull.

And she certainly couldn't trust her luck—it had clearly run out.

She let herself sag onto the uncomfortable support of the bramble and waited for her vision to clear. But there really was nothing—Strathcairn was gone.

Clever, interfering, bloody, relentless man. He must have secreted himself in the coach long before it drew up to the front of Winthrop House. She should have noticed that the curtains were all drawn closed, and the interior lamps put out. She should have remembered that he had baited the ball with his conveniently lost items, and was likely to bait a coach with a fat purse as well. She should have realized he was that clever. That determined. That relentless.

But she hadn't.

She had not done the one thing she knew, knew, knew she must—she had not clearly ascertained from whom she was stealing, a man who was, in hindsight, an associate of Strathcairn's.

She had let Strathcairn become her nemesis.

And she was most sorely sorry now.

Quince sat for a while longer contemplating her stupidity, husbanding her strength, and feeling her heart thump a weak tattoo in her chest. Waiting for the terror to subside.

After a while, when she could no longer hear her own blood in her ears, she tried to grapple her painful way to her feet. She ached in every bone and sinew of her body, and the pain left her dizzy, grappling onto a tuft of gorse to stay upright.

But the moment she tried to hold on to the bracken, savage pain tore up her right arm—from her wrist to her elbow—which had recovered from the strange temporary numbness, and was now radiating agonizing heat that rose up like a wave, drowning the breath from her lungs, and hitting her hard enough to knock her to her knees.

She tried to cradle her arm close to her body, but the

moment she did so, she could feel that her sleeve, and indeed the most of the right side of the black velvet suit, was sticky with warm wetness.

Quince held her open hand up to the fitful moon light—her palm was red with blood.

She was bleeding and in pain because she had been shot. Strathcairn had shot her.

Oh, holy bad, bad, bad, stupid luck. Stupid, stupid girl to get herself shot. Stupid girl to deserve it.

She was going to bleed to death on a heath miles and miles from home because she deserved to die. And they were never going to find her body, because it would be eaten by ravenous scavenging wolves, and no one would ever know it was she from the scattered, gnawed-upon bones.

And if she did die out on the heath, she would bloody well haunt him, and drive him mad with guilt and grief at what he had done.

But she did not die. The pain stayed strong, reminding her that she was indeed, miserably alive. And as she seemed not about to die at that moment, she had much better get herself home before she dripped to death on a gorse bush. If she could just get home, she would be all right. Her family would help her no matter what she had done. No matter what.

She would stay off the roads and take a circuitous route, because Strathcairn was clever and determined and relentless, and sure to come back. Sure to collect torches and those troopers from the Castle's garrison who had been acting as footmen, and roust them out to beat the bushes and track her down.

Just the thought was enough to get her moving.

She would have leaned upon her father's rapier like a cane, but she seemed to have lost it somewhere in the hedge. But she still had the sash, so she rigged it up as a sling the best she could, and she slowly, painfully, painstakingly set off in the direction the mare had been going when last Quince had seen her disappearing into the night.

She followed the rolling contours of the links, lurching along as she called to Piper with low clucks and quiet whistles. After a long half hour of stumbling progress the chill breeze finally brought back a low nicker, which led Quince toward the dim silhouette of the mare standing upon her own broken rein.

It was hell to hoist herself back into the saddle with only one good arm to pull herself upward, especially when the smell of blood made the mare skittish and jumpy. But she held on, clinging to Piper's mane as if it were a lifeline, because that would be all she needed—to be dumped back upon the heath concussed so she might be found by Strathcairn at first light.

Because he would be back. He was tenacious that way.

And if it had been bad enough to have him deduce she was his petty thief, it would be ten times as bad to have him finger her for a highwayman.

So she had best keep him from knowing.

Quince turned the mare southeast across the heath and rode for home. Except that she couldn't really ride—even at a walk, every bone in her body ached. Every stride jarred and drove the pain deeper until it was everything she could do just to grit her teeth, and hold on.

But hold on she did. *She* was tenacious that way.

Because she knew if she could just get home, everything would be all right. If she could just get home, she would never do it again. She would learn her lesson. She would give it all up and be good. If she could just get home.

Of course, Quince was realist enough to know there was no hiding what she had done—and had been doing for three long years now. She had been shot, and it would take more than just getting home to hush that up.

But if there were anybody who could keep Strathcairn at bay, it was her mother. Mama was no foolish, daft, reckless lass to give in to whatever intimidation Strathcairn might try to bring to bear. Nay.

Quince tried to keep that idea firmly in her mind, but it

was so hard to concentrate. The narrow streets seemed to twist and waver in front of her, and Quince had to shut her eyes to the bilious queasiness, and trust the mare to find her way around the foot of Abbey Hill and into Canongate, and stride by laborious stride, make her way home.

She only realized she had arrived when Piper stopped in the empty stable yard. Quince had only the strength to slide to the ground, and somehow shoulder the stable door open enough for the mare to walk in.

She abandoned Piper to her own devices, knowing the mare could find her own stall, and trusting that someone would eventually tend to the animal, and groped her own way along the stable wall to the garden gate. She was so close—nearly there. Nearly home and safe. All she had to do was cross the long lawn of the garden to reach the house.

The torches that had illuminated the terrace had burned out, and the garden was quiet and empty. Quince set her good arm against the wall that ran the length of the garden, using it to steer her home.

She walked onward, one step at a time as if in a dream, focusing her narrowing gaze on the glass house. Knowing that once she made it there, she could use the pump to draw water to wet her lips that had long since gone dry, and cool the hot ache in her arm, and wash away the worst of the blood. She could rest there, and recover, before she made her way into the sanctuary of the house.

If she just made it there, it would be all right. Because she would be home.

But she wasn't going to make it. Because the moment she finally reached the glasshouse, she heard that deep, deceptively even tone.

"I think you've gone far enough for one evening, don't you? You dropped your father's sword, wee Quince Winthrop."

Chapter 16

ALASDAIR WAS LIVID with something more towering than rage. He had thought to find a feckless youth robbing his coach, but the moment he heard her characteristically inventive oath, he knew his highwayman was none other than wee Quince Winthrop. So it would only been a matter of time before he caught her—he knew she would go to ground like the vixen she was. Animal instinct only ever got a person so far.

But wee Quince Winthrop wasn't listening. As usual. She staggered a little, but tried to open the locked glass house door.

"I'm warning you, Quince, I—"

The key fumbled from her hand. "Aye," she finally said, as she raised her empty hand in front of her, placating him. "I heard you the first time. There's no need to carry on."

"There's every need." His voice was as black as thunder. "You've crossed a line."

"Aye." She let out a strangely disassociated laugh that didn't match the dire seriousness of her predicament. "I crossed it a while ago. But first, I—"

"No explanations. No excuses. No—"

"Nay," she agreed before he could finish. "You're quite right." She wavered slightly. "He'll never forgive me."

"Who?" Alasdair pressed, hungry to get to the bottom of this ridiculous affair—a nineteen-year-old lass riding about Edinburgh, stealing from the rich, and robbing coaches at will. The broadsheets would have a field day. "Who will never forgive you? Whom are you working for? Give me his name."

She turned her face toward him, and the fullness of the moon painted her face a ghostly white. "My father."

Charles Winthrop, the Gardener Royal? A man who never seemed to speak unless it was of plants?

Alasdair was too stunned to speak, but she went on, her voice as thin and fragile as paper. "He'll never forgive me for bleeding all over his Antipodean Cabbage Palm. *Dracaena australis.*" She was looking at the plant at her feet. "Came all the way here on *Endeavor*, with Captain Cook."

"Bleeding?" She was hurt. "My God." He dropped the rapier, and started for her.

"I don't think your god has much interest in me. But perhaps he'll spare the *Dracaena*, because I'm afraid I'm about to expire upon the poor—"

"Don't you dare!" he yelled.

But of course, she disobeyed him in this as she had in everything else—her head lolled to the side, and then her entire body simply slumped straight for the ground. And she had no more control over her faint than he had over his impulse to catch her up in his arms before her head could hit the bricks upon which she had been so discreetly bleeding.

Damn him for every kind of fool. She had been shot.

He must have shot her.

He had fired over her head, hadn't he? He'd known she was the highwayman the moment she had uttered that remarkably characteristic curse. And he had been so bloody angry, so fucking betrayed, he had been dead set to stop her from doing anything more criminal or idiotic. To stop her before she got hurt.

But he was the one who had hurt her.

Alasdair laid her head on his knees to make a frantic search for the wound. Her hands, as well as her sleeve, were covered in blood, and the right side of her coat and breeches were sticky and wet to the touch. His hands slipped and shook as he fumbled with the buttons at the bottom of her waistcoat, trying desperately to open it up enough to see if she'd been gut shot.

He was hampered from yanking up the tail of her linen shirt and chemise because she had her arm clutched against her side. "Let me see, damn you," he muttered as he tried to peel back the clothing enough to find the wound. But instead of a welter of blood and guts, he found plain, although slightly bloodstained white cotton stays, an unadorned chemise, and smooth white skin.

It was...remarkably normal. And remarkably feminine for a lass who was attempting to be a notorious highwayman.

"You needn't swear at me, Strathcairn." Quince's eyes fluttered open for only a moment before they slid closed again. Her voice was nothing but breath and pain. "By all rights, don't you think I ought to be the one who gets to swear?"

Relief and rage made a strange brew in his gut. "Swear all you like, you heedless, thoughtless idiot."

"Aye. Heedless, I suppose. Not thoughtless. Thought it out very carefully, I did. Or thought I did. But you're too clever for me. I should have known you would bait me out on the road the same way you baited the ballroom."

"Aye, you should have."

"Ah, well. I've always been the sort of lass who learns the hard way." Her voice trailed away into nothingness.

Equal parts of fear and rage filled him like smoke, choking the heart out of him. "Quince!" He gripped her roughly. "Don't you dare die on me."

"Serve you right if I did." She sucked a breath in through

her teeth. "And I might still if you don't stop yelling at me."

Her voice had taken on a grudging, determined edge that he recognized. Relief let air creep back into his lungs. But not much—she was not out of danger. Not by a long shot.

A long shot that had apparently hit her. "Where exactly were you hit? Where is the pain?"

"My forearm. Hurts like hell."

Another measure of blessed relief made him clearer-headed. A forearm was not so bad. A forearm was not a belly wound. A surgeon could fix a forearm, or at least save it. Aye. He would take her to a surgeon. Edinburgh was thankfully bristling with able, well-trained medical and surgical men, damn her for needing one. "I imagine it does hurt. That's what getting shot feels like."

"Been shot yourself, have you?"

"Nay." He scooped her up into his arms, and made for the garden gate.

She immediately began to struggle. "Nay. Take me home." Her thrashing was weak, but she was tenacious, managing to get her boot braced against the doorjamb of the glasshouse.

It was all he needed for her to put a foot through the glass, and then where would they be? "Quince, you need a surgeon."

"Nay. Take me home. I must go home."

"Have it your way." Actually, it was a fine idea. If he took her into the house, her parents would have to know what had occurred. Not that he wanted them to know *he* had shot their daughter, but that their daughter had been out of their house, out on the roads, posing—nay, acting—as a highwayman, robbing Edinburgh's rich and powerful blind.

"Lord Cairn." It was Lady Plum, standing in the middle of the glass house in a night rail and dressing gown. "Whatever are you doing with my sister?"

Alasdair had not forgotten his last conversation with Lady Plum. So what came from his mouth was entirely due to his need to salvage his reputation as a gentleman.

"I was attempting to elope with her, if you must know, Lady Plum." But now that he had stated the obvious—that he was going to marry wee, inconvenient, inappropriate Quince Winthrop—he felt instantly better. He felt right. "But unfortunately, my beloved has gone and injured herself."

"I did not 'injure' myself," Quince objected against his chest. "You shot me."

"Oh, my God." Lady Plum rushed forward as if she would wrest her sister from his arms. "I knew you were in over your head with him. What on Earth happened?"

"Told you. He shot me." Quince was nothing if not tenacious with her point. "Though I will say I deserved it."

"No one *deserves* to be shot!" Lady Plum's glance was filled with frightened disbelief. "Did you?"

"Aye," he admitted with as much gentlemanly grace as possible. "It was a terrible mistake. I thought I had fired over her head—a warning shot."

"Warning? Oh, my God," Lady Plum repeated. "I told you that you were out of your depth with him," she chided her sister. "And now he's shot you. Carry her into the house, you horrible man," she ordered him. "I'll get Mama."

"Nay," Quince said against his chest.

"Aye. Get her mother. And her father." He held Quince more tightly lest she try to struggle out of his arms and injure herself further. "I will take my betrothed up to her room, if you would please bring her lady mother directly."

Lady Plum disappeared across the lawn at a run in search of Lady Winthrop, and Alasdair followed at a more measured pace, trying not to jar the slip of a lass in his arms.

Who held firm. "I'm not your betrothed."

He ignored her attempt at argument. "Which way?" he asked at the terrace door.

"Left to the servants' stair," she whispered, clearly fighting the pain. "Third floor, I'm afraid."

"I'll survive." He took the stairs two at a time. The lass in his arms looked even paler in the warm lamp light than she had in the blue refracted moonlight of the glass house.

She let out a careful, tight breath. "Holy painted trollops, it hurts." She sucked air back in through her teeth.

"You'd do better to faint again," he advised her, trying not to think about the pain he had caused. If he concentrated on what he was doing for her—trudging his way up three flights of stairs, he could see his way through this mess.

"Can't be done, I'm afraid," she said between her clenched teeth. "Didn't faint the first time."

He did not bother to argue with her. "We'll get some laudanum into you as soon as may be to blunt the pain." But to do that they'd need to get a surgeon to look at the wound, to see if the ball was still in her arm. And he had no idea who was the best local surgeon.

"I am sorry I can't seem to bear it any better." She was surprisingly agreeable when she was in pain. "And this is where you tell me I deserved it, I'm sure. The wages of sin and all."

He would have told her so if he had thought of it. Remarkable, frustrating, stupid lass. "Are you quoting the Bible at me?"

"It's normally a useful gambit." She let out a sigh that was nearly a groan. "I'm out of my mind, clearly. From the blood loss. It's a common result, or so I'm told." Even in pain, she was not done twitting him.

"How can you laugh?" he asked, as he paused briefly on the landing. "How can you pretend that nothing is wrong?"

"How can I not?" Her voice was weak, but lacking none of her characteristic insouciance. "Crying will not solve anything. And I look dreadful crying. Ugly. Troll-like. Best to avoid."

"Then I suppose I must be grateful for your morbid sense of humor."

"Just I am grateful for your bad aim. Laughing is the only thing that keeps me from being terrified."

Alasdair didn't know whether he was relieved or satisfied at this small show of sense—or if it wasn't sense, it was at least a show of humanity and vulnerability, which brought out his own sense of compassion. "I am sorry. Sorry I shot you."

"I'm sorry, too—sorry I made you shoot me. It hurts a bloody, awful lot." Her words came out in little pants of pain. "And I'm sorry for cursing."

"Curse all you like, if it helps." He started up the next flight.

"It doesn't help. It's bloody uncomfortable." Within his arms, she had curled herself into a tight little knot. "What an awful mess. I am sorry I got you into it. But no matter what, I'm not your betrothed. So whatever your reason for saying so to Plum—and I ken you must have a reason in that evil, ginger brain of yours—don't say so in front of Mama."

"Did I say that?" He knew exactly what he had said. And he was even coming to understand it. "Well, it's just as well."

"It is not just as well," she insisted through gritted teeth. "It's ridiculous. You'll have to hope Plum forgets you said it, and doesn't tell Mama."

Alasdair took a deep breath—not least because he had just climbed three sets of stairs, and had another still to go. "Actually, I think it best if she does tell both your parents. I think it best if we proceed under that assumption."

"That I'm your betrothed?" She tried to thump her fist against his chest, but she was so weak it barely registered. "Do you think it will keep people from knowing that you accidentally shot me?"

"No, I think it will keep people from knowing *why* I accidentally shot you. Or do you really want all of Edinburgh, from your father to the Lord Provost, to know that you are *Monsieur Minuit*? Well, *ma belle*?"

She considered the question in silence until they at last reached the landing. "I suppose not," she admitted.

"Then you had best marry me." His satisfaction was not nearly as…satisfying as it ought to have been. "Your secret will be safe with me if you consider yourself bloody well engaged."

"How else could I be engaged at the moment?" She

made a small gesture of raising her injured and bloody arm, but winced in pain.

"Keep still, damn you."

"You do growl at me so charmingly, it's a wonder I can resist you." She had closed her eyes again, and every word was laced with pain. "I will say we are engaged. But I will not marry you."

"You will," he insisted. Because there were too many reasons not to. Because now that he had made up his mind, he was certain. And because a wide-eyed maid had appeared at the top of the servants' stair, gaping at them. There was nothing for it. "Lady Quince's room?" he asked her.

"Just along here, sir." The lass scurried ahead to open the door to a bedchamber with a small fire in the grate.

"Thank you," he said as he laid Quince down on the bed. "Send for a doctor."

"Aye, sir." The poor maid's voice was full of terror. "I'll have Mrs. Mowatt—"

"Nay." Quince found her voice. "Annie, have Mrs. Mowatt send for the Reverend Mr. Talent, at the West Kirk of Saint Cuthbert's."

"Saint Cuthbert's? You don't need a priest. You're not going to die." Not if he could help it. And he could. He knew enough of the basics of field dressing to get the bleeding stopped. He stripped off his cravat and used it to apply pressure to the wound. "You need a surgeon."

"Ow, ow, ow," she protested at the pressure. "He is a doctor. A physician, trained at the university here in Edinburgh. He'll ken what to do even if he isn't a surgeon. He's close by. And he'll ken how to keep his mouth shut."

The image of the reverend doctor escorting Quince out of the orangerie earlier in the evening rose before Alasdair like a specter. And something else—some virulent, ugly feeling that was too close to jealousy for his taste—took root in his chest. "Patch you up a time or two already, has the good reverend doctor?"

"Nay." She gave him a pointed look out of the side of her eye. "You're the only person who's ever shot me."

"Lucky me. Do you think you might refrain from telling the whole of the world, Quince? For your sake, if not for mine?" He shot a speaking glance toward the maid. "Send for the Reverend Mr. Talent in his medical capability," he instructed the quivering girl, "from Saint Cuthbert's."

"Thank you" Quince said for his sake only, because the poor white-faced maid had already gone.

Alasdair kept his attention on the white-faced lass who remained on the bed. The blood had already soaked through his cravat. Devil take him if they really would need a priest by the time all was said and done.

Clearly, his worries were writ large across his face. "It can't be that bad, Strathcairn, though it does hurt like hell. But I fear you're right that it needs to be looked at." Quince took a few deeper breaths, and managed to push herself more upright. "Could you please help me get out of these clothes?"

"As attractive as that scenario might be to me at any other time, at the moment, I don't want to be caught by your mother or father in the process of taking your clothes off. Just let me see the wound." He crouched down next to her, and tried to take a better look at her arm. "Holding up coaches and getting yourself shot," he muttered. "Damn your eyes."

"No one in the other coaches managed to hit me." She screwed her face into a grimace at his gentle probe.

"And how many other coaches have there been?"

She took a breath or two before she admitted, "Only two."

Both he knew about—which meant that she had just started this more dangerous and more violent portion of her career quite recently. In fact, she had taken up highway robbery during the time he had become reacquainted with her.

The realization was a fist to his gut.

"How could you?"

"Very easily," she sighed. "More easily than you'd imagine."

He couldn't imagine. "Do you promise you won't do it again?"

She nodded. "You can be sure of that." She waited a few more shallow breaths before she added, "And you can also be sure I won't marry you."

"You will," he said grimly. "It's inevitable. The whole of our acquaintance has been pointing us toward marriage, even if it didn't seem like it until now. But now we must marry. My good name, not to mention yours, depends upon it."

"Nonsense. No one need know but my family. I can live with their censure. If I live."

He didn't want to think about her living or not, the damn daft lass. "Don't be in such a hurry to die. And frankly, it looks like the proverbial flesh wound." Though he knew as well as anyone that flesh wounds could still turn septic and putrid. "How about this—if you do die, you don't have to marry me."

"How comforting." A weak smile broke through her grimace. "I accept."

"Regardless of whether we marry or not, that coat needs must come off." He stood to try to ease the garment off her shoulders. "Easy. I'll hold the end of the sleeve, and you pull yourself out of it at your own pace."

She did as instructed, turning her shoulders, and carefully, slowly, bracing herself against the pain, she leaned her way out of the ruined garment. "You make an excellent valet," she commented between gasps.

He tossed the ruined velvet aside, and knelt back down beside her. "Aye. I'll make just as good a husband—the skills required are about the same. Now." He reached to tear away the tattered linen shirt. "Show me."

She had instinctively hunched over her arm in a protective posture, perhaps trying to ameliorate the pain. Or maybe she was just stubborn. "Nay. You might not think it serious enough, and try to shoot me again. You're tenacious that way."

He was both grateful and sorry that she was still

responding with her usual insouciant humor. Grateful, because if she could laugh, it couldn't be that bad. And sorry, because it made him feel as guilty as ever that he had made such a dreadful lapse of judgment as to allow himself to fire his gun in the first place.

"I think you've already bled a gratifyingly sufficient amount upon both the glasshouse floor and now the coverlet to prove the gravity of your injury."

"I aim to please. You aim—"

"Quince!" Lady Winthrop rushed into the room with the housekeeper hard on her heels. "Oh, sweet Lord, I've been worried sick about you. You disappeared—" She stopped short at the sight of him kneeling beside of her daughter's bed. "Lord Cairn. What on earth are you doing to my daughter?"

Alasdair squared his shoulders, but didn't rise from his knees. "I'm doing exactly as I should, my lady. I am proposing."

Chapter 17

ALASDAIR KNEW EXACTLY what he was doing—it was as if the words had been in his head, fully formed, and waiting for just the right moment to assert themselves. Desperate times called for desperate measures. And they were beyond desperate.

"My lady, forgive me." Alasdair rose to face his future mother-in-law. "But your daughter has been injured."

"Injured." Quince's voice was made petulant by the pain. "He shot me."

"My God, Quince!" Her mother was at the bed in an instant. "Where?"

"On the Leith Links."

"Oh, good heavens. I meant where on your *person*, though I hope there is also to be some explanation for why the two of you were out on the Leith Links shooting at each other in the middle of the night."

"By accident. Though he was the only one shooting. And it's my arm."

"Even so—" Lady Winthrop was already delicately peeling back the blood-caked linen.

"Along the side, there." Quince broke off, biting down on her lip hard enough to draw blood. She hissed another breath or two between her teeth before she went on. "I don't think anything is broken. You needn't take on so."

"I have already sent for a physician, my lady," Alasdair hastened to assure Lady Winthrop. "Though I think perhaps a surgeon ought also to be called."

"Mr. Talent will do," Quince insisted. "Even though he's a physician, he's not so particular and nice about titles, or so squeamish that he won't dirty his hands doing a surgeon's work."

"You seem to know this Reverend Talent fellow fairly well." Alasdair could not seem to help the derision in his tone. "You spent some considerable time alone with him this evening."

Quince didn't give anything away. "I know him well enough."

He was sure she would have tossed up her shoulder in a shrug if she had been able—that shrug that he was coming to recognize as meaning she was concealing something.

Lady Winthrop spoke over their fruitless exchange. "Mrs. Mowatt," she directed her housekeeper, "if you would see the physician up as discreetly as possible, please? And if you would furnish him with whatever necessary items he might request upon his arrival. But bring some dark cloths as soon as possible." She turned back to scold her daughter. "You're bleeding all over the coverlet."

"That's what I told him." Quince was still trying to be nonchalant, but he could see her lips were white with the effort to suppress the pain. "Pass me the basin from the stand, and I'll bleed into that."

"Yes." Lady Winthrop was as practical as her daughter, and held out her hand for Strathcairn to pass the basin and ewer to her. "My lord, if you would? And then you may leave."

"Certainly." He passed the articles in question. "But I should like to speak to you, and my Lord Winthrop, if I may."

Lady Winthrop spared him only the barest of looks. "Yes, when Quince has been tended to. Ah, thank you, Mrs. Mowatt." With the housekeeper's assistance, Lady Winthrop fussed over her daughter's arm, bringing over a table and a lamp upon which to place the basin and examine the long, oozing wound. It became readily, and rather bloodily, apparent that the long, ragged laceration, though shallow, was beyond either of their skill.

Lady Winthrop said, "We had best wait and let the doctor have a look."

Quince did not open her eyes from where she had laid her head back against the pillows. "Must be worse than I thought. You're a thorough fellow, Strathcairn."

Lady Winthrop's eyes were full of questions that could thankfully remain unanswered due to the timely arrival of the physician, who looked every inch the vicar in his somber black attire and grave demeanor.

"Lady Quince." The man's eyes were for no one else in the room, and he came to her with his hand outstretched, as if to greet her. "I came as fast as I could."

Or perhaps Alasdair had it wrong. Perhaps the reverend doctor was merely being professional in examining his patient, because Quince turned her head aside, and simply entrusted her damaged and bleeding arm to his care, and the physician beneath the black coat set to work examining the wound without any other outward sign of intimacy. "How did this happen?"

Quince's gaze flicked to Alasdair's. "An accident," was all she said.

"Aye," he nodded, trying to tell her without words that he would do everything he could to protect her—even lie. "An unfortunate accident."

"Very unfortunate," Lady Winthrop concurred. "And under the circumstances, I think it best you leave my daughter's bed chamber, Lord Cairn."

"I would prefer to stay with my betrothed."

The vicar's gaze snapped from Alasdair to Quince, and then back to Alasdair with such force and speed that the man was like to do his neck an injury. Good. But such petty satisfactions were beneath him—beneath them all, and beneath the gravity of the situation. Still.

"Quince," Lady Winthrop asked. "Is this true? Are you engaged?"

Under her mother's probing gaze Quince could no longer keep up her mask of bravado, and for the first time in their acquaintance, she looked entirely vulnerable—unequal to the moment.

"Aye, my lady." Alasdair answered for her, as if his surety could convince them all. "Your daughter has done me the honor of consenting to make me the happiest of men."

"Over pistols?"

There was the ghost of a smile from Quince at her mother's bone-dry tone.

"Aye, milady." He felt steamed heat creep up from under his collar. "Something like that. And I am most sorry for the accident. Happily, I will now have the rest of our lives to make it up to her."

Wee Quince Winthrop looked as surprised as Alasdair felt at uttering such a declaration, but by the time her mother turned back to look at her, Quince had closed her eyes and subsided back against the pillows.

"Quince?" Her mother asked again.

"Aye, it's true. We are…engaged."

It wasn't a yes, but for the time being, it would do. "Thank you," he murmured.

"I see," Lady Winthrop said. "In that case, perhaps you would be so good as to apprise Lord Winthrop that his consent is needed."

Alasdair took her sharp tone like a gentleman. "Yes, my lady," he agreed. "I'll speak to his lordship directly."

Alasdair stepped out into the corridor just as Lord Winthrop was all but being dragged along by Lady Plum.

"Lord Cairn." The eminent botanist held out his hand. "Now what's all this my Plum's been telling me?"

"My Lord Winthrop." Alasdair shook the man's hand. "I

should like to ask for the honor of your daughter's hand."

"Ah! No wonder my Plum was in such a hurry. Congratulations, my dear." Lord Winthrop kissed his daughter's cheek.

For a long moment Alasdair could not understand whom on earth Lord Winthrop could possibly mean. And then a quick surge of something only slightly less sharp than panic sliced through his chest. "Nay, sir. Not Plum. Lady Quince. I should like to marry your daughter Quince."

"Not Plum?" There was more than consternation on Lord Winthrop's face now—there was disbelief. "But Quince? Oh, no, no. I couldn't let ye do that."

Couldn't? It stung to be so summarily dismissed. "Why not?" Alasdair considered himself a damn fine prospect. He had his hair, his teeth, his wit, and his until-this-moment sterling reputation and laudable career. Which now hung in the balance. But his ruddy peerage—and a lineage going back bloody hundreds of years—was secure. Surely that was worth something? The dotty old man ought to be jumping at the chance to add a marquessate to the fruit of his family tree.

And the thought of failure was like chalk in his month.

"Why?" Lord Winthrop echoed. "Good Lord, she'd have ye for breakfast."

And Alasdair would have her for supper and dessert. "I insist," he found himself saying. "I insist upon offering for her given the circumstances, which I would otherwise hesitate to tell you. But unfortunately, Lady Quince has been…injured. Under most unusual circumstances." The second lie came more easily than the first. "When the two of us were alone together earlier this evening. And in order to protect her, marriage—to *me*," he added just in case the old man should start to think of anyone else, "—is her best hope."

"Ye can't be serious?" Lord Winthrop looked over the tops of his spectacles in an attempt to see him better.

"Aye, sir. I am." Having once made up his mind, he was determined. "Very."

"Is she in trouble?"

"Not yet," Alasdair hedged. "But she is injured, and things are...difficult." And delicate. And insanely complicated. And deceptively simple.

Lord Winthrop took a long look at him—from the bottom of the soles of his shoes to the very tip top of his ginger-haired, un-powdered head—as if he were one of the plants the man was attempting to catalogue. "Ye seem a fine enough specimen to me. Ye're not going to try and bargain with me to increase her fortune?"

"Nay." The thought had not entered Alasdair's mind.

"Well, then, it would be foolish of me not to accept such a bargain, eh?" Lord Winthrop laughed and stuck out his hand. "Take her with my blessing."

The relief that flooded Alasdair's chest was incendiary, burning away every other consideration, every thought of any different sort of wife.

"Thank you, sir. Of course, I shall send my man of business to you to confirm the formalities of the settlement, but you have my word. As a gentleman. But I believe the marriage ceremony itself should take place forthwith."

"Certainly. Best to get on with it as soon as possible. Give her no time to worm her way out, eh? Or do something else entirely foolish."

His daughter had already done enough that was entirely foolish. But had he? Was this marriage a bad, ill-conceived idea—so mad that she would want to worm her way out?

"I'll leave ye to it, then." Lord Winthrop was clapping him on the shoulder and turning to go.

"Don't you want to speak with her yourself? Tell her of your decision?" Give her his blessing? Quince was grievously injured—surely her father would want to assure himself that she was all right? "The vicar of Saint Cuthbert's, who is also a physician, is attending to Lady Quince, and I mean to see to the wedding straight away. Surely you'll want to stay for that?"

But Lord Winthrop waved off Alasdair's concern. "No, no. Best leave that to ye. I'm sure ye'll sort things out. And if ye can't convince her, well… Maybe her mother or sister can be of some help."

Alasdair began to see why wee Lady Quince might have been left to wander astray, with such disinterested parenting. But he would start as he meant to go on. "Thank you, sir, but I am well able to fend for myself."

Lord Winthrop smiled over his shoulder. "Aye, well, so is Quince, my Lord Cairn. So is Quince."

Alasdair returned to his now-betrothed's bedchamber to find the Reverend Talent still close within the bright circle of lamplight around his patient. "The ball passed by, but it's left a very long and jagged laceration. It will need to be tightly bound."

Quince endured the rest of the treatment with ashen-faced, white-lipped stoicism that Alasdair could only admire, though he did not want to be impressed—he didn't like the sense of obligation his admiration placed him under. But he was already obligated. And he had already spoken out loud, to all of her family. It only remained for him to convince Quince.

"You'll need to rest now, Lady Quince." The vicar turned to her mother. "See that she's kept from any strenuous activity for a fortnight, at least. The arm needs to be immobile if it is to heal. And—"

Quince stopped the vicar from speaking by taking his arm with her good one, and pulling him nearer so she could speak without being heard. Or perhaps she had not the strength to do more than whisper, though her grip on the vicar's sleeve belied such an idea.

But as she whispered low into the vicar's ear, a nasty shard of something juvenile and too much like jealousy for his tastes rove through him with all the finesse of an iron bar. God help him, he *was* jealous.

She was his. She should be whispering low into *his* ear. She had done so the night he had kissed her in his garden.

But whom else had she encouraged in such a way? She might have any number of beaux named Davie, or Cameron, or Talent, for all he knew.

Nay. She wasn't like that. She was loyal and sincere. Even if she did lie far too easily for a lass her age.

Perhaps her confidence to the vicar was a plea for absolution. Maybe she truly was sorry. Maybe she was repenting of her crimes. Pain and duress—pain and duress that *he* had caused—did strange things to a person. And she knew this vicar fellow well. Well enough to ask for him by name, and know his church, and his academic background and training. And he had seen her talking to the man twice. Maybe she did have some scruples wandering about aimlessly under that flibbertigibbet exterior.

The Reverend Talent finally stepped away from Quince, who seemed to have spent the last of her depleted strength on their conversation. She lay still and white in her black breeches on the bed.

"I'll see myself out," the vicar was saying to Lady Winthrop.

"A moment, Reverend Talent, if you would." Alasdair stayed the vicar—while the man was there, they might as well make good use of all of his qualifications, and engage him to conduct the ceremony directly. "There is another matter."

"No." Quince's voice was surprisingly strong for someone who looked so weak. "Not now."

"Quince." Alasdair went to her. "You know we must marry," he whispered low, trying to keep their conversation as private as it might be with such an interested audience. "You must."

"I don't like *must*, Strathcairn." Her answering whisper was taking on an edge of stubborn desperation. "I agreed to be engaged, not to marry. Surely that's unnecessary."

"It is very necessary," he assured her. "I've spoken to your father, and he has given his consent."

"Just like that?" What little color remained in her face left, leaving her as pale and colorless as the coverlet.

He didn't try to soften the blow. "Aye, just like that."

She put her hand to her forehead, as if the thought of marrying him was making her dizzy. "You ken I don't want to."

Her refusal hurt more than it ought. But she was hurt more than she ought to be, even if she had been robbing a coach. He softened his voice, and tried again. "Refusal is not an option, wee Quince." He spoke quietly but firmly, as one does when giving someone an unfortunate truth, and took her hand to demonstrate his sincerity. "But perhaps I need to assure you that you will make me the happiest of men, and that I will endeavor to see to it that you—"

She pulled her hand away. "I cannot possibly make you the happiest of men. I will make you the saddest. I will. I will—" Her whisper strangled to a halt, before she renewed her assault on his logic. "I will not make you a good wife. I won't make any mon a good wife, because I'm not good. If you think so, then you truly have lost your mind."

"Pray, give me leave to know my own mind, Quince." He kept on with that low, steady voice that worked with obstinate politicians. "I believe that once you have recovered yourself from what must be a considerable shock, you will see that we will suit quite well."

"We will not suit," she insisted with a frantic shake of her head. She put her good hand to her eyes, which had become suspiciously glassy. "We will not. We will be—" She looked from him to the others, as if one of them might save her.

Not the vicar. No matter what, he refused to let it be the damned solemn vicar.

If she thought she wouldn't suit Alasdair, she damn well wouldn't suit a staid, un-larky vicar. And he would do anything—say anything—to convince her of that fact.

He used the last weapon in his arsenal. "It has to be me, Quince. I am the only one who will keep you out of the Tollbooth Prison this morning."

Quince held his gaze, even with her eyes brimming with tears. "Truly? You would saddle yourself with me rather than see that happen?"

"Aye," Alasdair swore. "If we are wed, then in the eyes of the law we are one person, and I will be able to protect you as my wife."

"I don't understand—you are the eyes of the law, Strathcairn. How can you protect me from *yourself?*" Her whisper rose to a plea. "Why can you not protect me as your friend?"

Because they were not *friends*. They could never really be friends now, after what she had done. "You have a very strange idea of what a friend is, wee Quince."

She did not take his intended meaning. She had truths of her own. "And you have a very strange idea of what true friendship is, Strathcairn."

Alasdair felt his already worn composure start to give way. "We can argue all night long after we are married. But now, we are running out of time. No more baiting and debating." He took her good hand again. "Lady Quince, I would be honored if you would consent to be my wife. But let me be clear—I will insist."

"But—"

"No buts." He tried to harden his tone, to show her that he had made up his mind.

"You insist?" The fight was going out of her—she was worn down by pain, doubt and desperation.

"I do insist," he said, firming his resolve. "It's me or the Tollbooth."

It had to be said. Quince had to know exactly where she stood. And Alasdair wanted to have his way. He would examine the reasons why at a later date, when it was done.

"Such a charming proposal, Strathcairn. You quite overcome my maidenly sensibilities."

"You don't have maidenly sensibilities." Triumph and relief distilled themselves into a heady brew. "What you have instead is backbone. And far too much nerve. And I'm the only man who can see it." He met her blazing golden eyes. "It really is me or the Tollbooth, lass. Choose."

Chapter 18

WHAT QUINCE CHOSE was more time to consider. Because the ache in her arm had settled to an omnipresent throb that made it hard to think. But think she would—her future depended upon it.

She wet her lips to counter the dryness in her throat from all their furtive whispering. "May I please have a glass of water and a private moment alone to discuss the matter with the marquess?"

"There is nothing more to discuss," Strathcairn countered at the same time that her mother said, "Surely this can wait until Quince has had some time to recover? I see no reason for such unseemly haste."

There was every reason for haste with the law— embodied by Strathcairn—breathing down her sore neck. Which was bound to get sorer still if Strathcairn held to his threat of tossing her into Tollbooth Prison. She was well and truly caught between a rock and a hanging place, and she could not tell yet which was like to be the more lethal. "Please, Mama."

Perhaps it was the unaccustomed gravity in her tone. Perhaps it was the pain and weariness leeching into her voice. Whatever it was her mother heard, it was enough to move her to do as Quince asked.

"Reverend Talent? If you would be so good as to accompany me to my sitting room, we can see to the business of your fee."

"Don't go far," Strathcairn admonished their retreating backs. "We'll have need of you presently." And when the door had closed behind them, he returned to her side, standing by the bed, looming over her in that granite cliff sort of way he seemed to prefer. Trying to look impenetrable. "Well? Speak now, Quince, or forever hold your peace."

How like him to couch his threat with wedding language. "That's just the problem, Strathcairn—there is no possibility of peace. Not two hours ago you were furious at me—with good reason"—she held up a hand to prevent him from objecting and interrupting—"I grant you. But you were angry enough to shoot me, and now you want—nay, *insist* upon marrying me. Forgive me if I find you utterly confusing." Confusing because the ache in her arm decided to be democratic, and spread the pain around. Her temple started to pound.

"The feeling is entirely mutual, I assure you." He raked a hand through that glorious ginger mane, as if his brain were not unaffected either.

"Then why, reputation be damned—for you ken I care nothing for it—do you insist upon marriage? You ken you have but to tell my parents the undiluted truth—that I am the highwayman—and they would pack me off to Papa's brother in Nova Scotia, quick as you please. They've threatened it often enough in the past." She paused to catch her breath, and try to think clearly—clearly enough to understand Strathcairn. "The truth is, your problem—me— can be solved without resorting to a mis-thought marriage."

"Mis-thought? Is that even a word?" But her statement seemed to shake some of the insistence out of him. He gave up his looming and sat on the edge of her bed. "Would you really rather be exiled to Nova Scotia than marry me? Am I really that bad?"

"Nay." She had not expected such a personal appeal. A hot surge of sympathy—or was it empathy?—flooded her eyes. But sympathy was no reason to marry a man. Especially when the man in question was not entirely sympathetic to her.

It was all so confusing and exhausting, but she could not give in to either feeling. "You're really that good. I'm the one who's bad. I'm the one who is a thief and a liar and a highwayman, Strathcairn." It was an awful thing to say the words out loud, to admit to such faults. But whatever shreds of honesty and scruples she had left demanded it. She *liked* him too much to let him make such a dreadful mistake. "The best that can be said of me is that I'm a flibbertigibbet, but the worst is that I would be forever disappointing and infuriating you as much as I disappoint and infuriate you right now. Think very hard if you're prepared for a lifetime of that—a lifetime tied to an accomplished thief and liar."

"And a highwaywoman, don't forget." He was trying to be amusing and teasing, but his smile didn't quite reach his eyes. "Although I would hardly say you were accomplished in that area. Thievery and lying, however…"

"Aye. And if you had not stopped me this evening," she reminded him, "I would have kept on going in much the same vein until I did become accomplished."

"Nay." His voice was as sure as granite. "You would not. You would have outgrown such childish antics. We all do."

"And did you rob coaches and steal snuffboxes when you were young, Strathcairn?" She could not imagine anything so criminal from such a passionately upright and law-abiding man.

"No," he admitted. "But I did other stupid, though perhaps less larcenous, things."

"Like what?" She could not conceive of any serious misdeeds from honest, forthright Strathcairn, to whom deception of any kind was abhorrent.

But the image of him five years ago, all blazing ginger glory, smiling, laughing and teasing Linnea, filled her mind. She tried to swat the mental picture away, to concentrate on the here and painful now, but when she looked at him, sitting on the side of her bed in his shirtsleeves, ardent and rumpled and insistent and stained with her blood, she fancied she could still see that younger version of Strathcairn, all that drive and passion, just wrongly applied.

"Quince. We are not discussing my past, but your future."

"Our future, Strathcairn. One that looks rife with strife." Because if she looked away from him, and looked at herself, the fantasy of all that rumpled, appealing ardency faded away.

And he also looked at her then—really looked at her—as if those clear green eyes were seeing beyond the larking, dancing, flibbertigibbet exterior she had constructed. Seeing that she was scared, and tired, and in a bloody great deal of pain, and the worst prospect in the world for a wife because she had been *shot while robbing a coach.* "It's not pretty, is it, Strathcairn?"

His head rocked back slightly, as from a blow, but then he righted himself. And leaned closer, until she could smell the dangerously intriguing scent of night air and spent gunpowder on his skin. "On the contrary, wee Quince. It is very attractive." He reached out to brush a wayward strand of her hair from her forehead. "Bruises, bloodstains and all."

Her breath throttled up in her chest, tight and hot and aching. "You can't mean that, Strathcairn. One of us has got to *think.*"

He sat back from her, even as his gaze seemed to bring him closer. "Do you really not know? Has no one in all of Edinburgh warned you against me, or told you of my less than sterling past?"

"Nay," she began, but then hedged, "My mother did mention a rumor of an auld scandal. But I didn't believe it could be anything but rumor."

"Really?" He seemed suspicious of her claim.

"I *know* you, Strathcairn. You're *good*."

"My God." He passed his hand over his eyes. "But you have to understand that rumor is like stink, Quince—it fouls everything it touches. It cannot be contained, even if it isn't true. Especially if it isn't true."

"There. I knew it couldn't be true."

"But I can't afford—" Some strong emotion pushed him to his feet to pace away from her. "I can't take another five years to rebuild my name and reputation. I can't endure while another lass' name is linked to mine without the benefit of matrimony to clear the slate clean."

The words hung in the air between them like cold frost from a breath.

"Another lass?" Something icier than dread chilled its way into her bones—she was surprised she couldn't hear her knees shivering and knocking together. "What do you mean?"

He shut his eyes, and just like that his face closed off, as cold and immutable as stone. "I mean that we must marry." He took a deep breath and opened his eyes. "I mean, I insist."

The moment lengthened like a shadow, drawing out until she finally understood that he was not offering for her to salvage her reputation, but his.

She turned away, to hide the blazing heat burning her eyes, but his hand slid to cup her chin. "We have something between us, you and I." He met her eyes. "It may not be 'fellow-feeling' as you called it, but it's something far more powerful."

There was something in his touch, something fiercer than tenderness—an unrepentant ardor burning away all her cool resolve.

She closed her eyes to concentrate, to remember what she needed to say. "That's just lust, Strathcairn, a shaky, changeable beast at best. Hardly something to base a marriage upon. I have a lust for stealing things, plainly put, and look where that's got me."

"Aye." He considered her words. "With me. And I have a better idea of what we might do with all that lust you seem to have so carefully bottled up inside you."

Oh, holy helpful cherubs. He saw too much—and not enough. "There's nothing careful about it," she insisted, even as her voice cracked under all the heat building in her throat. "It's all rather heedless, and rubbishing—" The heat in her throat had climbed behind her eyes, scalding her.

"Quince." He took her face in his hands, and turned her chin up to him. "Lass, are you afraid? Of me?"

By jimble, he had got to the heart of her quick enough, hadn't he?

"I would be a fool not to be," she whispered. She was afraid of them both. Afraid of what she would become when the enticing lust wore itself out, as it inevitably would, and he no longer looked at her with such scorching tenderness. Afraid of what would happen to her if she started to believe the promise in his eyes. And his kiss.

Which he brought to her now, a quiet bittersweet gift of his lips upon hers. Offering her that insistent ardor. Seducing her with the promise of his glorious, blazing passion. Tempting her to believe.

Oh, holy stars in the sky, it would be so easy—so much easier—if she could let herself love him. But for all his insistence, the fact remained that he didn't, and couldn't love her. And he certainly didn't trust her.

He must have sensed her weakness. His kiss slid to the sensitive skin below her ear. "Have you any more objections?"

She had only one left. "I'll make you a dreadful wife, and an even more dreadful Marchioness of Cairn. " And with that idea came another. "I won't have children."

She took him entirely by surprise—he went still with consternation. "Won't or can't?"

How could she explain? How could she even begin to articulate the fears that filled her soul in the empty quiet hours when she had nothing to do to distract her from the ugly, unavoidable truth. "I'm the bad seed in the family greenhouse, Strathcairn. No amount of nurturing, or watering, or change of soil or gardener can change that."

She was tainted because she stole, not for charity or righteousness, but for the sheer unadulterated pleasure and illicit thrill. And that fact she could never, ever change.

"You've convinced yourself of this, haven't you—that you're no good, when what you really are is passionate and capable and bold."

"Not exactly sterling traits in a young lady."

"Rubbish," he contradicted. "They are sterling traits in a woman. And especially brilliant traits in a marchioness."

"A marchioness needs to bear an heir." Quince was growing too tired, too weary and sad to parse the truth into logical, palatable pieces. "So it is all the same, Strathcairn. You are a mon of property who will be in need of an heir. You should marry someone who can give you one."

"How do you know you cannot have children? Has some doctor—" He shot to his feet. "Are you not a virgin?"

She knew she was pale enough that the heat of her blush scorched her cheeks. "What if I weren't?" The moment the words were out of her mouth, she knew them for what they truly were—a test. A test to see just how far Strathcairn's like and affection and lust would let him go.

A test of her worth.

The moment stretched between them like a physical thing, pulling and weighing her down. And he was just as immobile, standing stock still in the middle of her bedchamber floor.

And when he answered, his voice was full of quiet conviction, of that unwavering, granite surety. "I would still want you."

She could not breathe. She could not think. "Want me enough to still marry me?"

"Aye."

She closed her eyes tight, as if she could stop what was coming. As if she could go back, and make a different choice in that moment his carriage had come at her from out of the night.

But she could not. And she could no longer hold back the feeling that this—that Strathcairn and she—were entirely inevitable. "Why? Why must we do this to each other? Why can we not just let each other be?"

"Oh, wee Quince." The mattress dipped from his weight.

She opened her burning eyes to find him inches away, looking at her with that strange mixture of exasperation and astonished wonder.

"You must know by now that I cannot possibly let you be." His voice slipped into that lovely brogue-y lilt he knew she had no power to resist. "We are in a world of trouble, you and me." He searched her face, poring over it with his eyes and his hands, tracing every curve and plane, as if he might find the answer to some question he had asked writ large across her forehead. "So I'll just have to ask you to believe me, and trust me."

Trust. It had all come down to trust.

She had to close her eyes to avoid the watchful intensity of his gaze. She had to hold on to the last leery piece of her breaking heart. "I am afraid."

"You, lass? You, who took to the roads as a highwayman?" He cradled her snugly against his chest. "What if I promise never to shoot you again?"

"It's not that easy, Strathcairn." Her voice was as hot and sticky as the tears she could feel accumulating at the corners of her eyes. "You can have no idea of the provocation you might face with me. And there will be provocation—I can't seem to help it. So why?" she asked again, needing to understand, needing to be sure—of herself as much as him. "Why would you want me, when you could have—when you *should* want—any other lass?"

He answered with a bittersweet smile that threatened to spill all of her carefully controlled tears. "Why would I want any other girl, when I could have a bold lass like you?"

There were a thousand and three reasons, but mostly just one. "You don't even like me."

"I do," he insisted with quiet conviction. "You know I do. We wouldn't be in this predicament—I wouldn't have laid my eyes and my hands upon you in the first place if it were otherwise. And you like me as well. Somewhere down deep inside, you like me fine. You never would have spent so much time aggravating me otherwise."

"This is terrible logic, Strathcairn, this idea that we antagonize each other out of love."

"Love, is it now?" His smile warmed the very corners of his handsome face.

"Nay." She could not shake her head while she was nestled so against his chest. "You ken that. I told you, I'm not romantic. I'm bad."

"You're not." He was just as insistent. "You're just young and bold and curious and too smart to let such an opportunity pass you by. The opportunity to be thrilled each and every night of your life. And some of the afternoons, as well as the mornings, too."

"Strathcairn." She swallowed her astonished amusement. "Are you trying to flirt me into marrying you?"

"Nay, lass. I'm trying to seduce you into marrying me. I'm sitting on your bed, with you in my arms, and your mother and your sister and a vicar right outside the door, and despite the copious bloodstains upon your shirt, I can still make out the outline of your magnificent wee breasts, and I want you so bad, I ache."

It was entirely, ridiculously wrong. But it was somehow the right answer.

She knew she had flaws that ran as deep as a loch, and that she would make him a miserable wife. But the truth was that she still wanted him to want her. Because, truth be told, he was the only sort of man—clever, amusing, attractive and experienced—that she could ever bring herself to marry. And he was something more. He was Strathcairn, the only man who had ever been bold enough to capture her imagination and invade her dreams. "Well, all right then. If you insist."

"I do, lass." He was sure in that scrupulous, granite sure way of his. "Wee Quince Winthrop, I must have you."

There was nothing she could do in the face of such

conviction but give in as gracefully as possible. "Then you shall, God help you."

The relief that washed across Strathcairn's face was so sweet it was heartening. "I'll call the vicar."

Mama, Plum, and Reverent Talent appeared with such alacrity that they must have been all but listening at the keyhole. At least Plum probably was. She burst through the door first. "Thank God for that. It took you long enough. Let's get you two married before one of you changes their mind."

Now that the moment was upon her, Quince felt impossibly unready—dirty and disheveled in person as well as in her mind. "If you'll give me a moment or two to make myself ready."

She gestured to her bloodstained, ruined shirt, and raised her eyebrows to remind him she was hiding the fact that she was wearing gentleman's breeks and boots under the cover of the bedclothes.

Strathcairn's voice returned to its crisp, public tones, but bless his enthusiasm, he managed to gaze at her as if she were still in fresh muslin. "You'll do quite nicely as you are, as well as where you are. The Reverend Talent says you are not to do anything strenuous, so it's best we keep the strain only to the saying of vows."

"Must we vow, when a handfast will do?" Handfasting would give them something of a trial marriage, which meant that there would still be a way out—a way to escape should she find that her ambivalence to marriage in general outpaced her lust and attraction to Strathcairn. Because while was she was not without affection for Strathcairn— she liked him plenty when they were dancing and flirting and kissing in the moonlight—binding herself to him for life did not seem like a very smart idea, even if he had promised not to shoot her again.

"Nay." Strathcairn's tone was adamant. "Handfasting will not do. It must at least be a civil union, by 'habit and repute' as it were. But it were better if the vicar married us both legally and religiously." He softened his tone, abandoning for the moment his Member of Parliament legalese. "It will all be fine, Quince. We'll start as we mean to go on." He took her hand within his own and interlaced their fingers. Meshing them together, so they were equal, and none was superior over the others. Holding them steady.

It was as close to a sign as she was like to get.

"Let us proceed before I faint from all the joy. Or the blood loss."

Strathcairn did not object to her sarcasm. Nor did he let go of her hand. In fact, he held it as if he never meant to let it go. "Reverend Talent?"

For a long moment, the vicar looked as if he might object. Or refuse outright. But finally, he fished a small, worn prayer book out of his medical bag and began his solemn invocation. "I require and charge you both, as you will answer at the dreadful day of judgment when the secrets of all hearts all be disclosed, that if either of you know any impediment why you may not be lawfully joined together in matrimony, you do now confess it."

How fitting. Today *was* her awful day of judgment, it seemed. Because the awful secrets of her heart had already been revealed. At least to Strathcairn. Quince could not but feel all the awful solemnity of the moment.

"Wilt thou—" He looked to Strathcairn to provide his name.

"Alasdair James MacNeal Colquhon, Marquess of Cairn."

Alasdair. She had never called him by his Christian name. To her he was Strathcairn, so much more and certainly no less. But he was to be Alasdair to her now.

"Do you, Alasdair James MacNeal Colquohon have this woman to thy wedded wife, to live together after God's ordinance in the holy estate of Matrimony? Wilt thou love her, comfort her, honor, and keep her in sickness and in health; and, forsaking all others, keep thee only unto her, so long as ye both shall live?"

Strathcairn's voice was calm and strong. "I will." Not Strathcairn—Alasdair.

It was...frightening and strange. But also lovely. She couldn't keep calling him Strathcairn in her usual nearly sarcastic matter if they were to be married. She had to act at least a little like a wife. And it might be nice, being able to call him Alasdair.

"Pay attention, brat."

The word snapped her out of her trance. And he could call her Quince. Or perhaps still, brat. But it almost sounded endearing when he said it now. "Would you repeat that, please?"

"And wilt thou, Quince Louise Alice Winthrop have this man to thy wedded husband, to live together after God's ordinance in the holy estate of matrimony? Wilt thou obey him, and serve him, love, honor, and keep him in sickness and in health; and, forsaking all others, keep thee only unto him, so long as ye both shall live?"

"Honor certainly." She shrugged at the gaping vicar before she swung her gaze back to the man standing beside her. "But obey? Not likely. Not even probably. It's not in my nature."

Quince thought the vein in the poor vicar's temple was going to burst and kill him before their eyes, until Strathcairn spoke in much the same vein.

"Well, loving you is probably not in my nature either, but you don't see me quibbling." His eyes were full of laughter—he was trying to be kind, and smooth it all over. And amuse her.

No one else in the world would—or ever had—put up with her so.

Quince had to swallow over the sudden lump in her throat to make her voice more than the barest whisper. "I will."

Strathcairn beamed at her as if she had done something wonderful instead of getting them both into the most awful mess.

"God the Father, God the Son, God the Holy Ghost, bless, preserve, and keep you; the Lord mercifully with his favor look upon you, and fill you with all spiritual benediction and grace; that ye may so live together in this life, that in the world to come ye may have life everlasting. Amen."

And so it was done.

Almost. "I don't have a register to sign," the vicar apologized. "But it's a legal civil union until that can be done. If you'll come on the morrow, or as soon as Lady Quince is better able to endure the carriage ride—"

"I suppose it is up to my lord and master." She looked at her new husband, to whom she was now bound more surely than she was even bound to her own blood family. "Wither thou goest," she quipped, not entirely willing to stop twitting him, even if they were married.

"So goest I," he finished. "I am glad to hear that, because as soon as you've had a few hours to recover and pack, we're leaving Edinburgh. We goeth north, to the mountains. We'll go directly to Cairn."

Chapter 19

DAWN CAME FAR too early—the summer sun slanted through the window well before the clock over the mantel had struck five o'clock in the morning. Not that she had slept much anyway. The teaspoon of laudanum that she had consented to take—and by jimble what vile, bitter stuff it was—had already worn off by the time the cock in the kitchen garden added his clamorous voice to the morning.

Though she was not exactly happy with what she viewed as her devil's bargain, Quince was at least curious as to what life with Strathcairn was going to be like. It had certainly been a curious thing to spend her wedding night—if the three brief hours between saying the vows and preparing to leave her father's house could even be called a night—alone.

And things were bound to get more curious still. Because Strathcairn was already below, waiting to take her away. Mama and Plum were in a flurry of packing of her trunks, as they found the general state of her wardrobe to be so inferior to what might be expected of a marchioness that all manner of loans and alterations had to be rapidly made.

Quince judged it best to let them have their way, and

even went so far toward graciousness to let them dress her in one of Plum's more ladylike gowns—a redingote-style traveling gown in creamy lemony silk, with the bodice and skirts embroidered all over in colorful flowers. The gown was everything Quince was not at five o'clock in the morning—cheerful, elegant and refined.

Despite her newfound elegant refinement, it was a subdued leave-taking, but no more than she deserved for having got herself into such a tangle.

"Take care of our lass," was her father's only instruction to Strathcairn after he had kissed her on the head, and stepped back, content to let his new son-in-law hand his youngest daughter into the carriage.

"Get better," Plum whispered. "And then give him all kinds of hell."

"Plum!" Quince was nearly overcome by sisterly affection. "In nineteen years, I don't think I've ever heard you swear before."

"A wedding present." Plum kissed her on both cheeks. "Write me. Every day. And tell me *all*."

Quince could feel heat suffuse her cheeks. "Not all," she whispered back. "But very near."

"Quince, my darling." A quick, fierce hug from Mama. "Be well," she instructed. "And do please *try* to be good. Write me if there is anything—"

And then Strathcairn was scooping her up, as if she were unable to walk the two steps into the carriage. And no sooner had the door snapped shut behind them than they were wheeling away, out the gravel drive, and west into the cool of the morning. Her married life had begun.

Strathcairn took his place close next to her on the forward facing seat, and immediately she moved to the opposite bench. He was too big, and too near, and too…everything.

If he asked, she would give him the excuse that she wanted to see her family until the last possible moment. But he did not ask, and before she knew it, the gates at the end of the drive had whipped past the window, and the only home she had known was left behind.

And she was alone with her husband.

Who crossed his very long legs—which seemed to span the whole of the carriage—propped them on the seat next to her, and regarded her from under his brows.

Quince turned her gaze resolutely out the carriage window, nearly pressing her nose close to the pane—if she had her way she'd put her head out the window like a dog trying to scent the breezes. She had seen too little of the world, and would take advantage of this opportunity to see it before she was shut away behind the gates of his estate in the countryside.

"How is your arm?"

Quince flicked a glance at Strathcairn. Who appeared all husbandly concern, with a line of query etched between his bright brows. "Aching."

"I regret the need for such a hasty departure, but I thought it best to remove ourselves from town to avoid any gossip."

"You have a strange notion of gossip if you think it can be avoided merely by leaving town. You yourself said rumor is like stink. Our hasty marriage will set tongues wagging whether we are present or not."

"I am aware." And now that she looked—really looked—he did look supremely aware. All well-fed tomcat, in an exquisitely fitted suit of dark bottle green that contrasted brilliantly with his russet hair. "Gossip can best be managed without participating directly."

Quince was instantly back on her guard. What she had left of her guard, anyway, which was severely worn down by the circumstances. "What have you said?"

His smile was almost too knowing. "It's to be a love match, naturally."

Something uncomfortable landed in the vicinity of her stomach, like cold porridge. But it was too early in the morning to examine one's feelings—one was so exhausted one might end up in tears. But sarcasm was a great fender-offer of tears. "Why Strathcairn, who knew? You're taking to lying very well for an amateur."

If anything, his smile widened. "I am a politician, Quince, and not in the least an amateur. Nothing I say is without a purpose."

Oh, aye. Plum had warned her to mind that aspect of his character, hadn't she? But Quince had blithely thought she knew better. And now she was married to the inconveniently perceptive man.

"Why don't you lean against me," he suggested. "It's bound to be more comfortable."

"I'm injured, but not an invalid, Strathcairn. You needn't coddle me."

"Perhaps I want to coddle you."

Quince didn't dare examine that sentiment—she was already too close to tears for her comfort. "Don't. It doesn't suit you. Or me."

"Well, if you aren't the contrariest girl this side of the Cairngorms." But he smiled as he said it, as if her show of independence amused him.

She put up her chin. "You should see me on the other side."

"I hope the view improves." With that, he left her to nurse her prickly feelings in quiet, and pulled his hat down over his eyes to doze, as if the rocking carriage were as comfortable as a bed.

She could find no such comfort. However well slung the traveling coach might be, she already ached from head to toe. Certainly her arm was the worst of it, but she also had bruises and scrapes aplenty from her fall and sojourn through the brambles.

She shifted to lean her left side against the padded backrest to make herself as comfortable as possible, leaning her head against the sash. Outside the city, the morning air smelled of hay and hedgerow flowers. Of ease and summer. She closed her eyes and tried not to think, not to worry and fret about what would come next, and let the heat of the sun melt away her aches and pains.

And the next thing she knew she was waking up with her

head on Strathcairn's lap. Or rather his thigh. His firm, long, sinewy thigh.

It was one thing to touch a man when one was standing on one's own two feet, dancing, or even asking to be kissed. It was quite another to wake up with one's head pillowed in what she could only term his nether regions.

Heat, and something more uncomfortably comfortable, blossomed up the column of her spine.

A glance told her Strathcairn had shifted her to his side of the coach, and now had his arm snugged around her waist, just below her breasts, holding her to him as she slept. And she in turn, had her bandaged arm curled over his thigh.

It was warm and cozy, and deeply, deeply intimate.

But the fact that he had done this—had moved her while she was asleep and couldn't object—bothered her in a way that she could not articulate, much less understand. She liked to be in charge of her own self. But that had all changed now, with marriage.

Quince couldn't stop from pushing herself to sitting. But her head spun from the sudden movement.

"You're awake, lass." Strathcairn gathered her against his shoulder to steady her, while his other hand brushed her hair away from her forehead—he must have taken off her stylish plumed tricorn hat. Or rather, Plum's hat. Not that she was going to speak of hats while he was caressing her face with such easy intimacy.

"It's all right. Stay where you are. You need the rest." And then he added, as if he perhaps felt the need to justify himself, "You were shivering."

"I don't feel cold." Not while she was held against the furnace that was her husband.

But Strathcairn's hand closed over hers where they fisted in her skirts. "Your hands are cold."

They were. And it was nice to have his fingers warming hers. But still, all this...closeness made her...ill at ease. Strangely agitated. Too aware of his size and heat and presence.

She looked away. "Where are we?" The shadows had lengthened considerably, and the heat had gone from the day.

"Some small way outside of Stirling, I should think." His words were spoken against her temple, warm and stirring against her skin. "Your hair is very soft. How strange when all the rest of you remains so steadfastly prickly." His voice was quiet and almost contemplative, as if he were trying not to pick an argument, but as if she were a puzzle he still could not solve.

That made two of them—she hardly understood herself, because uncomfortably comfortable as she was, she stayed in his arms.

But his strange compliment seemed to call for some answer. "I suppose it's only soft because I don't put a mountain of powder in it."

"How delightfully unfashionable of you."

Quince didn't want to argue, but she was herself. "I am more than unfashionable, Strathcairn. I am—what did you call me?—unapologetic. Pray don't fool yourself into hoping that I have changed overnight just because I am injured, and we are married."

He shifted away to regard her down the length of his perfectly straight nose. "Do you do this on purpose? Make it difficult for people to like you?"

Oh, holy glass houses. This was something more that intimacy—this was presumption. And an uncomfortably accurate assessment at that.

Heat and mortification at being so thoroughly discovered made her throat too tight to breathe. It was never particularly nice to hear such a frank assessment of one's character. While she had *not* actually tried to make it difficult for people to like her, the result had been the same—with everyone except the Marquess of Cairn.

Who continued to regard her in that minutely assessing fashion. "What a curious lass you are—borrowed gowns, no maid accompanying you, and a fairly small set of trunks, considering. One wonders what you did with all your ill-gotten gains?"

"Ill-gotten gains are still hard-gotten gains, Strathcairn." Her aching arm was proof enough of that.

"Are they?" He pulled his feet under him and sat up. "By the devil, then I almost feel sorry for you."

"Almost?" She matched the sarcasm in his voice. "But not quite."

Finally he smiled. "Not quite."

"Don't worry, Stratchcairn. I shan't ask you to play lady's maid. I am perfectly capable of taking care of myself."

He scoffed openly. "That point remains moot." He cast his gaze at her bandaged arm. "I doubt you can even cut meat."

"Then I shall eat soup."

"The contrariest lass this side of the Cairngorms," he muttered only half under his breath. "Have it your way. We are arriving at our inn."

"I had no idea it had grown so late."

"It has. The horses need rest. Unlike you, they have toiled instead of sleeping the day away. Though you look the better for the rest, I dare say."

"Careful, Strathcairn. That might almost be a compliment."

"Careful, Quince. It wasn't meant to be."

Quince could make nothing out of that comment, because they had indeed arrived, and Strathcairn was already climbing out and handing her carefully into the busy yard of the Bee and Thistle, a solid-looking gray stone inn bustling with ostlers and other coach passengers.

He escorted her across the inn yard, but despite her long sleep in the coach, or perhaps because of it, she was exhausted by the time she had followed him up the stairs to the small room he procured. She eyed the small, low ceilinged space under the eaves. "Are we to share?"

His brow rose precipitously. "If it doesn't offend your maidenly sensibilities." Strathcairn stepped aside to let her enter. "We are married, after all. Although frankly, I didn't think you had maidenly sensibilities."

"I suppose I don't. Must have sold them along with my scruples." He had to stoop to make it through the doorframe. And then she saw what answered for a bed— "You're too tall, for one thing. And for another you can't mean that I'm to fit in there with you?"

His eyebrows rose even higher, but he kept his face a careful blank. "We'll manage."

Quince was dubious. And weary, though she had done nothing but sit and evidently doze all the day through. But the pain in her arm had grown more than tiring—it was ruddy uncomfortable. Uncomfortable enough to seek out the tisane with laudanum her mother had pressed upon her in a vial, and gulp the bitter dose down without waiting to mix it into tea.

Strathcairn was watching her. "Is that wise?"

"If it isn't, it's done." Let him make from that what argument he would.

But he did not argue. He looked at her with that rueful half-smile that only just warmed the corners of his eyes. "Then let us get you comfortable and lying down as soon as may be."

"I'm perfectly capable," she began. But the truth was, she was not. The redingote, while gorgeous, had a long row of buttons marching down its front—buttons devilishly tricky for her to undo with one of her hands bandaged.

And Strathcairn, drat his perceptive eyes, saw all of that. "It's either me, or we scandalize my secretary by asking him to assist you. But as that would only serve to infuriate me, rather than scandalize you, you'll have to make do with me. So—"

He backed her into the bed until she was sitting, and then he went to his knees in front of her to unlace her shoes, which, unlike the borrowed redingote, were her own—the unfashionable, comfortable, worn half-boots she customarily wore. There were only so many sacrifices she was prepared to make in the name of fashion. Or vanity.

"Do a great deal of walking, do you?"

The question seemed strange. But what was strange was

that they really knew so little of each other, but for quips and kisses. She had no idea of his daily habits, of his true likes and dislikes, other than the fact that deception of any kind was abhorrent to him. What if he was indifferent to music? What if he didn't like animals? "Do you like dogs?"

He tilted his head in that way that made her think he was trying to see her better. "Aye. Why?"

"I should like one. I've always wanted one. Papa didn't want any about—he feared they would dig up his gardens. But I should like one of my own."

"Would you? There's bound to be a puppy or three, or eight, available at Cairn. When I was a boy, the place always seemed to be lousy with them."

"Thank you. I should like a puppy. For comfort."

What a strange thing to say. But she felt strange. An almost unpleasant warmth was blossoming within her chest, and spreading into her lungs. "I don't like this feeling." She tugged off her lace fichu, flinging it away so it was easier to breathe.

"And that will be the opium in that damn vial, no doubt," Strathcairn said obliquely.

She frowned at him. "I don't have opium."

"Laudanum is just a tincture of diluted opium, wee Quince. I thought you knew that." He brushed her hair off her face again, and Quince found the gesture infinitely more confusing than she had the last time. "Good to find you don't like it."

She might not have liked it, but it made her want to rub her face into the cradle of his hand, as an animal tamed to touch. And it made her want to touch his face the same way. To stroke her hands along the hard line of his jaw, and feel the scratchy bramble of his whiskers rising just below the surface. "I saw you in the brambles, you ken. Last night. You were very angry."

"I was," he confirmed. "But I'm not now."

No, now he was unbuttoning her redingote, and reaching up under her petticoats to tug free the ties of her garters, and divest her of her stockings. His clever, long fingers brushed against her skin, and she couldn't help the strange compulsion that had her pressing her knees together, trapping his hands. She was all over shivers and quivers and feelings dancing over the surface of her skin. "I'm not angry either. I'm..." She had no idea what she was.

"It's the opium, lass. Takes some like this." He eased her knees apart enough to take down her stockings, which he tossed over the arm of a nearby chair.

"Are you going to take me like this?" She wasn't exactly sure what she was asking.

"Nay, lass. Just set yourself at ease, and let me see to your comfort." He began to ease her redingote off her shoulders.

She rubbed herself against the heat of his hands, trying to ease the itchy need crawling across her skin. "I don't want comfort. I want—"

She wanted to touch him, to exercise the strange, itchy compulsion to press herself against him, to feel the rough texture of his skin against her cheek. And she couldn't seem to stop herself from doing just that—latching her arms about his neck and laying her lips to his mouth, tasting the rough tang of the nip of whisky he had taken from the ostler on his lips. Rubbing her bodice against his chest. Wrapping her legs around him as if she could climb him like a tree. A tall towering tree that smelled of spice and pleasure and passion—

"Easy now, lass. You've taken a bigger than advisable dose of laudanum." He plucked the vial from her hand.

"I don't care. I want you to kiss me. I want to kiss you, and touch you, and—" Appease the agitation skittering across her skin, making her feel strange and restless and weightless all at the same time.

"Aye, lass, sure," he murmured against her forehead. "There's plenty of time for more. No need to rush." He placed a gentle kiss on the corner of her mouth, and another on her nose. "I'm not going anywhere. We've all the time in the world."

The compulsion was working its way out of her, leaving

her strange and sad and tired. And he seemed to understand. He laid her back against the pillows, and stood.

He looked so tall and stern looming over her. But his rough voice was kind, if not gentle. "Save your breath, as well as your kisses, and rest, Quince. We've a whole lifetime to argue and make up."

Chapter 20

QUINCE WOKE TO a stream of early summer light in her eyes, the dawn call of the birds and sound of deep, heavy breathing in her ear. And the feeling of something stirring directly behind her. Not something. Someone.

In a burst of nonsensical panicked confusion, she catapulted herself from the bed and fell with a resounding thud onto the bare floorboards. And landed on her arm.

Agony echoed up and down her bones, and she let out a sound that was very near inhuman in its pain.

Another sound, louder and definitely human, roared from above. "Quince?"

Quince rolled onto her back to find Strathcairn towering above her, wearing only his small clothes, which were a ridiculous thing to call underclothes that weren't the least bit small, if you asked her. But no one did. Because they were alone.

She was alone in a bedroom with a half-naked Strathcairn. Who she seemed to recall she had thrown herself at, last evening.

"Holy naked trollops." She hauled a breath back her

lungs, and tried not act like the veriest, most inexperienced ninny. "Is this how you greet the dawn every day?"

He was already scooping her up from the floor. "Every day that I've been married to you."

"You can put me down, Strathcairn. I'm not a doll, or an invalid."

"So you've said." His voice was remarkably matter-of-fact. "But you couldn't manage to get out of bed without falling over." He deposited her on the edge of the bed.

"I didn't fall." She huffed. "I— Never mind." Because whatever else she thought she was going to say went straight out of her mind. Because the bed was smaller than a teacup. And the bedclothes were in an absolute tangle. And she was wearing only her chemise and stays. And he was bare-chested and in his small clothes.

Oh, holy glassy-eyed stares. Which was exactly what she was giving Strathcairn.

Who smiled down at her, all sleek stretching tomcat, running his hand through his glorious bright red hair. "Good morning to you, too."

"Oh, aye. Good morning." But her voice has lost all its volume and force.

Because his chest was entirely naked. And his skin looked warm and smooth and dotted with intriguing freckles in the morning light. And his hair—a slim line of that blazing, vibrant red trailed from the middle of his chest down past the waist of his small clothes. "You're a ginger all over."

"Aye." His smile slid to one corner of his mouth. "Very observant." That was also the moment she realized that he was still holding on to her good arm, rubbing his thumb back and forth a bit before asking, "Did you sleep comfortably enough in your stays?"

She eased away from her half-naked husband, trying to act everything cool and collected, as if she weren't entirely unequal to waking up next to, and covered with, a warm, half-naked man. "Aye," she finally answered. "Well enough."

"Good." He let go of her hand, and crossed to the other side of the room, and then, with his back to her, simply shucked his small clothes.

And she was left gaping at his pale, sculpted buttocks and his long, lean legs.

She knew she ought to turn away for modesty's, if not privacy's, sake, but his sculpted backside was like a flesh and blood rendering of the Apollo Belvedere she had seen in German drawing books at the bookshop off the Grass Market in Edinburgh. Except she certainly wasn't in a bookshop now.

She was in a country inn, alone with her entirely naked husband.

Unfortunately for her education, he pulled fresh small clothes and breeches on before he turned back to speak to her. "I'll get hot water."

"Oh." She hoped she nodded. "That's fine."

He stuck his head out into the hall, returned with two steaming pitchers that had been left right outside their door, and proceeded to pour some into a shallow bowl. "You're welcome to sit there, and watch me shave." He gestured to the bowl of shaving water. "But I should advise you that we need to get upon the road as soon as may be while the weather holds."

How extraordinarily straightforward and commonplace he was, standing there talking of shaving water. And how extraordinarily intimate it was, not only that they seemed to have slept together, but that even with his breeches covering his arse, the fine linen fabric left very little to her enlightened imagination.

What a finely built, braw man he was. Very finely built, indeed.

"Quince?"

"Aye?"

"You need to get up."

"I'm sure I do. Oh, aye." She pushed herself to her unsteady feet, and rummaged through the small valise with her toiletries and combs, to extract a flannel. Thought she hardly knew what to do with it in front of him. But if he could wash and dress himself in front of her—which it seemed he was doing—then she supposed she was required to do the same.

"Quince? Would you like some chocolate?"

"Hot? Ooh, aye!" The second pitcher was indeed full of steaming chocolate.

Quince immediately abandoned her flannel for something far more important to her morning, and poured herself a dishful. "Ahh. By jimble, that's good."

He regarded her in the mirror with lazy, narrowed eyes as he soaped his face. "Don't drink it all."

"Oh! Let me pour." She served him a dish full. "Only, don't get soap on the cup."

He smiled around his beard of foam. "Thank you. I'll wait until I'm done."

Quince put the cup on the washing stand and watched with something more than mere curiosity as he tossed a Turkish towel over his shoulder and then drew the razor down across his face, scraping a clear path across his cheek. Her insides felt all strange and warm and liquid—all swirled up like the hot milk she had just stirred into the chocolate. She was nearly spellbound by the sight of all that bare man and moving muscle and soapy foam as he stretched his chin up and scraped away another swath.

And then caught her eye in the mirror. "You can breathe now, brat."

"Oh." She felt entirely foolish. "I just didn't want to be responsible for startling you into slitting your throat on the day after our wedding. What would people say? "

His smile curved up one freshly sleek cheek. "It's the second day after our wedding. But I thank you for your concern."

He was taking such pains to be charming and convivial that she did the same. "You're welcome. This isn't so bad, this being married business."

He eyed her in the mirror. "Isn't it?"

"I'll admit to being rather put off by the whole idea. And

I was rather disconcerted when I woke to find you…there. But this isn't so bad."

"Faint praise, but praise nonetheless, so I'll take it." He turned his cheek and shaved a long swath down the other side of his neck, and dashed the last of the soapy foam off his razor into the basin. "And rather than press my luck in extending our not-so-bad interlude by offering to un-lace and re-lace you this morning, which will undoubtedly delay us by hours, I think I had best finish dressing quickly, and then send a chambermaid up to assist you."

Quince dismissed the strange fluttering in her stomach at the thought of Strathcairn disrobing her as hunger pangs— she hadn't eaten the previous day—added to the cacophony of other aches and pains making themselves felt this morning. "Thank you, Strathcairn."

He stood before her in all his shirtless, russet glory, looking down at her with a strange expression of pleased forbearance—all smiling eyes and sideways mouth. "Alasdair, I think, when I'm half-dressed, and alone with my wife."

Heat, and something else, something more dear, and therefore more worrisome, closed down her mouth.

For some reason she couldn't— No, she didn't *want* to say his name. It was too intimate. Too much of an invitation. An invitation she was not yet ready to give.

She was nobody's pet, to be jumping when she was called.

Quince waited until he had drawn his linen shirt over his head, looped a cravat around his neck, donned his coat, and was half way through the chamber door before she gave into the temptation. "Thank you, Alasdair."

ALASDAIR STOPPED IN the doorway. "You're very welcome, wee Quince." He took his time with her name, rolling it around his mouth like fine wine, enjoying the astringent tartness of the word on his tongue.

And soon, very soon, he would taste the rest of her in the very same way. As soon as he could manage. As soon as they reached the privacy of Cairn, where she could heal, and he could woo his curious, prickly, passionate bride in private.

It had been a tortuous heaven to lie next to her last night, after her amorous overture. But after the laudanum had worn off, it had been something of a revelation to see her for the first time without her defenses, unprotected by the chain mail of her formidably clever wit. He had stared at his new wife for nearly an hour, marveling at the twists and turns of fate that had made her his bride.

He had from the first thought her an attractive lass, but much of her charm had come from the vivacity of her over-large personality. In sleep, her lively, out-sized personality was less evident, less able to divert his attention or challenge his views. But she still possessed something that was more than mere beauty. Something more than the combination of sandy brown hair, golden eyes and fine, pale skin. Something beyond the delicate architecture of her strong chin, and the perfect bow of her lips.

Something quick and curious and playful and strong, which made it all the more difficult for him to understand how she could be so utterly feckless. How she could choose a life of larceny, violence and deception. How she could use her gifts—her strengths—for ill.

Yet her strength also made him hopeful for the woman she might become. What would she be like if all that playful curiosity and clever purpose were put to good use? What an ally and helpmeet she would make. If only she hadn't chosen—convinced herself—to be bad.

He would take her to Cairn and convince her otherwise. He would be clever and patient and would woo her while she healed. He would teach her how to go on in the world, and how to be good.

And she would remind him to laugh at himself now and again.

They made excellent progress through the morning, traveling on good roads higher into the hills. Such good progress that even after five and half hours, they were drawing close enough to Cairn for Alasdair to order the carriages to press on, north into the mountains toward home.

He was, after years away—years spent thinking only intermittently of his highland family home—suddenly anxious to be there. No, anxious was not the right word— hungry was what he was. Ravenous for the soft air and familiar comfort of a place that was as much a part of him as his bones.

His feeling must have been apparent. "Are we near?" his reluctant bride asked.

"Nearly. Within an hour's journey, if I remember correctly."

"Another hour, still? We've come so far north we must be running out of country soon."

She put her bandaged hand on the sash of the open window, as if she would lean out, and then instantly withdrew it as they passed close by a group of people—all clothes the color of dirt and wide, terrified eyes—who had flattened themselves against a stone wall to avoid being run down by the coach on the narrow country lane.

Alasdair was about to call a caution to his driver, when Quince forestalled him by immediately pounding on the roof. "Stop the coach!"

"What is wrong? Do you know those people?"

"Nay. Of course something is wrong," she contradicted herself. But she was already halfway out the door, clambering down into the lane, and heading back down the road toward the uneasy group before the coach had come to a complete stop.

"Quince!" He tried to call her back.

"In a minute." She didn't turn, but brusquely waved him off while she approached what he could now see was a family group, with a mother gathering her younger children to her skirts, and a father moving rather more bellicosely in front of the whole pack of ten or so.

"Quince." He followed at a slower pace, trying to put caution into his voice, to warn her to be wary, but Alasdair would certainly not stand back and watch—whatever it was he was watching—without being ready to take action.

But Quince ignored his call, paying neither Alasdair, nor the father of the group any mind, and instead went right to the woman, speaking to her in an earnest tone too low for Alasdair to hear.

Alasdair lengthened his stride.

"The Reverend Talent," she was saying. "West Kirk, also known as Saint Cuthbert's."

Alasdair stopped dead in the middle of the lane, as if his feet refused to take him any nearer the hated name. The damn vicar again. What was the clergyman to his wife? He kept cropping up at the most damnably inconvenient moments.

"On the west side of the city. Take this"—Quince passed something to the woman—"and tell him I sent you. No, don't tell him that." She contradicted herself again. "Say nothing of me. But go to him. Have you got that?"

The man and woman exchanged a look. "Aye," answered the woman. "*Thoir mo shoraidh le dùrachd.*"

It had been many, many years since Alasdair had heard the Gaelic tongue spoken, and he had spent a great deal of the intervening years speaking French, so he had little understanding of what words were exchanged between the peasant woman and his wife, only that it sounded vaguely like a blessing.

"It is the least I can do." Quince nodded briskly. "*Soraidh.* Farewell to you all."

They all—the travelers as well as he—watched her return to him. "I didn't know you spoke the Gaelic. What was that all about?"

"I gave them direction to a friend." Her sharp shrug told him she wasn't going to say more—she was too angry.

Alasdair felt his own confused ire rise in response. "Friend?" The image of the vicar rose like a ghost before his mind's eye. "The Reverend Talent is your friend?"

She shook her head. "Nay. But more importantly, he will be a friend to them."

The sour twist in his gut surprised him. He hadn't thought himself capable of such rampant, sustained jealousy. But jealous he was. "Why are they any concern of his? Or yours?"

"Whose concern should it be?" Quince had been striding purposefully for the carriage, as if getting there and getting underway might forestall the argument she felt bound and determined to start. But clearly she had changed her mind—she rounded on him, hands on hips. "You saw them, Strathcairn. Clearly they are dispossessed, and poorer and needier than church mice. Did you not see the pinched look on that woman's face?"

He had, but then again, he had seen thousands like her—in Edinburgh, London, and Paris. "Aye. But what—"

"Then you could see that she's been going without, to make sure her children and family have more. She's starving herself to feed them." Quince leveled the pointed blade of her gaze at him. "When was the last time you were fed, Strathcairn?" Her tone was rife with reproach.

"You know it was this morning. And what the devil has this got to do with me?" And where in the hell had this come from—this crusading creature all concerned with the poor, when not a day ago she had been a heedless, larcenous flibbertigibbet, bound on doing nothing but causing trouble?

"They came from Cairn land." She threw the words at him like an accusation—an opposition M.P. could not have addressed him with more disdain.

"Yes?" He looked at their retreating backs—the family were not anyone he recognized, but he had not lived at Cairn in many years. "There are many families on Cairn land and—"

"But not so many as before."

"Nay. Not so many as before," he agreed cautiously. "My grandfather did start to resettle people. It's been a terrible problem with the land being too hardscabble to support—"

"And so you've just thrown them out. With nowhere to go. Evicted and *starving!*"

He was buffeted back by the force of her anger and conviction—all that passion aroused against him, the man who had just rearranged the whole of his bloody life to save her. The thought made him want to get in the carriage, slam the door in her ungrateful face, and leave her misguided, ill-informed arse in the middle of the lane to find her own damn way home.

But chances were she would not find her way home, and then where would they both be? Chasing each other down the highway with flintlocks.

It was not, as she had so accurately predicted, a pretty picture.

So he took a deep breath, summoned all the rhetorical logic and political acumen he had spent the last five years acquiring, and tried like the devil not to shout. "Firstly, we are not yet on Cairn land, and if it is true that those people came from there, I cannot believe they would be starving. And secondly, while it did become necessary for my grandfather to move tenants off unprofitable crofts, he evicted no one. And neither have I. We are offering new jobs in carding mills we are building, or offering to buy out their leases and not simply end them, which is more than fair, and more than any other landlord that I know of has done, and damn expensive. So don't you dare accuse me of things which are not true and you don't know a damn thing about."

His voice, now that he was through, had clearly risen enough to still be echoing through the trees.

But Quince was not intimidated in the least—she advanced upon him, one small insistent step at a time. "But you are part of the government which says that it is perfectly legal, and perfectly sound policy to move the people off their land."

"It's not their land, Quince. And it's not that simple."

She turned away. "Feeding people should be simple, if

you ask me, which you don't because—"

"Which I don't, because I do not want to lose the last shred of my temper while arguing with my wife in the middle of a back country lane." He moved to hold the door open for her. "Let us please return to our journey."

She was not in the least bit amenable. "I'm not sure I want to make it."

The words were a slap in the face, hard and stinging. So he swung back, pointing his own finger at her face. "You, my Lady Cairn, have no choice."

He did not say he would toss her over her shoulder and carry her all the way to Cairn like a sack of grain, because he was not an idiot. Or a savage. He was Carin, and he was a gentleman. So he would damn well act like one.

He modulated his tone through sheer will alone. "I would be happy to discuss the merits of clearing agricultural land for pasturage, and entertain any real solutions to this terrible problem that you might like to put forth, at some other time, after I had had a chance to see for myself what changes my grandfather and his factors have wrought at Cairn. But I would bid you to please not accuse me of things without foundation or fact."

She crossed her arms over her chest, still mutinous. "It is a fact that they have been made to move."

"It is a conjecture until we can discover the facts at Cairn. Only then will I be happy to entertain whatever solutions you may have to propose—*if* you have anything to propose. But in the meantime, I would ask you to get into the damned coach."

He only just managed not to shout the last. But she got into the damned coach, and the journey recommenced in utter silence, save for the continuous grind of the wheels, and the rhythmic stamp of the horses' hooves against the grit of the road.

But not even the interval of some five and forty minutes could soften his young wife's indignance. She seated herself as far away from him as possible, in the backward facing seat, and hugged her arms around her as if she were trying to hold herself together. And she was eyeing him with disfavor.

Alasdair was conscious of neither provoking, nor being provoked into, an argument.

But Quince was of a more bellicose frame of mind. "All right." She put up her chin. "Go ahead."

"I beg your pardon?" He would make her work for her snit. "I have not the pleasure of understanding you, Lady Cairn."

"You've been *admirably* silent since this whole farce began." Her sarcasm was as sharp as ever. "But I can practically see the questions eating at your brain like a maggot. Have at it."

Alasdair managed to keep his temper by retaliating in kind. "By this farce, do you mean your flight into highway robbery, or our resulting marriage?"

She tipped that chin up in challenge. "Both."

"All right then, if you insist." He uncrossed his feet, and sat up. "I do have a question—why? Why did you take my buttons, and all those other things? Why did you rob Sir Harry Digby? And why in hell did you rob my coach?" It *had* been burning a hole through his brain, trying to understand what would drive a lass to such a dangerous, heedless act.

Her answer was immediate. "To get money."

It was an answer designed to say both as much, and as little, as possible. And for some reason that Alasdair could not yet put his finger upon, it did not ring true. "That is ridiculous, Quince. Your father is not rich, but he is a gentleman, and you've a sizable enough fortune."

The narrow-eyed look she sent him was so disdainful, it was scathing. "Looked into it, did you, before we eloped in this romantic fashion?"

"Eloped?" He hoped he gave her back an even more venomous dose of sarcasm. "An elopement is predicated upon a great deal more enthusiasm than you have brought to the current proceeding."

"I'm as enthusiastic as I can be with an arm torn up by a

ball, and a husband who does not trust me."

The accusation was another slap—another blow to his good intentions—however true. "I trusted you enough to marry you."

She scoffed. "You should not have done. I warned you, Strathcairn. I'm not good. I'm not nice, or obedient, or ladylike—I never have been. It's your fault if you ever believed I might be."

"Aye. I can see that now." He did himself the favor of looking out the window into the dappled shade of the forest, in order to draw an even breath into his lungs. She *had* told him she wasn't good within moments of their meeting, and he had the proof in her nearly suicidal, heedless behavior. So why did he continue to persist in his belief—his hope—that she was, under all that nerve and cheek, something better than she appeared, when the truth was that not only wasn't she good, she was barely even *good enough?*

"I'll try to remember," he said, more for his own benefit than hers. But she was very, very clever, and very good at turning conversations. "You've done it again. You've managed not to answer my question."

She looked out the window herself. "What a dog with a bone you are, Strathcairn."

He would not rise to the bait of her derision. "Considering you're the bone..." He answered with as much cynical amusement as he judged prudent, before leaned back in his seat, and crossed his arms over his chest. "Back to the question at hand—why would you steal for money when you have plenty?"

"I don't have plenty. You of all people should ken that my fortune, as you call it, goes to my husband, not to me. It's not as if I've been able to draw off the interest on the money my father set aside for my portion, to spend as I will. No, my fortune has nothing to do with this."

It was a surprisingly heartfelt diatribe. So heartfelt that he asked himself to accept it as truth. For the time being. "So what do you need the money for? Debts? Cards—

though I've never seen you gamble?"

"That's because I'm not allowed." She looked out the window briefly, as if she had not yet decided how much she would tell him, or how much fuel she wanted to pour on the bonfire of her anger. "I've long been forbidden the pleasure of card games, because early on I figured out how to cheat, and cheat well. And both my mother's and father's friends objected to being summarily fleeced by a lass still in the schoolroom, so my parents forbid all card games."

"Ah." A pity he had never played against her. A pity, and a very good thing, seeing as his grandfather had taught him all the dirty card tricks in the book so he could defend himself against cheats. What interesting card games he and his wife might have against each other. "So you found your thrill elsewhere."

She met his eye only briefly. "I did, as you so sagely discovered that night that now seems so long ago."

It seemed a lifetime ago. "And so instead of cheating at cards, you decided to steal."

"Aye, I did," she admitted without qualm. "I liked it, so I became very good at it. I stole all the items you were searching for in Edinburgh—the snuffboxes, vinaigrettes, card cases, lorgnettes, as well as your buttons. Three years' worth. It was all me."

The heady rush of vindication was tempered by the knowledge that she had so clearly, and so thoroughly, and so often, lied to him. "How?" was all he could manage at first. "How did you take my buttons?"

"Cut them right off your coat, with you none the wiser." She didn't try to hide her pride—he could hear it as loudly and clearly as a clanging gong.

"Were you deliberately trying to embarrass me? Or get my attention?"

His question surprised her—she frowned as if it had never occurred to her, and immediately shook her head. "Nay. It had nothing to do with you. Quite the opposite."

"Well, you've got my attention now, haven't you?"

And neither of them were pleased about it, were they?

Chapter 21

QUINCE SAVED HER breath to cool her porridge after that remarkably combative conversation. But it taught her that there would be no blank slate, with all her past deeds erased. There would be no forgive and forget. Strathcairn clearly meant to remember every one of her misdeeds, as if there were a tally sheet in his clever, ginger head.

And so she would give herself the small revenge of not telling him all. He may have married her to keep them both from scandal, but he had not married Jeannie or Charlie. She would be mad to confess anything about them.

And luckily, Strathcairn let go of his bone of contention, turning his attention to the countryside. The coach was rolling out of a wood and into the bright, crystalline sunshine of a wide valley, and all seemed instantly forgotten—Strathcairn's whole attitude changed dramatically. He sat up from his ease against the padded seat, and leaned forward toward the window, all avid eagerness, almost as if he were scenting the air. "This is the strath."

There was an intriguing reverence in his voice, as well as a hint of excitement.

"*The* strath?" she asked.

"A strath is a wide u-shaped valley," he explained, never once taking his eyes from the green and gold patchwork of fields. "While a glen is a narrow v-shaped valley. All of our place-names are determined by geography. How do you not know that, and call yourself Scots?"

"I ken enough," she humphed. "I ken a cairn is a heap of rocks. So Strathcairn is a heap of rocks in the middle of the valley. How fitting for you, Lord Cairn. The rock is granite, clearly."

His smile was all in the corners of his clear green eyes. "That warms the cockles of my auld Scot's heart, it does."

He was rather harder to resist when he was all smiling and golden and charming. But her resistance was running high. And she was still herself. "You look like the sort of fellow who would have cockles. You must keep them with your scruples."

"In a jar, by my bed."

A huff of laughter escaped, in spite of herself and her resentment. In fact, they were both smiling now, almost as if they were enjoying each other's company. Almost. There was still a healthy dose of something that had to be distrust—or at least wariness—in his smile. And it wouldn't do for her to repent, and see the error of her thieving ways too soon—where would be the challenge in that?

Quince turned her gaze to the bright summer countryside, where the rolling heather-clad hills were a haze of purple in the sunshine.

"You know," Strathcairn said from somewhere across the carriage. "You could probably like me if you weren't trying so hard not to do otherwise."

"We're already married, Strathcairn. There's no need to—"

"Alasdair," he corrected. "We've been married for two days now. You really ought to give my actual name a try."

She would do nothing of the kind at the present time.

"—to turn me up sweet."

"I think I had best do," he mused. "Arguing didn't help, so I think I ought to give turning up sweet at least a try."

She said nothing to that particular piece of provocation, because they were rolling up and over a charming little stone bridge, and entering through the turreted stone gates of an estate. And Strathcairn went still with pleasure.

"We're here."

Quince was torn between looking at the scenery of this place she had so long imagined, or looking at the remarkable sight of Strathcairn looking eager—and, dare she say it, boyish—as he put the window down and leaned nearly all the way out. He was as close to avid as she had ever seen him.

There was no carefully curated veneer to him now. This was the man in full—eager, engaged and ready for every challenge. And entirely, whole-heartedly happy.

The coach ground to a stop in the large gravel forecourt, and Strathcairn flung open the door and bounded down without waiting for assistance. "We are home."

"My Lord Cairn." A retainer liveried in plaid came forward from the ranks of servants mustered in front of a massive stone building that seemed to rise straight up into the air like a monolith. "Welcome home."

Behind him, Castle Cairn stood six stories high, softened here and there by the reflection from the odd window, like the glint in a giant's eye.

How apt a place for her husband—the man who was Cairn.

"Thank you, McNab." Strathcairn—Cairn—Alasdair—grasped the man's hand. "Let me present to you your new Marchioness." He turned to her in expectation.

Oh, holy stone castles. He was talking about her.

Quince scrambled out of the carriage and took the hand Strathcairn had politely extended, and immediately wished that she had taken greater care of her appearance this morning—at least enough to look more like a marchioness, and less like a gammy injured highwayman and thief who had married their laird under dicey circumstances.

But if the servants were shocked by her bandaged arm, and frankly rather shabby appearance without Plum to keep her from fashion ignominy, they hid it marvelously well. In fact, most were smiling as if she were not some scaffy, larcenous unknown, but a local favorite.

It almost made her want to be good, and worthy of their trust.

"My Lady Cairn, this is McNab, Steward of Castle Cairn."

The weathered-looking gentleman in tartan trews bowed deeply before her. "Welcome to Castle Cairn, my leddy."

"Thank you, sir." Quince tried to surreptitiously shake a crease out of her skirt.

"Just McNab, my leddy." The steward corrected her with a deferential bow.

"Oh, aye." What a splendidly medieval beginning. Quince didn't know which would take more getting used to—her to them, or them to her. "I thank you."

But Strathcairn— No, Cairn—it was time she thought of him as Cairn, and as her husband. Her husband, Lord Cairn, was already leading her across the gravel forecourt to a plump, spry woman with a ring of ancient keys clasped on her belt, and a beacon of a smile lighting up her mouth. "Castle Cairn's housekeeper, Mrs. Broom. My Marchioness, Quince, Lady Cairn."

"My leddy." The housekeeper sank into a deeply reverential curtsey, but seemed to be immediately lifted up by the natural buoyancy of her smile. "We're that pleased tae welcome ye to Cairn. It's sech a pleasure tae have wee Lord Alasdair—I beg yer pardon, yer lordship. It's sech a pleasure tae no' only have Lord Cairn come back tae us, but fra' him tae gee us a new mistress as weel."

Oh, this was better. Far less medieval, and a great deal little less feudally deferential. "Mrs. Broom." Quince returned her inviting smile. "Wee Lord Alasdair, was he?"

"Aye, he was a grand wee rascal, our laird was as a lad." She turned the warm ray of her smile upon him. "Just like his grandfather, God rest him. Loved tae roar with laughter all the day long with the wee lad. We could do with a bit of laughter here. But now ye've come back, and all will be sunshine and heather."

"Just so." Quince was delighted by Mrs. Broom's marvelous ability to make a blushing tinge of red creep over her new husband's shirt collar. "Sunshine and heather," she informed him.

Her husband pretended he heard nothing of irony in her tone. "You have your marching orders, Lady Cairn."

"Me? I rather think it's you, wee, scrupulous, staid Lord Alasdair, who have been given yours."

That hit of riddy color spilled nicely across his cheeks. It was marvelous to know he was not so stony and immune as he wanted her to think. "So I have. Let us show you into the house."

"Strathcairn." She could not seem to break herself of the pleasantly irreverent habit of calling him by his lesser title. But he did not seem to object, even in front of his people, so she gifted him with amusement. "This"—she gestured theatrically to the battlements rising several hundred feet above them—"can in no way be accurately described as a mere house."

He laughed. "Welcome to Cairn Castle, my dear. And welcome home."

My dear? She knew the endearment was only for the onlookers—a piece of domestic theater—but something warm and treacherous fluttered around in her belly, like moths drawn to the lethal warmth of his light.

Hope. That was what it was. Hope that perhaps, just this once, she might not be as bad as she pretended, or as bad as she had worked to become. Hope that maybe, just maybe, they might learn to rub along together just fine.

Her husband was every bit the gentlemanly bridegroom as he led her along the ranks of smiling, curtseying, bowing servants, whose names and faces she was trying to imprint upon her brain.

Until she came to the last, who stood between her and

the wide oak door. Whose face was already imprinted upon her brain—the African gentleman.

Oh, holy stony silence. The very man whose purse had precipitated *everything,* was standing on the doorstep of her new home looking as severe and unsmiling as a hanging judge.

Heat and humiliation replaced the hope, scorching up her neck and across her face. There would definitely be no forgetting, no blank slate—if ever Alasdair was tempted to forget her sins, this man would remember and remind him. In fact, she would lay odds that every servant in the place, every last gardener, gamekeeper and shepherd high on the dotted hills would know her secrets and sins within the week. Perhaps they already did. Perhaps that was the reason for the smiles.

The scorch of embarrassment cooled into a chill that crept down her spine. She could lie, of course, just as she had always done, staying one step ahead of the innuendo with her own campaign of misdirection. But that would never work with Strathcairn and his scruples and abhorrence of deception.

There was really nothing for it but to put up her chin and endure the humiliation. And what could not be avoided must be tackled straightaway. And there was no avoiding the man—Strathcairn's hand was at the small of her back, propelling her forward on legs that had gone treacherously shaky.

"My lady." The African gentleman made a stately, but shallow declination of his head, but his eyes were everything narrow and knowing, as if he didn't like what he saw, and he didn't care who knew it. "We meet again."

She knew that controlled, lawyer-like voice—he had been in the house with Strathcairn the night he had been accused of being the highwayman himself. No wonder he looked resentful. But he wasn't the only one who could nurse resentment.

Endurance be damned. Since there was nothing she could say with Strathcairn by her side, letting the man humiliate her, saying nothing in her defense, she said nothing. And walked on, into the castle.

"Quince?" The caution in Strathcairn's voice did not stop her, but in another moment, his ridiculously unfailing grip upon her wrist did. "Lady Cairn." His voice had already become several degrees chillier. "What do you think you are doing?"

They were alone in the cavernous entry, with a dark carved staircase rising like scaffolding above their heads.

She rounded her hand from his grasp, and asked a question of her own. "Who is that African mon?"

Strathcairn did not have to ask to whom she referred. "I assume you mean my secretary, Mr. Sebastian Oistins."

His secretary—a man permanently in his employ. A man who would permanently be part of *her* new life. But Strathcairn's use of the man's first name hinted at something beyond a disinterested business arrangement. This man—this man with whom he had obviously conspired to entrap her, this man who had witnessed Strathcairn shooting her—was his friend.

And Strathcairn was acting as such. "For your ignorant information, he is not African, but West Indian. And I will not stand idly by and see him suffer from such atrocious behavior. I expected better from you, of all people."

"Atrocious?" He was talking about her—her behavior? Oh, holy stone deaf statues. "If you expected me to submit meekly to this humiliation, my lord, then you have misjudged my character."

"Your character, Lady Cairn, is exactly what needs reforming." His voice was growing louder with every word, working up to a growling roar. "And that reformation will begin now, this instant, when you will turn around and go back outside and speak to Mr. Oistins in a civil voice, with every ounce of courtesy you possess, regardless of your prejudices against the color of his skin. You will behave in a manner worthy of the House of Cairn. Do you understand me, my lady?"

"What?" Quince stepped back. She did not understand

him, and clearly he did not understand her. "Nay—"

"Yes!" Strathcairn's ire echoed up the stair hall like thunder. "Understand this, my lady. Sebastian is not only under my patronage, and my protection, he is my friend. And I will not have him insulted by you or anyone, especially not by my wife. Not in my house. Not in the house I have offered him as his own. Not in the house I have offered *you*." Strathcairn practically hurled the words at her. "You're all for charity and the relief of the poor, all for beneficence, but only for those who look and speak exactly like you, is that it?"

He flung his hat across the foyer, as if he wished he could dispose of her as forcefully and easily. "Let me be very clear. I am an abolitionist, as are all the members of Mr. Pitt's cabinet. I may not be one of the orators whose speeches are copied and sold in copperplate pamphlets, but that cause is as near and dear to me as Cairn itself. It is a part of who I am, and what I have accomplished, and I will not stand by and let a spoiled lass with too great an opinion of herself, and too small an opinion of others, get in my way. Do I make myself very clear?"

"Eminently." Quince swallowed the lump of her pride. He thought she objected to Mr. Oistins simply because of the dark color of his skin, and not because he could stand in judgment of her past misdeeds. "But—"

"Do I make myself clear?" he roared.

Quince jumped at the force of his anger. "Aye." It was impossible not to be intimidated by him. Impossible not to be utterly humiliated by his assessment of her character.

"I'm disappointed in you, Lady Cairn." He straightened the fall of his immaculate coat. "Now, I'm going out to speak to my friend, and I will expect that by the time I have returned, you and your obnoxious opinions will have vacated my front hall. Do you understand?"

"Aye, but—"

He was through listening to her—or not listening to her, as it appeared. He had already turned on his heel, and left her standing in the hall alone, with a small army of servants nearby, pretending they had not heard every single word.

It was all suddenly too much—the failure and humiliation and marriage and pain. The ubiquitous ache she had held at bay in the excitement and hope of their arrival had returned with a vengeance. A vengeance named Strathcairn.

Every muscle and sinew shook from the strain. And the hot press of tears she had staved off with cheek and bravado and laudanum could no longer be stopped. Stinging heat spilled from her eyes, and trailed salty tracks down her cheeks. She squeezed her eyes shut to block it all out—the ignominy and humiliation, the eyes of the secretary, the ears of the servants, and the words of condemnation from her husband.

There was no blank slate.

But she would recover. She always did. But not now. Not now, when she could barely think for all the pain.

"There now, my leddy." Mrs Broom appeared from somewhere to put a gentle hand to her shoulder. "Ye must be fair done in frae yer journey. There, there, poor lamb."

Quince had never, not once in all her life been called any such pitiful, docile thing as a lamb. She swiped at her itchy eyes with her bandaged arm, and tried to salvage her pride. "I'm not delicate, Mrs. Broom. I'm only in pain." She swallowed and sniffed, and got her chin up, even if it did wobble. "You see his lordship shot me the day before yesterday." She took some savage satisfaction in saying it. "So I will admit to being rather done in as a result."

"Oh, gracious me! Sech a thing." The woman's face was creased with shocked sympathy. "We'll get ye up right away. Ye just lean your wee self against me, and let Mrs. Broom put it all tae rights."

If only. But Quince did lean against her, and let the housekeeper lead her upward, deep into the gray pile of stone, even if she had no confidence that her life could ever be restored to rights.

Chapter 22

EVERY TIME HE thought he had reached an accord with her—every time he thought they had come to a place where they might finally agree and settle into something more than intermittent sniping—Quince showed her true colors. And Alasdair was left wondering at the enormity of the mistake he had made.

He had been so sure. So sure that she was more than the shallow, heedless, larcenous, feckless flibbertigibbet she took such pains to appear to be. But clearly he had been wrong.

Alasdair strode up the stairs and into his private chamber, flinging off his gloves along with his foul mood. But the gloves landed on the floor—the chamber was bare.

"If I may, your lordship?" McNab hovered at the door. "I've taken the liberty of having your belongings moved to the laird's suite of rooms, sir."

The laird's suite was a grand sounding, but rather drafty set of ancient rooms in the older part of the castle. They were spacious and well appointed, but lacked some of the refinements the rooms in the later, more up-to-date parts of the buildings possessed.

But he was laird now—he was Cairn. If he insisted upon keeping his old rooms, where he had been happy and comfortable, it might be seen as some sort of an omen of lack of enthusiasm and commitment to Cairn. It was bad enough he had brought them a new, untried, unwilling, and very likely unworthy marchioness—he couldn't act like an unwilling marquess himself.

Mrs. Broom bustled past him with a steaming tray, headed down the corridor toward the newer wing. She bobbed him the shallowest of curtseys—so shallow her miff was palpable. "Very newly wed, are ye, my lord?"

"Aye, Mrs. Broom." The housekeeper's long tenure at Cairn—she had started as a housemaid the year his grandfather had come into the marquessate—had earned her the privilege of familiarity. "Only Tuesday last."

"Two days." She made a brusque sound of disapproval. "And was that afore, or after ye shot the poor lassie?"

Of course. Of course, the moment his back was turned, Quince would have been busy selling her particular brand of woe. "After. But no matter what my wife says, her injury was an accident, Mrs. Broom. An unfortunate accident."

"Most unfortunate," the housekeeper agreed. "Fair ript up she is. Lucky ye didn't take the arm off." Her round face was as puckered as a lemon. "If I may be so bold, sir?"

As if he might stop her. "In the twenty-six odd years I've known you, Mrs. Broom, when have you not?"

She pulled herself up to her full height of five feet. "I might caution ye, not only tae greater delicacy with a new young wife, but tae better aim."

Her salvo fired, Mrs. Broom sailed off down the corridor, leaving him in a sea of recrimination and regret. But it was not a sea he intended to swim in overlong—*he* was not the one in the wrong.

Alasdair found the door to the laird's chamber, a cavernous, circular room within the stone walls of the old turret tower.

He had not entered the room in a very long time. It had

been his grandfather's, and still seemed filled with reminders of the old gentleman's likes and dislikes—the big carved Tudor bed was hung with tartan, glass-fronted cabinets were full of oft-read books, and before the massive fireplace was a single, worn leather chair.

But when he stood in the middle of the room, Alasdair did not hear the ghost of his grandfather teaching him how to tie a proper feathered fly-fishing lure, or showing him the outlines of the Labrador coast in his atlas. What he heard was Mrs. Broom as clear as a mountain burn, chivvying her charge. "Now ye drink that down, my leddy, and rest, and get yerself better."

"I warn you, I don't like laudanum, or opium, Mrs. Broom."

"Och, we've none o' that here. Ye just gie that a try."

"You are a treasure, Mrs. Broom," said his young wife, sounding sweet and kind and everything biddable. "Whatever Cairn is paying you cannot possibly be enough. Ooh"—Quince made a near erotic sound of pleasure as she took a sip of something—"Holy painted castles, that's full marvelous."

Alasdair felt his body go instantly hard. There was no chance in the world that he could maintain his resentment in the face of such provocation.

"Go way wit' ye, and drink that doon." He could hear the pleased smile in the housekeeper's voice. "I'll come and check on ye myself, but we'll see to gettin' ye a lass of your own, as soon as ye feel up tae it."

"Thank you, Mrs. Broom. You are a wonder."

"That's all right, lamb. Get a good rest."

"Thank you, I will."

A lamb, his young wife was not. And she could rest after he had had his say.

As soon as the door to the hallway had closed behind Mrs. Broom, Alasdair strode through the connecting door from his chamber to find Quince with her eyes closed, propped up against a mountain of pillows like a doll beneath the massive, embroidered canopy.

But he could tell by her breathing that she was awake. "Would you mind very much not bribing my servants on your very first day here?"

She didn't even open her eyes. "Charity begins at home, Strathcairn."

Alasdair, he wanted to shout. But he had shouted at her not so very many minutes ago. And that had got him exactly nowhere.

He strove to keep his voice at an even volume. "So it does. And there is charity of the spirit, as well as of the purse. So I might also ask if you would please refrain from constantly advertising my mistake to all and sundry."

"Which mistake? The one I made in entering a life of crime? Or the one I made in thinking to steal from you, not once but twice? Or the mistake where you shot me? Or the one I made in entering a marriage with a mon who is never going to let me forget my mistakes? There seem to be many mistakes and regrets to choose from."

She had not committed mere mistakes—she had committed crimes. But with Quince, he decided it was best to deal with only one problem at a time. "Do you mean to tell everyone in the highlands that I shot you?"

Her mouth tipped up into a smile full of private amusement. And naturally, she only answered part of his question. "Not everyone. Only sympathetic types like your Mrs. Broom." She took another indelicate, slurping sip of her tea. "But the question, if you ask me, which you don't, but which I will ask anyway, is if you mean to let your Mr. Oistins tell everyone in the highlands that your new Marchioness of Cairn is a robber and a thief?" She held up a finger to correct herself. "Former robber and former thief."

He was very glad to hear her say "former"—her words were at least a statement of some intent to reform. "But what on earth makes you think that Sebastian would ever do such a thing? Have you just assumed he will because of—"

"His eyes," she said cryptically. "What is to keep him from laying information against me?"

"He is part of us, of Cairn." To Alasdair the answer was

obvious. "By your illogical way of thinking, what is to keep me from doing the same?"

But far from reassuring her, his answer had the opposite effect—her eyes opened wide, even as the rest of her went still.

"Oh, holy painted trollops. I am so stupid." Her eyes grew bright and shiny, and she passed a hand over her face to hide her welling tears. "I thought you wanted me because you liked me, despite yourself. But you don't really. You don't want me—the real me—at all, do you? You only want to stop me, to make sure that I couldn't possibly keep going, or thwart your plans, or embarrass you."

"Aye. To some degree," he agreed. "Surely you understood that you couldn't possibly go on?"

"I suppose I did understand that. But I thought it was a decision I had made. But it wasn't, was it? It was a choice you made for me." She turned away, nearly upsetting the teacup. Which spurred him closer to the bed to whisk away the cup before it was spilled across the counterpane.

But immediately he did so, Alasdair detected the pungent bouquet of strong whisky. "Have you been drinking?"

"I've been drinking tea," she sniffed. "Or rather a tisane of Mrs. Broom's own devising, she said."

Alasdair held the delicate bone-china cup up to his nose. "Tis straight Scotch whisky, lass. Which goes a long way toward explaining the tears."

"I am not crying. Though it does explain why the tea is rather peaty."

"You're drunk, lass, and only feeling sorry for yourself."

"I am very sorry. I don't like being drunk."

"I have a feeling you'll get used to it." He'd have to speak to Mrs. Broom about her concoctions. "But you'll see." He went back to the reason for her tears. "You'll see it's all for the best, no matter which of us—or both of us—made the choice. It was the right one."

She did not answer in words, but in a deep resigned sigh that reminded him that she was, in fact, still recovering from her injury, and that she had every right to be exhausted.

"The journey has worn you out." But even exhaustion looked good on her. It made her softer, pulled down her guard, and made her more approachable. More vulnerable, more human.

"Everything has worn me out." Another weary sigh. She turned her head on the pillow to regard him, and her hair fanned out behind her, and her sleeping gown slipped off her shoulder to reveal the tops of her enticingly soft-looking breasts. "My arm aches. Mrs. Broom says I need to rest. But they say a change is as good as a rest. And this certainly is a change."

"A change for the good." He had so many hopes. So many wishes for the two of them together—to work together for Cairn. To find something of fellow feeling along with the all-consuming attraction. To act on that damnable powerful attraction that had him reaching for her even now.

"The good." She made a wry face, and rearranged the bedcovers to cover those magnificent little breasts. "But I am not good, though for the record, I should like the chance to acquit myself of your charge against me."

"Which one? There are so many to choose from," he teased, not unkindly. "The one where you stole from half of Edinburgh?"

"Only the rich half."

"The one where you robbed Sir Harry Digby at gunpoint?"

"They weren't loaded. And they were your guns."

Alasdair rolled his eyes to the ceiling, and suppressed his groan. Of course she was telling him now, when it was all but impossible to remonstrate with her. He would have to take the issue of his missing pistols up with her at some later point. "Or the one you made in trying to rob me?"

"The one where I was so shallow that I judged your secretary upon the color of his skin alone."

Well, damn his eyes, but these Winthrop women certainly were direct. Points to her for not evading the subject, but this sin would be much harder to explain, much less forgive. "And?"

"Does it not occur to you, Strathcairn, that I might not want the worst part of my character known to all and sundry? That I might be afraid of a mon whose very presence and every look is a rebuke?"

"Afraid of Sebastian? No," he admitted. "It never occurred to me." It was something he had both admired and despaired of in her, her seeming lack of fear. "Are you sure? Are you sure your prejudice has not colored your thinking?"

"It is not his skin but his knowledge that frightens me," she clarified while her fingers plucked in nervousness at the counterpane.

He covered her cold fingers with his own. "Quince, I have that same knowledge, and you aren't afraid of me."

"Of course I am. Your knowledge frightens me, too. More. If I make another mistake—which I inevitably will—when I displease you, I will be entirely at your mercy."

"I have promised you already that I will not."

"But you can't make that promise for him."

He did her the honor of not lying. "No, I cannot. But I can tell you that I know his character and scruples as well as I know my own. And I think that perhaps it is not him, but yourself that you fear. I think the rebuke you heard in his voice or saw in his eye is no more than your own guilty conscience—your own long lost scruples—coming to claim you."

She let out a wee huff of something that wasn't quite laughter. But she did not let go of his hand. "Don't you dare accuse me of having scruples."

"It's all right," he assured her. "I won't tell anyone." He leaned over and kissed her whisky-wetted lips. "I promise."

She shifted toward him, and treated his over-weary eyes to the sight of her magnificent little breasts straining the fabric of his imagination. Even lying in bed, worn out and pale, she managed to be remarkably attractive. He would feel his steadfast resentments giving way to her dark fairy allure. And when she was like this—soft and warm and leaning into him—every fiber of his being, especially the less gentlemanly fibers, were drawn to her, as if she were a lodestone. His arms were already sliding around her warm, pliant back.

She sighed against his chest, and curled a hand into his lapel. "I suppose I should account myself lucky that it was you who apprehended me, or I might have fared much, much worse."

"I suppose." It had been his recurring nightmare the past two evenings—over and over in his dreams, he leveled his gun at her. "They might have been better shots." *He* might have been a better shot if he had been deliberately trying to injure her. Another inch or two lower, and he might have taken off her arm.

Alasdair ran a hand through his hair, as if he could hold on to whatever sense remained within his brain, and keep her from making him mad. "Of all the hare-brained ideas— highway robbery."

"Highway robbery was a perfectly serviceable idea," she countered, dropping her hand, "only made hare-brained by my stupid unwillingness to shoot you."

"And your inability to load a gun."

"Unwillingness, Strathcairn. I chose, just as you are so fond of making me do. Don't ever confuse a choice with inability."

In moments like these, when she spoke with such authority and an experience far beyond her nineteen years, she was stunning—she had stunned him. And he didn't much like it. "What am I to do with you, wee Quince?"

He wanted her to say, *why you're to kiss me, of course.* But she did not. She retreated into the bed linens. "I'm not wee. Stop saying that. It's as if you're trying to make me feel small, or dismiss me. And I won't have it." She turned her face into the pillows, but he could see the sheen of unspilled tears glossing her eyes.

"Lass, you're so damn over-sized, I'm only trying to cut you down to a manageable size."

"That's the problem for you, Strathcairn. I'm not in the least about to be managed."

AND TO PROVE it, she stayed in bed. She stayed in bed and slept so long, Alasdair began to think she might never wake up.

Every time he slipped into her rooms to check on her, he found her asleep. Or maids with their fingers to their lips, drawing the curtains. Or Mrs. Broom closing the door behind her, carrying medicines and tempting cups of broth that seemed to be returned cold and untouched. Or even McNab, damn his hoary old hide, tiptoeing about with a spray of heather in a vase, "To cheer the wee lassie up."

After three days, Alasdair's curiosity, not to mention his conscience, got the better of him.

"Ought we to send for a doctor?" he asked Mrs. Broom, when he ran his housekeeper to ground in her small parlor off the kitchens. "Is she really that ill? Has she taken a turn for the worse, and her wound suppurated?"

"Now, now, my lord. No need tae borrow trouble. She's as fine as can be. The arm seems tae be healing, but…" Mrs. Broom began to look a bit pinched between her brows, as if she were more worried than she let on. "I'm sure a good rest is what'll cure her."

"But..?"

"Oh, yer lordship. I dunno." Mrs. Broom pursed her lips. "Nothin' I've tried seems tae tempt her. 'I'm no' hungry,' she says, and then rolls right over and goes back tae sleep. I ken her body needs tae heal, but…"

"Have we any iced macaroons, Mrs. Broom?"

"Iced…?"

"Macaroons."

His housekeeper gaped at him. "No, yer lordship. I'm fashed to tell ye so, but we've no pastry chef here at Cairn as you mun had in London. But I'll try and find a receipt for cook, if it please ye."

"It does please me, Mrs. Broom, I thank you. But more

importantly, I believe it will please Lady Cairn."

"Am I tae understand her leddyship has a sweet tooth, my lord?"

"I am not exactly sure, Mrs. Broom, but I aim to find out."

"Oh, aye, I see. Iced macaroons it is then."

"Aye." He patted her shoulder in thanks and encouragement. "And perhaps lemon ice. Or tarts."

"Lemon, sir?"

"Yes, lemon tarts." He racked his brain. "And sticky toffee pudding."

"Oh, aye tae the pudding, my lord. Cook's a fair hand at a pudding. We'll have that tae her leddyship in a trice—for tea time, if ye like?"

"Excellent. I do like, Mrs. Broom. Very much. I thank you." His mission accomplished, Alasdair was better pleased to return to his book room to bury himself in estate work.

"Weel, I ne'er thought I'd see the day." Mrs. Broom let out a gusty sigh.

"Mrs. Broom?" He was almost afraid to ask. "And which day is that?"

"I ne'er thought I'd live to see the day our wee Alasdair was in love." She shook her head ruefully. "I thought they'd succeeded in shamin' the heart out of ye."

Everything within him stilled. And stopped. And started up again in painful cacophony, as if someone had taken a hammer to his ribs—he could barely draw breath.

Alasdair wasn't sure what shamed him more—the thought that he was in love with his magnificently inappropriate wife, or the fact that many of his servants, like Mrs. Broom, and McNab—who had served his grandfather for nigh unto fifty years—still remembered the youthful disgrace that had cost him his grandfather's esteem, and seen him all but banished from Cairn.

It all came back as if it were yesterday, instead of five years ago—his happy stupidity, his grievous error. He certainly could have given wee Quince Winthrop a run for her money in the heedlessness stakes. He had gambled with his allowance, and ridden his horses too fast, and generally been recklessly oblivious to the consequences of his actions. He had been as rash and generous and stupid as wee Quince Winthrop had ever been.

And he had spent the past five years atoning. "It was the rashness they shamed out of me, Mrs. Broom."

She pursed up her lips. "Is that what they called it?"

"I was young, Mrs. Broom. And in the wrong."

"That's not the way I heard it, Lord Alasdair."

It seemed an atrociously bad precedent to set—gossiping with one's housekeeper. He had made his peace with the past, and his part in it. He had atoned, and his grandfather had since passed away, secure in the knowledge that his grandson had become enough of a man to be Marquess of Cairn.

But all of Alasdair's accumulated self-discipline was not equal to resisting the chance to finally find out, "And what was it you heard, Mrs. Broom?"

"That ye helped a wee young leddy out of a sad jam that another young mon had put her in." She dusted her hands of imaginary dirt. "And simply, that ye'd done the right thing, the way a Cairn would, tho the diffy were no on account'a ye."

Diffy. What a charming euphemism for the overwhelming difficulty of the situation he, and the young lady, had been put in.

He had done what he thought was the right thing. But not exactly in the manner Mrs. Broom seemed to have thought. He had only done what needed to be done. "I was not all sainted selflessness, Mrs. Broom."

"Oh, aye, ye were a rascal, you and those bonny lads who were yer true friends, there's na doubt aboot that. But ye didn't have tae gie young Lady Lucy that money, and ye certainly didn't have tae take yer grandfather's blame."

He was as grateful for her honest kindness now as when he had been a lad, and she had tended his scraped elbows and knees. "Thank you, Broomie. But the fact was, I gave Lucy the money to emigrate because I could not make anyone else do the right thing. There was no one left but me to take the blame. And it was all my fault—the man who seduced her was my guest."

"Ye did what another should'a done, and then took the whole of yer grandfather's wrath for yer troubles."

"Just as he'd raised me to do, Mrs. Broom. I am a Strathcairn. I could do no less."

"Weel, ye certainly could do nae more. But ye let his lordship, bless his soul, go frae this world thinkin' ye'd been the one that done her. And that be what ye ne'er shoulda done. Ye shoulda told him the honest truth."

Alasdair shook his head. "He wouldn't have believed me, Broomie."

"Oh, lad. Certainly he would. I did." She laid her hand over her copious bosom. "I ne'er did think it e'er coulda been ye."

It was, if he were honest with himself, an absolution he had waited years to hear. Alasdair had to draw in a deep, steadying breath to combat the vertiginous gratitude that threatened to upend him. He had to act and speak in a manner befitting both his sacrifice, and the grandfather he had made that sacrifice for. "Your faith in me is very much appreciated, Mrs. Broom."

Her pleasure made pink buttons of her cheeks. "I liked it better when ye were calling me Broomie, like the old days. But ye'll soon have bairns running about the place, callin' me that, so I'll be satisfied soon enough. We'll just get your lass well—we'll tempt her with some sticky toffee puddin'—and ye'll be off the races."

Alasdair didn't have the heart to warn her that there might not be any bairns, much less any races. He didn't have the heart to face that particularly hard fact himself, especially since he had not yet reckoned out what sort of race he was going to run with his new bride.

He could not decide if his inability to engage the lass in marital relations was, in truth, unwillingness. If he was using her injury as an excuse to hold his unholy attraction, as well as his distrust, at bay. What he had decided, was that if and when he did give in to the lust that was all but choking him, it wouldn't be before she was good and ready, and all but throwing pebbles at his metaphorical windows to gain his attention.

Until that time, he could have to distract himself with work, and hope that sticky toffee pudding could do his work for him, and get the lass out of her bed. And into his.

Chapter 23

"STRATHCAIRN."

The insistent whisper woke him in the dark. Alasdair opened one eye enough to see by the low light of the fireplace embers that the clock over the mantelpiece read twelve minutes after two o'clock in the morning—not an hour conducive to receiving a visitor. Even if that visitor were one's difficult, reluctant, insistent wife.

"Strathcairn." Under the blanket of the dark the insistent whisperer had come closer—close enough that he felt the warm waft of her breath against his ear.

He pushed himself to his elbows, so she could see his scowl. "Are you ill? What is wrong?"

"Nothing. I couldn't sleep. Are you awake?"

He subsided back against the pillows in relief, and decided to choose the most obvious answer. "Nay."

He could almost hear her answering smile. "Good." Her weight settled onto the middle of the bed. "I want to talk to you."

"Talk to me in the morning."

"Technically, it is morning now." The bed creaked as she

shifted to sit somewhere closer by his legs. "And I can't sleep."

His eyes adjusted enough to the dark to reveal the astonishing sight of his young wife sitting cross-legged and bare-footed on his bed, wearing nothing but her chemise and a large tartan shawl. While the shawl did an obnoxiously thorough job of concealing her torso, the firelight did interesting things to her long unbound hair. And to her long legs. And his prone position also made it possible to see other, interesting things. Things which he knew she did not mean to offer him.

And a gentleman only ever accepted what was offered.

But still, his interest, as well as another, less well-mannered part of his anatomy, was piqued. He sat up. "Ring your maid for some warm milk."

"I don't have a maid, and Mrs. Broom will only try to drown me in one of those gammy concoctions she calls medicine, which seem to be made entirely of whisky, dirt and twigs. And I'm tired of being all ginny. And I'm sure it would be cruel to wake her at this at this hour just to keep me company."

"But it is somehow *not* cruel to wake me?" He shoved a pillow behind his head to prop himself up.

"Don't be silly. Mrs. Broom didn't pledge to love, honor and cherish. I feel quite certain that chats in the middle of the night fall under that particular clause. And I wanted to talk to you."

There was no hope for it. Alasdair leaned his weary skull against the headboard. "And what would you like to chat about at this particular hour?"

"By jimble." Quince crawled over to shove the bed-curtains wider, so the spill of light from the fire warmed the bed. "Strathcairn. Do you always sleep unclothed?"

"Alasdair," he muttered. But his answer at least was simple. "Aye."

"Holy painted tarts." She gaped at his chest for a good long moment.

So long, he crossed his arms across said chest, to show

her that he was a living, breathing man who wasn't to be trifled with in the middle of the night. Not even by his inconvenient, agile, interested little wife.

Who was definitely interested, even if she sat back on her heels. "Do you mean to say that you are entirely naked beneath the bed linens?"

Alasdair stretched his arms over his head with as much nonchalance as he could muster while still flexing a muscle or two. "Aye. I am."

"Entirely?"

"Absolutely entirely." He yawned again for good measure, as if he was so often naked while in the company of attractive young wives he had not yet bedded, that the thought bored him stiff. Which it did, for entirely different reasons. Which he did not tell her. It would do her good to think she had to work to earn her way back into his good graces. Although at two in the morning, his good graces were a great deal more lax and ready to be pleased than they would be in the cold, realistic light of dawn.

There was a pleasurably long silence while his wife contemplated his physique. He also wondered if his observant little wife was going to make note of his rather insistent cockstand.

"How curious," was all she finally said.

Since she didn't seem intent on ravishing him, Alasdair asked, "What was it you wanted, Quince?"

"Oh." She blinked at him, all rumpled bemusement. "I don't remember. I've quite forgot."

He would not be amused by her tame flibbertigibbet act. Nor charmed. He would not. "Then go back to sleep."

"I can't. I think I've slept too much. And I always seem to forget that you're ginger all over." She leaned fractionally closer, as if she wanted a better look.

He debated the wisdom of giving her one. "Aye. All over."

"It rather suits you," she allowed. "Very Scots."

"Thank you. Tis the reason why, when I was young, they called me Sandy."

This elicited a wide, rather wondrous smile. "Did they really? I had no idea."

"There are many things, I'm sure, that you don't know about me."

She rolled onto her stomach next to him on top of the bedclothes, and propped her chin on her hands, all acute attention. "Like what?"

"Like the fact that I don't like to be woken in the middle of the night."

She smiled and crossed her bare feet in the air. "No one likes to be woken in the middle of the night, or otherwise. Too common. Tell me something else."

He liked agile, acrobatic lasses wearing nothing but firelight and tartan. "You really ought to go back to bed. You've been injured. You need rest."

"Injured? You make it sound like the veriest accident, when we both ken different—that it was entirely my fault."

As glad as he was to hear her take responsibility, Alasdair was not about to be backhanded into an argument about the too-recent past. "It was an unfortunate accident," he insisted for what he swore was the last time. "Which is why you should go back to bed."

"Strathcairn, I've rested for days and days, until I'm tired of resting. I'm not going to die just because you put some trifling hole in me. I'm far too stubborn to oblige. And I'm in a bed."

"You're *on* a bed. Which is not yours."

"Hmm." She made a sound that was neither a yes nor a no, and settled herself more comfortably. "I didn't come here to argue with you. I came to thank you. For the pudding." She peeped up at him. "Mrs. Broom said it was all your doing. Though I don't ken if you had any part in it being liberally laced with whisky."

"Was it?" That explained why she was like a kitten in a sunbeam, all sweet animal satisfaction—she was perhaps a wee bit drunk. But even kittens had claws—he would be wise to be wary.

"Oh, aye. I think Mrs. Broom might own shares in a

distillery, the way she promotes the whisky for all available applications. I shouldn't be at all surprised to hear she uses it as a furniture polish."

He couldn't help his laugh. "Actually, I own the distillery. But I'm glad to find her so enthusiastic a patron. And I'm glad you liked it, the pudding."

"I did. So thank you."

"You're welcome. How is your arm?"

"Better." She rolled onto her back, and flexed the limb in question in demonstration. "It is only a wee bit sore and stiff. A bit pinchy, and a little itchy actually. But I suppose that means it's healing."

"Aye." The tartan shawl had become much less effective in shielding her person. Alasdair had to remind himself not to stare. Even if her wee breasts were magnificent. Pert and perfectly rounded. Just the right size for his hand.

He had to clear his throat. "Good. You should be more careful with it. Not take on too much, too soon."

"Not take too much on." She scoffed. "It's not as if I'm going to take to the roads of the Strath, terrorizing the local gentry. Oooh." She narrowed her eyes. "Is that what you're afraid of, that I'll take to the roads?"

"You're not going to take to the roads of the Strath."

"Nay. Certainly not without my mare." She rolled back towards him so he could see her teasing smile. "But if I promise not to take to the highway, do you think you could arrange for Piper to be brought north for me? I forgot to ask for her in all the flurry and haste of our leave-taking."

Something about the fact that she was asking him for something—almost the way a real, normal wife might ask something of her husband—thawed him a little. "Your co-conspirator? Your mare with an appropriately rebellious Scots name."

"Don't jump to unfounded conclusions, Strathcairn."

"Most of my conclusions about you are extraordinarily well-founded," he observed. "Did not the mare aid you in your larcenous endeavors?"

"Aye, she did. And very ably. But she does not have a

Scots name. Like everything else in the Winthrop household she is botanical: *Piper nigram*, the tree that gives us black pepper. By all rights her name ought to have been Pepper, but Papa named her because he bought her, so Piper she is."

"Fascinating." As was his wife, who seemed to be far better educated than he had thought—not many young ladies could readily recite botanical nomenclature. "Yes, I'll send for the horse, if your father will let her come." And if he remembered their last conversation on a bed together, he had also promised the kittenish Lady Cairn another animal. "You also asked for a dog, and according to McNab, the gamekeeper has a litter from which you can pick a puppy."

Quince clapped her hands together in delight. "Just like that? I begged Papa for years, and he never gave in. But while I am thinking of Papa, Strathcairn, I should like to speak to you of business."

She was like a kitten chasing a spider—all twitchy shifts of direction. All his wariness came creeping back up his spine. "What sort of business?"

"I assume you and Papa made some sort of settlement. Even in the rush to leave Edinburgh, you strike me as the type of mon who kens his worth, and would protect his patrimony from a heedless, larcenous lass like me. And while I have no interest in your money, I am interested in *mine*, so I should like to understand what sort of fortune I have, and what sort of husband you plan to be financially."

She rolled once more onto her belly, and propped her chin up on her elbow. And gave him an absolutely spectacular view of the delicate architecture of her shoulder and collarbone, as well as the sweet pale top of her breast.

His voice slid low, into the rough Scots burr he knew she liked. "I suppose the sort o' husband I plan to be will depend upon what sort of wife ye plan to be." He would take every advantage he could muster with wee, wily Quince Winthrop.

She sighed. "That, my dear Strathcairn, is what the philosophers would call a circular argument. We will go around and around until dawn, and still not find the answer.

So I will attempt to seize the moral high ground—although I am clearly not accustomed to such heights—and make a concession. I will *try* and be good. I will put my past behind me, and be scrupulously polite to your secretary, and promise not to steal the silver, or cheat your guests at cards, nor set up a running dice game with the footmen—"

"Devil take me," he laughed. She had astonished him out of his nebulous ideas of seduction. "Have you really run a dice game with footmen?"

"Gardeners mostly, since Winthrop House always ran short on footmen. And grooms, as well as the occasional ostler."

"Devil take you. I'll add running dice games to your long and varied lists of sins." He had meant to be teasing, but from the guarded look that instantly darkened her eyes, his jest had wounded rather than amused.

"I hadn't realized you were keeping a running list. Don't forget to add highway robbery."

"I haven't forgot." He was careful to keep his tone light. "It's right up there at the top."

Her sigh was quiet, but weary. "Are you ever going to forgive me, really?"

She had brought them neatly to the heart of the problem, because the truth was, he did not honestly know if he could ever truly forgive her—forgive her enough to forget what she was capable of. Forgive her enough to trust her.

To trust her with his heart. To trust her with his family.

Because what she had done was very nearly unforgivable—at least in the eyes of the law.

Which was why he needed to get the morally compromised lass off of his bed and into her own. Alone. Before he was tempted to take advantage of all that drowsy kitten softness, and get her in the family way. He was a man, and he was only human.

No better way to put her off than with honesty. "I don't know. I've never been married to a criminal before."

She absorbed that uncomfortable truth slowly before she spoke lightly. "I suppose I ought to be honored that I'm the first."

"You're meant to be." He tried to lighten the heaviness of the moment by reaching out to touch her, taking her hand.

She squeezed his fingers in response before she pulled a tight breath into her lungs. "I am truly sorry that I got you into this, Strathcairn. You ken it's not too late to find a way out—to annul the marriage." She drew in a tighter breath. "And then you can have the sort of wife you deserve. One who doesn't have to *try* to be good."

"Nay." He didn't want another wife. He wanted her. Only better.

"No? Do you really mean for this marriage to be lasting and binding?"

He had never in his life reneged or broken a promise, and he didn't mean to start now. He was a man of his word. "I do."

She inched closer, as if she wanted to read his face more clearly. "Forever—until death do us part—is a very long time. Unless you mean to have better aim next time."

"There won't be a next time, Quince. I spoke my troth." He was hanging out there in the breeze on this one, exposed from every angle. But it felt good—it felt like a thrill. "And it still seems best—the only way that I can keep you safe from all harm."

She took her turn at being philosophical. "No one can be safe from all harm, Strathcairn. And I don't want to be cosseted and kept. I can't think of anything more confining. Except perhaps, marrying without affection." She peered at his face. "Does it not bother you? To be married without affection?"

How devastatingly straightforward and forthright she was. But he had to be something more than straightforward—he had to be truthful. "I did not say I was without affection, Quince. Nor are you without some sort of affection for me. You wouldn't be here, lying comfortably on my bed, if you did not have at least some small affection for me, would you?"

"Nay," she said quietly, but just as truthfully. "I suppose not."

She edged closer, and closer still, until she had insinuated herself comfortably against his side, nestling naturally within the curve of his body, with her bandaged hand trailing across his chest, her fingers drawing idle circles on his flesh.

And somehow he had just as naturally put his arms around her, drawing her flush against his side, holding her comfortably against his chest.

And once she was there, so close, her mouth tipped up towards his, and it was the most natural thing in the world to kiss her, to taste the sweet gift she offered, to close his eyes and surrender to the inevitable rightness of having her in his arms.

He liked her this way—soft and open and honest, and sighing into his linen. It was deeply intimate, seeing her this way, with her hair unbound and her feet uncovered, undefended by the sharp claws of her wit.

How he ached to have her, this blazing, trusting, untrustworthy lass. But if she was a treasure worth having, she was a treasure worth waiting for until there were no more misunderstandings, no more recriminations or distrust. He felt it to his bones.

"It will all be fine, Quince." He said it as much to convince himself as her.

"Will it?" She did not seem at all so sure.

"It will. I promise."

She closed her eyes, and lay there with him, and he let her think about that for a good long time. Long enough for her breathing to become quiet and shallow. And he indulged himself for a further few minutes by snugging closer and simply watching her sleep. Plotting the constellation of her features—two doe-shaped eyes, with two straight, slanted eyebrows, one straight elegant nose, and one mouth.

Taken apart her features were normal—typical, even. But put together, the unique combination that was her face was magic. Even enchanting.

She had enchanted him. From the very beginning, he had

been susceptible to her dark fairy combination of mischief and excitement. And he was more than susceptible now.

So susceptible that he wanted nothing more than to roll toward her, and curl himself around her, and hold her close all through the rest of the night. But he was Cairn, and a gentleman, and the gentleman who wanted wee Quince Winthrop as his Marchioness of Cairn was going to have to wait until he was asked, even if he did have a cockstand that would surely keep him awake into the wee small hours.

So instead of spooning himself against his for-once-complaint wife's pliant back, Alasdair rose and tossed on a robe before walking around to the other side of the bed, where he slid his hands around his soft, warm wife. She stirred and rolled toward him, and came into his arms as if she were climbing a tree—all acrobatic arms and athletic legs wrapped around him, taut and warm and blissfully ardent.

It was everything he could do to stand still and wait, and endure the agony of arousal and half-hope that she would do something more. That she would stir, and rustle her agile, larcenous fingers through his hair. That she would ply her teeth to the side of his neck and bite down ever so gently, delicately abrading his flesh. That she would turn and taste him with lips and tongue, and kiss him until he was so dizzy with wanting it was everything he could do not to fall down.

And then she did.

She tasted of sugar and whisky and want, sweet and unbridled and untainted by the misgivings and hesitation that arose during the day.

He kissed her back, giving her everything he could, taking everything she offered until the ache of longing grew so strong it all but choked the heart from him. He turned away from the kiss, afraid she would taste the pain and uncertainty on his lips. Waiting for her to turn away from him, as well.

But still she clung to him, subsiding with a sigh onto his shoulder, so he carried her slowly back through the connecting door to her own bed. He laid her down, and took a minute to straighten the tangle that she had made of the covers.

"Good night, sweet Quince."

Her eyes blinked open for the merest moment. "You know," she said on the whisper of a sigh, "you really aren't so bad when you're being nice."

He smiled at her, even though she could no longer see him. "And you really aren't so bad when you're being good."

She smiled back, but didn't open her eyes. "Don't tell anyone."

That warm feeling welling in his chest was affection, and something more. Something sweeter. "Don't worry, brat. I won't."

Chapter 24

TURNABOUT WAS FAIR play, and Alasdair turned the
tables by taking himself into his wife's bedchamber
indecently early, just as the dawn was creasing the eastern
sky. He drew the curtains from the big bow window
overlooking the green park, and let the golden morning light
fill the room. "Good morning, sweet brat."

And yet, on she slept despite the streaming daylight.
Sweet, annoying brat.

"Time to get up." He reached for the delicate rounding
of her shoulder where she lay sprawled diagonally across the
bed, and gave her a rough shake. "Wake up."

"Why?" she groused, and pulled the covers tighter about
her.

"Because it is time to be up and about. There are things
to be done. Your days as a lady of lazy luxury are over."

"My days as a lady of lazy luxury have yet to begin." Her
voice was cottony, and full of sleepy discontent. "Go away."

He might have actually felt sorry for her if he hadn't
been so deprived of sleep himself. It had taken a very long
time for him to fall asleep again last night, for reasons he

would rather not examine too closely in the light of morning.

But he was not about to be swayed by a warm bedroom voice. Or aroused. Not yet. "Either you can get up on your own, or I can come into that bed and get you."

She opened one eye, and gave him a baleful stare. "Promises, promises," she muttered as she rolled onto her back. "If this is what having a husband is like, I'm not sure I want one."

Amusement, attraction, repressed need, and whatever else was sidling about his veins, made his blood sing. "You've got a husband anyway, so be nice to him. He's brought you chocolate."

The moment he said the word, her whole demeanor changed. "Have you really?" She groped her way to a sitting position, and made an instructively grabby motion with her hands. "You might not be such a bad husband after all. Give."

While he handed her the cup, her white cotton chemise slid off one shoulder, and made interesting twists around her trim torso, which he admired her as she took a tentative, delicate sip.

"Oh, holy chocolate tarts, yes." She took a more satisfying gulp of the unsweetened brew.

Trust Quince to like her morning chocolate bitter and dark. Trust him to like that about her.

She took another deep guzzle from her steaming cup. "Aaahh." She pushed that flowing, fall of hair out of her eyes, and blinked into the sunlight.

By God, she was beautiful. He wanted her with every fiber of his being, every pulse and breath and inch of tingling skin. She was temptation incarnate, moving and sighing with an innate animal grace that had him straining at the constraints of gentlemanly behavior, as well as the close of his breeches.

But if she had recovered from her injury enough to wake him up and arouse him in the middle of the night, she was well enough for a longer foray out of bed. Whatever else she might be ready for *within* the bed was a topic he would explore later. "Drink up and then come along. There is much to be done today."

"Like what?" She was the picture of tousled skepticism.

Like a hundred things. A thousand. He could make a list right there, on the spot. "Like acquainting you with the estate. Why don't you put on your riding habit?"

"Don't have one." She regarded him with something of her former mischievousness across the steam from her cup. "I rode in breeks, remember?"

As if he could forget. "I do. Quite vividly." He pushed aside the erotically charged image that came galloping into his brain—a treat to savor another time, on another sleepless night—and smiled at her anyway. "Then we'll walk."

It would take a great deal longer—days, even weeks—to show her the whole of the estate if they hiked, but perhaps that would be for the better. They would spend the time getting to know and understand and appreciate and hopefully enjoy each other in ways that they hadn't in Edinburgh. And her arse wouldn't be as sore from all the riding.

"All right," she said as if she were testing out the idea. "I think I'd like that. I'm rather fond of walking."

Yes, he could picture his Quince as a rambler—all independence, bracing fresh air and sturdy, sensible boots, like the ones he taken off for her at the inn at Stirling.

But now was perhaps not the best time to be reminiscing about undressing his wife, however briefly. If he did, they were unlikely to leave the house, much less get out on a walk. "I'll meet you in the entry hall."

Yes, outside in the fresh summer air was best. They could make a fresh start, as it were. He would begin his efforts to forgive her from this day forward. He had told her it would all be fine, and he meant to make it so.

She did not keep him waiting long—no sooner had Alasdair entered the imposing, high-ceilinged entrance hall, with its display of weapons blazing from the walls in all their well-honed glory, did she appear at the top of the stair. "Too hard, trying to pick just one?"

He laughed, and turned to find her attired in the same sort of sensible country clothes as he—all stout linen and well-worn boots. "Well, you are certainly dressed for walking. No worry that the mud will ruin that gown."

"I told you wit and not wardrobe is my motto."

"So you did. And while I appreciate your economy, I feel compelled to say you needn't worry you'll pauper me with a few gowns every now and again."

"No?" She turned that intelligent gaze upon him. "And are there no paupers in your portion of the highlands that might need your money more than I need a new gown?"

He acknowledged her point with a bow, determined not to start their day out on a cross foot. "A very good question, Lady Cairn. Why don't we go look at my highlands, and see what we can see?"

Alasdair steered her through the garden, as it was the most direct route. He had crunched up the gravel paths a thousand times in his youth—often on the same errand as today—and never once took any note of the horticultural offerings. But his quick, curious wife was all opinionated observation.

"These mixed beds are beautiful and charming," she commented. "While my Papa would doubtless be critical of the naturalistic planting scheme, I like all the gorgeous massed perennials for color. I especially like your allée of *Carpinus betulus*." At his nonplussed look she clarified. "The hornbeam trees, with their bright yellow-green leaves, underplanted with this abundance of bright purple puffs of *Agapanthus africanus*."

"I had no idea you were such a horticultural scholar." Although he should have guessed—despite that dedicated flibbertigibbet exterior, she was clever, and well educated enough to know obscure passages of Shakespeare. And her horticultural knowledge should come as no surprise—her father was the Gardener Royal.

She waved the attempted compliment aside. "Oh, I'm no

scholar. It's only that I remember things prodigiously well. But as to education… Mama quite despaired of me and my natural inclination to graft instead of industry."

She was so determined to be bad. "Says the girl who recites Latin plant taxonomy, knows her Shakespeare as well as her Bible, and speaks Latin and French—I have not forgot either your Q.E.D., nor your *Monsieur Minuit*." But if he could not be forgetful, he would try to be philosophical and forgiving. "It seems to me that your graft *was* rather spectacularly industrious."

She shot him a quick glance, as if she could not quite decide if he was attempting another compliment. But she did not argue, so he tried another gambit. "How should you like to have the direction of the garden turned over to you?"

"To me?" She looked astonished at such an idea. "Really? But I don't really know the first thing about gardening besides plant names."

"Certainly. And certainly you do—you just proved it with your talk of naturalistic planting schemes. You're curious and clever. You see things others don't. You have an eye for beauty. And you are not afraid to make decisions. You could learn."

"Careful Strathcairn, that almost sounds like a compliment."

"Careful, wee Quince, it might be one."

He could all but see the idea take root in her mind—pleasure bloomed slowly across her face. "I might, mightn't I?"

"I don't see why not. You learned to steal prodigiously well, and you taught yourself to rob a coach—I don't see why you might not dare to take on a garden. And the house. And more."

"What more?"

"Why don't we go see?" He pointed her up the path beyond the garden gate, toward one of the outbuildings, where McNab waited with Donne, the leathery-faced gamekeeper.

Behind them was a pen filled with a romping litter of

soft-eared spaniels, tumbling over each other in their eagerness to greet and impress their new mistress.

Who was running toward them with equal boisterous excitement. "Oh, by jimble." She fell among them, filling her arms with squirming, eager bundles of fur, kissing them just as avidly as they were kissing her.

Like attracted to like.

"Are they all for me? May I have them all?"

Typical of her to want to wade into the deep end of the pond straightaway. "Best to start with just one for beginners."

"Aye, mistress," the gamekeeper Donne confirmed. "And they're no ready tae leave their dam just yet. We've time aplenty for ye to find the right one."

She plucked the smallest of the lot up to gaze deeply into the tiny creature's eyes, nose to nose. And then she turned the full radiance of her smile upon him. "Oh, Alasdair."

Her use of his name hit him like a dart straight to the heart—or perhaps somewhere less choosy. But no matter where he was hit, he could not deny her effect upon him.

Nor his upon her. With any other lass he would have said that she looked at him with the whole of her heart shining in her eyes. But with Quince, he never knew—he was never certain he was seeing only what he wanted to see, and not what was really there. Perhaps he never would.

HER HEART WAS too full—she was too happy to speak. They were only puppies—adorable, warm, fuzzy, soft puppies—but still, they were a gift. The first gift her new husband had given her. And exactly what she wanted—something of her very own she hadn't begged, borrowed or stolen. "Thank you so very, very much, Alasdair."

"You are very welcome."

"How long will it be until I can pick one, and take it home with me?"

"In tae the Castle, mistress? I don' ken 'bout that, but 'twill be another four week or so, afore ye can take one."

"So in the meantime," Alasdair advised, "you can think of a name."

A cheeky answer was on the tip of her tongue—she would call her Larceny or Graft, or some other scaffy name. But the truth was she had never had the naming of an animal before, and it felt like too precious a gift to take so characteristically lightly. "I will do."

"We'll visit the puppies again soon," he promised. "But there is more to see this morning."

She grudgingly let herself be led away, casting her glance back over her shoulder toward the kennel, until the rough way called for greater attention. Alasdair led her on in companionable and peaceful silence, until they reached the stile over the fieldstone fence marking the end of the pastures and rough paths beyond.

"Here, let me help you." He didn't wait for either her consent or her refusal, but simply swept her up into his arms to carry her across the mud puddle at the bottom.

He was rewarded for his chivalry when she instinctively looped her arms around his neck, bringing her so intimately close she could smell the crisp scent of starch rising from his linen, but still she felt bound to protest. "You can put me down, Strathcairn. I am made for action, not idleness. I need to regain my strength."

"Alasdair," he corrected. "And you're not a prizefighter, wee Quince."

"Neither am I made of spun glass. You needn't be so careful of me. I daresay I could even take a tumble and emerge unscathed."

"Let's not test that theory, shall we?" But he set her down upon the path, and held out his hand, palm up. Offering his assistance, instead of insisting.

"Thank you." She put her hand carefully into his, and relished the tingle of sensation that hummed all the way up her arm and settled warm and comfortable in her chest. So warm and comfortable and companionable, that when he laced his fingers through hers, and let their hands swing freely between them, she felt almost faint with hopefulness.

Free and equal, almost. At least as freely as possible, given that he was so much taller.

But still it was nice. Friendly. Equitable. Intimate in a way that had nothing to do with lessons in kissing, and everything to do with learning each other as people, instead of husband and wife.

Or maybe it was enjoying each other *like* a husband and wife. Like they had last night.

This time the riddy heat that crept across her face at the memory of being all stretched out next to him last night, and in his arms, felt comfortable and warming. And right— he was her husband.

At the first crest of the hill, he stopped and turned her back to the view. "And there is the castle. I'm sure Mrs. Broom will give you a full tour of the interior, if she has not already. But what she may not tell you is that you have my full leave to suit your own taste in the furnishings. The whole place is an antique, with ancient furniture that has been in this place or that since the days of the clans, and could likely use a fresh eye and a deft hand."

She gaped at him instead of the battlement walls. "Would you really give the run of your house and gardens?"

"My dear Quince, I am trying to give you the run of the whole damn place. You are mistress here now—the house and garden as yours to do with as you please, so long as you leave me the grouse moors. And speaking of which, we go this way."

He took her hand again, and towed her up the meandering path to the ridge of the hill. The air around them was full of sound and sunshine—the summer breeze dancing through the pine trees, the bees humming industriously in the wildflowers, and the tiny animals she could not name rustling through the underbrush.

In another few minutes they reached the second crest of the hill, where the landscape opened up to the glorious vista of the moor stretching as far as the eye could see, saturated with the purple and pink haze of heather.

This was Cairn. This was home.

Quince gasped at the sheer beauty of the place. Or perhaps she was only gasping for air from climbing a hill after staying in bed for nigh unto a week. Either way, she found a convenient boulder to rest upon.

"And what is this place?" she asked when she had caught her breath.

"This is the Vale. The Vale of Strathcairn. This is Cairn."

She could hear the depth of feeling in his voice, the pride and possessiveness he felt when he looked out over the land stretching away toward the loch—the land where his family had lived and prospered for hundreds of years. She could see all the honor, and all the responsibility, he felt at being the steward of such a spectacularly special place.

"That's Loch Cairn, and also the River Cairn." He point out the familiar landmarks. "The house and park come to there"—he pointed back down the ridge—"and the home farm starts from there." He took in a deep breath of the bracing air, and then let it all out on a laugh, as if he couldn't possibly contain it—as if he was drunk on all the heather and sunshine. "All in all, Cairn runs to about fourteen thousand acres."

"Is that all?"

"Aye." He didn't care if she was teasing him—he looked happy, all intoxicated pride and contentment. "The woodlands up on the hillsides"—he pointed off to a pocket of pine forest on their right—"run to about seventeen hundred and eighty acres."

"Been counting carefully, have you?"

"I'm Scots, lass. No other way to count." He was all unguarded enthusiasm and admiration for his home. "The home farm, which is most of the land on the valley floor, is about forty-two hundred acres of mixed arable—put to plow—and pasturage."

"As far as the eye can see."

"Aye. And farther." His gaze remained on the brilliantly vibrant landscape, as if he could easily picture every last inch of the place. "Our quarry is over the back of that hill, coming in just under a hundred acres—ninety-eight to be exact, though it's one of the largest in the highlands. The rest though—" Here he paused, and drew in another lung full of the fresh, summer air. "The rest is moorland. Thousands and thousands of acres of heather and gorse and hills and rock and grouse. And sheep." He turned to look at her, and something in his delirious gaze came back down to earth. "And unfortunately, you were right—crofters have been put off the land. The decision was made because the land was deemed too scrubby, too unsuited to arable agriculture for a number of reasons—steepness, rainfall, rocky soil—and only suitable for grazing by small numbers of sheep."

He held up a hand to forestall her from speaking too soon. "So I am trying do more for Cairn's former crofters, and do what's right for our dependents. I've set one scheme in particular—a carding, dying and weaving mill up the glen—that I'm keen on, but that is a discussion and tour for another day. Today I just want to look at this"—he turned back to the vista across the moorland—"because, by God, it's beautiful. It's heaven."

Heaven. Never in a hundred years would she have thought that the raw, craggy, soaring beauty of the place would fill her with the same wonder that made her husband's chest expand with pure, undiluted happiness.

"This is home," he said simply. "The one place on this earth I know I am meant to be. Devil take me, but I should have come home sooner."

It was as if the whole of his heart was in his eyes and in his voice.

"Aye," he said, as if she had spoken out loud "I thought it was the whole of the wide world when I was a child."

She heard something else in his voice—an ache for something lost. "And now you know better?"

"Nay." His voice grew strained. "I know more, surely. But better? I think not."

A day ago—even an hour ago—she would have teased

him for being a romantic. But now that she was here, now that she breathed the nectar-laden air, she could only agree. "I wish this were the whole of the world. I wish that there was no need ever to return to Edinburgh."

Out here, with the clean wind streaking through her hair, blowing the dust and cobwebs and dirty, twisted secrets from her mind, there was no past to contend with, no future to worry about. Here everything seemed good and possible. As good as Alasdair, who seemed more completely himself, as if he were distilled down to his essence, like sharp mountain whisky.

"You are a romantic, after all."

He smiled back at her, his sunny mood undimmed by any of her native cynicism. "Perhaps I am. Perhaps I am old-fashioned. But today, I really don't care."

"Look at you," she teased. "Why on earth are you a politician and not a farmer?"

The happiness shining from his face dimmed a little, as if a cloud had passed in front of his sun. "It seemed impossible to be both, at first."

"But now you must be both. Although I will say, I've never heard you talk about London, and the government the way you've been talking about Cairn, with—dare I say it— pleasure. You've not said one word about duty." Because here, duty was devotion. Here, doing right by Cairn and its people was what he did, regardless of his personal feelings or inclinations. Or perhaps his personal feeling were more visible to her here—the granite foundation of his character. "Whatever persuaded you to leave?"

"NOT WHAT—WHO." Alasdair picked up a small rock from the path, and exercised his discomfort by tossing it clattering against the stacked boulders of a stone fence in the distance.

He toyed for the merest moment with the thought of

telling her something other than the uncomfortable truth. But deception of any kind was truly abhorrent to him. And lies always made everything worse. And she needed to hear this particular truth as much as he needed to tell her. "My grandfather. I disappointed him. He all but threw me out of Cairn."

His young wife gaped at him. "I cannot believe it—of him or of you."

It was kind and rather loyal for her to say so, but then again she had always seemed loyal to him—when she wasn't trying to rob him, anyway. And to be fair, she hadn't known she was robbing him.

But the truth was still the truth. "It wasn't my grandfather's fault, entirely." Alasdair tried to sort through the convoluted tangle of blackmail and accusation, betrayal and shame, and crushing, crushing disappointment that still sat heavy in his chest. "I forced his hand, I suppose. I let him believe an untruth, because..." His reasons—pride, embarrassment, resentment, and a very real concern for the privacy of the truly injured party—all seemed so thin and ridiculous now, when he had the sage benefit of hindsight.

"Alasdair, did you...lie?" There was no triumph in her voice, no snide innuendo—only genuine shock. Much like his grandfather had evinced at the time.

"I lied by omission." It gave him no pleasure to admit the fault. Only regret for all the years he had missed Cairn. And missed his grandfather's unfailing support. "I took the blame for something I had not done out of a misguided sense of loyalty. Out of the heedless, headstrong belief that I had to be right. But I wasn't. I trusted the wrong person—a person I had been warned against—and so it was my duty to take the blame."

She was all solemn curiosity. "Alasdair, you'd best tell me what really happened."

How like her not to let him evade discovery, or couch his admission in euphemism. "An acquaintance, a man I had unthinkingly invited here to Cairn, violated a young lady, another guest." He tried to choose the politest way possible to say what was impossibly impolite, and in reality, simply criminal. "He forced himself upon her in the most dastardly, *bastardly*"—he didn't mind giving vent to curses with Quince—"manner possible, and then denied all responsibility. So I offered for her. There, actually"—he pointed back down the hill—"under those ruddy hornbeams, in the garden. But for whatever reasons, she wouldn't have me. Instead, she took my offer of money to help her do what she preferred, which was leave Scotland behind. It would have been a simple case of helping a friend in need, but the bastard blackmailed me over the whole affair, claiming he would tell everyone that I had been the one with the lass. And that I had paid her off." He scrubbed a hand through his hair, as if he could brush away the memories. "But I wouldn't pay him. I hit him, if you'll recall my saying. And he told his lies to my grandfather."

Her mouth opened in a silent "o" of affronted astonishment. "Is that why you went to London so suddenly?"

"It is why I stayed there. I was not to be allowed home until I mended my ways, and made something of myself."

She pulled a face—all appalled disbelief. "I can't imagine you not making something of yourself. It beggars the imagination. If anyone was bound for greatness, it was certainly you."

Something very close to pride filled his chest. No, not pride—gratitude. "I thank you for your confidence, but at the time, it certainly wasn't a forgone conclusion. I wasn't even sure I had come up to his mark until the end, and he called me back. But by then he was dying. And unfortunately, he died before I made it back."

It was a blow every time he thought of it—how many years his bad decisions had cost him. And all he could hope was that his experience could serve as a cautionary tale for a certain someone else who had made her fair share of whopping bad decisions.

A certain someone who stared into the middle distance for a bit, and then brought her quizzical gaze back to his.

"All right, so you wanted to make your mark upon the world. Why politics? Why not…something else?"

This, at least, was easy. "No interest in the army, no inclination for the church."

Her eyes searched his face, all frowning indignity on his behalf. "But you're the heir. Usually it's the second sons who are spiffed up and stood for Parliament—your Mr. Pitt the Younger is a perfect example."

Her indignance on his behalf was charming. "It was felt I might have an affinity for government. If only I would apply myself with attentiveness and restraint."

She leaned back, as if she were putting a certain distance—however slight—between them. "This is a warning for me, then, this attentiveness and restraint?"

"Nay. Not entirely. It was my grandfather's admonition to me." Alasdair was careful not to lecture. "But he was right—politics did suit my ambitions. Although originally I joined Pitt's government because I was mad to make a name for myself, to correct the world's bad impression of me, I eventually began to realize the opportunities and the power I had to effect change—that I could make a real difference in the world by making the right choices for the populace. It is still my ambition today. The world is changing rapidly, as you have so presciently pointed out to me, and we must keep up with it, or be left behind."

Quince drew in a deep breath of the bracing air. "There are days when I most ardently wish to be left behind."

Was that real regret he heard in her voice? It seemed too much to hope. But he hoped anyway. "Me too. But don't tell anyone."

His admission surprised a wee smile back across her lips. "Your secret is safe with me."

"Thank you. Because it is important, you see, for you to understand my position."

"Oh. You mean as your wife." She shifted a little uncomfortably on the rock. "I need to understand your position within the government—the Home Office, is it?"

"Aye. Because—you will like this—what I do as Home

Secretary is issue instructions on matters of law and order to officers of the Crown, like the Lord Lieutenants and magistrates—the Lord Provost in Edinburgh, for example. I am sure the deep irony of my situation—our situation—has not escaped you. It has certainly not escaped me."

Understanding blew across her face like a stiff wind, buffeting her back. "Oh, Alasdair. If it became known that you helped me evade prosecution then you would be removed from your post?"

"Aye, most likely. Assuredly." But the tightness in his chest—the nagging worry that had bound him up like a truss—eased a little. It was a relief to see that she finally understood.

But it was as if he had passed his unease directly to her—she looked utterly appalled. "And you married me anyway? Knowing it could cost you all?"

How like her to cut directly to the heart of the matter. Though he was not ashamed to admit it, but he still felt rather exposed. "Aye."

But mercifully, she did not immediately ask him why he had married her anyway. Her mind was already racing ahead to other, more practical consequences. "And what will happen if someone—someone who matters or someone who wishes you political harm—finds out?"

He shrugged, and bent to examine a heather shoot. He had already thought it out—he had thought of little else from the first moment he had found her bleeding in her father's glass house. "I brought you here so no one will find out. But I will lose everything—everything but Cairn. I have seen to it that Cairn is legally protected, no matter what. I have written already some letters explaining my decision and involvement, and have put contingency plans in place should I be forced out. But it would not be the end of the world. I would retreat here, to become a full-time farmer."

"Oh, by jimble, Alasdair. You've given this serious thought."

"I have," he confirmed. "I am nothing without my plans. And today, with all this in front of me"—his arm swept across the vista—"it does not seem a punishment if I were to decide to stay."

"But you would miss it—London and the government?"

He had long since made up his mind. "Some of it, aye. There are some causes that I believe in absolutely, that I would work for even if I were no longer part of the government."

"Like abolition."

It was more than a relief to be so well understood—it was very nearly a pleasure. "Aye, exactly like abolition. But that is a discussion for another day. And today I have tired you out. You look weary." He reached toward her, thinking to touch her face, or brush her hair from her forehead as he had done previously, to regain the sweet intimacy of their night.

But their truce, this honest peace they had made between them was too new, too fragile to withstand too much pressure. He diverted his direction, and pulled a leaf from the brim of her hat. And stood. "Come. Enough for one day. Let me take you home."

Home. Quince looked back across the vale to where the house stood like a rock outcropping, solid and immovable in the distance. As if she had not yet decided if it would be a punishment to stay at Cairn. As if she had not yet decided she could call it home.

But he had made inroads, he was sure. She was softening toward him, as well as Cairn, bit by tiny, inevitable bit.

Chapter 25

HER HUSBAND WAS courting her.

Quince was sure of it. Throughout the next few days Strathcairn was unfailingly polite, witty and amusing, parrying all attempts at argument, and avoiding all subjects intended to incite a row with remarkable calm and skillful tact.

He was everything utterly and delightfully charming. And just, dash it all, out of reach.

If he touched her at all—her hand as he led her through a tour of the dairy, her hair when the wind blew it across her eyes, the small of her back when he walked beside her—it was just for a moment, no more. Just enough to leave her with the fleeting impression of warmth and weight, and leave her yearning for more. Teasing her so subtly, so nonchalantly, so naturally, she doubted he knew he was slowly driving her mad.

But there was only so much casual intimacy a lass of her particularly impetuous and impatient character could take before she was driven mad. So she decided to do what she did best—take action. And do the unexpected.

Turnabout, as Strathcairn liked to say, was fair play.

And so, in an unprecedented but thoroughly provoking move, she let Mrs. Broom dress her in one of Plum's just-ever-so-slightly-too-small gowns.

The provocation she chose was a fresh green printed silk, with a marvelously full silk skirt that whispered secrets when she walked, and more importantly, possessed an astonishingly low-cut bodice that displayed her manifest charms to perfection.

Quince quite purposefully left off the modest lace fichu, giving her husband a rather spectacular view of the pale tops of the magnificent wee breasts Alasdair had so admired.

Mama always said a man couldn't think, or argue, or keep to himself, while looking at breasts.

"Good morning, Strathcairn." She slipped into a seat opposite him in the breakfast room, instead of taking her chocolate in her chamber, as had been her wont.

Strathcairn looked at her over the top of his morning newspaper. And stilled. And cleared his throat. "That, my dear brat"—he folded the newspaper with a decided snap—"is a beautiful gown you're almost wearing."

By jimble.

"Do you like it?" She leaned forward just enough to be encouraging. "Mrs. Broom chose it out of my wardrobe, but then had to sew me into it, in the manner of the French. I have no idea how I am to be gotten out of it."

He made a rude sound that indicated without words his disparagement of the French, and gowns that couldn't be gotten out of.

She rewarded his lovely discomfort with a concerned frown, and a strategic little shift of her stays. "I am sorry, Strathcairn. I thought you of all people would appreciate the gown better than I, having lived among the French."

He leaned back in his chair, as if he needed to put distance between them. "I find myself remarkably out of charity with the French this morning."

"So long as you aren't out of charity with me, my Lord Cairn." She indicated herself by laying a hand across her bodice, drawing his eye. "Alasdair."

Oh, no fool, Mama.

Alasdair put down his coffee cup with an audible clank. "Let me be sure I understand you, my Lady Cairn—are you flirting with me?"

She looked up at him from under her lashes. "I am *trying*, my lord."

He stood so abruptly his chair tipped over behind him. "You are *doing* remarkably well."

Quince welcomed the blaze of heat his voice and gaze kindled under her skin, letting it push her to standing as well. Heat blossomed under her bodice. And she liked it. She had finally pushed her un-pushable husband over his personal brink. "I've missed our lessons in kissing, Alasdair."

"As have I, brat. And I've a mind to—"

"I say, Alasdair?" An unknown voice called out from somewhere in the house, interrupting and ending her hopes all in one moment. "Alasdair, where are ye?" The voice was followed by the sound of heavy footfalls striding up the corridor. "What are ye doing, auld mon?"

Alasdair's voice was low and intimate, and for her ears alone. "Attempting to be seduced by my wee wife. My wee, half-undressed wife."

Quince fished her fichu out of her pocket. "Who on Earth is it?" she asked. Besides someone with execrable timing.

"My auld and very good friend Ewan Cameron," Alasdair explained, straightening his own clothing, "who is supposed to be in his own home with his dogs, or up on his moor shooting, or doing any number of harmless country pursuits that do not include barging in on my breakfast with my wife. But whom I cannot turn away. Yet I hope we may continue this discussion later, at a more convenient time, my lady?"

"I am at your disposal, my Lord Cairn." Quince tugged her bodice to a more modest configuration, and tied her fichu around her neck in preparation to meet their guest.

When she was presentable, Alasdair raised his voice. "Go away, Ewan."

"Ah." The still unseen friend drew nearer. "Breakfast room, is it, McNab?"

"Aye, Your Grace," came the steward's overloud reply from just outside the door.

And then this friend was there—a giant of a man, filling the small room with his presence. "What ho, Alasdair." The behemoth crushed her husband in a bruising embrace that owed more to a wrestling match than an introduction. "I came as soon as I heard. This must be your wife, the new Lady Cairn I've heard so much about."

Quince was immediately engulfed in a similarly crushing embrace, full of warmth and genuine welcome. But despite the warmth, or perhaps because of it, she was immediately on her guard—despite Strathcairn's assurances that neither he, nor Mr. Oistins would tell a soul the sad, sordid story of how she had become Lady Cairn, she was a realist when it came to all things rumor and scandal. She did not yet believe him. She braced herself for the worst.

In contrast, Alasdair was all relaxed, smiling enthusiasm. "It must be." He played the gallant, reaching for her hand, looking at her from under his brows as he brought it to his lips. "Ewan Cameron, may I present my wife, Quince, Lady Cairn. Quince, I give you my good friend, Ewan, also known as His Grace, the Duke of Crieff."

"My Lady Cairn." His Grace made her a slow, measured bow. "What a singular pleasure to meet ye. We thought auld Alasdair would never be brought to book."

"No, Your Grace?" Quince recovered enough of her usual aplomb to give the duke a ratchety little curtsey. "You underestimate your friend's manifest charms."

"Alasdair, charming? Auld cork like him?" His Grace of Crieff's square forehead folded into a frown. "You're joking."

"I am not." Quince's smile was all for her husband, even as she hedged her bets. "I can't even begin to tell you the lengths I was forced to go to in order to secure his hand."

After all, Alasdair said it was to be a *romance*.

Her husband was all smiling, amused appreciation. "Just so."

Which left his friend gaping. "Good Lord. I wouldn't have guessed stodgy auld Alasdair worth any effort."

"Oh, you are quite wrong." Quince returned to her seat, and indicated that the gentlemen might take theirs. "I account myself very well satisfied with my side of the bargain."

It was not a gross exaggeration, and therefore not an outright lie. The truth lay somewhere in the middle—mostly because she was still looking forward to the fulfillment of her devil's bargain. Which she was not going to be able to fulfill at present, and with a guest in her house.

What a waste of a dress.

Evidently her husband's thoughts were much the same. "What brings you to darken Cairn's door, Ewan?" Alasdair asked.

"The promise of breakfast," was the big man's answer. "I'm for Edinburgh, and thought I would call on my way."

"Ewan's estate, Crieff, lies some small distance to the north," Alasdair explained. "Then you will not stay?"

"Nay." For such a big man—the Duke of Crieff was easily twice her husband's breadth, and nearly as tall—he took his seat with surprising grace. "The other chaps said best not to disturb a mon and his new wife, but once I got Alasdair's letter, I couldn't rest until I'd come and met the woman who made him change his ways. And I also wanted to make sure ye weren't a figment of his poor imagination."

Quince decided she rather liked his casual abuse of her husband. It reminded her of her own teasing style of conversing, which Strathcairn always seemed to enjoy. And here was the reason—he was quite at home squabbling so amiably with his friends. "I assure you, I am quite real, Your Grace."

"Call me Ewan, please."

"And you must call me Quince. I hope you shall take breakfast with us, and we should be delighted for you to stay as long as you like. Wouldn't we, Alasdair?"

She signaled a footman to bring a plate of country ham and eggs, but in reality, she was not exactly delighted. It was hard enough trying to capture Alasdair's undivided attention in a house and estate as large as Cairn without the additional diversion of a friend. But she was Marchioness of Cairn now, with the run of the house, as Alasdair had told her, and standards must be upheld, and friendships maintained. She was nothing it not unfailingly loyal.

Luckily, the Duke of Crieff stuck to his plans. He accepted the plate of country ham and eggs, but not the invitation to say. "I thank you, my Lady Quince, but I must be off within the hour if I am to make Edinburgh in good time to meet with my solicitors."

"Not that I am encouraging you to stay, you understand, but you seem to be in an uncharacteristic rush," Alasdair observed.

"Aye, I am," the Duke agreed. "I'm getting married."

Alasdair's fork and knife fell to the plate with a clatter. "What now? After all these years? You've been engaged to be married for what seems like forever."

"For eight years," Crieff clarified. "I have been betrothed to Lady Greer Douglas since the age of eighteen."

"So what on Earth brought this on now?" Alasdair demanded. "Why the unseemly rush?"

"Says the mon who told no one of his own impetuous, lightning-quick wooing and wedding. It is time," His Grace said simply, looking from Alasdair to her and back. "It is time I was married."

"Let us be the first to wish you happy, Your Grace," Quince put in, lest Alasdair's shock be interpreted as disaffection, or worse, dissatisfaction with the married state—though her husband had perhaps more reason than most to be dissatisfied. "Congratulations."

"Thank you, Lady Cairn. And if I may trespass on an auld friendship, I should very much like a quick consultation with your husband on a few matters legal before I go."

"Certainly." As His Grace's tone was more confidential

than condescending, Quince didn't mind leaving them to their coffee and private talk.

But it did make her think of her own matters legal—her marriage settlements to be exact, about which she knew next to nothing.

But there was in the house someone who doubtless did know about such things. And now was as good a time as any to speak to Alasdair's secretary, Mr. Oistins—to make her amends while she was feeling fresh and optimistic, and could mind her uneven temper.

"If you'll excuse me, gentlemen."

The gentlemen stood, and Quince was happy to find Alasdair's gaze followed her from the room. She would need all the confidence and courage she could get before she bearded the lion of the library. Mr. Oistins, she had found through careful listening, was greatly esteemed by the rest of the staff, but also a little feared—his stoic, reserved demeanor kept the other servants at a distance.

But Mr. Oistins was not a mere servant—he was Strathcairn's friend. And she judged, his protector.

Quince made sure to check that her appearance was everything demure, wifely, and correct in one of the mirrors decorating the corridor before she entered the library, where she found Mr. Oistins attending to his work at one side of a huge desk.

He rose upon her entrance, and bowed gravely. "Your pardon, my lady. I believe his lordship to be in the breakfast room. I believe his visitor the Duke of Crieff to be with him."

"Aye, I thank you, I've just come from there." She gathered a larger measure of courage and composure to wrap around her in the same protective manner as the fichu. "It is you, Mr. Oistins, who I wanted to see."

Mr. Oistins inclined his head in that characteristic manner that was not a bow, but was still entirely civil. "Then I assume you wish to know that the post, with your letters, has arrived from Edinburgh."

"My letters? I haven't written any letters." Not even to

Plum, who wanted to know all. Mostly because Quince had yet to experience *all*, drat it.

Mr. Oistins made her another correct nod in acknowledgement of the truth of her statement. "Perhaps I misspoke, my lady. I mean to say that letters addressed to you have arrived."

There was something about the secretary's tone that served as a warning—against what, she could not guess, but that alert sense of alarm came padding across her shoulders like a stealthy barn cat. "Oh, I am sure they must be from my mother. Or sisters." She had no other correspondence. Jeanne knew her numbers, and could read, but she did not write enough for a letter. "How nice."

Mr. Oistins made no comment while he unlocked a desk drawer and drew out the letters, but even before she saw the missives, Quince could tell from his measured, almost weighty manner, that they would not be from her mother.

That stealthy sense of alarm scratched up her spine, and almost kept Quince from accepting the two letters from his outstretched palm. Because now she could see the direction, written in a cramped but decisive hand, with her name slashed across the paper. Written by someone who was most assuredly not her mother. Someone who had written not one, but two private, painstakingly folded and sealed letters to Lady Quince Cairn, from the address of Saint Cuthbert's, West Kirk, Edinburgh—the Reverend Talent.

A small measure of relief eased the tension in her shoulders.

"Oh, it is only the Reverend Talent." Who could object to a clergyman's letter—other than her? But still, she felt compelled to offer some explanation for correspondence with a man who was not her husband—even if she was not the person initiating that correspondence. "How kind of him to write. He tended to my arm, you see."

Mr. Oistin's eyebrows flicked upward for the barest of moments. "Yes, my lady."

Quince stuffed the letters deep into her pockets—she would read them later, if she read them at all. "Thank you,

Mr. Oistins."

"Lady Cairn." His bow was minimal, but rather elegant at that—a slow stately inclination of his head. Still, there was a wealth of judgment in his eyes.

Or maybe Strathcairn was right, and what she saw in the man's eyes was nothing more than the product of her own guilty conscience. Or maybe not.

The secretary raised one eyebrow in slow, unmistakable judgement. "Is there any other way I might assist you, my lady?"

"Aye, I thank you." She smoothed her hand across her skirts to quell a nervous clench. "Forgive me if I am wrong, Mr. Oistins, but I detect a rather large note of disapproval in your regard."

His stoic expression barely changed. Barely. "Not at all, my lady."

If she had not been looking for it, she might not have noticed the change—she doubted that most people would have seen what she saw. "Unlike me, Mr. Oistins, *you* are not a very good liar—though I will say it speaks highly of your sterling character that you cannot even tell a polite, civil lie to your employer's wife without betraying your conscience."

Quince thought she could see a flicker of something that looked a very little like admiration, or at the very least acknowledgement of her truth. And something else. "Or perhaps," Quince added in a moment of insight, "you have grown so weary of having to make polite lies, Mr. Oistins, you have simply given them up?"

This time the light in the man's eyes was surely admiration, if not respect for her acuity. "Just so, my lady."

"Just so. It is a stance I admire, even if I cannot emulate it."

He inclined his head in that intriguing manner than was acknowledgement without agreement, civility without obeisance.

"As we are attempting to be friends," she continued. "Or at least I am attempting to abide by my Lord Cairn's request that I become more of a friend to you, Mr. Oistins—I will tell you that your nostrils flare just the tiniest amount when you tell an untruth, as if the stink of mendacity is too much for you."

His face barely changed, but the expression in the corner of his eyes softened just as bit, but no more. "I thank you for that observation, my lady."

"You are welcome." She strove to keep anything of nervousness from her tone—she could not read Mr. Oistins the way she could other men. Probably because he was proving remarkably immune to her particular charms. "And through my observation, I can tell that you are a mon of careful, measured responses."

"A man in my position has to be, my lady."

"Your position as my lord's secretary, protégé and friend?"

"No, my lady, my position as a man. You ask if we may be friends, my lady, but I do not know if we can be," he said frankly. "For in my world, in my situation—a West Indian man who came to this country in bondage from Barbados— a friend is a rare and precious thing indeed. A treasure to be earned."

"I see." Quince understood at once, despite his steely tone. Or rather because of it. "And Lord Cairn is that rare and precious thing. He is your friend."

"Yes, and it is not a friendship that either he, or I, take lightly, my lady. He has remained my friend and supporter steadfastly, through both easy and difficult times, though it has cost him to do so—the derision of his peers in society, and the opposition of his colleagues in Parliament and in the government, has been a steep price that he has gladly paid for my sake. I would do the same for him, Lady Cairn."

"Aye, he's like that isn't he? Loyal and true. Once he makes up his mind about the right of something, I doubt any mon, or woman for that matter, could dissuade him from his chosen path. I ken I could not. But I am glad of it, for he has done that very same kindness for me, you see, demonstrating his loyalty and steadfastness and commitment by marrying me."

Mr. Oistins raised one eyebrow in that lethal manner, but finally inclined his head to acknowledge her point. "I suppose he has."

"You ken I am no good, Mr. Oistins, for you saw me upon the heath with your own eyes. But I am not a wholly bad, either. I am told I have misjudged you, and I owe you an apology. And so I give it to you—please forgive any slight I may have served you. I will not do so again."

"I do not take account of slights, for there are too many to count. But I thank you for your civility, my lady."

"You are welcome." But still she felt there was something more to say. "I am, and will be, as loyal and steadfast to my husband as he has been to me, Mr. Oistins. It would pain me if you continued to think me unworthy of his trust."

"I must think as I see fit, Lady Cairn, for no man can make me do otherwise. No woman either." He inclined his head once more. "I will watch, and observe, and reserve my judgment."

"As you watched and saw and looked for my mistake the night I held up your carriage." It wasn't really a question— she just wanted to get it all out in the open.

"Yes. Just so."

"You're not a very forgiving mon, are you, Mr. Oistins?"

"It is not my place in this world to forgive, Lady Cairn. That I leave to God. My job is to guard his lordship, and be vigilant."

"And work with his lordship to pass a bill to end slavery."

He agreed with another stately nod. "Just so, my lady."

"I should like to join your fight, Mr. Oistins. Firstly, because anything near and dear to my husband is now near and dear to me. And secondly, because I have been wrong about a great many things, and I should like to become right, both in your eyes, and more importantly, in his."

Mr. Oistins inclined his head to her. "I would welcome your assistance, my lady. But I will not be any less vigilant."

She gave him a nod of her own. "Just so, Mr. Oistins.

Just so."

And so should she be vigilant, for she had finally met a man who was not only determined, but quite able to resist her all of her charm.

It was most unsettling. It put her right off her game.

So she was not in the least bit prepared to open the first of her two letters, and read the only words the Reverend Talent had written—*You must come meet me at once.*

Chapter 26

ALASDAIR SAW EWAN into his traveling coach, wished his friend godspeed, waved him upon his way, and went in search of his wee, alluring, enticingly-dressed young wife.

Who proved very difficult to find.

"On 'er way up to 'er bed chamber, milord," seemed a promising direction from one of the housemaids, until that room proved empty.

"Oh, the library, milord," was Mrs. Broom's suggestion. "She was speakin' with Mr. Oistins."

Was she now? That boded well, he hoped.

But in the library, he found Sebastian working alone. "Good morning, my lord. I take it your visit with His Grace of Crieff went well?"

"Tolerably well, aye. He sends his regards. He's getting married. Have you seen my wife?"

"Felicitations, to His Grace and Lady Greer Douglas, my lord." Sebastian indicated several neat piles of papers on the desk. "There are a number of matters that require your attention, my lord, chief among them, the conversion and refurbishment of the old granary into the dye and carding houses alongside the new mill for wool production, my lord."

"That's at least two too many 'my lords' for the applicable sentence, Sebastian." Alasdair moved behind the desk, and paged through the papers that his secretary had arranged for his perusal.

"My apologies, my lord." At Alasdair's obvious hesitation, he prompted, "Will you sit, my lord?"

"Nay. I think not." On any other day, the conversion of the estate's old medieval granary would have consumed his attention, as he was deeply concerned about the displacement of the crofters from the hill farms—a concern that had arisen from his young wife's all too pointed, but ultimately true accusations. And he had come to be as adamant as she was that there be some alternative local employment available to the crofters. So rather than ship the wool from Cairn flocks off somewhere else to be processed and woven into material, he was determined to make Cairn a center of woolen production, using the buildings and natural resources readily available—the river spilling in and out of the loch—to power waterwheels for mills fulling, carding, teasing and spinning woolen yarns.

"I'm sorry." His mind was elsewhere. "Did I ask if you'd seen my wife? Mrs. Broom seemed to think Lady Cairn came in here."

"Yes, my lord," Sebastian answered in his grave manner. "She was here. But she left. She had some private letters that she wanted to read."

There was something in Sebastian's tone, some subtle warning that Alasdair had no time to fathom, because he could swear that Quince's head skimmed past the window outside. "Never mind. There she is."

Alasdair crossed to peer through the watery pane into the garden. It must have been Quince, though she was dressed like a housemaid. But no housemaid at Cairn walked with that characteristic quick, skipping pace. And he had seen that nondescript, practical ensemble of jacket and quilted petticoat before, the day he had come upon Quince, her mother and sister on the High Street in Edinburgh on their way to their dressmakers.

He unlatched the window and shoved up the sash despite the summer rainstorm that began to pelt against the panes. "Quince?" He raised his voice to carry across the garden, but the rain drowned him out.

Alasdair shoved himself away from the window. "You'll excuse me, Sebastian. There is an important matter—" The matter of his wife flirting and very clearly wanting to be seduced. And he aimed to please. As soon as possible.

He tore after her like the greenest of lads, eager for a kiss, instead of like a mature, experienced man of six and twenty. He was through the old oak door and down the old circular stairway that led to the servants' kitchen entrance, and striding into the garden only in time to see the tailing hem of her long, forest green cloak whisk out of sight at the far end of the allée of trees that led toward the wood edging the burn.

But she was too quick—by the time he had reached the bank of the burn, his lass was out of earshot, well away down the winding path that led to the village. She went entirely alone, but unlike him, who had run out unprepared for the weather, she was dressed against the summer downpour.

Still, it was no time to be about. And stranger still, she also chose the longer, more circuitous route along the burn, instead of taking the open lane that ran in a straight line from the Castle to the village. The path along the burn provided more cover.

Cover for what? The rain wasn't that hard—for Scotland, where it was very often horizontal—and there were trees along the open lane, too, shielding her from the heavy summer shower. But not from view.

The memory of the subtle warming of Sebastian's tone pushed him closer to alarm. And once he had started, Alasdair could not seem to stop himself from thinking there was something distinctly furtive in the way Quince twice stopped to check the path ahead and behind. Something distinctly clandestine, that made him think she was up to no good.

His heart stuttered painfully in his chest—either that or his new wife was giving him an ulcer of the stomach. How many times had she warned him that she was not good? Too many times to count.

And now she was flitting surreptitiously through his woods. As if she had an assignation.

Nay. Who could she meet? She had not left the castle before, and had no acquaintance that he knew of in the highlands. He was inventing problems—borrowing trouble, Mrs. Broom would have said. He would catch up with his wife, and put all his fears and distrust to rest.

But she had already slipped past the stone gates that marked the boundary of the estate, and was upon the wet, puddle-strewn path to the outer village. And her destination, some fifty feet down the lane, proved not to be the village, but the village kirk.

Alasdair's mind blanked—nothing was more innocuous than a church. And it was only right that Lady Cairn should involve herself with the spiritual well-being of the village. He should be glad she was involving herself.

But he couldn't make himself believe it. Not entirely.

Quince paused only briefly in the kirkyard to look across the lane over the hedge toward the grey stone vicarage before she disappeared through the lone low doorway.

But Alasdair didn't follow her.

For reasons that he did not want to examine or admit, Alasdair stood in the rain in the shadow of the gate, debating what to do next, wrestling with his scruples. There were any number of perfectly innocent reasons why she might have gone to the church. She might be praying—God knew, she had sins aplenty for which she might want to atone.

But because he was the man he was, and because she was the woman she was, Alasdair did not think Quince was praying. And even though a good husband would have turned around, and gone home, and waited patiently for his young wife to return in her own good time, he did not. He could not be that man. He did not trust her.

And he could not put off what needed to be done. *Incipe*—he would begin at once.

On the shaded north side of the church, a leaded-glass window was tipped open to let in the soft summer air. Alasdair damned his scruples, and headed for the spot, hugging the wall just below the window, trying to make out words over the steady drone of the rain.

He could discern only two voices—Quince's and a man. A younger man, whose voice could not be that of Reverend Ramsay, the aged rector of Cairn Kirk.

A younger man whose voice—though he could not immediately place it—sounded vaguely familiar.

Alasdair plastered himself against the wall, and made himself stop, and think, and decide if he really were going to eavesdrop on his young wife. He made himself wonder if he was prepared for his young wife to serve him another nasty surprise as shocking as the last, when he had been driven by sheer fury and frustration to shoot at her.

Despite the potentially dire consequences, he chose to peer through the wavy glass into the dim interior anyway.

In the narrow view of the nave afforded by the open sliver of window, he could make out Quince standing at the front of the pews, her hand gripping the railing so tightly her knuckles looked white. In front of her was the dark shadow of a man—a vicar to be sure, judging by his round-brimmed back hat and black coat.

The Reverend Mr. Talent, damn his holy eyes.

The same man Alasdair had interrupted with Quince at a ball, not once but twice. The man Quince had sent for when she had been injured. The man who had reluctantly married them. The man who had likely sent his wife that private letter Sebastian had so carefully mentioned. The man who was in Cairn village, when he ought to have been at Saint Cuthbert's West Kirk in Edinburgh, one hundred-odd miles to the south.

Alasdair turned away and shut his eyes, and realized it

was his turn to pray.

"REVEREND TALENT." QUINCE pushed back her wet hood, and approached the tall clergyman at the altar rail without waiting for him to greet her. "I received your note. What is so urgent that you must come all this way to see me?"

Her heart was hammering away at her conscience—she was beyond worried that somehow, someway, despite Strathcairn's rushed wedding and rumors of romance, she had been found out. Or worse, that Jeannie or Charlie had.

But the Reverend Mr. Talent wore a stolid, unconcerned smile, as if there were no crisis or urgency. "My lady."

"Sir." She essayed the barest curtsey, anxious to discover the reasons for his unexpected presence. "What are you doing in Cairn? What is wrong that you have come here?"

His cheeks colored is what she could only assume was chagrin. "I had hoped you would welcome my call."

Quince did not bother to hide her consternation. "Certainly, but if you had wanted to call, why did you not call at the Castle, instead of sending for me in this frankly alarming fashion?"

"I admit some reluctance to see you at Castle Cairn." His bright cheeks made his eyes shine with his characteristic self-effacement. "But I came because I could not rest until I had satisfied myself that you were well, and happy, my lady."

Quince was entirely taken aback. "That is very good in you, I'm sure. But as you see, sir, I am well. Surely you have not come all this way north merely to check on my health?"

"I can see you are well," he hedged. "But I flatter myself I cannot see that you are happy."

As she was in a kirk, Quince thought it best to pray that her confidence and temper—already a little frayed from her conversation with Mr. Oistins—would hold. Mr. Talent did indeed flatter himself. To excess. "I assure you, sir, there are qualified physicians here, as well as admirably talented healers. My housekeeper, Mrs. Broom, has looked after my injury with every care. I thank you for your concern, but I fear you have wasted a very long and arduous journey north for nothing."

"But the abrupt manner in which you quit town..."

Quince felt the heat of her own embarrassment scald her cheeks. This was more than idle flattery—this was intrusion. But however mortified she felt, she was herself, and had an answer. She smiled at the intrusive man. "Pray, must I explain romance, Reverend, in all its impetuous variety?"

"Forgive me for speaking plainly, my lady, but you did not seem entirely willing to be married at the time."

Oh, by jimble. Of all the cheek! Not that she hadn't been a wee bit unwilling, but they had sorted that out, she and Alasdair, and she had chosen to marry. But now she feared that in choosing to call the Reverend Talent to tend to her injury, she had somehow engendered some feeling from him other than gratitude. At the time, she had thought that as he was rather beholden to her, he would do a better job of keeping his mouth shut.

"I had been injured, Mr. Talent, as you may recall. An accident, as I assured you then, that colored my thinking. Blood loss will do that I'm told."

"Yes. So will fear."

The feeling that streaked across her skin was something more chilling than embarrassment—it was as stealthy and sharp-clawed as alarm. Her palms went instantly cold and clammy within her gloves. But she put up her chin. "I was not afraid of Lord Cairn, Mr. Talent. Nor am I now."

He smiled and shook his head, as if he were talking to a recalcitrant child. "Perhaps you ought to be, my lady."

Her alarm grew talons, the cold claws sinking deeper into her spine. "How do you mean, sir?"

"I should be very afraid of what Lord Cairn, the Home Secretary, the minister in charge of prisons and probations, should think if I were you."

Holy painted saints on a church wall. It was as if he had unsheathed a sword—Quince could almost hear the sound of sharp metal slicing through the air. At least he *thought* he was unsheathing a sword—he could not know the threat was empty because Strathcairn already knew her worst.

But who would have thought the stolid reverend was ever a sword player? Clearly not she.

But now that she was on her guard, she could see that trying to serve him up a riposte—telling him that Strathcairn already knew all—would be pointless, and potentially damaging. The less the reverend knew, the better.

"I thank you for your concern, Reverend Talent." She stood, and gave him the shallowest curtsey in her repertoire. "Good day." It were best if she left before she allowed herself to become fully angry.

But Talent was not ready to be dismissed—he stopped her with a surprisingly strong hand to her elbow. "Surely, my lady, you don't think we can get along without you?"

The fine hairs on her forearm lifted, and fear slid under her skin, cracking and chequering like a fast rime of ice—his grip was purposefully hurtful.

But Quince husbanded enough anger to match the fear. She wrenched her elbow from his grip. "The situation has changed, sir." She hoped her voice was nothing but frost and ire. "I am no longer available to help you."

He frowned down at her, as if he could not believe what he was hearing—as if he could not grasp that her days of donating to Saint Cuthbert's charity must be done. "Surely there is something you can do? You are Marchioness of Cairn, now. Surely you have more to give."

"Nay," she insisted. "I will give here if there is any giving to be done. Surely you understand that?"

"What is to stop you from doing both?"

Nothing but a rapidly growing distrust. Quince made up the most convenient, and most unassailable excuse upon the spot. "I no longer have any control over my own finances. My husband controls my fortune now, not I."

It was not entirely a lie—the truth was she had no idea of her settlements. But the law was fairly cut and dried, and fairly *un*-fair, on the subject of a wife's fortune—it belonged almost entirely to the husband. But she would not protest the law at this moment if it meant she could be shed of Talent.

The vicar moved closer—too close, backing her against a pew—and lowered his voice to speak as if they were intimates. "My lady, I think we both know you have…other means of assisting us."

Everything within her went instantly cold and still, as if she had frozen up inside. Something close to abject terror squeezed her chest tight.

She had never admitted the full extent of what she had done to anyone but Alasdair. She had been careful with Talent, wary of letting him know too much, protective of Jeannie and Charlie, happy to encourage the convenient lie that the money she gave to West Kirk came from a generous allowance.

"There are no other means, sir." She tried to keep her voice even, firm and factual. But she could hear the first faint cracks of fear creaking through her words. "Let me repeat, sir—my husband controls all of my fortune, every last penny and pin. Pray apply yourself to him."

Talent shook his head. "I don't think Lord Cairn would like that. Nor would I. I doubt he has anything like your dedication to the poor, my lady. You have always been such a reliable champion of God's unfortunates. And there are, sadly, too few people like you."

Quince tried to push air back into her lungs. If he thought she was a saint, she would be happy to disabuse him. "There are many people like me, sir, so perhaps you need to cultivate a wider circle of acquaintances and donors, now that, sadly, I cannot be one of them."

He shook his head in dogged disagreement. "Where there is a will, my lady, there is a way."

Quince was tired of polite, well-couched double-speak. "Let me speak plainly, Mr. Talent. I regret, sir, that there is no longer a will. I cannot help you in Edinburgh. I am mistress of Cairn now. My responsibilities are here."

The reverend continued to be everything inconveniently

obstinate and ridiculously sure. "Surely as the mistress and Marchioness of Cairn, you can find a way to support the Lord's work both here and at home?"

Home. Just yesterday she might have used the same word to describe Edinburgh, but on Talent's lips the reference felt strange. And wrong.

"Nay." And to make sure he felt the prick of her point, she sharpened up her sarcasm. "You are very sure about a great many things, sir—things which you want other people to do *for* you."

But nothing could ruffle the reverend's calm. "It is easy to be sure in the Lord, my lady. Surely you know this. Surely you have always known that when one is doing the Lord's work, the ends can be made to justify the means."

Holy sainted fishmongers in a stall. It was nothing more than what she had always thought, and often said to herself to justify her thievery. But somehow, from Reverend Mr. Talent's mouth, the platitude seemed completely and catastrophically wrong.

He carried on in the same vein. "And you, my lady, have always been willing to aid West Kirk and the poor we serve—why just last week, a family came to us, saying that you had met them upon the road, and sent them to us."

Of all the times to be caught out as a saint. "Aye. I did send them. And that is what I will continue to do here at Cairn, should the need arise. I did my best to support you, as I could, and when I could, Reverend. But I can no longer do so."

"My lady." He shook his head. "You are too important to us to simply let go."

Quince's frustration got the better of her. "Let me be sure I understand you, Reverend Talent"—she borrowed Alasdair's words—"with no double-speak, or idiotically polite euphemisms. What exactly do you expect of me?"

He was unembarrassed—nay, eager—to share his plans. "I think it would be beneficial to both of us, my lady, if we were able to continue on as we were before. Without Lord Cairn's interference."

Quince felt as if she would scream if she had to explain herself one more time. But she bit her tongue, and made herself speak plainly. "I have told you that I cannot do so." The time had come for a change. The time had come for her to put away childish things.

"I think I would behoove you to do so, my lady." Talent's easy smile was unnerving. "The West Kirk can ill afford your departure, and you can ill afford the stain to your reputation should people—should Lord Cairn, among others—discover what you have been doing."

The chill sliced through her spine, leaving her numb with fear—not for herself, but for Alasdair. But she had to be absolutely clear that her fear was well-founded. "And just what have I been doing?"

"Giving away what was not really yours to give, was it, Lady Quince?"

Oh, holy, holy, holy.

Well-founded, indeed.

"How do you ken that?" Her breath was nothing but a ghost of bravado.

"I made it my business to know all that I could about our most dependable donor. You are not the only observant person in Edinburgh, you know, my lady."

Oh, holy gaping holes to hell. She had been more than wrong about Talent—she had been utterly deceived. "I'm not?"

"No. You are very easily recognized, a well-known young woman, and easy enough to follow, or set beggar children to following."

She was stunned into silence, sick with shock. She had thought herself so clever and rare, so careful and successful, it had never occurred to her that she was being watched as carefully by the despicable likes of the Reverent Talent, as she had been watching others. "I suppose you are to be congratulated, sir."

He preened just the tiniest amount, putting his hand up to smooth his lapel. "Thank you, my lady."

Vanity, thy name was Talent. But perhaps she could use

that twisted vanity to some purpose. "You're supposed to be a mon of God, Reverend. And yet you've been sneaking about, following me?"

He was not in the least bit ashamed. "While you were sneaking about giving stolen money to the church? Yes. The Lord truly works in mysterious ways."

She struck back with the sharpest weapons to hand, her wits. "And blackmail is one of the sacred mysteries of the church now, is it?"

He laughed, and the sound echoed strangely in the empty church. "Yes, I suppose now it is. The ends always justify the means for our Lord."

She was beginning to see the twisted lines of his logic. She was only ashamed to admit that hers had, until quite recently—until nearly that very minute—been the same.

"Of course," he went on. "But your Lord Cairn, he's another question entirely." He smiled.

The effect was chilling.

To combat the sense of mortal cold, she was desperate for some fire to throw in his face. She was on the verge of telling him in no uncertain terms that Lord Cairn was well aware of her larcenous habits, if not her support of Talent's church, but something that must have been prudence stopped up her mouth.

She did not always have to rush in where angels feared to tread.

"What do you mean?" she asked instead.

"I mean that unless you want your Lord Cairn, the Minister in charge of justice, to know that you've been the one stealing from Edinburgh society for the past three years, you'd best find something new to steal, Lady Cairn. Your castle looked prosperous enough. You can send the things directly to me. No need to involve your friends Jeannie or Charlie Smith anymore, is there?"

Oh, that was the last of it. Alasdair's name was nothing compared to Jeannie and Charlie. Alasdair could look out for himself and Cairn, but Jeannie and Charlie, whom she thought she had protected, were vulnerable. Talent's cruelly casual mention of their names left her gasping. Heat choked up her throat and burned behind her eyes. And made her furious.

"Thank you, Reverend Talent, for making yourself so clear."

He smiled and bowed, oblivious and impervious to her sarcasm. "You understand me then, my lady? We must let nothing stand in the way of doing the Lord's work, and glorifying his name."

Her throat was tight, and her eyes burned with unshed tears just waiting for her to be free of his loathsome presence before they could fall. There was absolutely nothing witty or clever she could possibly say to him that wouldn't give away the totality of her disgust and her fear.

But she tried anyway. "I understand you perfectly, Dr. Talent. Perfectly."

But she had absolutely no idea what on Earth she was going to be able to do about it.

THE RAIN CAME down so hard Alasdair could make out nothing of what Quince and Talent were saying beyond a word or two, but he could pick up some sense of tone of voice—Talent's low and in control, Quince's defensive and increasingly emotional. But increasingly emotional about what, he had no idea.

He had almost given up torturing himself with the ineffectual eavesdropping, and given in to his desire to simply charge into the kirk in a straightforward manner, and strangle the lies out of the damned interfering reverend, when the old oaken door of the church slammed open, and his wife came pelting out from under the gloom of the stone porch.

His guilt over listening without making his presence known kept him pinned to his place along the wall, and he could only watch as she passed so close that he could see the raw look upon her face—beneath her hood, her eyes were red-rimmed and bloodshot, her nose was pink and dripping, and her face was suspiciously blotchy.

She was crying.

Quince, who never cared what people said. Quince, who had shrugged off more of his best insults the first evening they had met than most men could endure in a fortnight of debate in the House of Commons. Quince, his unapologetic, unassailable brat, was weeping.

He was beyond astonished—his chest contracted with something uncomfortably close to fellow feeling. And anger.

And all the questions that had been swirling around in his head dissolved into only one—what could that bastard Talent have said to make his wife cry?

On second thought, another question intruded—was it he, with his insistence upon marrying her, and bringing her to his corner of the highlands, cut off from all her friends and family, who had made her cry?

Alasdair could find no answer in her ravaged face, or in the composed face of the Reverend Talent, who came out to watch her depart, and then turned up his black collar, and headed toward the village, leaving Alasdair alone to decide.

And try as he might, he could not. The strong sympathy he had felt only moments ago was met by an equally strong, more painful feeling—rampant, distrustful jealousy.

This man, Talent—what the devil was he to Quince?

A suitor, at least. No man followed a lass who was not his wife to the highland village of her husband without being quite strongly attached to her. But was she equally attached to him? Alasdair didn't think so—if Quince had not kissed half the lads in Edinburgh, she certainly had not kissed someone so stodgy as a vicar.

But there was something between them. Something to draw the clergyman one hundred and eight miles north from his home parish. Something that upset Quince deeply enough to make her weep.

Alasdair took a deep breath, and purposefully knocked the back of his head hard against the cold, stone wall of the kirk, as if he could smack some sense into his brain, when what he really wanted to do was smack the Reverend Talent down to the ground, and leave him there, wallowing in the mud.

But that was not the way of the rule of law. He was Cairn—he had to *be* the law, and the law did not go about beating people up just because they had discommoded one's wife.

Especially if it was really Alasdair who had done the discommoding.

He forced his feet in the opposite direction from Talent—he did not completely trust himself not to set upon the damn fellow, and beat the bloody pulp out of him.

But neither did he trust himself with Quince at that particular moment.

She had warned him that she would make him a bad wife. She had insisted that they wouldn't suit. What if she did share her fellow feeling with Talent? What if she did want to leave Cairn? What if she wanted leave him?

Nay. The thought was a punch to the gut. It was not to be borne. But bear it he must, even if the aching doubt brought him to a bloody standstill in the cold rain. Even if the hot pain cleaved his chest like an axe blade. Even if everything within him roared out in protest and denial—she was his.

She was *his* wife. His joy and his burden and his weakness—the chink in the armor he had manufactured of his life. She was the temptation he could not seem to resist.

Yet resist he must, even if he did not want to give her up. Because he could not keep her, like a pet in a cage, locked up in Cairn for his pleasure. Quince was no one's pet, least of all his.

But if she were going to leave him, he had much rather not watch.

He turned his steps toward the wild moor, and the scouring solace of the windswept hills.

Chapter 27

QUINCE TRUDGED HOMEWARD, nursing her anger as assiduously as her fear, and scrubbing the scratchy heat out of her eyes with her damp sleeve.

She had to think, and for the first time in her life, think her way beyond doing the first rash or impetuous thing that came into her mind. She had to think her way beyond the fear—the fear that this last straw would be the weight that would break the last bond of affection Alasdair might still hold for her.

All her life—and certainly all of the past three years—she had been so sure. Sure that she held the moral high ground. Sure that she was *right*, when she had been nothing but wrong.

All that time, she had been justifying her sins by filling her mind with anticipating the next move, and staying one step ahead of the consequences. Delighting in the dance. But the music had stopped, and she had stranded herself flat-footed in the middle of the floor. Hoping she still had a partner.

Hoping he would be willing to help her. Hoping that he

could help her. Hoping that he would not, at long last, find the cost too high.

She would have to trust the one instinct she had left— the instinct that whispered that if she just went to him, and laid the whole of her troubles bare with no holding back, no sparing her feelings, it would all be all right.

If she just trusted him, all would be sunshine on heather.

Even when it was pouring rain.

And if it wasn't already too late.

Quince broke into a run, gaining speed as she tore into the castle, calling for him. "Alasdair! Alasdair?"

But on this day of downpours, he was nowhere to be found. Neither McNab, nor Mrs. Broom, who seemed to know everything there was to be known at Cairn, could say where his lordship had gone. Only that he had gone.

Only Mr. Oistins, with his all-seeing eyes and constant vigilance, had an answer. "He went out to find you in the garden, my lady, after you passed by."

Oh, nay.

"But I did not see him." And she had looked, checking the path behind as well as ahead, hadn't she? If Strathcairn had followed her, she would have seen him, wouldn't she?

Dread seeped under the dam she had made of her hope, weakening the walls, eroding the strength of her trust. But she had to trust someone.

"Mr. Oistins." She swallowed the last bitter remains of her pride. "I have made a terrible mistake, and I need Alasdair to…to help me make it right. I need him. And I need you to help me find him."

The air is the room seemed to become thin in the long wait for Mr. Oistins to answer. "You will not find him if he does not wish to be found."

"Oh, stop it!" she cried. Her temper—never the most even, especially on such a day when it had been hopelessly frayed—snapped. "You needn't speak to me in riddles, to suss out if I am worthy of your trust. I'm not." Her voice rose, high and scratchy, full of heat and desperation. "But *he* is. And I have to speak to Alasdair for no other purpose than to warn him so he can protect himself and Cairn. But if you will not help me—"

"If he is not in the castle, my lady, there is really only one other place to look—the hills."

"Of course. Thank you." Quince was astonished to feel the hot press of gratitude gathering behind her eyes. She dashed the tears away. "I ken just the place."

She took the path across the garden at a run, retracing their steps through the hornbeams and over the stile, taking herself through the welling puddles without a care for her skirts or muddying her boots. She climbed higher onto the wet, windswept moorland, relishing the exertion that kept her mind from having to think and doubt and worry. Saving her breath to marshal her arguments.

Nay. She would not argue.

If she had learned anything from Alasdair, it was that argument didn't help, and that she would be far better off to simply admit the uncomfortable truth—that everything he had feared and tried to prevent was coming to pass. All because of her reckless, unthinking choices.

The rain clamored over the moorland, clattering on stones and heather, chiding her with its incessant whisper— *too late, too late.*

And she began to think the rain was right when she found the spot at the crest of the hill empty. She had already overdrawn her strength—being hit on one's blindside by a blackmailer could do that to a person—and she collapsed upon the same boulder as she had the first day Alasdair had brought her up here, to catch her breath, and decide what to do next. Because Mr. Oistins was right—she was not going to find Alasdair if he did not want to be found.

And if he did not want to be found, or did not want to help her, she needed to face the facts, and do what she must to keep Alasdair from being forever tarred with her paintbrush.

She must leave Cairn. She must leave him.

A pain like no other pierced her heart—regret, it seemed, was the sharpest sword of all.

"Quince?"

He was there all at once, her Alasdair, looming over her and the moor, looking wet and weary and wonderful.

But her relief was both only momentary, and bittersweet, because he was not regarding her in the same way—her Alasdair looked none too pleased to see her. "What are you doing up here?"

This answer at least was easy. "Looking for you."

"You've found me. And I you." His voice was rough and weary, as if he were already tired of the excuses she had yet to give. "You look cold. And done in."

How like him to think of others before himself. "Aye," she agreed. "I am. But it's no better than I deserve. You look little better."

He shrugged, not making her way any easier. "I am sorry," he said only. And he looked sorry indeed—his face was a mask of a sort of resigned loss, a warding off of greater pain to come. And he kept his distance. As if he knew.

She could not meet his acute green gaze, so she looked out across the expanse of moor and sky, as if it might give her the answers she sought. "There's a lovely solitude up here, isn't there? I can see why you once thought it the whole of the world. I wish it were, too."

"Do you?" His brow rose slowly, weighing her sincerity more carefully than an undertaker.

"Aye. But it's not, is it?" She made herself meet his eye. "And I have unthinkingly brought the whole of the world here to ruin it all. To ruin Cairn and you."

The muscles along his jaw went tight, as if he were preparing to fend off a blow. "Have you?"

"You know I have. How much did you hear?"

He shook his head. "Nothing, really. Couldn't hear over the rain." He looked her in the eye. "Is it over then?"

"Over? Nay." She didn't understand him. "I fear it's only beginning."

He heaved in a great breath and blew it out. "That's some relief, then. Let me take you home, lass. You can tell me all in the comfort of a warm fire, where you won't catch your death of a chill."

"Nay," she insisted. She deserved no such comfort. Not until she had earned it. "I need to tell you now, before I lose my nerve."

His face screwed down into a wince, even as his mouth twisted up in a wry, sideways smile. "Hard to imagine you, lass, without your nerve."

"Aye. It's unnerving."

The wry smile slid to the other side of his mouth. "Well, have at it, lass. Do your worst, for it can't get better until you do."

She wanted to move closer, to be able to read his face clearly. To be able to touch him, and hold him close and convince him—

"Just tell me what happened today, Quince. Tell me what has made you weep?"

He saw too much, and not enough, her Alasdair.

Quince pushed a tight, unhappy exhalation out of her chest, and raised her chin so she could look him in the eye. "My conscience came to call."

"Is that what he calls himself?" He moved closer to the boulder, standing so that he blocked the worst of the blowing rain. "That doesn't sound entirely pleasant."

"It was awful, if you must know." The heat in her chest and throat and eyes was mortification, and no less than she deserved.

"I think I must know, wee Quince." He came close enough to slip an arm around her shoulder, bracing her—or himself, she could not tell—for the worst.

She allowed herself the luxury of leaning against him a little, and warming herself for a moment or two on his surety, borrowing his strength. "Do you remember," she chose her words carefully, "when I told you I would lie for you, if you asked me?"

"The night the Lord Provost came to my house."

"Aye." She tried to read his face. "And I would still, now, to protect you. Because that's what you, did in a way, when you married me. You didn't exactly lie, but you stood up for me, and saved us both from the necessity of lying by marrying me, which was nearly the same thing."

"The end result," he admitted reluctantly, "was to keep you safe."

"The end result was also to keep you safe, as well." It had eased her conscience, and made her decision easier, knowing there had been benefits to them both. "And I always thought that the ends justified the means, but now I am not so sure."

Alasdair cut through her prevarication. "What happened today, Quince?"

What happened was that she found herself upon the edge of a great yawning precipice, poised upon on a knife's edge. "What would you do if you were ever blackmailed?"

"I'd break his nose."

Quince was so astonished, she gaped at him. "You would? How remarkably bloodthirsty of you."

"Aye," he agreed. "I did break the nose of the last bastard who tried to blackmail me. It was the mon I told you about, the friend for whom I had taken the blame. I left him flat on his arse on the cobbles, dripping in his own blood. Of course, he took his tale to my grandfather, so much good it did me. Though the bloodletting did give me a certain satisfaction."

"Alasdair, you surprise me." Quince felt her mouth curve into a wry smile. "You always manage to surprise me. But unsurprisingly, as well as unfortunately, I have acquired another nose for you to break, if you would be so kind."

"What a remarkably bloodthirsty lass *you* are. But I like that about you. You don't quiver and quail in the face of adversity."

She noted that he did not ask whose nose. "I am sorry to disappoint you, Alasdair, but I am nothing but quivering and quailing now. Because the good Reverend Talent is blackmailing me." The name tasted like poison on her lips.

"The vicar? That dirty, dicky bastard." Alasdair's face screwed up as if he had tasted the same vile drink. "But what I can't understand is how a clergyman is even mixed up in all this?"

"He knows the whole of it. Because—"

Alasdair interrupted her by turning her chin up to him. "Do *I* know the whole of it?"

"Mostly, but not his part."

He dropped her chin and stood, putting distance between them. "And what is his part?"

"Firstly, he threatened to tell you. He could not know that I had already confessed—"

"Is that what you call getting caught red-handed, with a pair of pistols filling your grip?"

He was teasing her—she could tell by that lopsided crook of a smile. And also because he took her hand, and held it against his chest where she could feel the strong, steady beat of his heart. Telling her without words that he was protecting her.

"Aye, euphemistically."

"I still cannot fathom how Reverend Talent should be involved in any way?"

Quince took a deep breath. "There was this lad, you see—it all began with him, a long, long time ago. He was out at Winthrop House's gate, all alone. And he was even younger than me at the time." She felt the chill of the damp boulder beneath her, as if the burden of the old story, of carrying it all these years, was weighting her down. "Or at least he seemed younger. He was a scaffy wee thing—small and thin. Malnourished, I understand now. And even if I didn't understand it then, I could see that he was hungry. That he was dirty. And that he was on his own. Orphaned I supposed. Or one of too many mouths to feed with not enough food."

"It's a common enough story." His expression grew serious. "Paris, London, Glasgow, Manchester, Birmingham—they're all littered with such children."

"*Littered.* Listen to yourself. As if they were rubbish, to be thrown away."

"I didn't mean it like that, Quince."

"Well, I did." She could hear the fury rising in her voice, but she didn't care. "Because people talked as if they're lazy and sinful to *let* themselves get hungry. Because in the end, that child was thrown away. He died on our street corner from the hunger, curled up like a rag, and they just threw him into the back of a cart, and hauled him away. I decided when I was old enough to do something about it, that even though I hadn't fed him, I would feed the rest of them." Heat bottled up in her throat, and her heart was slamming against her chest, but it was the truth, and it needed to be said. She raised her voice against the shriek of the wind. "And I'm not sorry in the least. Not in the least. I'm only sorry I got caught."

THERE IT WAS—the truth at last. The whole of the truth, with all the misshapen, unlikely puzzle pieces falling into place at last. It all made such daft sense. "My God. I've married a zealot."

"I'm not a zealot," she insisted, visibly stung by the charge. "I just can't stand idly by, or shrug and say 'That's the way of the world,' when it needn't be."

He astonished her by not arguing, and by instead bringing her hand to his lips. "You really are the most extraordinary lass." The words rumbled out from deep in his chest, because he knew it now more than ever. The truth came to him with all the speed and power of a storm sweeping across the moor. "Devil take you. You gave Talent your ill-gotten gains. For the crofters. Like that family on the road you sent to Saint Cuthbert's. You gave the money to support the charity workhouse there. He was the reason you stole."

She wasn't in the least bit a heedless flibbertigibbet—she was as cunning and resourceful as a she-fox. And as to those scruples she claimed not to have—

"Nay, not the reason. Much as I would like to, I can't

blame either Talent or that poor lad. I became a thief quite on my own. Aye, I did give the money to West Kirk workhouse, but anonymously—I put it in the Poor Box at Saint Cuthbert's. Do good by stealth, as the Bible says. And I never told him where the money came from—I never even spoke to the Reverend Talent before that night at the masquerade."

"My God, Quince. You certainly did give away a great deal of things, but I am coming to see that you never did do away with your scruples. I rather think, despite what you'd like me to think, you kept a firm hold of them."

"Nay," she insisted, determined to make him see the bad along with the good. "I didn't steal so I could give the money away. I gave the money away so I would have an excuse to steal. It is a terrible thing to have to admit about myself, and an even more terrible thing to await your judgment of my character. But the bare truth is I stole because I liked it."

"Ah, lass." He shook his head, and hugged her as if he could possibly contain all the impossible, contradictory feeling careering around within him. "Devil take me, I was right. I did know a thrill-seeker when I saw one."

He wrapped his arms tight around her, to show her what she meant to him. To prove to her that he did not mean to let her go.

"You did," she agreed, looping her own arms around his neck just as tightly. "Though I don't ken how you did, you staid, upstanding politician."

"Quince. Did you never wonder how I knew? Did you never wonder why a staid politician would be attracted to such an inappropriate, thrill-seeking lass?"

She looked at him warily, as if she had been too afraid to allow herself to wonder. "Nay."

He felt as if he had waited forever to tell her. "Because you, my darling wee Quince, are my secret thrill."

"I can't be," she whispered, even as she clung to him. Even as the first faint dawning of hope shone in her face. "You must understand—it's as if something is broken inside me, Alasdair. Like my mother's Sevres vase that I tipped over years ago, smashing into a hundred pieces. I worked for days and days, weeks, carefully gluing and piecing the vase back together to make up for what I had done. But still there was something missing, something irretrievably gone. The cracks were permanent and couldn't be hid."

He took her beautiful, solemn, heart-shaped face in his hands. "I refuse to let you think your character is irretrievable, Quince. Your means were wrong, but your heart was in the right place."

"Don't make me into a saint, Alasdair," she pled.

"All right, I shan't put you upon a pedestal—I shall keep you down here, with me." He put words to action, holding her so close he could feel the strong beat of her brave, ambitious, reckless heart. "But how much was it, in all—the money you gave?"

"I didn't keep a formal ledger, mind you—it didn't seem prudent."

"And Prudence is your middle name." He gave her a warm, teasing squeeze.

"No, it is Louise Alice, actually."

"It ought to be Heedless Unapologetic, if you ask me, which you don't." He teased her with her own acrobatic style of talk. "I begin to see all the puzzle pieces for the first time. But is there any more I don't know?"

Quince nodded, as if she were eager to finally get the whole of it off her chest. "I never did tell Talent where I got the money, but he sussed it out. He had me followed, you see. I thought I was careful—I got away with it for three years, after all—but he had me followed, and discovered where the money came from, and how it got from snuffboxes and buttons to pounds sterling." She took a deep, fearful breath. "Alasdair, you must promise me that you won't use what I'm about to say against…anyone."

Every time he thought he had come to some kind of accord with her, there was another twist, another unforeseen turn. Alasdair closed his eyes and turned his face up to the pouring sky, praying for patience, and understanding, and acceptance. "Against Talent? That, I won't, and can't promise. And I thought you wanted me to break the bastard's nose?"

"Nay. I was not speaking of him, but...others."

"You have confederates?" Alasdair braced himself anew—one nineteen-year-old lass could hardly have caused so much havoc alone. "I don't know if I can promise that, Quince."

"You promised to help me."

"I married you to help you, knowing that our marriage would keep you from any further crime, and thereby removing the problem. But if there are others still—"

"Nay. No one is doing any stealing. That's all stopped." She was emphatic. "I stopped the pilfering immediately after you came."

"But not the highway robbery," he noted. "And so?"

She twisted her nervous fingers into his coat. "I am more afraid than I've ever been to trust you with this, Alasdair."

He answered carefully. "I will try to honor that trust, Quince, but I cannot control every circumstance that might arise to make it impossible."

"But you will try? You will try to keep this confidence, on your honor as a gentleman?"

Everything within him stilled—the charge that he might not be acting as a gentleman never failed to wound him. "Why would you question my honor as a gentleman?"

"I don't question it. I *rely* upon it, which is why I'm asking—"

His relief was such a visceral thing—like an animal released from a cage—that he could barely contain it. So he kissed her—a hard, heartfelt kiss on the lips that was not nearly enough to assuage the hunger and sheer beating joy that burst through him. "You have my word. Upon my honor I will keep your trust to the best of my ability."

Quince took another deep, sustaining breath and forged ahead. "There were others who helped me—not steal, mind you—but to convert the things I stole into ready money. My maid, Jeannie—"

Another piece of the puzzle. "The dressmaker. Her shop lies in Menleith Close."

"Aye. What a distressingly precise memory you have, Alasdair." She drew in another careful, fortifying breath. "And her brother, Charlie, as well, who is a blacksmith."

And there it was—the whole of the picture. "And he melted the goods down, snuffboxes and buttons alike?"

"Aye. That's why I only ever took precious metals and not jewels. Nothing that needed to be pawned or sold in its original form. Although I do still have Lady Digby's pearls, but I had decided to raise my stakes by then. I was planning to send them to Amsterdam eventually."

"My God. Quince." She was nothing if not a spectacularly ambitious brat.

"I ken I'm no good." The worry was back on her face, pleating a line between her brows. "But Jeannie and Charlie are. They only helped me because they felt beholden—the first of the money did help set up Jeannie's shop, and Charlie's forge. But after that, we kept none of it."

"You gave it all to the Reverend Dr. Talent? And how much was it, do you reckon, all told?

"Somewhere in the region of four thousand pounds. Give or take a few florins."

"Pounds sterling?" He was all admiration and incredulity. "That's a bloody fortune."

"Is there any other kind? I told you, Alasdair, I knew what I was about."

"You did, damn you. No wonder Talent doesn't want to give you up. Devil take me, what a puzzle you are."

"That does not seem like a good thing, Alasdair."

"You're a bloody strange, marvelous, rare thing, wee Quince Winthrop." He shook his head, even as he smiled. "In my experience most people, when they descend into a life of crime, do so out of poverty, and want. At least the poorer ones do. Conversely, those who start out in a position of wealth and privilege—as it may be argued you did—turn to crime out of greed and selfishness, and a desire to take from an undeserving world all that they can. They risk their good names, but rarely their very lives, for gain. While you—"

He shook his head, and ran his hands through his dripping hair, and generally made all manner of exasperated gestures to keep him from grabbing her, and laying her down upon the rock as if it were a granite bed, and showing her just what he thought of all her nerve and darling and ambition and bravery. "But you, brat—try as I might to find some personal gain—you have nothing to show for all your troubles."

"I have you as a husband to show for my troubles."

This time he was sure he could see the whole of her heart in her face. "Aye, you do, lass. And none other."

She finally smiled. "None other."

But before he took her home, and put paid to all the disagreements and misapprehensions between them, he wanted to be perfectly, completely sure. "So, just to be perfectly clear, you're not in love with that bastard Talent? And you aren't going to elope in some ridiculously romantic fashion?"

"Holy gods and little fishes, nay! How could you think that?" She was so shocked, she hit him square upon his chest. "I want to break his nose. Which was a great deal less than he—"

"—deserves. Aye. How restrained of you." Alasdair closed his eyes and took a deep breath, in a vain effort to contain the flood of gratitude and relief coursing through him. "My darling brat, you may safely leave the mon to me."

And something that seemed suspiciously like tears of gratitude shone in the corners of her eyes. "Alasdair, that is very kind in you, I'm sure. But I created this awful situation, and I shall have to see myself out of it."

"Must you?" He leaned in to kiss her cheek. Softly. Gently. But also, he hoped, enticingly. "I thought that maybe you'd let me assist and protect you. Just this once. As a sop to my pride."

"Well, Alasdair, when you put it like that. Perhaps just this once. As a sop to your pride."

He enveloped her in a hug so tight, he was half-afraid he might hurt her "My pride thanks you."

She didn't object. "Your pride is quite welcome."

"And what does *your* pride think we ought to do?" He nuzzled along the side of her jaw.

"Tell him to be damned, and tell who he likes. After I have had a chance to warn Charlie and Jeannie, of course. But what do you think we ought to do?"

"I think you're not much of a politician, wee Quince." He punctuated his answer with a kiss. "But I am." He kissed along her brow. "I think I aim to have a nice quiet talk with the reverend—if he thinks he can prove that the money he accepted from you came from stolen goods, then I can prove he was complicit as well."

"Oh, by jimble, that is lovely news. But it bothers me, Alasdair, that I am asking you to bend and use the law to defend me, when I am the one in the wrong."

"And there are those scruples you claim to have sold," he teased. "You have paid your price, wee Quince—you gave up your freedom to marry me. Talent has yet to pay his piper."

"Well, as your scruples have been so much better exercised than mine, I feel certain I can safely rely upon them without question." She sighed against his chest with what he hoped was contentment. "But marrying you is not a punishment, Alasdair."

Her voice was so quiet, he was not sure he heard her correctly. "Is it not?"

"Nay." She turned up her chin, so her warm, clever lips were but inches from his. "In fact, it's rather nice."

He kissed her emphatically, with unmistakable promise and passion. "Only nice, my Lady Cairn? I could offer to make it exquisite."

"My dear Lord Cairn, I do wish you would."

He swept his wife into his arms. "Come away with me, lass, and let me take ye home."

Chapter 28

THE MOMENT ALASDAIR got her out of the rain, and
into the house, he took her face in his hands, carefully,
slowly, giving her all the time in the world to change her
mind, letting his thumb rub across her skin, soft and warm,
until he well and truly lit the spark between them, and she
was all but begging for his touch.

He kissed her gently, lightly, not wanting to press either
his luck, or his urgency upon her. Because the moment his
lips touched hers, he could feel the iron-willed self-control
that had seen him through two days of sitting beside her in
the coach, and a long night of sleeping beside her at the inn,
and days of waiting for her to recover, and another sleepless
night in his own bed, slip away like the rain dripping from
the heavens, falling away to nothing.

Because no matter her larcenous skills, or her avowed
lack of scruples, or her surprising moral core, he wanted her
so badly he ached. But she was young, and tired, and wet,
and chilled, and emotionally wrung out. And he was a
gentleman.

He kissed the corner of her mouth, and then the taut,

sweet slide of her cheekbone, before he put his lips behind her ear, to kiss his way down the exquisite, sensitive tendon. "I'll have you warm in no time, lass."

Quince let out a soft exhalation of pleasure, and tipped her head away to give him access. The scent of rain and citrus evaporated off her skin, filling his head. "Orange blossom—a bridal scent. Who would have thought you so sentimental?"

"I'm not sentimental," she whispered back. "But oh, by jimble, I have missed our lessons in kissing."

He found the very edge of her ear lobe with his teeth. "How unfortunate for you."

She shivered, and turned toward him, seeking his mouth. "How so?"

He took what she offered, tasting the sweet pliancy of her lips. "Because," he whispered against the corner of her mouth. "We are married now, lass, and any tuition"—he let that rough Scots rumble she liked so much drench his voice—"would naturally be more advanced. And involved."

"Oh, aye," was her breathless encouragement.

He left her lips, and took a deep breath. Because this was too important to get wrong. "Let me be sure I understand you, wee Quince." He tipped her chin up so she would see that he was being serious, even as he teased and kissed and smiled. "You would not object to me leading you upstairs at this very moment, and divesting you of each and every piece of your clothing, and making passionate, but entirely thorough love to you?"

"So long as you don't object to me doing the same."

"I most assuredly do not object."

"Good. I thought you'd never ask, Alasdair." She gave him the gift of his name with that wonderfully mischievous, inviting smile. "And we don't even have to go all the way upstairs. We could kiss, and make passionate love somewhere nearer to hand."

"Nay." He resisted her pull upon his hand. "There are plenty of days for making love upon the dining room tables, and smashing every plate in the house, if we so choose.

We've all the time in the world to be impetuous and exuberant, and loud and laughing at some later date. But today, I am going to make love to you properly, with a soft, comfortable, clean bed at your back. Because we have only one first time, wee Quince. And we're going to take our time. And get it right."

"Alasdair." Her laugh was nearly giddy. "You are such a romantic."

"For you—for us—I'm prepared to be. And I like the way you've taken to calling me Alasdair. But when the time comes, you're going to call me Strathcairn. But not yet. Not for a little while. Not until you're naked upon that clean, warm bed, and you are breathless with longing, and you say please, Strathcairn, please."

"Please, Strathcairn, please let us do that now," she said immediately, to let him know she wasn't going to completely give him his way.

But she had met her match in him. "Not yet." Though he laced his fingers with hers, and drew her hand to his lips. "Because we have a few scores that needs must be settled, you and I."

"I don't think I like the sound of that, Alasdair."

He felt her withdrawing, but he didn't let her retreat too far—he held her hand, and kept her close enough to unhook the clasp of her cloak.

"Quince." Once the wet cloak fell away, he began to seek out her hairpins, pulling them out of her fox-bright fall of hair, one by one. "You do realize that in the course of the aforesaid stripping of clothes, and making thorough, passionate love that we will both be quite, quite naked?"

"Quite." Her eyes brightened with interest. "Though my education was most irregular, I do understand how it's done, Alasdair."

He wouldn't let the fact that she was lavishing his name upon him like a gift deter him from his point. "And you do also realize that in the course of such thorough, passionate love making, that you may, in the natural course of things, fall pregnant."

"*Fall* pregnant—what a ridiculous thing to say, Alasdair. Such things don't exactly *befall* a woman all by herself."

"Exactly. But let me be more specific—you, my sweet wee Quince, may become pregnant. Which is something, you may recall, that was a barrier to your marrying me."

"Aye." She drew back, with a frown—a single line pleated itself between her brows, as if remembering. Or reconsidering—he could only hope. "I did."

"And have your wishes changed?" he asked quietly.

Her sigh was answer enough, before she added, "Nay."

The crash of disappointment hit him like a cold wave, dousing his hopes. "Devil take it." He let out a deep sigh of his own. "That is most unfortunate."

"Alasdair." It was she who reached for his hand this time. "Why must it be?"

"Because Quince, it is a request that is impossible for me to honor."

"Why? Can't we—you—do something?"

"Something?"

"Take precautions," she insisted. "I know such things exist."

"You do? What an astonishing sort of education you seem to have gotten, lass."

"Alasdair, you ken what I mean—I've *heard* things. Married women talk about such things all the time when they think no one else is listening."

"And you're always listening."

"Always. And don't give me that look, Alasdair, because I ken you're always listening, too."

"I am, but not to talk about preventing pregnancy." A gentleman had to have standards.

She was all curiosity and frustration. "I thought you had been educated in France?"

"Alas, my education seems to have a serious gap. I did, however, concentrate on learning other skills." He set to demonstrating one such skill, kissing his way from the delicate turn of her wrist, up along the sensitive skin of her inner arm to her elbow.

"How studious of you, Alasdair." Her voice was taking on that soft, blurry edge. "Top marks for initiative."

He took another initiative, and moved to stand behind her, and kiss his way across her nape. "Very studious. Very skillful."

"Then what, my very skilled friend"—she turned, and looked up at him with a bright, encouraging gaze—"can be done?"

He kissed the end of her lovely sweep of nose. "I—we—can take precautions. But they are not entirely effective. So even if we did take precautions, we would still be taking a very great chance. A very, very great chance. So if you want your lesson in anything more than kissing, you're going to have to choose."

She thumped his chest with her forehead—taking him to task. "How inconveniently like you to confront me with such a choice."

He wrapped his arms around her trim little waist and held her tight against him, and rained gentle kisses along her collarbone. "Why don't you think of it, wee Quince"—his lips found the sweet spot just at the very side of her neck below her ear, where he could bite down gently—"as a dare."

"Oh, by jimble, Alasdair." He felt rather than saw the slow dawning of her smile. "Under all those scruples, you're a scoundrel, Alasdair. It's almost as if you ken that I'm the sort of lass who can't resist temptation."

"Oh, I know, lass." He took her mouth in a kiss that he intended to be so tempting it was just short of immoral. "I know."

"Oh, holy sweet cream tea," she said when she came up for air. "I'll take your ruddy dare."

"THANK GOD." HE caught her up in his arms, kissing her deeply before letting her slide down the lovely warm wall of his chest. So deeply she couldn't quite feel her feet touch the ground.

But she was still herself, and could not give herself over entirely to sunshine and heather. "But does it not frighten you?" she asked, since the moment seemed to call for complete candor. "The idea that I could have a child just like me—a thieving, secretive magpie. It's not just frightening—it's terrifying."

"Nonsense. A wee lassie like you? I'd love it. I'd love her," he insisted. "And give her proper attention so she would find and exercise her passions in the right side of the law."

"But what if it were a boy—an unruly, larcenous lad—"

"Stop it, lass. You're borrowing trouble." He heaved out a long-suffering sigh. "Why can you not see the good in yourself? Why do you insist on being bad?"

"Because I am myself." She had to make him understand what a ruddy chore it was to be good, and how much better she had loved being bad. "And I had so much rather be bad and have a lark. Larkiness is good for the soul."

Alasdair shook his head. "But bad for the heart, lass," he said quietly. "Bad for *my* heart."

Something that had to be her own heart suffered a pang of regret. "Oh, Alasdair. I didn't mean—

"And if you have one scruple left in the whole of your body—which I know you do—you'll know that it is bad for your heart as well."

Quince discovering she did have at least one scruple left, because she ached for him, this man who had stood by her through so much. "I do have a heart, Alasdair. Which I was rather thinking about giving to you."

He waited no more than a second to pull her into his arms, and crush her against his chest. "And you said you weren't romantic."

Relief, and some far, far sweeter emotion, made her unexpectedly teary. "And I'm not. I'm practical, and realistic, and—"

"Romantic," he insisted, kissing the corners of her hot

eyes.

"All right," she conceded. "Maybe. Probably. If only you'll stop all this palaver, and take me upstairs and have your way with me, I will be as romantic as you like."

"I thought you'd never ask." And then he swept her into his arms.

Quince wrapped her arms tight about his neck and didn't say another word. She did not stop him, nor pause to give herself a moment more to think on what she was about to do—about to do at last.

She relished the giddy shiver of anticipation that raced across her skin, and seeped deep into her bones like warm honey. She allowed herself to settle comfortably against his chest as he carried her through the hall and up the main staircase, thought she was rather flummoxed to find herself almost paraded through the house, like a triumphal prize.

She knew what to do when she was on her own two feet—she could think then. "Alasdair, you must put me down."

"Nay. You're shivering."

"Not from the cold."

"Can't be too sure, lass. I need to get you out of these wet clothes"—he took the stairs two at a time—"and warm you up. And I have great many useful skills for warming a lass up, each of which I would be delighted to demonstrate for you."

"Very kind of you, Alasdair. I appreciate your thoroughness, but do you think you might hurry—"

"Nay." He gave her his absolute wickedest smile yet, but did not climb the long staircase any faster. "Everything we've ever done has been in a rush, in the dark, out of sight. Today, I'm going to take my own sweet time with you. And nothing you can say will stay me."

For once in her life, Quince didn't want to say anything to stop him. She felt as if it were she, and not he, who had climbed up the long stair, so breathless was she by the time they reached the top, that her heart was hammering in her ears as if her stays were too tight.

They would be loosened soon enough.

Because at last Alasdair was kicking open the carved oak door to the Laird's suite, and carrying her into the high, vaulted bedchamber.

The room was nearly round—part of the original tower of the first moated castle built upon the site, Mrs. Broom had said. But Quince didn't want to think about Mrs. Broom or castles, or history, or anything that wasn't the tall, imposing man who set her down at the foot of a high, imposing, Tudor carved bed. "It's quite impressive."

The impressive man did not entirely take her meaning. "We're not going to talk about architecture, Quince. We're going to talk about your wet clothes, and how we might best get them off you."

As she was wearing her own country clothes—a simple, well-worn jacket that had seen better days, Quince had no attachment whatsoever to the garment. "We get it off like this—" She simply fisted up her lapel and ripped, tearing off all but the last, tenacious button.

"Very efficient. And impressively impetuous." Alasdair put his hands over hers. "But allow me."

Where she would have rushed, he took his time, standing close and sliding his fingers against the soft material, pressing into the barrier of her stays so that she felt the heat of his fingers all the way through the intervening layers of material, all the way across the surface of her skin. When she would have thrown the jacket to the floor, he eased the garment from her shoulders carefully, lingeringly, guiding her free of the tight sleeves, standing so close she could smell the rain on his hair and skin. Rain she wanted to taste.

"Alasdair." She looped her arms around his neck and did just that, kissing the drops from his neck. "I'm not made of spun glass."

"Ah, lass. So impatient. So impetuous." But he said it with a low appreciative murmur of approval that hummed down her spine and stayed, warm and delightful, in her middle. And he allayed her need for closeness by wrapping his own arms around her, crushing her against his chest. He ran his hands down the column of her spine, and around the curve of her bottom, lifting and wrapping her legs around his waist so his torso was pressing against the heat of her.

She gasped at the contact, at the shivers racing across her skin and the sudden glorious tightening of everything within, as he carried her to the edge of the bed, and set her down.

"Boots next." He pushed up the froth of her petticoats.

"I can to that." She bent to unlace the threadbare old things. She knew well enough what to do when they were kissing, but all this preliminary undressing, and leading-up-to, was making her positively nervy. She was made for action, not idleness.

But Alasdair was his own unruffled self, pushing her hands away. "I know you can, but let me, Quince. It gives me pleasure to undress my wife."

"I can't see how," she whispered, her voice lost somewhere at the bottom of the well of feeling echoing through her body as his hands cupped the back of her calf. "Seeing as you've never had a wife before."

His smile grew wider. "And that is why I'm going to take my time, and savor you." His fingers slid northward, exploring the hollow at the back of her knees, gently urging her legs apart. "I'd like to start as I mean to go on. For years and years."

And to demonstrate just exactly what she could look forward to savoring in the coming years, he pushed her knees wide, slowly sliding his palms along the length of her thighs.

She felt as if she were crawling out of her skin, with the need to do something besides sit still and *feel*—her breath felt hot and tight, as if she couldn't breathe. But she didn't care, because on the next breath, he was smiling at her, that gleaming, nearly mischievous, full-butter boat smile that lit her up, and instead of going up in flames, made her feel as if she were melting in the sun. "Oh, by jimble."

"Exactly, lass." And then he slipped one boot free, and put his thumb into the sensitive, ticklish arch of her foot, and pressed, just so.

Just so, a sound of pure animal delight and pleasure slid right out of her mouth and danced down her spine.

"You like that?" He shied one eyebrow over his laughing eyes.

"Oh, holy iced macaroons." She had never felt such unadulterated physical bliss in the entirety of her life. "It feels like morning chocolate tastes, only better." If she had not already been seated she would have toppled over. "Do it again."

He did, kneading deep with of his clever, long, strong, fingers.

The bliss made her topple over anyway. "Oh, Alasdair. If this is any indication of what you are capable, I'm rather sorry I didn't throw myself at you that first night, at Lady Inverness's ball."

"You did throw yourself at me, wee Quince. And I caught you. And I'm very glad I did." He flipped off her other boot and dug his knuckles into her arch. "There's more to come. Much more." And to prove it, he slid his fingers up the back of her legs to untie her garters. Which he did without ever taking his eyes from hers.

She was as spellbound by his look as she was by his clever fingers, brushing along her skin, tugging at the ties of her garters, heating her by degrees as he slowly, slowly rolled her stockings down until her legs were bare.

"And we're just beginning, wee Quince."

She felt joyous, and light, and stupid, as if every touch stole her good sense along with her breath. "You had better not call me wee when you're looking at my breasts, Strathcairn."

Alasdair gave her that wicked, lazy, tomcat smile and drew her to her feet. "Why don't we take a wee look under those stays, and find out? But as I recall, lass, they're magnificent."

Pleasure curled her toes into the thick Persian carpet. Every sensation felt exquisite, every touch a delight. He shivered his palms across her collarbones, and lingered, playing his fingertips in the dips and hollows at the base of her throat. "So lovely."

Beneath the confines of her stays and chemise, her breasts felt tight and swollen. She felt giddy and light-headed and happy. So happy she wanted to share the delight. She reached for his buttons of his waistcoat. "I want to see you, too."

"All in good time, wee Quince. And first things"—he put his lips to the spot where his fingers had just been, while his clever fingers plucked at the ties of her quilted petticoat—"first."

He was taking his time with her, she knew, drawing out each touch, each sensation, lingering and waiting while a yearning worked its way through her. He was clever, her Alasdair, letting the pleasure seep deep into her bones so she was already wanting more of the gorgeous feelings. Already eager for each step toward passion.

He was slow and cautious and oh, so thorough when she wanted to throw herself at him, and have done all at once, in one glorious headlong rush.

But Alasdair would not rush—he sipped when she would have gulped, savoring the pleasure slowly, as if she were a delicate teacup of a woman who might shatter under any pressure.

Well, she wanted to shatter. She was strong enough to break apart and make something new. She wasn't tepid tea, she was strong Scots whisky, hot and volatile, ready to go up in flames. Ready to take him up in flames with her.

Chapter 29

"PATIENCE, LASS," HE breathed against her skin. And no sooner had the heavier outer petticoat come down, that he was already at the lighter underskirt, tugging the tapes free to fall to the floor in a *shush* of fabric that pooled and lapped around her ankles.

Quince stepped out of the soft puddle of material, while Alasdair circled behind her, just out of sight. But not out of mind. Nor out of reach. She could feel the heat of his strong, solid body close against her back, as he brushed his hand through her loose hair, raking his fingers through the length of it, lifting it aside to bare her nape.

Quince curved her head aside, silently granting him access, closing her eyes to give herself over to the exquisite experience of his touch, his care, his love—for that was what he gave her, fully and unconditionally. And that was everything and all she wanted.

His touch was feather light but sure, the gentle impression of warmth and sensuality, as he stroked the backs of his fingers down the arc of her neck, then turned his hand to sweep his palms along the taut tendons, and out across the bridge of her collarbone to her shoulder.

Her skin blossomed with heat and anticipation—from the top of her head to the bottom of her bare toes, she tingled with awareness and longing for more of his touch.

"Tell me what you like, lass," he instructed into her ear.

"I like this." She hadn't sufficient experience to imagine more that the delicious sensations he was currently arousing. "But you tell me what you like, too."

"Oh, aye. I like to look at you." His hands circled the slim span of her waist, just as they had that first night in the darkened room at the ball. But this time his touch held no anger, only reverence and passion. "To look down your wee bodice, at those magnificent breasts."

Beneath his gaze, those small breasts grew full and tight and so aching with pleasure that she couldn't contain the low, breathless murmur of delight that slid off her lips. "Tell me more."

"Aye, lass. I'll tell you." He tucked his chin over her shoulder, and eased her flush against his chest, letting her feel the full length of his arousal between them, showing her that he was a man, with a man's appetites and desires.

The heat of his body warmed her through, but still she shivered.

"I've got you, lass." He flicked the tapes of her shoulder straps loose, and brushed aside her chemise, bending his head to nip and salve the sensitive slide of her shoulder. His mouth rounded to the hollow of her throat, and she could feel the rising cadence of her pulse where it beat against his lips.

"Alasdair." It was a delight to give him the gift of his name. A delight to reach back and find his familiar face, and stroke the strong stark angles along his granite jaw.

He turned his face into her hand, rubbing the rough texture of his incipient beard into her palm, chafing her in a way that was discomfort and pleasure all at once. Pleasure that she wanted to experience with hands and lips and tongue.

She gave him her mouth eagerly, turning into the kiss,

but once their lips met, and she tasted his desire, she gave him her mouth completely, all hungry lips and dancing tongue, bending back to him with the strength of her own desire.

While they kissed, his hands were not idle—he stripped the laces from her stays with sure, strong strokes that tugged and released, tugged and released, until her stays fell away, tossed onto the heap of her petticoats, and she stood before him in nothing more than a chemise of thinnest, most translucent cotton.

Never had she felt more vulnerable, or more strong. More ready. Ready for his touch. Ready for his love.

He set his hands to roaming, tracing the size and span of her through the thin layer of cotton, delineating the flare of her ribs and the warm curve beneath her breasts. He spread his clever fingers out, grazing across her body from belly to breasts, stroking his thumbs back and forth, until awareness and deep saturated pleasure flooded across the surface of her skin. Until she was straining and arching into his hand, silently urging her breasts into the cups of his palms. And then not so silently. "Alasdair, please."

"Aye, my wee Quince. Keep saying my name like that. Keep saying *please* in that lovely, wanton, needy voice, and I will grant every last one of your desires." He picked her up, and carried her to the bed, where he came down on top of her, pressing her into the soft mattress with his weight and his strength and his need.

She could feel the length of his arousal between them from the crease of her thigh to her belly. And when he moved, easing himself against her, her own body rose of its own accord, rubbing against him like a cat, eager for his touch, meeting his need with her own desire.

And eager to touch for herself. She clutched his back, greedy for the weight and length of him atop her body, greedy for the kisses that grew hotter and bolder still, until she could think and feel and taste nothing but the lazy, breathless rapture of his tongue twining with hers.

Quince breathed in the taste and scent of him—the clean

drink of rain, the exotic dash of spice mixed with the aura of experience—and let it go to her head. She was intoxicated with him—she had been from the first moment she saw him, tempting her from across the ballroom, her own red, forbidden fruit.

And she was hungry for him. She wanted to taste that fruit of his knowledge, to share everything and all that she was with him. He had already seen her at her most naked, most flawed, and he had not turned away.

She was suddenly anxious for him to be naked in reality, to shed the last vestiges of cover between them. She went at his clothing with careless abandon, heedless of buttons and seams, anxious to feel the breadth and curve of his firm muscles beneath her palms. To feel the sleek bliss of his skin against hers.

Alasdair laughed and lifted away from her enough to shuck his coat and waistcoat, sending them sailing across the room to land on some unseen piece of furniture, before he reared back on his knees to peel his linen shirt off over his head, and she could marvel and ogle him as she had that day in the inn.

But now she could touch him as well. She could skate her hands across the firm boundaries of his chest, and tease the flat of his nipples into tight contraction, and trace the line of bright ginger hair down to the waist of his breeches. "Are you really going to be ginger all over?"

He laughed. "We'll find out, won't we? But not yet. Not just yet. There's more I'm curious about, as well." He curled his hand around her breast, cupping and touching her through the fine cotton lawn of her chemise, thumbing her until the sensitive peak of her nipple contracted into a tight bud, and something darker and more demanding than mere need spiked through her with all the finesse of a thunderclap.

And then his lips replaced his hands, and he was kissing her, wetting and nipping through the layer of fabric until his mouth closed around her nipple.

"Please," was all she could think to say—all other words

but entreaty abandoned her. All other thoughts dissolved until she was nothing but want and need and shivering, wondrous desire.

But she didn't care. Not when he bared his teeth and bit down gently, teasing and abrading her nipple until she arced up into the blissfully painful pleasure.

Alasdair was a fair man, and transferred his attentions to her other breast, kneading and kissing the tight pink bud into an exquisite peak with his hands and mouth.

That familiar slippery jangle of anticipatory excitement burst within her veins, spreading like an opiate, until want became physical desire, an insistent demand that drove her on. She fisted up the chemise, dragging it up and off her skin.

He leaned away, lifting himself on elbows and then hands, and then levering himself to kneeling, as she drew the thin fabric up and over her head.

And she was naked and wanting before him. Just as he had said she would be.

"Strathcairn." She said his name because she wanted him to know. Wanted him to understand.

And he did. He looked at her, letting this hands trail where his eyes led, smoothing around the curve of her breast, stroking down the sides of her ribcage, and sweeping down across the flat of her belly to the flesh of her thighs. "Milky white," he said. "I knew they would be."

He came over her, laying his long lean body over hers once more, teaching her the shock of sensation as the rough fabric of his breeches rubbed against her sensitive skin, and the buttons on his breeks bit teasingly into her flesh.

"They would, wouldn't they, being your buttons."

He could not possibly understand her, but he smiled anyway—she felt it in the warm hum of vibration as he bent his head to toy with the sensitized peaks of her breasts. He speared his fingers into her hair, his big hand cradling her skull, holding her as he ravaged her with pleasure.

She wasn't idle, or passive—she wanted to touch him as well. To run her own fingers through the bright fall of his russet hair, press her palms flat to the warmth of his muscles, and taste the salty tang of his smooth skin.

She wrapped her hand around his neck, and pulled him to her so she could kiss his face and let her lips skate across the smooth planes of his cheekbones, along the firm pliancy of his mouth, and along the rougher, raspier skin of his strong jaw.

She filled her hands with him, reaching between them to cover the length of his arousal where it pressed into the soft flesh of her belly.

"Oh, God, aye, lass," he breathed, before he backed off the bed and stood, toeing off his boots and stomping out of his stockings. Urgency finally had him in her greedy grip, and Quince watched with equal parts wonder and awe as he rapidly unbuttoned the row of fasteners down the placket of his breeches.

And then he was shucking the breeches off, flinging them over his shoulder to join her discarded clothing scattered across the floor and furniture. And then he was there, crawling back over her, and his mouth was on hers, filling her senses until every thought and feeling began and ended with his kiss.

Quince held on tight, running the flat of her palms along the sinuous line of his shoulders, leaner and harder than any man who lived in London had a right to be. "What on Earth do you do there, to make you like this?"

She didn't wait for an answer, as he could have no idea what she was talking about, but went on with her admiration of him, stroking down the sleek muscles of his back and up the long straight column of his spine.

She kissed him with everything she had within her, all her wit and cleverness and exuberance. But all her charms were nothing compared to him, and his skill and experience and subtlety. He touched her and every thought disappeared, every obstacle fell away, until they were rolling, tumbling together with his long legs scissoring through hers. Until she was giddy with happiness and the rush of pleasure that came from knowing they were at last together. That nothing was ever going to keep them apart.

Her legs tangled with his, twisting and lacing them together until they were one body, one heart, one mind. And they were kissing and kissing until she began to laugh out loud from simple silly happiness.

This was what she wanted. This. This man. This love.

His hand once again covered the roundness of her breast, before his lips followed to kiss her flesh into tight peaks. "Magnificent,' he said, his voice turning rough. "Magnificent and mine."

And she was arching into him, giving herself to him, abandoning herself to the exquisite pleasure that blossomed deep as the pull of his lips created a tight needy heat low in her belly.

The warm summer air caressed her bare skin as he rose above her, and let his hand trail down the line of her inner thigh, making tight, lazy circles across the surface of her skin with the tips of his fingers, slowly tantalizing her.

She felt his touch all the way through her, deep inside, a tight constriction of want that spread through her, leaving her breathless and rising into his hand. Needy for some stronger touch.

"Strathcairn," was all she could say to try and articulate the heedless hunger that was rising within. "Alasdair."

She wanted to say more, to find the words to tell him what she wanted, but he stopped her mouth with a kiss, and came down on top of her, his long, strong body fitting over hers with perfectly imperfect symmetry, like the two halves of a lock, meshing together.

She closed her eyes and gave herself over to him, to the soul deep pleasure that burned under her skin as his hands drew down the long run of her legs, and back up, nearer and nearer to the center of her pain and pleasure.

Again and again he stroked up and down until she was moving beneath him, arching and twisting in needy anticipation, opening to him as wave after wave of sensation pushed her higher and higher on the crest of desire.

She felt stretched beyond the limits of what was possible,

taut and ready—ready for the pleasure he gave her like a gift. Her skin was on fire with anticipation as his long clever fingers teased at the tight heat at the junction of her thighs. Her body was moving of its own accord, arcing toward his hand, opening to the exquisite torture of wanting more. More than she had. More than she understood.

And then he gave her more.

He bent his head toward her heat and kissed her there. There, where the tip of his tongue slid inside her, and she was nothing but bliss and need bound together, gasping for air and holding her breath all at the same time.

"Quince." Her name on his lips was a sound of approval and encouragement that vibrated into her core and echoed down through her body like a shout. The warmth of his mouth filled her, arousing and soothing all at once, kindling her desire into flame, stoking the fire higher, until she was rising, soaring on the pleasure he lavished upon her.

And then with one exquisite touch, he licked her once more, and she felt as if she were bursting into flame, burning away her edges, spending and renewing the growing, glowing heat within.

She made a breathless sound of want, as if she were desperate for air, desperate for water to quench the flame.

But he touched her with his tongue again, and again, swirling the hot passion through her until it reached the palms of her hands, and still it spread until there was no place left for it to go, nothing left but him and his mouth and bliss pouring over her.

And then she went higher still. He slipped a finger inside her, touching her deeply, stroking gently and strongly all at the same time, until a pleasure so sweet and so intense it was almost pain rained down inside her.

Her hands closed into fists in his long, gorgeous, russet hair, holding him to her. Holding him tight. Holding her love.

But she couldn't contain all the need and desperate yearning. Another sound, a gasp of hunger and want poured out of her, but he heard her and understood, because that moment another long articulate finger followed the first, and she began to feel filled up to the brim of her longing.

With his fingers in her, his tongue swirled over her one last time, and she threw herself out—out into the heat and sunshine, out into the warm oblivion, soaring into the hot, happy bliss.

It was minutes—hours, days—before she came back awareness, to find herself in the soft comfort of her husband's bed. He was on his knees before her, watching her, smiling with a grave sort of wonder.

"Is something wrong?" she asked. Not that she really cared. She felt dazed and lazy and so happy she couldn't be bothered with thinking.

"Impossible," he assured her. His voice came closer, and the mattress shifted as he leaned down to kiss first one, then the other eyelid closed. "Just go on as you've begun."

"Begun?"

"Only just begun, lass. There's more. So much more."

She closed her eyes obligingly, and then the pad of his thumb brushed against her lower lip, a gentle invitation to a kiss. His mouth followed his hand, deepening the kiss, asking her to open to him, to the heat and smooth friction of his tongue. To the hunger that reasserted itself at the first taste of him.

But she was not alone in her hunger. He kissed her with the same sort of appetite, as if he were fast exhausting his share of patience and prudence and caution. As if he too had a need that only she could fill.

The weight of his body pressed her deeper into the soft mattress, and her senses were filled with him—with the taut texture of his mouth, with the soft fall of his long red hair as it brushed against her breasts, with the sharp rasp of his teeth as he kissed his rough way along the sensitive line of her jaw.

Her head fell back into the pillows, letting him have his wicked way with her, nipping and laving the hollow at the base of her throat, moving lower still until his tongue and lips were on her breasts, teasing and tugging, unraveling the twisted skein of her soul. And she was arching up to meet him, giving him all that she had, offering up the entirety of her being, if only he would give her more of the pleasure as potent as whisky.

She cradled his skull, holding him to her, holding herself tight against the potent rush of pleasure that coiled within.

He levered himself away, and she felt the loss of him— of his heat and his weight and his reassurance. But before she could pull him back, he found her hands, and interlaced her fingers with his, holding her in a different way as he placed their hands over her head.

And then he was kneeling between her legs, kneeing her thighs apart, and she was open to him, stretched past the limits of experience and imagination, as his body settled between her hips. And he was pushing into her, stretching and filling her slowly, making his way into her body until he was fully sheathed within.

"Quince." He said her name like an oath, like a prayer.

But she couldn't speak, couldn't answer him. She felt heat and pressure, and pleasure and pain all swirling together, tumbling her up like a mountain burn, rumbling through her. She wanted to move, and he was moving with her, flowing into her, ebbing and advancing, reaching higher and higher with every surge of his body into hers.

He made a sound that was both elation and anguish, and he gripped her fingers as if he, too, feared being swept away. As if he could no longer hold back the force of the want.

He leaned his weight onto his hands where they were joined above her head, and she felt her body bow upward, toward him as he surged into her, pushing deep into her core. And then deeper still, because he bent his head and took her breasts between his lips and teeth, closing down around her peaked nipples, sucking and laving and sending a burst of hot bliss showering through her body.

And still she was greedy, hungry for more—more of the playful torture of his teeth on her skin, more of the erotic friction of his belly against hers, more of his strength. More.

And then he let go of her hands, and she was loose and

soaring, untethered to the earth, held aloft on pleasure. He skimmed his own hand down the side of her ribs, sliding along the flat of her belly, grazing across the dark chestnut hair that covered her mons. He stroked her there, before he parted her flesh and brushed a feather light touch across the exact spot where his tongue had been before.

Heat built into a sensation that burst within, and she was gone, rushing over the edge.

And he was with her, shouting her name, holding her fast, swept away with her, falling and floating down the wide river of their love.

She stayed there, floating, gasping for air, listening as their breathing and heartbeats eventually slowed, and their bodies cooled. It seemed forever before she even wanted to open her eyes. But there he was.

"Strathcairn," she breathed his name. "You certainly do ken how to give a lass a thrill."

Alasdair lay on his side next to her, stroking her tangled hair away from her temple. He leaned over to kiss her there. "Thrilled enough to be wanting more?"

"Aye." She was lingering in the last of the drowsy bliss, in no rush to let the languorous feeling of peace and rightness dissipate. "Give me a moment, or two, and I will certainly want more."

Chapter 30

ALASDAIR HAD THE Reverend Talent run to ground like the rat he was early the next morning, because, as his young wife had so perceptively said, what could not be avoided ought to be tackled straightaway.

And so straightaway, Sebastian was enlisted to put his cool perceptiveness to work. His secretary quickly discovered the rat holed up close by, at the village inn. It was as Alasdair had predicted—animal instinct only ever got a person so far. But to make sure that the reverend got no farther, he had Seb, backed by two of Castle Cairn's brawer gamekeepers—a pair of rough, strong-legged lads—make sure the reverend accepted Alasdair's invitation to join him at the Castle.

They waited together, he and Quince, hand in hand, united against their common enemy.

"Oh, by jimble. There's something you should know." Quince turned to him with whispered urgency, as footsteps could be heard in the corridor. "Do you remember how you called me a zealot?"

"Aye?" Alasdair smiled in acknowledgment.

"Well, I am strictly an amateur in comparison to the reverend. He is the real zealot. 'The ends always justify the means when doing the Lord's work,' he said. Or something very near. But you get the gist."

"I do, indeed."

"He's utterly devoted," she went on. "All that mattered to him is that the money I gave could be used to glorify the Lord, and nothing should be put in the way of me continuing to do that."

"I see." Alasdair squeezed her hand in reassurance. "Thank you for telling me."

"And he's smart, and imperturbable. Nothing I said, no attempt at logic would sway him." He could hear the worry in her voice.

"It will be all right, Quince. I promise." Though he was sure had Quince been trained up for the law, she would have made a formidable speaker. He himself *had* trained both in Parliament and the government for just such a moment, and he was more than prepared to use every rhetorical trick at his disposal to get and keep an edge ahead of Talent.

And then their nemesis was there, the Reverend Talent, shown into the estate office by McNab. Sebastian and the lads hung back in the corridor, and let the reverend come in alone.

"My Lord Cairn." Talent bowed, hat in hand, very correctly. "You wanted to see me?"

"I did." Alasdair said nothing more, but gestured to a chair on the other side of the desk, wanting to take his time and proceed in a thorough, controlled manner.

"Lady Cairn." Talent acknowledged Quince with a smile so snidely pleasant it was guaranteed to make Alasdair's blood boil.

He managed to control himself, and kept a firm grasp upon his temper. But at his side, Quince was not so deliberate—she was almost twitching with an itchy restlessness. Patience and deliberation were clearly not her strong suits—a sort of straightforward bravery was.

"It's no use, Reverend Talent. I've told my husband all. I've told him that you're blackmailing me, and why."

Talent absorbed that information in silence, with only a

raised brow and a tight smile that told Alasdair the reverend wasn't quite sure if he believed her.

So Alasdair decided to make it more complicated.

"I don't believe her, either. Not that you aren't trying to extort money from her—that I believe—but that she has actually done any of the things she says you've accused her of. I can't believe her capable."

Beside him, Quince gasped at such an unexpected gambit.

To strengthen his argument, Alasdair let go of Quince's hand and strolled around to sit on the edge of the desk directly in front of Talent. "No, I don't believe her at all."

"You should," the reverend maintained. "You—"

Alasdair cut him off, determined to keep him off balance. "And am I to take the word of an admitted blackmailer?"

Alasdair's accusation caught Talent off guard. "No. I— I didn't admit to—"

"Of course, you just did. " Alasdair slapped the flat of his palm against the desk as if he were hammering a judge's gavel. "Your very presence here today is an admission of that fact. Your very presence in this village, over a hundred miles away from your parish, is evidence of the fact that you came here with the express purpose of luring a wife away from the influence of her husband and the sanctity of her marriage—a marriage you yourself performed. What on Earth were you thinking, Talent, to be so devious? To act in so ungodly a manner. What on Earth do you expect your bishop will say? Good Lord, Talent, you have got yourself into a world of trouble."

"My bishop? But you should want to keep him from knowing. Her ladyship—"

"Do you have proof of her ladyship's involvement?" Alasdair pressed, leaning forward to physically loom over Talent. "Can you show me this beyond a shadow of a doubt?"

"Well," he hedged. "You have my word—I know exactly what and where—"

"Exactly what, if you have no proof other than the word of a blackmailer?"

Talent drew himself together. "Rumor and innuendo will be enough to see her ruined."

"Ruined for what?" Alasdair immediately fired back. "Her prospects? I've already married her."

"Her standing in society," Talent countered. "Edinburgh—"

"Society?" Alasdair roared. "Think, mon! If I don't believe you, who do you think will?"

"But the rumor will get out, and—"

"Think, you addlepated preacher. That's the terrible thing about rumor, Talent—it will get out, most assuredly. And nothing travels faster than its stink. But it fouls everything it comes into contact with, Reverend. Everything and everyone—Saint Cuthbert's, the charity workhouse and all the good work you've done there, and you yourself. No one will escape being tarred with a fouled brush. Think hard before you choose to ruin everything you've worked so hard to achieve."

"But—"

"If the rumor that the workhouse has knowingly been running on the proceeds from stolen goods—certainly aiding, if not abetting a criminal activity—reached the Edinburgh Presbytery, or God help you, the General Assembly of the Kirk of Scotland, I've no doubt they would close the workhouse down, and transfer you God knows where. Even here, to serve my village. Wouldn't that be an apt punishment?"

Talent paled, but rallied. "But either you believe she did it—or none of those things you are talking about could have happened."

"Of course not," Alasdair agreed to confuse him, before he ground on. "It's the rumor, Reverend. Once you let that particularly stinking cat out of the bag you'll never stuff it back in. You won't be able to keep it from going places you didn't even know existed—the Rector of Saint Cuthbert's, the Presbytery, the General Counsel of the Kirk. No, no," he counseled in his best and most prudent ministerial tone. "Best not to even start, but go home and keep your peace. Then all will be well."

"But what about her?" Talent pointed at Quince in accusation. "What about all the wrong she's done?"

"If she did it—and I still await your absolute proof that such a decided and well-known flibbertigibbet could have done even half of the things of which you accuse her—it was all in the service of God. And who is like to object to that? Besides the Presbytery and the General Council, who take a graver view of such moral matters?"

"But—"

"No. Leave it be," he advised.

But Talent still showed signs of rebellion—his face was flushed with ruddy heat, and his eyes glittered with that zealous need to be right.

So Alasdair rose and moved closer. So close Talent had to move his feet, lest they be stepped on. And he leaned over the clergyman in such a way that Talent had to crane his neck and look almost directly upward to meet Alasdair's eyes. "And furthermore, Talent, if you persist in this foolish enterprise, I find I'll have to simply break your goddamned nose. Or better yet, I'll let my wife break your nose herself, while I hold you. She's got a hell of a right."

"What?" Talent shot out of his chair, knocking it over, scrambling backwards, gaping at Alasdair and Quince alike. "But she's—"

"Entirely capable," Alasdair finished with a vast deal of satisfaction. "Never underestimate the power of a woman to accomplish what's right, Talent. Never."

Talent backed toward the door.

"Mr. Oistins?" Alasdair called.

"My Lord?" Sebastian was immediately at the door, his braw lads behind him.

"Please see that the reverend is safely put on the Post leaving for Edinburgh, so he might return to his parish in peace. And in one piece. No need to mention this to the staff, of any of the villagers, or I doubt I should be able to answer for Mr. Talent's safety."

"Most assuredly, my lord." Sebastian bowed in his restrained, vigilant way. "I will see to the reverend's safety myself."

"No!" the reverend cried, clearly unnerved at such a prospect. "Don't touch me. I'll see myself out. I'll get my own transport back to Edinburgh."

"Nevertheless…" Alasdair let the thought—innuendo and threat—hang in the air. "Do what you will, Reverend Talent. Let your conscience be your guide. But remember, everything—all actions—have a cost. Be sure you are prepared to pay yours."

His words were met with silence for a long time, until Talent finally said, "I understand you perfectly, my lord."

"Good. Have a pleasant journey, Mr. Talent. I don't expect we'll be seeing you again. Ever. Good day." And with that he turned his back upon the door, and waited until he heard the latch firmly close, before he turned to his wife. "And that, I will wager you, is the last we shall ever see of the bad Reverend Talent.

His darling, disreputable wife launched herself into his arms. "Oh, Alasdair. You were magnificent. Truly. And I am the luckiest lass in all of the land." She buried her face against his neck, but he could still hear her words. "Because I get to make my home with you, and keep you by me for all the time I have in this life. And that is full fair marvelous."

"My darling brat." He wrapped his arms around her, and nothing had ever felt so good, and so right.

QUINCE DECIDED TO order a simple supper for two laid out in the dining room.

She dressed carefully for her husband's company. A marchioness has to be seen to be believed, her Mama had once said, and Quince would give Alasdair something to believe in.

She chose one of the more opulent of her borrowed gowns—an old-fashioned, narrow-waisted confection of white satin with decorative lacing—that was neither too grand, nor too ordinary, but did show her décolletage off to best advantage.

"That is a lovely gown you're almost wearing," was her husband's marvelously predictable greeting as he came to her dressing table and kissed her on the shoulder. "You look a treat."

"Thank you, Alasdair. So do you. That crimson velvet is my absolute favorite. Even without the buttons."

"I'm glad you approve." But his eyes were all for her. "As do I—that gown does wonderful things to your manifest charms. It makes me damn glad I forced you to marry me."

He was teasing her, so she could not help but laugh. "You forced *me*? Alasdair, we both know that's not how it was. And you should know enough of me by now to ken that I can't ever be forced to do something I don't want to."

"Nonetheless, I arranged it." He moved in front of her to prop himself on the edge of her dressing table, partially blocking her view of the mirror. Not that she particularly minded, as the mirror showed off his trim backside to all kinds of perfection. "Don't forget I went to all the trouble of shooting you, just to make sure you couldn't escape me. Aye. " He lowered his voice to that deep Scots rumble she so liked. "From the very moment I pictured you stuffing my buttons down between your very lovely, very white breasts, everything I have done has been to the single purpose of being able to see more of those very lovely white breasts. More of you." He looked her in the eye. "All of you."

His words hit her like a soft blow—she staggered just a bit. Or would have, had she not already been sitting. But still, she was moved enough that he could see she was not as immune to him as she wanted him to think. "Stop it. You'll make us miss our supper."

"Perhaps I have something else in mind?" He leaned back against the edge of the table, and let her think. And more importantly feel. What his hands might feel like if his fingers were caressing her as intimately as his eyes.

Until he frowned at her. "Something, I fear, is missing."

"What?" she leaned around to peer at herself in the looking glass. "I don't like to powder my hair, and I can't stand wearing feathers. Or—"

Alasdair stopped her by placing a very old-looking, flat, rectangular, blue leather box in front of her.

"Alasdair," she said when she had found her voice. "Please tell me you are not tempting me with jewels."

"I am." He flipped open the box. "The Strathcairn emeralds."

"Oh, by jimble," she whispered. She had seen such a demi-parure of matching stones before, and even been tempted to steal them. But she never had. And she had never, not once in all her years of magpie larceny, ever thought she would ever be gifted with such incomparable jewels.

"My mother never wore them, I'm told, nor did my grandmother, who felt the green stones didn't favor her complexion. But you"—he shook his head as he smiled— "I'll wager your fortune they will favor you."

"Alasdair, they're beautiful." Her voice was low and quiet and rough—full of the most wretched gratitude. "They must be worth a fortune."

"Why does it matter what they are worth?" he asked just as quietly.

"Because," was her only answer.

"I had wondered if you might like them better if you got to steal them? I could leave them lying about for you to find." His voice was full of warmth, and he was smiling, so she knew he was teasing. "Or are you instead tempted to pack them off to Amsterdam and pawn them?"

"Alasdair, be serious. They are too precious, and too old, and too stunning to do something as ridiculous as pawn. You had best not to give them to me. Don't tempt me beyond endurance."

"My poor, darling brat." He pressed a kiss to her

forehead. "Most women would be tempted to steal such jewels to keep for themselves. But you are tempted to sell them away." He stood and walked behind her. "But they are your jewels now, and you may do with them as you please. Sell them or not, it is up to you."

"You can't mean it." Her eyes burned with the most wretched gratitude.

"I do mean it, Quince. You are the Marchioness of Cairn now."

"Aye, I know, and I've given you a sorry excuse for one."

"You misunderstand. Do you not see and understand that instead of stealing your bits and bobs from ballrooms, and pressing pound after pound into the poor box, you might harness the power of society to what is both good and right? Did you never think that as Marchioness of Cairn, you could take all your hidden scruples and bring them out into the light and make real change? Not spare florins and pennies change, but real change that will amount to far more than the cost of an old set of jewels. Use them as you like—as a start. They are yours. And you are far more valuable to me than their cost."

"Oh, Alasdair." Quince didn't know when she had felt so completely, entirely, peacefully happy. "You really are the most wonderful mon, scruples and all." Heat and gratitude and love and ridiculous need to laugh all piled up behind her eyes. "Don't you dare make me cry. I'll look a wreck at dinner."

"I will not notice your red eyes if you wear these. Here." He plucked the heavy necklace out of its satin lined nest, and placed it about her neck. "I was right. They do look as if they were made for you."

The green jewels looked warm and glowing against the white of her skin. "Oh, Alasdair, the jewels are beautiful."

"Are they? I was talking about your rather magnificent breasts," he clarified.

"Alasdair." She lowered her chin and looked up at him from under her lashes just the way he liked. "You're only saying that so I'll let you—"

"Take greater liberties? Make you late for supper?" He bent to kiss and warm her neck just above the cool stones. "Aye. Aye, I am. But I also aim to let you take greater liberties with me, as well. As many as you'd like. But as you've become such a shy, demure type, I reckon you need encouragement in your liberties. Instruction, even. And opportunity."

She stood and turned to him, leaning into the solid strength of his chest. "I'm neither shy, nor demure, and well you know it."

Alasdair wrapped his hands around her waist and pulled her tight against him. "No," he breathed his agreement, "you're all blistering cheek and bravado."

She made her tone full of the aforementioned cheek. "Is this to be another one of your lessons in kissing?"

"I reckon this just might be rather more than kissing." And to demonstrate exactly what he was talking about, he traced a finger along the top of her bodice, across the sensitive swells of her breasts, protected only by layers of cotton and lace and satin, like so much armor. "In fact, I think there might not be very much kissing at all."

"But I like kissing."

He smudged his thumb along the ripe ridge of her lip. "And so you do. And so do I. But let us see if you might like something…else as well as you do kissing."

"Something else?" Her voice had gone soft and slightly breathless.

"Something more intimate," he whispered. His breath fanned along her temple, disarranging her artfully arranged curls. "Something much more personal."

She went up on tiptoe until his lips were mere inches from his. "More personal than kissing?"

"Oh, I don't know." He let his hands skim down the column of her neck and across the delicate sensitive skin of her collarbone. His voice was gently chiding. Teasing her softly. "How intimate is this?"

The ripe, pink tip of her breast just barely crested above the lace and fine lawn of her chemise. He let his clever fingers skim over her once, twice, until she was arching into the weight of his palm, digging her fists into his velvet sleeve.

Her breath came shallow and fast as he cupped her more firmly, and thumbed the sweet peak into a tight furl of pleasure. "Well. I was wrong." His voice was distracted, and vaguely wondrous. "I think there's bound to be some kissing after all."

He set his lips to her breast, and pleasure blossomed under her skin, speeding heat and heady bliss. Hunger for something other than soup had her in its greedy grip. And she really didn't mind. "I think I've had quite enough lessons on kissing." She began to fist up the yards and yards of fabric that made up her skirts.

"I disagree. Quite passionately. We've only just begun to skim the surface of what goes on in the business of kissing. Although you're coming along quite nicely. Very nicely if I may say so." He crushed her against his chest. "Come."

"Where?"

"To bed."

"Too far." She swept her brushes off the table and onto the floor, although she was a bit more careful with the powder—she only wanted to make love to her husband, not ruin the carpets—sliding the box well out of the way. "This mahogany looks sturdy enough."

"I want to make love to you properly, Quince. In a bed, like a goddamned lady."

She shrieked with laughter. "We both know I'm not much of a lady."

"You're enough, brat. More than enough. Even if you're not lady, you're my wife."

He hooked a finger beneath her neckline, and found the tight peak of her breast. The sound she made was as exuberant as it was unrestrained. "And you are wearing a dress that gives me an absolutely spectacular view of your magnificent breasts—"

"I choose it with just such a view in mind."

"Clever, clever lass." He kissed the sass off her lips.

"And as a reward, I'll have to ravish my wife upon her dressing table, in the most impetuous, heedless manner—" He tugged at the bodice. "Are you sewn into this thing?"

"I am. But I've my wee dirk"—she slid her old ring knife out of the side of her bodice—"that I used to use to steal buttons, to make it that much easier for you."

"Oh, Lady Cairn." He could feel his grin slide straight across his face. "Extra points for being prepared."

"Thank you, Alasdair." Her hands were at the ribbon of his queue. "I try to have a sense of occasion."

She laughed and laughed as he picked her up and sat her on the table amid the profusion of her skirts, like an exquisite bloom. She leaned back and gripped the edge of the table in inviting readiness. Everything within her encouraged him—her lips, her hands urgent at his hips, her voice. "Shall we break all the china?"

"All." And he was looking at her in that way that was so intent it was embarrassing and mesmerizing and angelic and wicked all at the same time. He looked at her as if she were a puzzle he had no hope of solving, but was enjoying anyway. He looked at her as if there were nothing else and no one upon the earth at which to direct his focused gaze. He looked at her as if, despite her many and spectacular faults, she mattered to him. Just as much as he mattered to her.

"I love you, Alasdair." He was perfect. Perfectly flawed. Perfectly human. And most perfectly hers.

"I know, brat. And I love you, too. In all the world, you're the only temptation I can't resist."

And that was exactly how she liked it.

Please turn the page for an exciting excerpt from
Elizabeth Essex's next Highland Brides novel

*MAD, BAD, AND
DANGEROUS TO MARRY*

Coming Soon!

MAD, BAD & DANGEROUS TO MARRY

Castle Crieff, Scottish Highlands
1792

IT WAS ALWAYS going to be a delicate, tricky thing, to marry a man one had never met before one's wedding day. But until the moment the carriage rolled into the forecourt of Crieff Castle, Lady Greer Douglas had not suffered a single twinge of worry. For all that she had never met her bridegroom in person, she and the Duke of Crieff knew each other well.

Well enough to marry, sight unseen.

She knew him by the hundreds of letters they had exchanged since the day she turned fourteen years old, some eight years ago. Letters he had faithfully, and hopefully joyfully, written up until one month ago. That last letter—the one telling her he was at last ready to marry, if she was also—was folded deep in the pockets beneath her petticoat, tucked away for safekeeping, like a talisman she could touch for strength and reassurance.

And she needed reassurance now, as the coach rolled to a stop, and the grey gravel crunched under the grooms feet. This was the moment it all began—the life she had been waiting, preparing, planning to lead.

From the backward facing seat, Papa beamed at her. "You look beautiful."

"And you *are* beautiful." Beside her, mama gave her words an entirely different, but no less heartfelt, meaning.

"Thank you. Thank you both." Greer knew she was not a conventional beauty—she was too-flamed haired to be considered pretty anywhere but Scotland—but she knew she was loved. And she knew that gave one a different sort of beauty—a beauty that came from confidence in one's merits.

And if her knees were knocking together, it was from excitement, not apprehension. Because the day had at last come for her to meet the man she loved. Any moment now, Ewan Cameron, His Grace the Duke of Crieff was going to throw open his doors, and greet her with the smile she had been waiting eight years to receive.

She herself was already smiling in readiness, happy to receive him, at last.

And yet, he and his smile did not come. The door remained closed.

"Curious," was all papa said before stepped down from the coach, and took a fraction of a moment to straighten his coat. "Robert," he instructed the footman, "pray ply the bell and inform them that his grace's betrothed has arrived."

She certainly felt as if she had indeed arrived—in more ways than merely standing on the doorstep of her soon-to-be-new home. Greer sat another moment or two, admiring the beautiful proportions of the Palladian mansion, and buff stone balance and pleasuring symmetry. Ewan had described it so perfectly she felt like she were coming home instead of coming to a place she had never been.

On the seat beside her, Mama took her hand and gave her a reassuring squeeze.

"It's quite alright, Mama." She made herself everything calm and unruffled, like a swan gliding along the top of the water, while beneath all was determined work. "I am sure it will all be right as rain."

"Good girl." Mama patted her silk and lace clad arm. "No need to fret or fash."

And yet there was a need for…something.

She had expected that he would have set up a signal from the gatehouse, and been out on the forecourt waiting for her—she would have been, if their situations had been reversed.

"Come, my dear." Papa handed her out just in time, because the huge oaken door finally opened to revel a man in black who must be the house steward.

He was just as Ewan had described him—thin, angular and proud, with a stoic demeanor. "My leddy." He bowed deeply at the waist. "I welcome ye to Crieff."

"Thank you." Greer very composedly smoothed down her embroidered silk skirts, and moved toward the door on her own, as papa handed out mama. "You must be MacIntosh. His grace has told me so much about you."

The man looked so pained that for a moment Greer feared she had said the wrong thing. "His words were everything complimentary," she assured him.

"Thank ye, my leddy." But somehow he looked more anguished at such a compliment.

It was most awkward.

"You are quite welcome. I know I shall come to value you just as greatly as his grace does." And speaking of her duke. "And his grace?"

The steward pleated his lips between his teeth. "It pains me, my leddy—"

"I am here."

Greer turned and felt the warm smile freeze to her face.

This couldn't be her Ewan. Nothing about the sharp-faced, unsmiling man in the grey powdered wig and black embroidered silk suit—which, by the way needed tailoring to make it fit him properly—was familiar. His hair was not blond. His eyes were not green. He was not so tall and ungainly that he might frighten children, as Ewan had once told her he was.

And furthermore, no spark of welcome, no soft flare of recognition lighted his eye. Everything was stiffness and unease.

"Welcome to Crieff, my lady."

He was as correctly polite and formal as if they were strangers. As if she did not already know the private longings of his heart, and he hers.

Greer curtseyed because she knew she should, and because several other men, Creiff's—and very soon her own—retainers had come out into the forecourt. But she could not keep from asking, "Are you Ewan Cameron?"

Perhaps it was her patent disbelief, but there was a twinge, a twitch of narrowing at the corner of his clear blue eyes, as well as a clenching along his jawline, before he covered his discomfort with a pleasant smile. "I am his grace."

Which was not what she had asked.

Because she had been raised to be everything polished and polite, Greer did not allow her annoyance to show. But neither did she falter—she stuck to her point like a burr. "But you are not Ewan Cameron. You cannot be." Everything about him was wrong—different. Unless…

An unwelcome, entirely disloyal thought jumped into her head—what if all his letters, all the words she had cherished and practically memorized for the past eight years, were a lie?

His answer was another almost imperceptible twinge— this one at the corner of his wide, mouth—before the man finally spoke. "No," he admitted. "I am Murdock Cameron, his cousin, and Duke of Crieff now." He looked away, as if he did not like to meet her eyes. "Ewan Cameron is dead."

THANK YOU FOR READING

Thank you for reading *Mad About the Marquess*. I hope you'll take a few minutes out of your day to review this book – your honest opinion is much appreciated. Reviews help introduce readers to new authors they wouldn't otherwise meet.

THE HIGHLAND BRIDES

Mad About the Marquess is the first book in The Highland Brides. While each book reads as a stand-alone, the series is best enjoyed in chronological order.

Mad for Love
Mad About the Marquess
Mad, Bad, and Dangerous to Marry
Mad Dogs and Englishwomen

To keep up to date on The Highland Brides, sign up for Elizabeth's newsletter and get exclusive excerpts, contests, and more
http://www.elizabethessex.com/contest/

BOOKS BY ELIZABETH ESSEX

Dartmouth Brides
The Pursuit of Pleasure
A Sense of Sin
The Danger of Desire

Reckless Brides
Almost a Scandal
A Breath of Scandal
Scandal in the Night
The Scandal Before Christmas
After the Scandal
A Scandal to Remember

ABOUT THE AUTHOR

Elizabeth Essex is the award-winning author of the critically acclaimed Reckless Brides historical romance series. When not rereading Jane Austen, mucking about in her garden or simply messing about with boats, Elizabeth can be always be found with her laptop, making up stories about heroes and heroines who live far more exciting lives than she. It wasn't always so. Long before she ever set pen to paper, Elizabeth graduated from Hollins College with a BA in Classics and Art History, and then earned her MA in Nautical Archaeology from Texas A&M University. While she loved the life of an underwater archaeologist, she has found her true calling writing lush, lyrical historical romance full of passion, daring and adventure.

Elizabeth lives in Texas with her husband, the indispensable Mr. Essex, and her active and exuberant family in an old house filled to the brim with books.

Elizabeth loves to hear from readers, so please feel free to contact her at the following places:
E-mail: elizabeth@elizabethessex.com
Web: http://elizabethessex.com
Twitter: https://twitter.com/EssexRomance
Facebook Page:
https://www.facebook.com/elizabeth.essex.37
Pinterest: https://www.pinterest.com/elizabethessex/
Goodreads:
http://www.goodreads.com/author/show/4070864.El izabeth_Essex

76214638R00223

Made in the USA
Columbia, SC
03 September 2017